OUR DAYS ARE NUMBERED

By

Jill Hogben

*"You can no more analyse love
than you can analyse beauty
and the reasoning of
a hundred brains cannot explain
or explain away the motives
and emotions of the heart"*

Published by Aurelian Publishing 2016

This novel is predominantly a work of fiction, but draws upon documents written by the author's Mother, and Grand-father discovered after her death. The poems and letters in the book are authentic, and the quotes at the start of each chapter are drawn from the author's mother's poems. However, except where consent has been given, names have been changed, and the characters portrayed are a product of the author's imagination and any resemblance of them to a real person, living or dead, is purely coincidental.

First published in Great Britain in 2016 by:
Aurelian Publishing

tjfh@hotmail.co.uk

Jill Hogben

This book is dedicated to my Mother.

Our Days Are Numbered

CHAPTER 1

*"Remember one has to make some sacrifices in life
for the sake of principles"*

Sarah bounced along the dusty pavement – it was a
blazing hot sunny afternoon in suburban south
London. She was a pretty girl in her late teens, with a
fresh complexion, rosy cheeks, green eyes and dark
brown hair, slightly frizzy from a perm and the heat.
She wore a floral printed dress caught at the waist with
a belt of the same material and her legs were devoid of
stockings, she wore smart sandals with a small heel. She
swung her white bag as she walked and casually tossed
her cardigan over her shoulder. She was very happy,
relieved and was longing to tell her mother of her
achievements.

London in high summer was very uncomfortable
until the cool of the evening set in. The houses
themselves seemed to groan and creak under the
burden of stifling acrid air and dry heat. The doors of
the houses were all open to let in any breeze going,
shaded by brightly coloured striped canvas curtains.
Roses in front gardens wilted sadly, and lawns once
green and lush with spring rain were withered and
brown.

Sarah turned into the gate, jumped though the
colourful sun curtain swaying in the breeze and called
out gaily to her mother.

"Mummy darling! Where are you? I have some
brilliant news!"

Hilda emerged from the kitchen wiping floury hands
down her all-enveloping pinafore. She was a cheery
rosy-cheeked lady of ample proportions, at her

happiest when in her small tiled kitchen cooking wonderfully tasty food for her family.

"Whatever is it darling?" Sarah grabbed her by the hands and danced her around the hall.

"I have passed my shorthand and typing exams. I managed my 70 wpm – at last!"

Hilda laughed at her daughter as Sarah enveloped her in a bear hug.

"Why, you have now got flour all over you from my pinny!" her mother exclaimed, and she put her hands into her front pocket, drew out a clean hanky, moistened a corner and proceeded to wipe specks of flour from her daughter's face gleaned from their embrace.

Sarah had been struggling at her commercial college for a while. Her aims to become a stenographer at one point had seemed dim, as Mr. Pitman's method of shorthand had erstwhile eluded her, but today she had triumphed at last.

"We will have to ask Daddy to look for a secretarial job for you in the bank, darling," said her mother. "Would you like that?"

"Oh, I would love to work with darling Daddy – but will I ever be really good enough?"

"Well, we'll just have to see. Now go and wash for dinner, it is almost ready."

Sarah ran upstairs just as her elder brother George came in, tired and hot from his commute into London where he worked in the tea trade.

"Hello, Mummy dearest!" George kissed his mother on the forehead. "Dratted heat! I'm fair pooped, the train was murder, absolutely stifling. I find it difficult to function efficiently in this weather. My eczema has flared up again, and I itch so much!"

His mother sighed sympathetically, as she set the table for dinner. "Poor dear! Go and wash for dinner and I will put some cream on your hands when you come down."

The dining room faced a large pretty garden. When it was very hot the French windows were propped open to allow a cool breeze, on which the scent of the myriads of flowers, tended carefully by Hilda, wafted into the house.

Hilda had prepared home-made lemonade which the three of them quaffed while they ate their meal. Halfway through eating, Mr. Langman, the patriarch of the family, came home. He was a gentle Scot of medium build, balding, with twinkling blue eyes that could be stern but were mainly kindly, especially where his family was concerned.

Joe Langman worked in the city, in a large bank, and used his ability for figure work as treasurer at the local Presbyterian Church where he was also an Elder. He spent a lot of time at the church. This devotion was rather resented by his wife Hilda; she wished he would not do so much, as he tired easily and was not in the best of health.

The Langmans were a happy loving family: hugs and kisses were the norm, and much familial affection flew around and between them all. George teased his little sister, and although he was eight years older they were very close. He would often give her pocket money from his wages. Sometimes, when the mood took them, Sarah and George would wind up the mahogany record player standing in the corner of the dining room and, clearing a space, would dance together around the room to Harry Hall and his dance band.

As a boy George found having a baby sister a bit of a bore and would protest when having to look after her. Once he was asked to take her to the park, and abandoned her in the pram and went off to play cricket. His mother was not best pleased. However, as they both grew, a close relationship between them blossomed. Sarah loved and admired her brother, and they had great fun in each other's company.

Sometimes he would put her on his bike cross-bar and whizz down the hill of their road at great speed, much to their mother's horror and Sarah's great glee. She shouted "Whoopee!" as they sped along with the wind in their faces.

Sarah absolutely adored her mother and they shared many loving times together. Sarah had been a late baby, possibly a much loved after-thought, as her mother was well into her forties when she gave birth.

Hilda took Sarah, as a special treat, to see Madam Butterfly at the Royal Opera House. They were lucky enough to be given up-graded tickets as someone had cancelled, so they had the best seats. The opera really grabbed Sarah; she was thrilled by the pathos of the story, and turned to see her mother watching with tears coursing down her cheeks when Butterfly killed herself and the music swelled to a mighty crescendo of pain and anguish. Throughout her life Sarah never forgot her first experience of opera. The gift of musical appreciation was encouraged by her beloved mother and also her brother, who surprised her shortly after their outing by leaving the LP record of Madam Butterfly on the turntable of the gramophone, much to Sarah's profound glee at his thoughtfulness.

George and Sarah both played the old piano which stood in a corner, neither of them reaching heights of excellence, just enjoying thumping out tunes. George was passionate about music and loved Rachmaninov, the Russian expert in romanticism, and he taught Sarah to listen and love piano concertos. She especially loved Chopin, and while she realised that her application at the piano would never do that composer justice, she diligently practised and could play his works tolerably well.

A short while earlier George, normally a happy-go-lucky sort of young man, had become depressed as he had found it very difficult to obtain work despite his education at one of the most prestigious local colleges, paid for by his hard working father. Gainful employment, even for the well-educated, had been very hard to come by recently and George himself had despaired of getting his first job.

Finally, however, he found a job in the tea trade and he enjoyed his time learning all about the different teas, often bringing home choice blends for his mother. He had given her a beautiful mahogany tea caddy from which he had plied his trade.

So there they are, the Langmans, living in their three-bedroomed comfortable suburban house, just before the dark clouds of the Second World War overcame them. It was an enchanted time of peace in between two world wars, when life seemed safe, gentle and had a certain comfortable naiveté. The trials of unemployment during the great depression of the early 1930s were mainly over and the country was slowly getting back on its feet, blissfully unaware of the horrors to come.

CHAPTER TWO

"You have written a memory on my memory page"

Henry Treleaven neatly folded his crisp white handkerchief and placed it carefully in the top left-hand pocket of his immaculate pin-striped suit. His shoes were polished to perfection, his cuff-links carefully chosen and his hair slicked back with a special blend – personal to him – of gentleman's hair oil which enabled him to exude a whiff of aromatic masculinity and cleanliness. He was clean-shaven but had a carefully trimmed smart moustache, as was the trend to be seen in any cinema. Film stars on screen, such as Clark Gable and Errol Flynn, were responsible for many men proudly sporting growth above their upper lips.

Henry took his furled umbrella and rain-coat, the best that money could buy at the local gentleman's outfitters, donned his trilby and set off from his flat to the local station for his commute to London. The grey dreariness of the day made him long for his native Cornwall, where the sun seemed to shine incessantly as he was growing up in Truro. He had a great yearning for the streams, woods, and golden beaches with crashing azure surf, frequented in his youth. His heart was in Cornwall, but circumstances had brought him to dismal London, on the brink of war, as his mother had moved up to the suburbs with her step-sister when their brother died in Cornwall.

Mrs. Treleaven had benefited greatly from her brother's generosity, and her inheritance had bought a comfortable four-bedroomed house in the same road as the Langman family. In essence Henry felt he was trapped in London, realising that he had to stay near his mother and step-aunt as they were both ageing. Besides, his sister Violet had returned from Malaya with her husband and they had settled in Beckenham nearby, so there was no real reason for Henry to return to the county of his birth.

As a boy in Cornwall he had attended the cathedral school as a chorister. He once sang a solo during a service, something that he kept quiet from his devoted mother. She would have cheerfully sat behind a pillar to hear her son sing in his clear treble, but Henry had been afraid of a ragging by his fellow choristers.

He had always been very underweight, being premature at birth; he was skinny and the smallest chap in his class. He had been subject to much bullying and teasing by other boys. During cross-country running he was the only one up to his neck in the river whilst the other boys crossed waist high with ease. However, he had a certain amount of resilience; he was not of Cornish stock for nothing!

Henry's father, William Treleaven, had been a gold miner in the southern Transvaal. Mining, was an occupation that had proven fatal to both he and his brother Matthew, who had chosen to mine in Colorado, U.S.A. Like many Cornish miners, they had gone abroad to find work as the Cornish mines shut down. They both sadly succumbed in their thirties to the miners' lung disease phthisis.

Henry and his sister Violet were brought up by their uncle Arnold, who, being single, had taken his young widowed sister Annie and the children under his wing and provided for them as if they were his own. Arnold Francis was a high-earning bank inspector who compiled the cathedral's accounts, and was therefore well able to send Henry and Violet to public schools.

The irony was that they would not have had such fine schooling had their father lived.

Thus, while Henry and his sister missed out on a father's presence as they grew up, both gained from the benevolence and guidance of their uncle. Henry Treleaven benefited from excellent musical education at the cathedral choir school, whilst Violet was educated at the local girls' public school instead of attending a village school and went on to train as a teacher.

After matriculation Henry was also sent to teacher training at St. Luke's College in Exeter, but unfortunately he found that he could not keep discipline in the classroom and so gave up teaching as a career. He would have loved to have had a little watch repairing business as he was very good at mending things. His life would have been bliss working, with tiny instruments peering down a magnifying eye glass at the movements in watch cases, making them tick again. However that mode of employment was not to be his, and so he made the best of things in the bank.

Henry boarded the steam train, which took him to London Bridge; from there it was a short walk to his place of work, where he was employed at the head office of a large bank. This job had been obtained through his uncle's influence: given his former role as a bank inspector, Arnold had been able to pull a few strings to get Henry his position. There he became much-respected member of the ledger department. Henry's colleagues admired his neat and accurate figure-work – and he was often the last to leave the bank, tidying up after others had finished. He was a reliable sort of chap.

Henry would often meet with his brother-in-law Herbert, who worked in the City, for a drink or a game of billiards in a club after work. Inevitably, the conversation turned to the possibility of war.

"Well, old boy, what do you think of the situation in Europe?"

Herbert chalked his cue, shook his head ruefully and looked at Henry.

"Violet and I have even called off our normal camping trip 'sur-la-continent'. She does not want to be away from home and our son Francis at this time. She says she feels in her bones that evil is coming – and your sister has that Cornish ability to sense things!"

"Do you reckon old Chamberlain will pull off a pact for peace?" Henry potted a sitter neatly into the pocket.

"Oh, good shot old boy!" said Herbert admiringly. "I really have no idea, but all I know is that rum cove Hitler is a force to be reckoned with. Going by the news reports he has such a profound far-right influence over the German people. He epitomises sheer evil to me; he is a dangerous one, all right." The two men chattered on over their game.

The clouds of war had been gathering for a while and the English people had been experiencing a growing sense of unease, even though Neville Chamberlain, the Prime Minister, believed totally in his foreign policy of appeasement and had returned the year before from signing the Munich Agreement waving papers triumphantly. There was no doubt that when the Germans invaded Poland there was no niceties of treaty – and thus England declared war on Hitler and the German nation.

In 1939 life continued as normal for the majority of Londoners. The first air raids had not begun, but all had been given gas masks. Children were evacuated to the country, well away from danger, and ordinary citizens made preparations to protect themselves and their families. Many dug Andersen shelters into their gardens, half below the ground with round corrugated roofs for protection against bombs. Everywhere sandbags were propped up against doors and windows to prevent blast damage, and there was an air of anxiety in the faces of the passers-by, a dreadful fear of the devastation to come.

Henry and Herbert carried on with their occupations, learning to run for cover when air raid sirens blasted out. Many offices used their cellars as air raid shelters, and they endeavoured to cope with the fact that their homes may not be standing when they finally finished their work for the day.

The bulldog spirit of the British people meant - that wherever it could – business carried on as normal.

CHAPTER 3

"Then when this ceases to be, I will draw on its memory"

Gary walked alone along the golden sands of a Cornish beach. He kicked the odd pebble in a desultory way. He was sad, fed up and just really didn't know what to do to make his marriage work. The sheer stunning beauty of the wide sandy beach and sparkling sea in the afternoon sun couldn't touch Gary's misery.

He was in his thirties, and was a tall handsome man with fair curly hair, tending on the lean side with very long gangly legs. He was unhappily married, with two small children whom he loved dearly. The disagreements with his wife were getting him down, there seemed to be no pleasing her – and sometimes he just had to take the dog out for a long walk down by the sea to clear his head.

Rusty, a Welsh Springer spaniel, always made him feel better. He was full of the joys of life, for ever bringing bits of driftwood back to his master for him to throw, especially into the sea. The little dog's abundant energy and eagerness to please and to rush headlong into the rough waves to fetch a stick always cheered Gary. The dog's unconditional devotion to him, Spaniel grin, tongue lolling and saliva dripping, seemed to epitomize totally the love that Gary did not receive from his wife.

Gary's parents were aware of their son's unhappiness, and tried to support him and the whole family as best as they could, but they took a concerned back seat and hoped that their daughter-in-law and son could sort out their many differences. They lived back in Wales, in Glamorgan where Gary had been brought up, and they didn't have much money to travel to see their family in Cornwall, so most of their support for their son had been in the form of letters and phone calls. This disharmony in their family was a source of great sadness to them, compounding the loss of their younger daughter some years ago after the birth of her only child.

Sometimes Gary just longed to be back in Wales. Although he felt in many ways Cornwall had the same Celtic heritage: a love of male voice choirs, fine choral singing, supporting rugby with a passion and sharing the occupations of mining, farming and fishing. Glamorgan's rich coal seams once matched the plenteous tin mining of Cornwall. However the Vale of Glamorgan pulled Gary, who had an overwhelming and fierce passion for his homeland. He had climbed Crag y Llyn as a youth and had felt as if his heart would burst with Welsh pride when he reached the summit and surveyed the astounding beauty of the many rich shades of green, as far as the eye could see.

His longing for Wales was exacerbated by his unhappiness in Cornwall. His wife Helen was Cornish, and they had moved to the Penwith Peninsular when they married. He had been lucky to swiftly secure a post at the Camborne School of Engineering. His children were both born in Cornwall and he had tried his best to integrate into the Cornish community, attending Camborne Chapel and going to watch Rugby at the Mennaye Field as often as he could.

Gary loved music, especially anything by Rachmaninov, one of his favourite composers. He could play the piano tolerably well and would give Chopin etude Opus 10 number 1 in C Major his best shot. He possessed long fingers and a wide span; this and many hours of practice, meant he could do justice to cascading arpeggios, creating a delightful waterfall image. However, for fun he loved to play his accordion to amuse the children, singing songs in a high falsetto voice and making them laugh.

Gary was trained as an engineer. He had always had a fascination for engines, especially those of aeroplanes, and many times he visited the Land's End School of Flying, helping behind the scenes. He eventually managed to persuade several of the chaps running the school that he could cheerfully carry out some maintenance of their planes in return for the odd flying lesson, which he enjoyed immensely. He had a natural aptitude for flying and was very at home at the controls of a plane, and soon obtained his pilot's licence. He found the exhilaration of soaring above the beautiful rugged coastline of West Penwith totally absorbing, and it took his mind away from his unhappy home life.

In fact, he couldn't get enough of flying and was fed up when wet weather precluded the use of the grass runway at Land's End. The sheer excitement of opening up the throttle and moving at high speed towards the cliff edge, only to lift off over the turbulent sea at the last minute, never failed to thrill him. The blue sea below him would foam and boil as it hit the jagged granite cliffs, and the sea birds would scream and wheel about. Often along the coast he would spy basking seals, and at sea the occasional pod of dolphins gambolling behind a small tosher, or a large Penzance fishing smack, with its wide booms outspread trawling nets behind it.

From high up one could really appreciate the translucence of the water around the rugged Cornish coast, especially towards Porthcurnow where the sea took on a turquoise hue, reflecting light from the white sands beneath. In high summer gigantic basking sharks would wend their slow progress through the clear waters, mouths open to catch krill, much to the fascination of the many tourists visiting the Minack Theatre, skilfully cut into the open rock face.

Yes, flying really helped to lift Gary's heavy heart for a while. He could forget his problems and soar to the sun. He adored his son and daughter – they made his home life bearable, and he would take them out for walks and to playgrounds, just to get away from everything. Their laughter and antics on the swings made him smile again. Yet he was also afraid for their future, as the likelihood of their lives being normal was looking dim. Even down in Cornwall people were beginning to mutter amongst themselves and to be afraid of the threat from Germany.

CHAPTER 4

*"For all the tender love you gave,
for every sacrifice you made"*

Henry Treleaven got in from work. It had been a long
hard day and the ledgers had not balanced easily, so he
had had to stay late to sort it all out. He made a cup of
coffee and felt too fatigued to cook himself a meal, so
he made a sandwich and sat down to open an official
looking letter. It was his call-up papers. He sighed. He
so wanted to defend his country, but had a feeling that
joining up would not be possible.

He was right, he attended a medical and failed on
two counts. He had dreadful varicose veins in his legs
from endless standing behind a desk working as a bank
cashier. Also, in his twenties he had suffered a mild
heart attack. Unfortunately, the forces required one to
be reasonably fit. He was also underweight; he had
been a premature baby and had never put on weight
and muscle like the other boys at school and college.
He felt a complete failure but the doctor was very
understanding and told him that he could still serve his
country as a Fire Warden. He was told that fire
watching was a very important role, as he would be
protecting factories as well as local shops and houses.
He would be issued with a uniform, a blue serge suit
and a white hard hat, a stirrup pump and a sand
bucket, his duties were to prevent large conflagrations
by extinguish small fires. Henry was relieved that he
could still play an important part in the defence of his
country.

The next day was Saturday and, after working at the
bank in the morning, Henry went round to his

mother's house to tell her the news. His aunt opened the door.

"Why Henry, nice to see you, do come in," said Mamie. "Mother has just gone round the corner to the shops. She will be back in a minute."

His aunt Mamie was a little old lady and Henry loved her dearly. She resembled a little bird: she had a kindly and much wrinkled little face and a rather pointed nose, which reminded one of a beak. When they lived in Truro, she had virtually raised Henry and his sister Violet, as, after their father died, Annie had to go out to work. Mamie had given up her teaching job to stay at home and look after the children, who were very young.

"Hello Auntie," he said, and kissed his aunt affectionately on her paper-thin cheek.

"I have just received the news that I cannot join up to fight for my country. I am to stay and work in my job and fire watch whenever I can."

"Well now," Mamie said. "Fire watching is a very vital service, Henry dear. You must not feel that you won't be doing your bit for your country in this war."

Secretly Mamie was very relieved. She loved Henry as if he were her own, and it would have broken her heart if he had gone off to fight. This way, although his job had its dangers, he would still be nearby to support both of the sisters. They were not getting any younger, and they relied upon his car to take them around, and she actually didn't know how they would have managed without him.

The two went into the long garden room, which had high moulded ceilings and French windows overlooking the small but neat garden. The lace curtains were pulled back to let in the sun, and fragrant roses covered the trellis, nodding their heads in the light breeze. The trellis divided the lawn from a paved area, sending dappled shade onto the pebble-dash of the house.

They had only recently moved into this house in Sydenham, South London. They had purchased it from a nervous widow who had actually constructed a brick air-raid shelter in the garden room, so worried was she about the bombing. Mrs. Treleaven soon had the shelter demolished. She was a no-nonsense type of lady, cocking a snoot at Hitler and his bombs; she might be shaking inside, but she put on a brave face to reassure her rather nervous half-sister Mamie. Besides, she was very eager to furnish her new house using the legacy she had received the year before, when her well-to-do brother in Truro had died and left both of the sisters quite comfortably off.

The house was Edwardian, built just after the old Queen died, and was of generous proportions. There were four bedrooms, two reception rooms and a large kitchen and scullery for the maid. Each room was equipped with a bell with which to summon servants – even in the bathroom one could call for assistance, using a bell on the wall next to the bath. There were very modern gas fires in all the bedrooms, set in little green-tiled fire surrounds in which open fires were once lit. The moulded hoods were decorated in the Art Nouveau fashion with curling leaves and mythical flowers, mostly fashioned in cast iron, but in the main drawing room a burnished copper hood graced the room.

Mrs. Treleaven, Annie, settled easily into her new life in south London, but Mamie missed the peaceful market town of Truro and all her friends. She was not

happy in Sydenham – it was generally too noisy, the
bombing was terrifying and she hated the copious
traffic which made her very nervous. Her relationship
with her sister was also very strained. Annie had not
really wanted her sister to come and live with her, and
took her in from a sense of duty when the Truro house
was sold.

However, both Henry and his sister Violet adored
Mamie, and knowing that she was now nearer to them
both made her life bearable. Mamie made tea for
herself and Henry and took it into the garden where
they sat companionably in the afternoon sun.

"How are things at the office dear?" she asked
Henry, passing him a tea cup.

"Oh, just the usual bodge-ups in the ledger
department," Henry said, as he helped himself to
sugar. "I ticked-up the ledger just in time the other day.
We seem to have such a heavy load of work, nowadays.
People are nervous because of the war, and would
rather stuff their money under their mattress than trust
a bank at the moment."

They sat and stirred their teacups in synchronised
rhythm. "I say, Auntie, these heavy cakes are rather
scrumptious!"

"Well, I had hoped you would call this weekend,
and made them especially for you," his aunt said.

"I know you are fond of Cornish hevva cakes. I
made them with the best currants and lard that I could
find. Luckily Miss Slade round the corner has still quite
a few provisions tucked away at the back of her rather
dark shop – for her best customers, of course!"

"That was kind of you. May I take one or two home
with me for later?" Henry asked, smiling at his aunt.
Mamie answered in the affirmative.

"Really, you know, business has to go on as usual despite the devastation of bombed offices and blocked streets around us, and the increasing difficulty in travelling to work. So many delays on the trains! I had even considered taking the car up to London, but petrol is rationed and scarce."

Just then Annie came in. "Hello Mother! I was turned down for the forces, you know." He stood up and kissed his mother.

"Well, I am very glad to hear that, Henry dear. I couldn't bear to lose you, you know. I should have been so worried while you were away. Mrs. Johnson at the grocery shop told me that several of the large houses in Venner Road have been hit by a bomb. Even in Newlands Park there is a huge gap, as it seems a very large bomb hit two substantial Victorian houses there during last night's raid. I haven't heard about casualties yet. That was too close for comfort, I must admit."

Annie sighed wearily. "Perhaps we shouldn't have come up from Cornwall after all. While Penzance and Truro are suffering raids too, they will not be as intense as up here. The blasted Jerrys are aiming for London, to facilitate the greatest devastation and cause the most deaths. I don't know what the world is coming to, really I don't – such a tragic loss of life and much destruction. We never thought after the last war that there would be another so soon. You wouldn't believe that there would be so much hatred in the world; just smell the perfume of the roses in this lovely sunshine, what more could people want?"

She took her shopping into the kitchen and called out of the window. "Would you like to stay for supper, Henry dear? I managed to get a couple of large kippers and they will stretch to three."

"No thank you, Mother. I really must be getting back as I don't know when I will be instructed about my fire watching, and I believe I have to pick up my uniform from Boag's. Everyone is doing their bit, we are all pulling together to keep morale up – and the shopkeepers are no exception!"

Henry kissed his mother and aunt affectionately on their cheeks and left them sitting in the warmth of the afternoon sun. He thought he might go to the State cinema this evening as he heard there was a good flick on and he felt he needed a bit of escapism to cheer him up. He was often lonely and had almost given up the idea of love in his life. He had various girl friends in the past, but for one reason or another these relationships had fizzled out, and his mother had despaired of him ever settling down to wedlock and a family. He was very fond of his nephew Francis, who was mostly away at boarding school. They spent time together and played cricket together when Francis was home, and Henry longed for a son of his own. He was particularly anxious to carry on the family name. Down in Cornwall all his cousins were female, and he felt a duty to procreate and produce a son.

"First find a wife," thought Henry. "Easier said than done!"

CHAPTER FIVE

"What is this thing called time?
It makes no sense to me"

Gary opened the sealed brown envelope. This was it, his call up papers. He had a choice: Army, Navy or Air Force; and for him there was no other Service except the Air Force. His love of flying, his pilot's licence and engineering knowledge of planes, would hopefully stand him in good stead.

Two weeks later, leaving his dear blond-haired children was heart-breaking: their sad little faces and blue eyes bright with tears, not understanding why Daddy had to go away. He didn't know when he would see them again, if ever. Even his wife was less cold towards him. She was a modicum less grumpy and more supportive, but things had been so bad recently that he would really be relieved to put some space between them. Not that he wanted to fight a war, but he did want to serve his country. Helen knew this and was grudgingly helpful and packed his things in a large trunk, and they all went to Penzance station in a taxi to see him off.

It was a clear, bright day as he waved goodbye to his family. The sun was shining and the sea sparkling, and the large steam engine grunted and heaved as it moved slowly out of the station. As the steam cleared he could see his family getting smaller, waving on the platform. He wondered if he would ever see his children again, and his heart was heavy. He sank back into his seat and watched St. Michael's Mount, majestic in the sea and glistening in the bright air, as the train gathered speed.

Other men shared his compartment. "Would you like a smoke mate?" a friendly chap in his twenties offered. "Got to keep the old spirits up, haven't we? This war sure is a rum do, and no mistake."

"Thank you very much," Gary said, settling back with a cigarette. "Where are you posted?" he asked the young man.

"Oh, I am going to Portsmouth to the join the Royal Navy – the Senior Service, you know!" The chap grinned. "I have always wanted to go to sea, but not in this way! I used to help on the luggers down Newlyn harbour, and went out on the odd fishing trip, and once I had stopped throwing up I had a marvellous time, fresh sea air in the old bellows, you know – although, of course, not so good in a force nine gale! So I will be happy on board ship; however, this whole fighting business, well it fair makes me knees knock! How about you?"

"I'm joining the RAF, and going to Northumberland for basic training. I am already in my thirties, so I'm older than most, plus I can already fly. I hope I will find it fairly easy to master war planes. I have always loved flying, but of course, defending one's country is a lot different from flying for pleasure."

"I know, chum, we don't really know what is going to befall us all. I did notice that this train seems to be full to bursting with really young chaps, some still in their late teens, obviously all on their way to fight for King and Country. It is all very daunting, isn't it? Still, we cannot let old Hitler have his way in our country as he seems to be doing in Europe, can we? Well, good luck with whatever befalls you, anyway."

They sank back into reverie, and spent the rest of the journey in silence looking out at the beauty of the

Cornish countryside. Soon they passed into Devon with its rolling green hills, little thatched cottages and farms, cows and sheep grazing peacefully. It all seemed so daft that on such a glorious sun-filled day they were all under a cloud of war.

Gary travelled for many miles, changing trains at London for his final destination in Northumberland.

As he travelled, his mind mulled over the change in his wife since she had had their children. He had supposed that having children would make her happy; but, no, she regarded their two as a real nuisance, impinging on her life. She was an academic and wanted to study. Having children meant she never had time for her books and writings. Thus she resented their presence and the incessant interruptions of having to cook, clean and care for the family. This resentment spilled over in her relationship with Gary. She seemed to blame him for everything, even the children. She longed for freedom from domestic chores: to be able to write and study was all that possessed her waking time. Now, of course, the war had made her lot even more difficult as Gary wouldn't be there to relieve her of housewifely duties, not even at the weekends. She found the idea of being trapped by domesticity even more daunting than the fact that her husband had gone to war.

Gary knew this and thought that at least his parents may travel from Wales, to help with the children while he was away. However, once he reached the RAF base he could not spend much time thinking of his family; his long journey had worn him out and he was very hungry and weary. After reporting in and receiving his uniform, he was shown his meagre bed. He already felt homesick and full of anxiety about what was to come.

However his travel weariness sent him quickly into the land of nod, despite the lumpy mattress and the snoring of the other occupants of his billet.

In the morning he realised that he was among many other such chaps, apprehensive about the future. As many were younger than himself, he found it easy to play the 'elder brother', and chivvy them on as their training panned out. When chatting to the other chaps he tried to reassure them by saying that it wouldn't be so bad, and that at least they were all in it together and would look out for each other.

An amazing camaraderie soon became apparent between all the new blokes. They supported each other, each having a tale to tell of their homes. A lot of chaps had come from London, cockney sparrows, full of cheerful tales of their families, and with lots of wisecracks and joshing. The early days of service were filled with learning to handle armaments, partaking in various drills and marching practice. Square bashing took extreme concentration and thus lifted the spirits, but these were dashed somewhat by a visit to the Mess, for the food was nothing to write home about.

Thus the days of Gary's basic training passed. He was a very quick learner, and he was shipped out to Canada for a few months where he learned to fly fighter planes – a different kettle of fish from the small planes he flew in Cornwall.

CHAPTER SIX

"And now my happiness complete"

Sarah Langman opened her eyes. Her nose hurt dreadfully and she was black and blue after a nasal operation to cure her rhinitis. She sank back into the soft feather pillows and contemplated the sky outside her bedroom window. England was at war with Germany. She felt very fearful for her family and her friends. What would happen? Would her brother George have to go and fight? Would their happy lives change unbelievably and for ever?

Her best friend from school days, Joyce, who lived a few doors away down the hill, had already told her that they were likely to be called to serve their country. The thought of leaving her home and parents filled her with great dread.

At that moment the air raid sirens began their mournful wail, and her mother called up to her: "Put your dressing gown and slippers on Sarah, we must go and shelter!"

"Coming, Mummy," she replied. Sarah reluctantly got out of her warm bed, her head and nose aching, and made her way downstairs to join her mother. Hilda wrapped her daughter in one of her father's large warm coats. They walked quickly down the road to the house of their good friends Jessie and Mary Twentyman, who had a large cellar in which to shelter.

The two sisters shared the old house, having once kept home for their parents who had passed away. They had adapted their cellar with camp beds, plenty of blankets and pillows, and flasks for hot drinks while Hitler's Luftwaffe did its level best to blow everyone to smithereens. Their cellar was open for any needy neighbour and could be quite crowded, everyone trying to cheer the others along, but all were really quaking in their shoes and wincing at every blast, which sounded so very near. The London blitz had begun.

As they sat in the cellar, they sang songs to keep their spirits up, and the two sisters sat busily knitting to keep their hands from shaking with fear. Their neighbours, Bob and Flossie Chambers, and Sarah's best friend Joyce were in the shelter, as were the Richardsons with their young baby Sheila.

The women discussed the shortages of food and rationing, which had just come in, stretching their culinary skills to the limit in trying to feed their families on meagre stores.

The men discussed the best way to dig up their lawns to provide more home-grown vegetables, mulling over which varieties would suit the heavy, but fertile, London clay to be found in most back gardens in the suburbs.

All agreed that potatoes would be a valuable first crop, to be followed by as many of the brassica and legume family that could be sown.

"Daddy says he has managed to get you an interview at the bank next week, darling," said Sarah's mother.

"Oh, Mummy! How can I go to an interview with my nose all sore and my face bruised?" Sarah asked her mother.

"Well, I will bathe your face with witch hazel to help the bruising. Don't worry, I'm sure it will be gone by then, you see if I'm not right!"

The all-clear siren blared out its triumphal wail. "Phew! Well, there didn't seem to be much damage in our area, at least," Jessie Twentyman said. "Come on, let's get back upstairs. I need to make some pastry with my last bit of lard. This food rationing makes cooking very difficult."

They all climbed back up the steps into the hall and went their separate ways home, exchanging pleasantries as they parted.

Sarah wrapped her dressing gown and Joe's warm coat around her and walked back up the hill to their home with her mother. "Whatever should I wear to this interview?" She wondered out loud.

Her mother thought for a while. She really needed a new smart suit, but where on earth would one get such a thing in this time of rationing. The family had just received their clothing coupons, sixty-six per year each for every man, woman and child. Fourteen coupons for one coat, Hilda sighed. Goodness gracious, she couldn't afford to waste coupons on a new suit for her daughter. Then she suddenly remembered her navy tailored suit in the back of her wardrobe, which could probably be altered to fit Sarah. With the addition of a crisp white blouse and a pretty turquoise broach from her own collection, her daughter would be well turned out for the interview. She would even fashion some shoulder pads to make the suit up-to-date for her daughter, and luckily Sarah already had some smart navy court shoes with a small heel which would finish off the ensemble nicely.

When they reached their house they were relieved to see that it was, thankfully, still standing and undamaged by blast. Hilda fetched her suit from the depths of her wardrobe, took it out and shook it to remove creases. It did need a lot of work to tailor it to her daughter's slim frame, and it smelled quite strongly of camphor mothballs, but she cheerfully set to with her ancient sewing machine, set on a treadle, and began to take the suit in, darting here and nipping there, taking up the hem, until it was finished.

The front door banged as the hall clock struck seven. Mr. Langman and his son came in together. They had met on the station and caught the same train as the raid had disrupted the train times and George had to wait for his Father's train to arrive in order to get home.

"Oh goodness, is that the time, Joe? Hello, George darling! I have been so busy with Sarah's suit that I haven't even begun to think of the dinner. I'll quickly make a corned beef stew; luckily I have a tin in my store cupboard, and it won't take long. How was your day at the office? Did any of those cruel bombs fall near you?"

Joe kissed his wife on the head affectionately and replied: "Well, it was a pretty near thing. The sandbags helped protect our building, but an office at the end of the street bought it. This destruction is so evil, people are very afraid. We won't be able to get any petrol soon the garages are running out fast. Last year's rationing is taking its toll. Already there is a dearth of blackout material for the office windows. We are having to use thick brown paper to cover the windows and door-lights wherever we can. Every night we seem to suffer appalling raids, the Blitz is upon us, I'm afraid."

Hilda peeled the vegetables for the stew and said: "Earlier today the sirens wailed and we sheltered in the Twentyman's cellar. I luckily managed to get some blackout material before the raid in the high street. It was the last lot that Boag's had. We will fix it up as best we can tonight. I also managed to get some torch batteries. We will need them to go down to the shelter

if there is a raid in the middle of the night, and there
were not many of those either. We will have to resort
to candles, so I also bought a score of those for use if
the power goes off. Thank goodness we have a good
supply of coal in the bunker. I asked Sarah to count the
bags when the coal man came, luckily he still manages
to keep his horse. Ben is such a lovely old Clydesdale;
he seems as if nothing would faze him, but he cannot
understand all the noise of the bombs. I believe he is
safely stabled under the railway arches in Green Lane.
Domestic animals are also suffering, I hear Mrs.
Summers has lost her cat, he just ran off, and she
cannot find him anywhere. Poor Boocles is prostrate
with fear when there is a raid – I have to shut him in his
cat box with some choice tit-bits, and put him outside
in the coal shed before we go to the shelter."

The family chatted over their meal. Sarah had hers
on a tray in her bed. Her head was still aching and she
wasn't very hungry.

Later that evening in a semblance of normality the
Twentyman sisters and their friend, old Captain
Pendred, came up to the Langman's house for a game
of cards. The dining room table was cleared of plates
and dishes and the green baize cloth was laid over the
table. The square pink and yellow fringed gaming light
was lowered by means of a pulley and the games began
in earnest. All loved card games of whist, rummy and
pelmanism. They also played Newmarket, in which
small bets were placed, usually in pennies or half-
pence; however, when young people such as Sarah
were present, spent matches were used instead. The
four old friends concentrated hard over their cards and
then after an hour Hilda brought in steaming mugs of

hot cocoa and some griddle pancakes with home-made blackcurrant jam.

"With eggs and margarine rationed, I soon won't be able to make many more of these," sighed Hilda. "I wonder if we could have a couple of chickens in a coop down the bottom of our garden. We could then share our eggs with neighbours. I think that would be a good idea; what do you think Joe?"

Her husband, being a canny Scot, liked the idea and promised to build a coop with an outside run. "Just a couple would be no good, we would have to have at least six hens to make it worthwhile."

They chatted on, and luckily that night there was no raid to disturb their camaraderie.

"I'm so relieved my children were safe today," Mary said. She ran a small Dame School in an old Edwardian house in the next road. "I fear for their future, I really do! Most of them have been evacuated but just a few remain, they will be leaving any day now, to the country or the seaside out of danger, I understand."

"What a terrible wrench for their mothers," put in Hilda. "I know I could not have borne having to be parted from George or Sarah, especially at such a young age, although of course, they will be safer away from London. The goodbyes on the stations must be hell."

The old friends munched contentedly and sat gazing in companionable silence at the glowing embers of the fire.

"Oh well, we must away to our beds. Mine is definitely calling me," said Joseph, as he escorted the ladies to the hall and helped them on with their coats.

The grandfather clock on the wall struck 10.00 p.m. as they took their leave.

"Let's hope we have a quiet night tonight. I don't want Sarah out of bed again until her nose is less swollen and she is feeling better."

"Goodnight Jessie, bless you Mary, see you soon." Joseph closed the front door and went into the kitchen where Hilda was washing up.

"Is Boocles in dear?" he asked his wife. Hilda wiped her hands and pointed to the cat basket under the table, where their old tabby cat was curled up snug and warm.

"Since the raids began he doesn't stray far from the house. He, like us, must feel his whole world has descended into chaos."

Hilda went up the stairs to bed and Joseph wound the old clock in the hall, using a large brass key. His mind was full of anxiety for his family. He knew it would only be a matter of time before his son and daughter would be called up to serve their country and leave home.

In the Great War he had been a V.A.D. volunteer. His health precluded his joining up, so he had helped all he could to organise and facilitate the care of wounded soldiers and sailors. He well remembered the horrors of that war, and that made him doubly afraid of the devastation and death of this war to come.

Joe's strong faith helped; his Presbyterian church came second only to his family. He shook his head and ascended the stairs thinking, we are all in the hands of our Father in heaven. He will care for His children, we must trust in Him.

CHAPTER SEVEN

"To make the darkness light"

Sarah had been working at the bank for a year or so.
She was rather a square peg in a round hole, but
wanted to do her best for her father, who had managed
to get her an interview at the head office of one of the
top five London banks.

On the day of her interview, she had been very
nervous before setting out for head office, having to
visit the lavatory several times. However, once she was
in the interview room she smiled disarmingly and
presented a very polite and very respectable
demeanour, which, coupled with the background of her
private education, including extra elocution classes,
meant that she came across very well in front of the
Board. She charmed the straight-laced bank officials to
such an extent that, to her amazement, she was given a
job straight away. She was so proud of obtaining the
post, but modestly did not put this accomplishment
down to her own personality; instead she was sure that
it was because she was wearing the smart suit that her
dear mother had fashioned for her.

Owing to the outbreak of war and resultant staff
shortages, the bank did not give her an arithmetic test,
which was fortunate as it would have made it obvious
that she was really hopeless at figure work. Although
her secretarial skills were good, and her command of
the English language was excellent, her job entailed
ledger work. This really made her brassed off as, no
matter how hard she tried, the figures did not behave as
they should. She hated the moment when all had to
tally up before the bank employees could go home.

Sarah always seemed to be the one to cause a problem
with her ledger, and she began to dread the end of each
working day.

Henry Treleaven had noticed the pretty dark-haired
new recruit to the office, and thought her extremely
attractive. She was much too young for him, of course,
but still he could admire her trim figure and ready
smile.

He also realised that she was struggling with her
ledger work. He was a kindly man, and didn't like to
see another suffering, so he would offer to help her
balance her books. For that she was extremely grateful.

"Thank you so much, Mr. Treleaven," Sarah said
gratefully. "I know I am hopeless, and you must think
me such a dunce, but I just don't seem to be able to get
the hang of these figures."

"Not at all, Miss Langman," said Henry kindly.
"These books are not that easy, and every single penny
has to be accounted for at the end of the day. They just
have to balance. I have been doing them for years, so I
can see where you are going wrong, and perhaps I can
point out a few short cuts to make your life easier."

Sarah rather liked Mr. Treleaven; he was so well
turned out, and smelled very nice when he bent over
her work. He had kindly brown eyes and she noted his
long, elegant fingers and large gold watch and signet
ring as he helped her put things right. She thought he
was probably in his thirties, much older than her, and
was surprised that he bothered to assist her. None of
the other men in the office seemed to care at all, and
were only irritated that her failing book-keeping was
preventing them from going home.

Sarah's concentration was not helped by the fact that
she was also very nervous. Bombing raids were

increasing, and she was terrified that she would not find her beloved home still standing when she returned each evening. Her mother was so brave and stoical and always greeted her daughter with a smile and a kiss and brushed away her fears. She simply could not bear the thought of losing her family, and this background anxiety coloured her life every single day.

During the Blitz there were few nights when the sirens didn't wail their mournful sonorous wavering warning, so the people of London did not get much sleep. The Langman family tried to make the best of things, constantly having to get up out of their warm beds to go down to the Twentyman's shelter. Broken nights did not help the morale of those living in these anxious times, and tempers often frayed.

"Blast!" Sarah exclaimed. "I have just badly laddered my stockings, I shall have to run and change them, and now I will probably miss my train." She disappeared upstairs in a flurry, and her mother waited in the hall to hand her the sandwiches she always made for her daughter's lunch at the office.

George came down in a hurry. "Mother! Where *is* my brown striped tie? I cannot find it anywhere."

"It is on your tie rack, darling," said Hilda patiently.

"Joe, I have cooked you an egg – it is the only one you will have this week, I'm afraid."

Joseph Langman ran past his son down the stairs. "Goodness, I have overslept Hilda my dear," he panted. "I really have no time for breakfast this morning. Last night's raid has made me very tired and crotchety."

"I will quickly make a sandwich with the egg for you darling," Hilda said calmly. "There is a pot of freshly brewed coffee on the table. Have some, and that will perk you up."

She seemed to be the only one in the family who was in a good mood that morning. She bustled away into the kitchen to rescue the egg.

Sarah rushed in. "Thank goodness, Mummy! At last I have found another pair of nylons with a seam, my very last ones. They are all but absent from the shops now. I shall just have to stain my legs brown and draw seams on the back with a pen – all the girls are resorting to that tactic – or I shall have to wear those dreadful old thick lisle stockings, ugh! Do you think my aunts in Plymouth may be able to find me some down in the West Country shops?"

"I'll write and ask them but I don't hold out much hope. Plymouth has been hit with a lot of devastating bombing raids recently. Sadly, the lovely old parish church of St. Andrews in the city centre has been hit."

"That is a great shame, such a beautiful church. Oh, I forgot to say," said Sarah. "Joyce and I are going to the flicks tonight, Mummy, as long as there are no raids. There is a good flick on at The Rink with one of my favourite actors, James Stewart. Do you know he is in the American Air Force and has flown his twelfth combat mission, leading the second bombing wing in an attack on Berlin? Can you imagine that? He is sooo dreamy, and handsome, and funny."

"He is a very brave man, are you, perhaps, losing your heart to him, darling?" her mother asked, "What about Gary Cooper? Have you deserted him?"

"No – not darling Gary." Sarah had kept a scrap book of his films ever since she was a teenager. "I could never forsake HIM!"

"All right, sweetheart, here are your sandwiches. Now be off with you!"

She kissed her daughter's soft cheek, and noticed how pretty she was looking. Sarah didn't use much make-up, unlike some of the girls, just a touch of pink face powder and red lipstick. With her sparkling green eyes and pretty hair, Hilda thought her daughter was quite beautiful. She was also wearing a touch of her favourite L'Aimant perfume, by Coty, which made her smell delicious.

With a bang of the front door Joe, George and Sarah all departed for the railway station and on to their places of work, and peace descended once again on the little suburban house.

"Now Boocles," Hilda addressed the cat, meowing at her feet. "Let us see what we can find for your morning titbit. Then I really must get the wash tub and blue bag out to tackle some sheets, as it looks like a fine day to hang out the washing."

CHAPTER EIGHT

"Enriching and filling my treasure store"

Henry wore his dark overalls; he had obtained his stirrup-pump, Fire Watcher's SFP armband and hard hat. It was tiring work as he watched the skies criss-crossed by searchlights, and it was lonely as he made his solitary rounds in the dark.

He had had a particularly difficult and long day at the office. There was a chap in the office that he disliked intensely. Old Cochran made Henry's life very difficult sometimes: he seemed to go out of his way to antagonise, deliberately causing problems where really there should be none. Henry put it down to a desire on the other man's part to be top dog, and as Henry generally got on well with everyone else at work, including the manager, he supposed this cantankerousness to be down to a sense of one-upmanship or rivalry. Henry was all for a quiet life and just liked to be left alone to get on with his job; after all, the war created far more financial work than normal, and he very much felt that the staff all needed to pull together. Working life was tough enough, and pettiness was definitely not on his agenda.

He was responsible for a couple of factories situated near his home. Sometimes he was out virtually all night, watching for incendiary bombs and warning the authorities of any fires caused by them. It was tedious work, as he had to patrol the factories constantly, and he still had a full day to face at the office the next day. Often he felt dog tired, but at least he knew he was doing his bit to keep Sydenham free from fire damage.

Piling on the pressure was the fact that it was getting more and more difficult to travel by train to work. Railway lines were being bombed all over London, and whilst Henry's line to work was still just about functioning, stations were being wrecked along the way, making buying tickets very difficult. He decided he must begin driving up to the office. Maybe he could even offer lifts to other members of staff, picking them up en route. It would be an answer to the transport problem if he could only get the petrol, and perhaps the office could help in that department.

He was worried about his mother and aunt. They were getting quite nervous living in south London, and in fact he was thinking that it may be a better idea to ship them off to Gloucester, where his sister Violet had gone temporarily with Francis her son. However, when he broached the idea with his mother she said she wouldn't hear of leaving him, and there was nothing he could do about it as she could be very obstinate. Henry realised he would just have to keep the two ladies as safe as he could. He had checked that their blackout boards fitted the many windows in their large house, and told them to go into the cupboard under the stairs if there was a raid and if they had to shelter in a hurry, to get under the kitchen table. He realised that his mother's arthritis would probably preclude that action, but it was the best option if ever they heard the warning siren.

Despite all this misery and anxiety caused by the conflict, Henry was aware of a strange stirring in his heart. He found himself looking for the new recruit, Sarah, each day when he arrived for work. He was pleased to help her in balancing her ledger. She really seemed to be struggling with the figures, and he couldn't bear to see her in distress.

During their working together Henry ascertained that Sarah was keen on music, especially Chopin, one of his favourite composers; thus the two had begun a friendship. He wondered if he dared ask her out for a bite to eat. He knew he was much too old for her, but he found her passion for classical music a great attraction. He had recently purchased a mahogany upright piano and he just loved to spend hours playing it when he had the time.

He had noticed one Saturday morning, when the trains were still running, that as he alighted at Sydenham railway station Sarah seemed to be on the platform too. He must have been on her train, further down in another carriage. He followed her down the high street a little way, to see where she was going; however he lost her in the crowd. Henry wondered if, indeed, she lived in the same place as him. That will make my asking her out a bit easier, thought Henry, maybe I will look for her on the platform in the morning, and we can travel up to work together. Or, he suddenly had another idea, I could offer her a lift to work with one or two others in my car. Lately the office had offered to do what they could to help procure petrol for their staff travelling to work. That would be a good way to get to know her better. Our line to London has been partially damaged by bombing, so I think I will take it up next week.

Sure enough, after the weekend, he spotted Sarah waiting on the platform and went up to her, and raised his hat in greeting: "Well, hello there!"

Sarah turned around and when she saw it was Henry, gave a beaming grin.

"Good morning Mr. Treleaven," she said. "What a lovely day!"

"Please, call me Trel," said Henry. "Everyone else does – Treleaven is a mouthful – and I have been known as 'Trel' ever since my school days in Truro. I live here, and so, I presume, must you – seeing as we are catching the same train."

"Yes. I live with my parents in Tannsfeld road, No. 15."

"Well, well! Just fancy that! My mother bought a house in that road fairly recently, No. 113, so your parents live at the top and my mother lives at the bottom, down the hill by the park. What a coincidence! Now, as we are so close, I wonder if you would be interested in a lift up to town. I am going to start taking my car to work soon and am offering lifts to anyone I can pick up, and fit in, on the way. This railway line of ours is just about open but could be bombed at any time and we would be stuck." He smiled.

"Well, we *could* take a bus, but that would take forever, and we would have to leave at the crack of dawn," Sarah observed wryly. "Yes, please, Mr. Treleaven, a lift would be absolutely marvellous. Thank you."

The train arrived into the station with a whoosh and flurry of steam, making any more conversation impossible. Henry and Sarah carried on chatting in the compartment about the office, their work, and the coincidence of living in the same place. They also chatted about Sarah's anxiety, as her elder brother George had been called up and had joined the Royal West Kent Regiment, and she was afraid for him.

That evening they missed each other going home because Sarah left early, as she had a dental appointment.

Later that very night they suffered a large raid, and their railway line to London was hit, so early next morning Henry telephoned all those he could pick up en route – first, of course, was Sarah.

The lifts to and from the office carried on as long as Henry was able to obtain petrol. As predicted, his chief stepped in and helped Henry to locate the scarce filling stations that still had fuel, and also sorted out some extra petrol coupons, so he continued taking staff into London for some months. During this time Henry had been introduced to Sarah's family as he picked her up in the morning, and thus was even able to occasionally take Sarah, her mother, his mother and aunt on the odd jaunt into the countryside at the weekend for a welcome breath of fresh air.

Sarah's mother Hilda and his mother Annie got on very well, and Sarah and Henry were able to leave them gossiping, sitting in their picnic chairs, while they went off together and chatted. They spoke about their mutual passion for Chopin and classical music, especially piano concertos, and these subjects made for some lively discussions on the techniques of various pianists and their performances. They laughed and joked and kicked the fallen leaves as they walked along together.

I must ask her to come with me to that concert, thought Henry, as he drove them all home through the autumn twilight. The trees blazed in their dying colours and the sun touched the dark clouds with gold and pink as it waned.

After dropping his mother and aunt home and then bidding goodnight to Sarah's mother, Henry plucked up the courage and asked Sarah to a concert he had seen in the local paper. One of her favourite pieces of Chopin was to be performed in Upper Norwood. To his tremendous pleasure she agreed to accompany him.

Their first outing together was a great success. They both enjoyed the music immensely and afterwards they went on for a bite to eat at Cobb's restaurant, at the top of Sydenham high street.

Sarah liked Henry very much; she admired his well-turned out appearance, his trim moustache and kindly brown eyes. He was also the perfect gentleman when they were together, making sure she was comfortable, taking her wrap, making sure she was not sitting in a draft. He was solicitous towards her in every way. A bit like her dear father, Sarah thought. She enjoyed his attention to detail: the best seats at the concert, the best table in the window of a restaurant. An older man knows how do to these things well, Sarah pondered, and she relished his thoughtfulness.

Henry was totally smitten with Sarah. It was great fun being with a much younger, pretty woman, and her ability to laugh at a moment's notice and her cheerfulness began to creep into his heart. He knew he was falling in love, and they were spending a lot of time together. Sarah often came to his flat on a Saturday afternoon for a cuppa and chat, mainly about office politics that week, and they became firm friends. A relationship was blossoming that Henry hadn't experienced for many years. Henry would play his piano for Sarah and, as she could play a bit too, they played a few duets together – amid much laughter from Sarah when she went wrong.

Henry tried to be cautious, however, because of their age difference. However, being with Sarah made him realise how empty his life was when she went home, and he now longed even more to get married and settle down, but he realised that Sarah was probably not ready for that yet.

I will just have to bide my time, he thought. If I have a chance to make her my wife she will be worth waiting for, and that is a fact! So he resolved to be patient and meanwhile just to relish her delightful company.

CHAPTER NINE

"When did you endear yourself to me?"

Gary really felt very happy during his time in Canada, learning to fly the planes of war. He spent six months overseas and soon was able to handle the fighting planes with consummate ease. He enjoyed his training; the Canadian Air Force men were very friendly. If it hadn't been for the war in Europe he'd have simply felt elated to be able to fly, his main passion, well away from the pressures of the front line and to certain extent his unhappy home life.

He won his wings, which he wore with great pride, and was sent back to Blighty to commence his life as a Flight Sergeant. He was posted to Kent, to the RAF base on the east coast at Manston on the Isle of Thanet. This was far from Cornwall, and Gary was a bit fed up at being sent seemingly to the other side of England.

However, he was very adaptable, made the most of things and settled in fairly well to his new RAF life at the air base. He had to complete a few more weeks of training in the Flying School at Manston, just to familiarise himself with the Spitfires, Mosquitoes, Halifaxes and Lancasters: the 'kites' as RAF colleagues called the planes of war. They were mostly involved in flying low-level sorties in K1 Spitfires, which had been brought into service in August 1938 and were reported to be the most versatile fighter planes, manoeuvrable and fast. However, recently the RAF had brought in a faster Spitfire model, the Mark XIV, which was more able to compete equally with the German Focke-Wulf 190. Gary had much admiration for the new plane. He had heard that it handled very well; no wonder it cost as much as £5,000! It was worth every penny, so responsive and easy to fly. This could turn on a sixpence, he thought.

He much enjoyed flying around the coast of Thanet, testing planes that had been repaired, observing from above the landscape that was so different from wild Cornwall. He flew over the wide flat marshy bay at Pegwell and the southern approach to Manston RAF base. Beneath him passed the white cliffs of Ramsgate, the corner of North Foreland and the golden sands at Margate, Westgate and Minnis Bay. At least the flying is over the sea, mused Gary, so not really that different from home. He pondered on the similarity between the peninsula of Penwith and the Isle of Thanet. They were roughly about the same width and almost totally surrounded by the sea. Both were at the east and west extremities of the widest part of England, too. Although the sea was more of a mud colour in Kent rather than the blue-green of Cornwall, the sunsets over the North Sea were just amazing. It wasn't surprising that Turner liked to paint here, he thought.

Back at the airfield he had made friends; after all, the other chaps were in the same boat, coming from all over England, Scotland and Wales. There were even a couple from Cornwall. Most were very young, all were missing their homes and were thrown in to air combat. Taught to look out for each other, a real camaraderie grew amongst those lately posted to Manston. Gary found that it was a great comfort to meet chaps from Wales, the land of his birth. He could still speak a bit of the language and felt a great kindred spirit with them. One of his best pals was a chap called Reg, a friendly sort of cove. Reg was one of the invaluable ground crew who worked on the kites when they landed with engine trouble. Manston was one of the first ports of call when damaged planes returned to England. Some of them only just made the airfield, or were so battered that they sadly crashed. Reg and his crew spent all of their time patching up these planes, ready for their next excursion to enemy territory. They worked on farmland belonging to Alland Grange, just beside the 'drome.

During further training Gary flew across the Channel and along the Kent coast. During a night raid he learned to dodge anti-aircraft guns and enemy searchlights, how to use his ejector seat and parachute to reach the safety of terra firma. His first parachute jump was exhilarating as well as terrifying, and he nearly lost his breakfast in the fear of waiting for the command to "Go!"

At one point he was temporarily made a 'tail-end Charlie', a rear gunner in a Lancaster bomber, part of a pathfinder unit whose job it was to lead the way. All the men had interchangeable jobs: the pilots became navigators, and vice versa. Each man had to be able to handle and direct the planes in case one was picked out and killed by gunfire, ensuring the safety of the crew.

However, as time passed Gary was asked to fly less often. Although he attained the rank of Flight Sergeant, he was mainly assigned to testing planes reassembled by Reg and his crew. Gary realised that this was probably because of his age, and to his chagrin his Adjutant put him in charge of Admin, in one of the huts, making sure the paperwork of the unit was up to date. He had several WAAF clerks working for him. He got on well with these ladies. They were a happy lot and although the work was tedious and long they always managed to

have a laugh and a joke along the way. He was a bit of a
charmer, and soon he had one or two of the girls
making him 'special' cups of coffee or bringing the odd
biscuit to his desk.

There had been many buildings flattened by a large
bombing raid at Manston in 1940, so all staff were
billeted out of the camp. The WAAFs were staying at
the nearby Ursuline Convent in Westgate which had
been adapted from classrooms to dormitories. This
had been a great upheaval for the gentle nuns. Only a
few remained at the convent as most had been sent out
to help in other areas. Those that remained enjoyed the
company of the lively young Women's Auxiliary Air
Force recruits. The schoolgirls had all been evacuated,
so the big old red brick building had seemed very
empty and lonely without their noise and bustle. Now,
however, the arrival of the WAAFs helped to bring the
old building back to life again, with their lively
chattering and general clattering noise.

The RAF men were billeted at a large old house,
once the Hockeredge Hotel, along the Canterbury
Road, and both sexes had to cycle or walk to the
'drome every day. This was a pleasant ride along
country lanes through the fields of Thanet, which were
usually planted with cauliflowers and did not smell too
good at certain times of the year!

Gary sometimes walked across fields to and from
the 'drome. He enjoyed his time out in the fresh air.
Eventually he was given an ancient bike, and although
he wasn't brilliant at riding it, he soon got used to
bowling along early in the morning to breakfast at the
camp. He especially appreciated the vastness of the flat
land and huge skies. The dawns and sunsets in Thanet
were stunningly beautiful, and the ever-changing

colours of the clouds over the fading sun filled him with awe. He had an eye for the beauty of nature and had even tried his hand at painting. I'm no Turner, though! He mused, but he was very inspired by the land and seascapes of Margate. He did not appreciate it, however, when the wind blew in from the North Sea and made the early morning treks to get breakfast pretty grim, even after he was kitted out with a thick RAF blue issue overcoat and muffled up in a scarf of grey with maroon and navy stripes.

He was getting used to life at Manston. At least he was now in one place, and wouldn't be sent to other postings for the moment. It was a very long way from Cornwall though. Sometimes he was very homesick, and he missed his children very much. He wrote long letters to them, coupled with newsy letters to his wife. He included little drawings for his children, of local landmarks such as the twin towers at Reculver. This area had once contained a Roman fort, but now the twin towers of the church were the local landmark. They had gained notoriety in 1943 when the Barnes Wallis bouncing bomb was tested in that area before the successful Operation Chastise carried out by the Dam Busters. He wrote about the Roman fort to his son, who, at nine years old was keen on history.

Gary's wife wrote the odd line or two in return, but the letters were never very loving, just filled with the practicalities of looking after two young children with the constraints of war, rationing of food and clothing, the general difficulties of which Gary would have taken on as he was the one who usually washed and dressed the children and put them to bed. His wife was still too much involved with her academic research, and found the children a burden. She let Gary know this in no uncertain terms, almost castigating him for not being there as if it was his fault there was a war on.

It began to get very cold at Manston during the winter of 1943/44. The wind whistled cruelly in from the North Sea, the morning trek to the 'drome was difficult, the roads were icy and snow fell intermittently. Spring was very late that year. The dark mornings were miserable and the tortoise stove in the Admin hut seemed primarily to belch out smoke and fumes and did not give out much warmth. Morale was low. Gary did his best to chivvy the typists along but they complained bitterly.

They all sat in a tremendous draught. The Admin hut faced north to south and the wind howled in under one door and raced out the other. Working under the duress of the incessant bitter cold made all the girls feel very fed up.

"Coo! Stone the crows! My chilblains are playing me up something awful. Having constantly cold feet doesn't help," said Phyllis, a brown haired bespectacled girl who was a typist. "I really need some new thicker lisle stockings, but I have run out of clothing coupons for this month."

"Never mind ducks," her pretty dark-haired friend, Jill, replied. "I have a spare pair you can borrow. Just lend me some of your lipstick, would you? I feel so undressed without a bit of face powder and my ruby red lips. My Mum thinks I have the look of Margaret Lockwood when I am made up, you know!"

"Margaret Lockwood!!! You must be joking! No amount of make-up will make you look anything more than yourself, dear," retorted Phyllis with a grin.

"Well, thanks for that, chum! At least I can dream! You know, I think I am losing weight – that is why I am so cold. What doesn't help matters is that the food here is bloomin' awful. My breakfast sausage was running with syrup as they put everything on one plate. At least we *all* may lost a bit of weight with all this walking in freezing weather, and the disgusting rations!"

"The work load goes on and on. I have so many of these leave dockets to do, and this morning I have to escort a prisoner to the C.O. One of our lot went AWOL and was nabbed in Margate in a pub, after hours. She is for the hop and no mistake! I wouldn't like to be in her shoes. She will get jankers, maybe in the form of extra duties, and probably be confined to camp indefinitely with no weekend pass or any chance to go on leave. All for the sake of a drink or two! Still, I hope she enjoyed herself for a while – that is what we all need at the moment. Mind you, I could kill for a bar of chocolate. Some hopes of that!"

"Well, you cannot blame her really, this weather means there are no shakey-dos to cheer us girls up. Nothing like a bit of a dance to put the roses back in our cheeks! All we get to do is mend our stockings and polish our buttons for inspection. I ask you, all this and freezing feet too!"

Gary knew there was no lightening the mood of the girls. The cold and the interminable war had just got to them, and morale was low in the camp generally. His wisecracks and friendly teasing fell on deaf ears. It was his duty to keep the girls working well, but he couldn't blame them for their moaning. He tried hard to boost the heat from the old stove and stuffed some sacking under the doors to try and raise the temperature. The girls resorted to wearing fingerless mittens to try and keep their hands warm. They even took to wearing their thick RAF scarves round their necks indoors, and that helped a bit.

Manston, despite the bad weather, had lately become part of the Second Tactical Air Force, and the base was increasingly coping with the many damaged bombers that just made it to the East Kent coast. This all engendered more paperwork, and the work load was incessant. Dockets created for this, that and the other came through the Admin hut. The girls worked as fast as they could, but they were mostly behind, and Gary knew he would get it in the neck if he couldn't remedy the situation. Hopefully, he had been informed that there would be a new contingent of WAAFs coming in from other stations to ease things in the near future.

It began to snow very heavily, so Gary arranged for early transport to take the girls back to the Ursuline Convent. At least they would not have to walk back that evening, and with any luck he could hitch a lift back to his billet too, as he was sure ready for his bed. He wondered when he would be flying again. Probably not in this weather, no chance!

CHAPTER 10

"My harbour of tranquillity"

Sarah's relationship with Henry had been gathering momentum. She knew he was very keen on her and was inclined to be a bit serious at times. She laughed at his seriousness, and at twenty-two years of age she was having fun going out with a man of thirty-seven. Well, that was something, for a young lady: he paid for everything, and even when she got her purse out to pay for the odd drink, no, he would not hear of it!

They had been to concerts – they both enjoyed piano concertos, in fact their musical taste was very similar – and they enjoyed going to see the latest films at The Rink cinema. Henry told Sarah that it was so called as it was once an ice rink. It was now converted, with cosy red velvet seating and crimson curtains with gold tassels, and was very swanky! Sarah had always wondered about that name, and now she understood.

They were able to discuss the films when they came home from the office together, in Henry's car. They enjoyed lively analysis of the characters and the plot, sometimes agreeing but mostly disagreeing, in a friendly fashion.

Henry was a very good dancer. As he was very slim he was light on his feet, and he was able to steer Sarah around the dance floor with great aplomb. His hero was Fred Astaire, and he longed to be able to emulate that genius of Terpsichore, and Sarah became his Ginger Rogers for the evening as they whirled around to the sounds of a local band. Sarah loved to dance; she found it very romantic, being held lightly yet firmly by Henry who smelt divine. She loved his cologne, and she was very happy as they sashayed around the dance floor.

Henry always took Sarah out for a bite to eat after a show or when they had been dancing. One evening they went to a very smart dinner dance in London. Sarah was all dressed up in a white satin dress with a pretty sparkly brooch on her shoulder, borrowed from her mother, set to hold the floral corsage that Henry had bought for her. She felt very grown up and glamorous as he presented it to her in a box, tied with pink satin ribbon. Her cheeks were flushed and her eyes sparkled at the magnificence of the dance venue. Even in the middle of a war, in the true British bulldog spirit, London kept entertainments going, and the big hotels put on the best show they could under difficult circumstances.

Yes, Sarah really liked Henry and was very glad to have him to take her out to the best places. He was also very kind to her, very solicitous and thoughtful, always looking after and her making sure she was not too hot or cold, wrapping her up in her evening stole so she felt cherished.

When they said goodnight at her garden gate, he pulled her towards him and gave her a soft kiss on the cheek. His moustache momentarily tickled her, so she giggled with glee. He treated her with respect, even though Sarah would have liked a little more from him. He was taking things slowly, and that is the way her parents would have wanted things to progress.

Both Joe and Hilda liked Henry. His good manners and polite conversation endeared him to them, as did, of course, his assurances that he would look after their daughter during their evenings out. Henry particularly got on well with Hilda: her West Country jolliness and warmth was in stark contrast to his own mother, who tended to be a little stern and cold at times. Annie Treleaven couldn't really be blamed as she had endured a hard life, and it had reflected in a lack of physical warmth in her personality, whereas Hilda always welcomed Henry to the house with a loving hug and Joe Langman came and shook his hand warmly.

The Treleavens often took tea with the Langmans on a Sunday afternoon. Mrs. Langman could still turn out a passable table, with cakes and scones made with powdered egg, and there was always a full teapot on the go for anyone with a thirst.

Often these convivial tea parties would include the Twentyman sisters and so a party would be made up ready for an evening of card games, air raids permitting. Henry loved to have his mother with him. The Langmans really made her feel at home too, there was much laughing and joking which ensued as various games were won and lost. Joe Langman was a canny Scot and was good at winning games, whereas his wife was happy to lose. She really enjoyed having so many people in her cosy home as it took her mind off the harshness of war, just for an evening or two. Her son George had been called up and was now serving in the Royal West Kent regiment as a Captain. She was very proud of him but also full of dread, and prayed earnestly to God every night for his safe-keeping.

Henry loved having a piano in his flat. He rushed home every evening to practise *'Liebestraum'* or *'Moonlight Sonata'*, although secretly he would have loved to be able to vamp like Charlie Kunz and just play all the latest songs in an easy way, or even boogie-woogie sometimes. His piano gave him great pleasure. It had a matching stool and barley twist ash-tray which stood beside it to hold his cigarette, smouldering and sending out a slow spiral of smoke while he played.

He also played the musical saw with much vibrato and wobbling of his knee. He managed to make it sound very eerie, just right for a horror programme on the Home Service. His musical accomplishments stretched to playing the accordion. He would occasionally, fire warden duties allowing, take it round to their house and play to entertain his mother and aunt while they did their mending on cold winter nights.

Life carried on as normally as people could manage, but a great change was to come for Sarah when she received her call-up papers at last.

CHAPTER 11

"The chain of thought remains intact"

There was the dreaded buff envelope, waiting for Sarah on the hall table.

Hilda knew what it meant and was filled with anxiety for her daughter. In 1940 George had been spared taking part in the Dunkirk evacuations because of his eczema. His painful skin condition had worsened, possibly being exacerbated by worry because his Regiment, in which he was a Captain, was very much involved in various dangerous missions. He was thankfully still safe and sound, but now her only daughter might be put in peril in the services.

She sat down in the kitchen on her own by the stove and had a little weep into her pinny. When on earth will this dreadful war end? She asked herself. She just couldn't bear the fact that her beloved daughter would have to go away from her. Even though Sarah was now twenty-two, she had never been away from home on her own before and Hilda wondered how she would cope. She was also very afraid. War was so evil, bringing so much death, destruction and heartache, and that was a grim fact.

The door banged and Sarah came in with a flurry of snow. She said hallo to her mother and announced that she was absolutely freezing and her teeth were chattering but then noticed the buff envelope. She struggled to get her coat and furry gloves off in a hurry.

At last she opened the envelope and said: "OOOh Mummy! My call-up papers have arrived. Oh goodness me! How very scary! Well, I think it will be the Royal Air Force and the WAAFs for me! I really don't fancy going to sea – I have no sea-legs at all – and the Army does not interest me either. At least in the RAF I won't have to wear khaki. Blue is more my colour! I really don't want to leave you, Mummy dearest, and darling Daddy neither! I will miss my home so much."

"You are funny, darling," said her mother. "I cannot think that anyone else would consider their appearance at such a time!" Her mother reached out and gave her daughter a reassuring hug. "We will always be here, waiting for you to come home."

"I know, Mummy," Sarah said. "Now I must simply go and tell Joyce."

"Well, don't be too long, will you? Your meal is all ready, and piping hot."

"Oh, if it is ready now, I will eat and then go down to Joyce. I don't want your lovely meal to spoil."

Later, Sarah donned her coat again and slithered down the road through the snow to her friend Joyce's house. She had also received her call-up papers and was very apprehensive about it all.

"How will we cope away from home?" Joyce was peeling potatoes for her mother in the kitchen. "I mean, I cannot imagine living away from my dear parents, and we may be posted miles and miles away from them."

"We could be near enough to come home at the weekends," Sarah said cheerfully, trying to buoy up her pal. "You and I can certainly write to each other as well. Have you another knife? I could help do a few spuds with you. I have already eaten."

"You are lucky, you know, to have a mother at home, mine works and I help cook the evening meal as often as she gets home late and is so tired. In fact, I don't know how she will manage when I enlist."

They both tried in vain to look on the positive side, but really in their hearts they felt sad, and very frightened at what the future would bring.

Sarah was not looking forward to telling Henry that she had been called up. She had begun to call him Trel, a shortened form of Treleaven, as everyone in the office knew him. She knew he would miss her, and also knew that he really wanted to get married. He had hinted several times to her that he was well set up in a good job, and was of mature years and ready to settle down. The war would certainly come between them. In a way she was thankful because, although she had become very fond of Trel, the prospect of married life was something she could not contemplate yet. She was still young and wanted to enjoy herself, perhaps to go out with other chaps and play the field a bit. She was a vivacious, pretty girl and was well aware that her charms produced admiring glances from other male staff members at work.

She called to see Trel at his neat little flat, where he was ironing his shirts ready for the next week.

"My call-up papers have come," she said, noting Trel's forlorn expression. "I shall be leaving in a couple of weeks, I have to report to an RAF base to learn the ropes."

Trel, who had been dreading this moment, gave her a hug and said sadly. "Well, darling, so you have chosen the Air Force, have you? You know I will miss you every single minute you are away. I will pray for your safety, and also that you will soon return to me. I have been so busy these nights on my fire-watching duty that we have not had much time for each other lately, have we? When will you be going and where? We must have a last evening out together before you leave."

Sarah and Trel did have a wonderful evening out together. They went to The Rink cinema to watch "Give us the Moon" with Margaret Lockwood and then on for a slap-up supper at Cobb's Corner Restaurant.

The evening together was very precious. Trel kept stroking Sarah's hand and reassuring her, trying to allay her anxieties. He really loved her so much, and she was looking so lovely that evening. Her dark, curly hair had been recently styled and her green eyes shone like deep pools in the dim light of the restaurant. She smiled at him and playfully tweaked his moustache. "Will you wait for me, then?" She tipped her head on one side. "You may get lonely and go after one of the other young ladies in the office. I expect you will go up to the West End without me, maybe meeting up with Herbert – I reckon you will soon be a proper Piccadilly playboy, and no mistake," she teased.

"You know I only have eyes for you, Toodles," Trel said gently. "Besides, the other girls are all good at maths and don't need me to help them tick up their ledgers at the end of the day!" He laughed, catching hold of her hand.

They drank their coffee almost in silence, their hands touching, but despite this warmth between them it was not a very happy meal.

Trel and Sarah walked back to her parent's house. The evening was cold and crisp, the pavements sparkled with frost and luckily there had been no raids that evening. He left Sarah at her family home, kissed her goodbye and said:

"Take care of yourself, darling one. God bless you and bring you safely back to me."

"You look after yourself too, Trel," said Sarah leaning back to look into his eyes. "Make sure you wear warm clothing, and eat well too. Please give my regards to your mother and aunt when next you see them."

Sarah always had a caring attitude when she spoke to Trel, although he was much older than her. She had a natural ability to nurture and always wanted to make sure he looked after himself. She was very fond of him, enjoying their evenings out together and also their time as colleagues in the bank. Quite honestly, if it hadn't been for Trel's kindness she was sure she would have received her cards long ago. He always covered up the mathematical discrepancies in her ledger, so that no-one found out what a dunce she was! She also knew he cared a good deal for her and hoped that one day she would be able to care for him properly too, as his kindness to her had certainly earned her affections.

CHAPTER 12

"I will keep it close to my heart"

Within two weeks Sarah was travelling to
Northumberland, where she met many other girls who
were just as nervous and homesick as herself. They
learned the pattern of RAF life, received their
uniforms, tried them on with much giggling, and were
designated jobs. Sarah, with her secretarial training, was
made a C.G.D. – Clerk, General Duties.

One of the tasks that Sarah enjoyed very much was
marching. They were taught to square bash. "Reach
forward, reach back," their rather austere C.O.
bellowed. "Keep those arms well up, straight, and
pointed at the shoulders of the girl in front. Left, right,
left, right. Company halt!"

There was a great sense of camaraderie that
stemmed from marching, moving as one unit instead of
individuals. Occasionally she would catch the eye of
another girl and they would exchange smiles. For the
first time Sarah felt that life in the RAF was not going to
be all bad.

Sarah did get in a muddle with marching, turning this
way and that as she never could remember her right
from her left, but she and the other girls had a lot of
fun learning. They were taught to salute the ranks
above them. "Longest way up, shortest way down," was
their mantra. The new life of discipline was certainly
different from Civvy Street and took a lot of getting
used to: their freedom had disappeared. The young
women were learning to look out for each other and to

act, not as individuals, but as a close team, each doing
their bit towards winning the war.

After two months' basic training, Sarah found
herself on a train winging its way down south again,
towards London and home. However, she had no time
to visit her folks. She made her way with other WAAFs
to Victoria Station and caught the train down to
Westgate on the east coast of Kent. She had been
posted to RAF Manston, and was very pleased to think
that she was much nearer her home and that maybe
she could get back for the occasional weekend's leave.

The train sped through the freezing dark night,
flurries of snow stuck to the windows and slowly slid
down the panes. The girls had each been given a packet
of sandwiches and they shared them with each other as
they sped along.

"What have you got in yours?" asked a friendly
auburn-haired girl. "I've got what looks like ham, but I
think it is the new Spam, mock ham, really."

Sarah opened her packet and replied: "Yes, I have
that too. It is not at all bad. Gosh, look at the weather!
It seems so odd to be going to Margate in the middle of
winter. My parents often travelled down on a steamer
in the summer, landing at the pier, and we have spent
many happy days on the sandy beaches."

The snow seemed to be getting thicker, the windows
of the train were now almost totally obscured by a thick
white blanket and the wind was howling outside as they
sped onwards, all feeling a trifle anxious.

They were met at Westgate station by an RAF
transport vehicle, and soon they were bouncing along
snowy country lanes to the RAF Aerodrome at
Manston. They met their Commanding Officer, a
rather stout lady with a loud voice. She briefed them

with their duties for the next day, and then the girls were taken to their billet at the nearby Ursuline Convent which had been especially adapted to house the WAAFs. They were given steaming mugs of hot cocoa and a few biscuits, after which they had a quick tour of the convent. They were then issued with their uniforms, shoes, towels and pyjamas.

"Please try on your uniforms before you go to bed, and report any that do not fit. In the morning, you must quickly wash, dress, have a cup of tea here and then transport will be sent to take you to the 'drome. If any caps don't fit, swap them around among yourselves, and report to me if you cannot find one suitable. Breakfast will be served at the Airmen's Mess at Manston. You will be up early so get some sleep as soon as you can." The C.O. saluted and it was returned.

The girls settled into their dormitories where they sat chatting on their hard, single beds and tried to keep warm, as the convent was not without draughts and the temperature outside was freezing. They changed into their RAF issue blue and white striped pyjamas, laughing and joking at the sight of each other. Some of their pyjama legs were far too long, and the more petite girls were falling over them and giggling.

"Well, here we go, girls," remarked one girl. "We will just have to keep together and buoy each other up and see this through. At least these 'jamas are quite thick – I have never worn anything but a long nightie in bed and I feel like a bloke in these!"

Sobs were heard coming from one of the beds. "I cannot bear it, it is soo cold, and I do so miss my parents and my home!"

"We all feel like that, ducks" said the blonde girl. "It won't be so bad, you will see." She went over to the heap under the blankets and patted the sobbing girl's head reassuringly.

"I'd kill for a hot water bottle," Sarah said. "I shall ask Mummy to send some bedsocks, my chilblains are aching so much. Let us all try and get some shut eye now, and see what tomorrow will bring. Not sure that I will be able to sleep with these blessed convent bells pealing every hour."

Silence fell on the dormitory, broken only by the howling of the wind outside and quiet sobbing of a couple of the girls. Soon all was still. Sarah did not sleep immediately; she was too overwhelmed by her new life away from home. Eventually her fatigue overcame her as it had been a long day, and despite the hourly bell chiming, she slept.

CHAPTER THIRTEEN

"Why do I say, if I meet you today,
it will make my day"

A shrill whistle cut through the dark dormitory.
Blackout curtains were swept aside.

"Time to get up girls, hurry with your ablutions, the
transport lorry will be outside in half-an-hour. There is
a cup of tea downstairs for you before you leave!" The
booming voice of the C.O. shattered any dreams the
girls may have been having and, after a lot of yawning
and stretching, they made their way to the cold
bathrooms.

Sarah was reluctant to leave her bed; hard though
the mattress was, at least it was warmer than the dorm.
She hurriedly slipped her feet into her slippers and
walked to the ablutions. There she encountered a girl
stripped to the waist, washing and singing at the top of
her voice: "Oh what a beautiful morning... tra la la!"
This was rather a contradiction in terms considering the
snow that was still falling outside, not that it could be
seen through the amazingly beautiful frost patterns on
the insides of the dorm windows.

Sarah hesitated – should one cough or something?
When the other girl spotted her.

"Come on in ducks," she said cheerfully. "Don't just
stand there! You will miss your cuppa if you don't look
slippy!"

Sarah went in and began to wash in the tepid water,
quickly using her flannel with a small bit of soap. She
was shivering so much she found it difficult to clean her
teeth. *'A lick and a promise'*, her mother would have
called her ablutions that day; but she had no time to be

sentimental, dried herself in a hurry, put on her
uniform, great-coat and cap, and rushed down in time
to gulp her lukewarm tea and ran out to jump into the
transport lorry with the other girls.

"Gosh, I am sooo hungry!" One girl said. "I shall
have to get a packet of biscuits if it takes this long to get
breakfast. Yuk! That tea was disgusting."

The girls chattered together and huddled for
warmth, hanging on for dear life to straps at the side of
the vehicle as it clattered, bumped and skidded along
the country lanes; tracks had been cut out of the deep
snow, with drifts piled up either side. The driver said
that the whole country was suffering from extreme
snow falls, and ice was preventing the movement of
troops and much needed food.

"There will be no flying from Manston tonight," the
driver continued. "Our planes are near frozen in their
hangars, even with the heaters blasting them. At least
this blizzard will allow little sight for Jerry's Luftwaffe: it
is a small comfort, but even the German planes won't
be flying in this weather! I hear most of Europe is in the
grip of the icy weather. East Kent tends to get the brunt
of it when the wind is in the north."

After an uncomfortable bumpy ride the girls arrived
at Manston and, crunching over the snow, they made
their way to the Mess for breakfast.

After their meagre repast, consisting mainly of
prunes and 'yellow peril' powdered egg scrambled on
toast, they received their milk ration. Only the
airwomen were allowed fresh milk; airmen had to put
up with powdered milk. After breakfast they were all
detailed to different areas of the 'drome. A pretty fair-
haired girl called Eleanor, a jolly girl going by the name

of Rhona, and Jill, who had been talking to Sarah, were all sent to the Admin hut.

They knocked politely on the door, only to be grabbed as soon as the door opened and nearly flung inside.

"Don't stand on ceremony in this weather!" The Flight Sergeant said. "Just come in as quickly as possible. It is very difficult to keep this hut warm, even at the best of times."

He had a kindly face, even though his manner was gruff, and the girls saluted him after shaking the snow from their shoes. He returned their salute, showed them where to hang their great-coats and took them through to the main office.

"Now, who have we here?" He asked, head on one side. Sarah noticed that he had a shock of curly fair hair; he was very tall and lanky, and he had a kindly face. She reckoned he must have been in his middle thirties.

He showed the girls to their desks after letting them warm themselves on the pitifully inadequate tortoise stove, the chimney of which went up through the room and out through the ceiling. The girls were glad at least to thaw their hands and left their gloves on a chair back near to the stove to steam gently and dry out.

The Flight Sergeant sat behind his desk called them and the girls lined up in front of him. He smiled at them, thinking to himself that they all looked very young, and said: "Good morning Ladies, you are all very welcome here as we are absolutely up to our eyes in work; and I, in particular, have looked forward to your coming to help us. I'm afraid there is a dreadful back-log, so I need you to get stuck in and not to chatter so we may have a chance to clear the in tray. I gather – well, I hope – that you are well versed in turning out normal RAF dockets, leave documents, official signals, flight plans, etc. I trust you had some prior training in what is expected of a CGD, at your holding camp?"

"Yes sir, we were taught what was expected of us." Sarah reassured him. "We will work hard and hope to help clear the work-load as best we can. We will, however, have to get used to the way you work here at Manston."

"Of course, of course – I know it will take a time to get to know our ways here, and allowances will be made, but as long as you knuckle down and get on with things I'm sure we will rub along fine. Now, here is a little information for you all:

RAF Manston's motto is 'Arise to Protect', and we are known as No. 11 Fighter Group. I am sure that what you accomplish here with us will go a long way to fulfilling that dictum, and that you will be proud to serve your country here in Kent." He smiled.

"Before you commence work you need to know this important safety information. If the air-raid siren should start to wail, just leave everything and make your way at a gallop to the shelters, which are situated all over the 'drome. Ours is just to the left of the hut next to this one. There are large pointers showing the way, just keep with me and run like hell. Although, in this weather bombers will probably not be flying, so we may relax a bit. Normally the kites – sorry, planes – are hidden in farm buildings, but in order prevent them freezing up we have them in the large hangars, with heaters blasting away."

"Pity we are not in one of those cosy hangars!" Sarah said cheekily, and at that very moment the tortoise stove belched out a cloud of black smoke, setting the girls coughing and spluttering and giggling.

Then they moved down the middle of the hut, each taking a desk with a typewriter, and perused the work waiting for them.

Well, thought the Flight Sergeant, at least this lot of WAAFs have a sense of humour. He left the girls to get acquainted with their typewriters and, with quick nods and smiles to the other girls already beavering away, the new recruits got stuck in.

"He is quite cute," whispered Rhona. "At least he seems human, and I'm sure he will help us learn the job. Gosh! I never thought I would be pleased to be wearing these thick woollen passion-killer stockings, but at least they are warmer than nylons!"

Sarah privately thought that the mound of paperwork on her desk looked impossible to lighten, but set to with gusto and was soon lost in her job – so much so that, when the call came to break for lunch, she was totally engrossed. She found the work very interesting: the machinations of an aerodrome in wartime, everyone pulling together to help the war effort, she thought. I am doing some good, rewarding work at last. This is a lot better than the bank – at least I don't have to add anything up! My English is good, so maybe I have a chance to make this a success.

Later they fought their way through blinding snow to the Mess again, grateful for a hot meal, even though it seemed to have no taste. Sarah thought longingly of her mother's wonderful cooking as she ate her insipid mince, tasteless mash, soggy cabbage and runny gravy. However, all the girls were hungry, and at least with the meal they had steaming hot tin mugs of cocoa, made

with their allowance of fresh milk, they felt blessedly
warm as they clasped them in their cold hands.

When they had eaten a rather stodgy suet pudding
with syrup, they made their way back across the white
waste to the hut, chattering all the way, their grey
woollen RAF scarves tightly wound around their faces
to keep out the cold. They giggled as they slid and
slipped on the ice and a couple of the girls made
snowballs and threw them at each other. At least they
had a warm glow to their cheeks by the time they
gained the hut.

They also were cheered by a passing crew of airmen
who whistled appreciatively at them and called out:
"Wot yer doing tonight ducks? Are you free for the
shakey-do?" The girls giggled again and waved back.

"Whatever is a shakey-do?" Sarah enquired of one
of the older girls.

"Oh, it's a dance, and this one is being held in the
NAAFI Club," she said. "We have them regularly; they
are quite fun and at least it allows us to meet the chaps
at the 'drome, you know, socially. Some of them are
half decent!"

"You have to watch if they have had a drink
though," put in another girl, laughing. "Then it is fight
for your life – or your honour! Don't wear French
knickers when you go out, either: they are known as
'easy feelers' by the lads, so you can imagine how they
try it on! Have you heard of knickers known as 'harvest
festivals'? All is safely gathered in!" They all fell about
laughing at that.

They reached the hut and rushed in through the
door in a flurry of snow and stamping of feet. After
saluting the Flight Sergeant, they settled down to their
work and the hut was soon filled with the clacking of

typewriters. The wind howled outside, and every now and again when the door opened a bitter draught hit the girls. The windows were obscured with snow and it was difficult to see. It seemed to be getting darker and colder.

"By the way, girls," their Flight-Sergeant said, standing in front of them. "Before we call it a day, I wanted you to know a few interesting facts about this RAF base." He sat on one of the desks, and leaned forward to talk to them.

"I wonder, did you know that RAF Manston was virtually razed to the ground by bombs during the Battle of Britain in 1940? That is why you girls are billeted at the Ursuline Convent, well away from the 'drome at night, at least. We men have to slum it wherever we can! See how precious you ladies are to the RAF!" Gary smiled reassuringly.

"Another fact, which is not general knowledge, is that Manston is considered such an important airfield that it has its own battalion of soldiers to protect it against enemy paratroopers. They have been known to land anywhere on or around this airfield. These army chaps are here to keep us all safe. We also have a cell block here to hold prisoners of war.

You may also hear over the tannoy that a plane is coming in without landing gear. Sadly that happens all too often, and airmen and women have to be made aware of the potential dangers to life of an unstable damaged kite. If it happens, take cover.

Also, there is a fascinating piece of information which should make you very proud to be detailed to serve the RAF here. That is, Manston has been given a very specific role in this war, the defence of our historic cathedral city of Canterbury. Obviously Canterbury

Cathedral holds a very special place in the hearts of the people of England and, as the bombing of our wonderful medieval Christian centre of worship would be too terrible to contemplate, Manston has been put on standby to protect it. No. 11 Group Head Air Commander Trafford Leigh-Mallory has sent Hawker Typhoon kites to the base, which are kept on permanent stand-by. I only wish I could have a crack at flying one myself."

He stood up. "Now, I think we will have to call it a day, girls. This weather is not going to let up, and we don't want you all stuck in a snow drift on your way back to the convent. So pack up now and be back here bright and early tomorrow. Thank you all for your hard work. You seem to be a good lot of girls, not given to idle chatter, and for that I am grateful. See you all tomorrow. Dis-miss!"

The girls packed up their typewriters, saluted their Flight Sergeant, donned their warm RAF great-coats and boarded the waiting lorry. They chatted gaily to the other WAAFs, who had been at Manston for a while. The transport vehicle again slipped and slithered its way back to Westgate. Chains had been put on its tyres so that at least it had a bit of purchase on the ice along the snowy lanes.

The three girls were pleased to get back to the convent, and to relax for a while. There was a common room with a cheerful fire where they sat after their evening meal. The nuns came in and asked them a bit about themselves, and a pleasant evening of chat about their families and homes ensued. They were also able to reassure the nuns that their local RAF base was detailed to protect Canterbury cathedral. This fact pleased the nuns greatly, and they chatted about it amongst themselves. Sarah took the opportunity to polish her buttons and clean her shoes, as there would be a uniform inspection in the morning.

This is not too bad, thought Sarah. At least Mummy, Daddy and Trel are only about sixty-five miles away, and I can probably get home on leave for the odd weekend. That wouldn't have happened had I been permanently posted up north or somewhere.

In the dorm she settled down to write a couple of letters, one to Henry (or Trel, as she now was used to calling him), and one to her beloved parents, to reassure them that she was fine and life at Manston was quite bearable. She begged her parents to send her some more warm vests and some mittens, as her chilblains were really giving her gip.

All the girls found it easier to settle down that night, as they were now used to the hourly convent bells.

Meanwhile the freeing wind howled outside, and very soon all that could be heard in the dorm was gentle breathing. The girls were tired out and, although their beds were not comfortable, they slept the sleep of the weary.

CHAPTER FOURTEEN

"Nothing can surpass your treasured memory"

Sarah soon relaxed into the routine of work with the other girls. The weather slowly improved, snow and ice melted and by March it was balmy enough for the girls to cycle to the 'drome. A keen north wind still blew off the sea, making riding very hard, and they arrived at Manston with pink cheeks and not a little puffed at the effort.

The lanes were white with sloe blossom, and primroses and early daffodils sprouted in the hedgerows. When the sun was out the girls enjoyed the ride across the fields to Manston, but when the skies were grey and the rain threatened it was not at all as pleasant, and they had to watch out for the odd hoar frost making the lanes slippery.

Sarah was still losing weight, what with the cycling and the fact that the camp food was not up to much, and the girls were worked very hard in their admin capacity. They kept the 'drome going, typing away and producing endless official documents. She was pleased she had lost weight, in a way: she had always been slightly chubby with a large bust, and the fashions of the day had not really suited her figure as it had been. Perhaps the new fashion of squared padded shoulders and slinky dresses would suit her better, now she was slimmer. Being short in stature, she was determined to save up her shoe ration points to buy a pair of the latest chic two-tone white and navy high-heeled courts.

As the lighter evenings drew out the girls found cycling back and forth really quite pleasant. The flat fields and the sea in the distance made for wonderful views.

They often had to be on parade early for inspections, and they had to keep practising their square bashing. Everyone at Manston was talking about the news of the Nuremberg bombing raid which was filtering through. The RAF had suffered its worst night ever. Whole squadrons were destroyed by enemy gunfire, their aircraft simply exploding in mid-air. Each one was nothing but a monstrous firework, packed with at least three tons of bombs, one thousand five hundred gallons of aviation fuel and seven brave men. One hundred and six bombers and five hundred and forty-five men were lost that March night.

One of the girls had a brother who was a gunner, she had recently seen him as his plane luckily made it to Manston. She met up with him in the medical wing. He was in a pretty bad, shocked state. He said he had been dumbstruck, sitting in the tail end of a Lancaster bomber watching his comrades' funeral pyres over the German country side as they stretched sixty miles into the distance. Those airmen who parachuted to the ground faced being captured and shot; in fact, he had heard that fifty Allied airmen were executed on Hitler's orders. In one night the RAF had lost more men than in the entire Battle of Britain.

Manston was busy receiving crippled planes. Lancaster and Halifaxes limped in; these were the lucky ones that were shot up but largely had dodged the German anti-aircraft gunfire. The damaged planes couldn't safely make it back to their own bases. The men received a hero's welcome and a place to stay and rest after their ordeal. All this made a lot of extra paperwork in the Admin department, but the girls cheerfully set to and stayed late to shift it all.

Although their work was hard there were compensations in the form of occasional visits to the local cinema – if one managed to catch the liberty bus into town. Quite frankly they needed the break, as their paperwork described some of the horrors of war in the air, and they certainly needed taking out of themselves and away from all the news of the carnage.

One cinema in Margate had already fallen under an air raid. The only one left was a bit of a flea pit, but at least the films offered a little escapism. There were dances locally, and at the 'drome they had a Music Club. Sarah persuaded Rhona, Jill and Eleanor to attend it with her.

The Music Club was held in one of the rooms of the whitewashed brick built Officers' Mess. There were chairs set around in a circle, and an ancient gramophone stood in the middle of the room. A tall Flight Lieutenant with a wonderful handlebar moustache was in charge of the proceedings. He played Elgar, Bach and Mozart, speaking at length on each piece; he was very knowledgeable and was able to answer any questions, especially those on the various characters that Elgar portrayed in his music. However, Sarah wished he would shut up for a while, so she could just sit and relax. His pronounced lisp made it hard not to giggle. She was careful not to catch Rhona's eye, as every time he lisped the ends of his magnificent moustache quivered alarmingly. She so wanted him to just allow the music to speak for itself. The Enigma Variations had just started when the door gently opened and their Flight Sergeant quietly sat down, with apologetic looks and smiles all round.

The evening was enjoyable in spite of the fact that the girls were all tired. The seats were comfortably padded, and it was just pleasant to sit and relax and listen to the rather scratchy records. When it was over they applauded and got up, and their boss came over to them.

"Hallo, you ladies," he said. The girls immediately stood to attention and saluted him. "Sir!" He returned their salute and smiled. "At ease now, this is a relaxation time for all. What did you think of the quivering moustache?" The girls laughed and relaxed.

"Actually, he is a damn good pilot, one of the best, and he is passionate about his music. I have seen him limping in after a bad sortie, and the skill with which he handled his damaged kite was just tremendous. He was very lucky not to have a bad prang on landing – a brave flyer indeed!"

"He is very well informed about music, and certainly knows his Bach from his Beethoven," observed Rhona.

"Yes," agreed Sarah. "I just wish he wouldn't try to inform *us* quite so much! Although I do feel a greater admiration, now you have told us of his flying skills. You pilots are such brave men."

"We just get on with the job," their Flight Sergeant said. "I only wish I could be doing more flying, but it seems I am relegated to just being on stand-by. However, I have quite a job overseeing you lot, now! Still, I could be called upon to fly at any time." They walked into the night air together.

"Transport is just leaving for the convent girls, so goodnight – and see you tomorrow."

He waved goodbye and winked at Sarah. He is really rather nice, she thought. She had heard bad reports from other new girls, whose bosses were horrid and expected the WAAFs to wait on them hand and foot. One girl said that she even had to dust her boss's desk, at his insistence.

At least our Flight is kindly, she mused, and he appreciates our hard work. We are indeed very fortunate to work for him.

CHAPTER FIFTEEN

"Now, we meet only in dreams"

Henry was missing Sarah sorely, but at last she wrote to say she had a '48-hour's leave' and would be home this coming weekend. He busied himself in planning a special evening out for them both. It would have to be only a local outing, as transport up to the West End was really difficult now. He decided to take her to a favourite restaurant of her mother's in near-by Catford. He hoped she would like his choice of venue.

Sarah was so longing to see her dear parents – and, of course, Trel! She was very pleased when he met her at the station in his car.

"How are you darling?" Trel asked. He noticed that she had lost quite a lot of weight. It suited her, but part of her charm for him was her cuddly figure, and he hoped she wouldn't lose any more.

They chatted on the drive back to her home. Sarah kissed him and said she would see him the next day. He was hoping to be asked in, but understood that she was tired and wanted to be with her family, so he bade her goodnight and drove home.

Sarah opened the front door with her key and ran eagerly into the house.

"Mummy, Daddy, I'm home!" she cried, flinging her coat over the hall stand. Joe and Hilda both rushed into the hall and engulfed her in hugs and kisses, saying how pleased they were to see her home, safe and sound.

"It was very decent of Trel to meet you, dear," said her father. "We have seen quite a bit of him since you have been away. He is lonely, and often comes round for supper."

"That is very kind of you, Daddy. Now what else have I missed?"

"You have heard of the Twentyman's house, darling?" Her mother asked. "Their windows all blew out as the result of a nearby bomb blast. They have gone home now, but they stayed with us while repairs were effected."

"Oh, Mummy, you are so kind," said Sarah, playfully putting her arms around her mother's ample waist.

"Nonsense, dear! They are kind enough to share their cellar with us, during raids, so I could do no less. Now, then, I want to hear all about what you have been up to, and it looks like you could do with a good feed, my young lady." She held Sarah away from her. "My word, you have certainly lost a bit of weight, dearest, but you look very well on it."

"Yes, I am well, Mummy. I get lots of exercise and we are kept really busy, and I have lots of new friends. Of course the food is dire but life in the RAF is at least bearable. In fact, I think it is not at all bad – except, of course, that I miss you and darling Daddy lots and lots.

"Also, George, how is he? I cannot believe his new girlfriend Monica is now his fiancée, and I cannot wait to meet her. Just fancy, a wedding! How exciting, and afterwards I shall be a step-aunt to Monica's daughter. What is she like, little Penelope? I bet she is very sweet!"

"Yes, she is a dear, with a freckly nose and lots of lovely golden curls, and George is very happy. Remember, things go on a lot quicker in war time; no-one has time to wait around, and when George met

Monica he just knew she was right for him. She needs a husband, and a father for her little girl after her pilot husband lost his life. I am sure they will be happy together. George loves her very much and he is very good with Penny – you know how much he loves children.

Now go upstairs, young lady, wash your hands and come down for your meal!"

Coming home was bliss for Sarah, and she tucked into her Mother's home-made food with gusto. The three of them chatted a hundred to the dozen. Sarah had so much to say, and her parents just listened with pride at their daughter's new vocation.

Mrs. Langman was a skilled cook, but even she was hard pressed to make good food with the meagre rations they were allowed. Luckily, Joe had always cultivated their vegetable patch at the bottom of their long garden, so the slogan 'Dig for Victory' only made him step up his production. Potatoes were plenteous, as were all the winter vegetables: sprouts, cauliflower and cabbages, all as a result of his hard work. Fruit was produced in abundance too; there was rhubarb, blackberries, apples and loads of shining blackcurrants.

Hilda made jam and chutneys, bottling and preserving as much as she could of this produce in season. These may not have been as sweet as she would have liked with sugar rationing, but they were the occasional bottle wholesome and sated the family's hunger. She managed to get enough cream off the top of the rare bottle of fresh milk to scald and make her version of Devonshire cream, from the county of her childhood. This went very well with Joe's favourite, Scottish griddle scones, which she still could bake occasionally, saving up all her ration of flour for when her daughter or son came home on leave.

As Hilda had recounted to her daughter, she catered for two more mouths while her offspring were away in the forces. Her two dear friends, the sisters Jessie and Mary Twentyman, had suffered blast damage to their house from a parachute bomb that fell in nearby Newlands Park. Although Mary had covered their windows with gauze, the two elderly sisters could not live in their house until the windows had been repaired, so they stayed with Joe and Hilda up the road. Their food ration coupons came in very useful and Hilda had been able to stretch everything just that little bit further to produce plain but nourishing meals for all of them. She missed Sarah and George, but Jessie and Mary had livened up the house with their funny little ways of quarrelling over absolutely everything. They loved each other dearly but their ideas of the way to do things were diametrically opposite.

Mary had been a school teacher and in fact had taught the young Sarah at her little dame school, situated in a Victorian house in the next road. She was a brilliant mathematician, while her younger sister was a talented artist with not a mathematical bone in her body. Mary was precise and efficient; Jessie was totally absorbed and scatter-brained as many artists are, when their minds are focussed on their latest creation. So the two of them clashed, but in a very loving way, and they always ironed out their differences. However, the frequent squabbling had made sharing a home with them a trifle tedious. Luckily, Hilda was stoical and easy going in her nature, so she just left them to it and enjoyed their company when they were being nice to each other.

Joe knew his wife was struggling with the powdered egg allowance so, true to his word, when he got wind from someone in his congregation whose broody hen had hatched out a clutch of eggs, he asked the chap to reserve two for him. Later on when they had matured, he picked up two healthy little point of lay pullets and took them home in a cardboard box. He had really wanted at least six hens so that some could be bred for the table, but two was all he had been allowed.

Hilda was really pleased with her 'girlies', as she called them, and watched as they made themselves at home in a coop and run constructed by Joe, using chicken wire and odd bits of wood he kept in the shed. She loved to walk down the garden with cooked oatmeal, cabbage leaves and spare bits of fat or bread crusts to give them. They soon recognised her call and came running to greet her. Boocles the cat ran down the garden and sniffed at them a couple of times, but with a flick of his tail he turned on his dainty paws with much disdain as if the hens were not even worthy of his notice.

Soon the young chickens were laying well, providing eggs for the table. They lived mainly on table scraps, weeds from the garden and bran to make a mash, when Joe could get hold of it from Boag's. They occasionally had chicken meal but it was in short supply, as was oyster shell, so Joe ground shells down for them, begged from the fishmonger. He was even able to promise the occasional couple of eggs to the Misses Twentyman, when they returned to their own home. The two sisters were very grateful for his largesse.

Hilda took Sarah down the garden after their repast to see the little brown hens. "What are you going to call them, Mother dear?" Asked Sarah, bending down to stroke the hens and giving them a couple of crusts saved from her meal. "Isn't it funny that they squat down when you stroke them?"

"That is because they think your touch is the rooster jumping on them to mate, so they automatically squat down."

"What happens when you haven't got a rooster?" She picked up one hen and was happily stroking its head.

"Well, you don't have to put up with crowing at all hours of the day and night, for one thing! Hens don't need a cockerel to lay eggs, their bodies just get on with it; but of course the eggs they lay are infertile. That is all right by me, as they still taste wonderful. They come running to my calling out 'girlies', but if you like, you could give them individual names." Hilda reached into the nesting box and brought out a couple of large brown eggs.

"Those look good! They are quite big too." Sarah thought for a while and then said. "How about naming them Gert and Daisy, after the two comediennes?"

"That is a good idea. Gert and Daisy, yes I like those names, well done. By jingo! It is getting a trifle chilly out here! I will shut Gert and Daisy in their house and we can go in now for some cocoa, only with powdered milk I'm afraid, and then bed for you my darling girl."

Sarah took the eggs from her mother, carried them with care and ran happily into the house.

CHAPTER SIXTEEN

"The joy in recapturing hours"

The next evening Henry called for Sarah.

Mr. Langman opened the door at his knock. "Come a-wee in laddie. Brrr! That wind is getting up a bit, and it is very cold out. She'll be down in a trice, she is just titivating herself, no doubt! Won't you come and warm yourself for a minute?"

Trel thanked Joe and they went into the cosy front room, with a fire crackling merrily in the grate, and he sat on the chintz chesterfield and began chatting to Hilda as she was doing her mending.

"The raids have been terrible lately haven't they?" Trel said, holding his hands to warm them in front of the flames.

"Aye, laddie, they have that. Some bombs have been too close for comfort," Joe remarked, settling down in his arm chair.

Hilda looked up from her mending and said "I do envy your mother and aunt down in Cornwall, Trel dear. I wish I were in the country away from all this bombing, but I will not leave Joe, and he will not leave his job at the bank. These sleepless nights really get one down. Everything is so hard, and I fear for my children's safety." She began to cry softly.

"There, there, dear," said Joe kindly, putting his arm about his wife. "Dinna fash yoursel'. God will provide, just trust in Him. Oh dear! Look at that dratted weather!" Sleet had begun to dash itself against the window panes.

At that point Sarah came into the room, wearing a pale blue woollen frock and her new two-tone navy and white high heels.

"Good evening, Trel," she said. "Oh, Mummy, whatever is the matter?"

"Don't you take any notice of me, my girl, I'm just being silly. You go out and enjoy yourself, the pair of you. I understand you are going to Cominetti's? Mind you wear my musquash coat, darling – it is sleeting outside, and I think you need a warm cardigan with that lovely dress."

"Really? Oh bother the weather. Lucky you have your car, Trel." She turned to Henry, who said they would be fine and dry as he had umbrellas in the car.

"How truly lovely, we are going to dine at your very favourite restaurant, Mummy."

"That is correct, darling, good old Cominetti's. I don't know how they keep going in this climate. I would love to eat there again. You just go off and have a lovely meal, and let me know what he serves up! Have a wonderful time."

Joe and Hilda kissed their daughter, shook Henry's hand, watched them through the window, driving off, and then turned to fit their blackouts.

"He is a verra nice man." Joe tapped his pipe on the side of the fireplace. "Sarah could do very well married to him. He is comfortably off and will look after her well, plus there's the fact that she would only be living a wee way down the road from us. You can see that Henry is fair besotted with her. Och! she is still verra young though, and I suppose should walk out wi' a few more laddies before settling down."

"It all depends on how long Henry is prepared to wait for her," said Hilda, getting on with her darning.

They drove with dimmed headlights through the blackened out streets at the mandatory 20 mph to nearby Catford; managed to park the car away from the main road and went to the small Italian restaurant, Casa Cominetti. It was much frequented by various famous show-biz personalities, as evidenced by the many photos on the wall of the stars enjoying Mr. Cominetti's wonderful Italian food.

Henry led Sarah to a secluded table and ordered some wine. They both chose from the menu. Sarah was very pleased to see that her favourite chestnut gateau was still available.

"I don't know how Mr. C. can still produce such wonderful food," said Sarah, as they tucked into their meal.

"I expect he has his own way of obtaining ingredients. Maybe he has a secret supply; he has lots of friends in London who love his cooking and would probably help him out," said Henry. He was so enjoying the evening. Sarah was in a jolly mood, laughing and joking good deal and full of things to tell him about the RAF.

However, Henry did try and steer her away from talking so much about her Manston life by hinting here and there about how much he was looking forward to their future together.

Sarah tended to laugh off any serious talk that Henry made. She felt that life in Civvy Street was a long way off. After all, she had had to sign up for four years in the forces. To her, their future together was just a hazy picture, and not really relevant in her eyes.

They chatted about the bank and of their mutual acquaintances, many of whom were also now in the forces.

They finished their delicious meal with a coffee, and Henry produced a small package and gave it to her.

Sarah's tummy did a quick flip. Was this an engagement ring? She hoped not. Her fingers fumbled a bit as she undid the package. Yes, inside was a jewellery box and she trembled even further. She was not ready for marriage yet, whatever could she say to him?

She opened the velvet lined box to find... a really pretty silver Celtic knot brooch! What a relief!

"Thank you so much, Trel, it is absolutely adorable. I shall be proud to wear it on my best coat."

"I thought you would like it, darling. I chose it because it represents the link we have together, both of Celtic origin – you Scots and me Cornish. It brings us close together, somehow, don't you think?"

Sarah smiled at Trel and leaned over and kissed his cheek. She should have realised that he wouldn't just spring a proposal on her, and that he just wanted her to have something nice as a token of his affection for her.

He drove her home and they had a little kiss and cuddle in the car. "I'll take you to the station tomorrow, darling."

"That would be lovely, thank you," replied Sarah. "I have a heavy kit bag of clean necessities and a nice warm dressing gown the parents have kindly bought me to keep out the cold of the draughty convent, and it would have been a struggle on the bus."

They parted. One day, life with Trel as a husband will be very comfortable, Sarah thought, as she walked up the garden path. He is such a dear and so very kind.

Her parents were still up, the fire embers were still glowing and Hilda was just putting her mending away. "Did you have a lovely meal, darling?" Hilda asked Sarah.

"Oh, yes, Mummy dear, it was absolutely wizzo. Mr. Cominetti is still working his culinary magic, despite the war."

"Joe, we will have to go over there when George comes home; perhaps we can take Monica and Penny too, for lunch. That would be nice".

Joe was winding the old chiming clock in the hall. "Time for bed, now," he said.

"Oh, wait a minute," Sarah said. "I've got something to show you both."

She took the velvet lined box from her bag and opened it to show her parents the brooch.

"Why, that is absolutely lovely!" Hilda exclaimed.

"Yes, it is really grand," said Joe. "Celtic too, what a thoughtful choice. You are a lucky one, my girl. That wee man really cares for you."

"I know, darling Daddy," said Sarah, hugging her Father and kissing him resoundingly on his cheek. "He looks after me, just as you have done."

With that the family retired upstairs to bed and a stillness encompassed the old house. The cat stretched and yawned in front of the dying fire. No raids disturbed the night and the family slept in peace.

CHAPTER SEVENTEEN

"You healed the wound and bridged the cleft"

The mad March days with occasional frost and biting wind soon gave way to milder April, the sun was shining and in the hedgerows the first pink and white hawthorn buds were bursting through. Local children picked and ate these buds, calling them "bread and cheese".

Many RAF personnel attended St. Catherine's church at Manston on Sunday. Their boots and buttons were shining as they made an extra effort to be smart, and after Matins quite a few of them would repair to The Jolly Farmer pub over the road – known locally as the 'RAF inn' – for a drink before the walk back to the 'drome.

Sarah, Eleanor, Rhona and Jill came out of the little Victorian church. "That was a good service," Rhona remarked. "The vicar is a dear, and certainly his sermon did not send me to sleep. It was nice and short!"

"Yes, there were good rousing hymns and those sweet choir boys sang really well. Oh, I do wish I could have a little boy one day that looked like an angel, with blond hair and blue eyes!" Jill said wistfully.

"Not much chance of that, with your dark hair and brown eyes," the others laughed.

"Oh, I only want girls when I have children, perhaps a lovely wee girl with curly hair, as I'm really not sure if I could cope with boys. I shall name her after you, Jill!" Sarah smiled at her friend.

"Well, that is very nice of you, but just make sure she is not called Gillian. Oh, how I hated that name!"

They stood outside the church for a while. The sky was looking a little threatening, and thick black clouds were blowing their way.

"Well, girls, what do we do now? Shall we try the pub, and perhaps have a snifter?" Eleanor asked. "Looking at the sky, I reckon we could miss the rain if we stopped here for a while."

"That would be a topping idea," said Jill. So the friends went across the road to the quaint little roadside pub. It was packed to the hilt with RAF personnel, but luckily they managed to find a table in the corner. Sarah and Eleanor fought their way to the bar to order coffees.

"Make way for the girls!" Some RAF chaps smiled and let the girls get through. "Welcome, ladies, what may I get you?" enquired the jovial bartender.

"Oh, we just want four sweet sherries, please," Eleanor asked politely, and smiled.

"Want a bit o' rum in those, or whiskey to warm the cockles o' your hearts, girls?" one chap said, taking off his cap and pushing his hair back.

"No, thank you," Sarah said politely, and endeavoured to carry the drinks through the jostling crowd.

"Here, let me help you with that." Their Flight Sergeant appeared from nowhere and escorted them back to their table, carrying the tray for them.

"I saw you in church," he said to Sarah. "It was a good service, wasn't it? Not quite the same as the chapel I am used to, but very nice and reasonably short, I'm pleased to say, and at least the singing was good. I do enjoy a good rousing hymn or two," he laughed.

"Enjoy your drinks girls, and don't get tiddly! Let me know when you want to go back to the convent. I have a transport vehicle outside and can drop you back."

"Oh, thank you, that would be lovely. It would certainly save us a walk, and it looks as if it is coming on to rain."

He left them to chat.

"Flight is rather a dear," said Eleanor. "I wonder if he is married. He has such lovely twinkling eyes and a friendly smile."

"Now, now Ellie," said Jill. "You cannot go falling for your boss you know, it wouldn't do at all!"

They laughed and chatted, sipping their drinks. True to his word, when they had finished their boss brought the Liberty vehicle up to the pub and the girls climbed in the back.

"There is room in front for a little one," said Flight. "Come on, Miss Langman, jump in."

Sarah got up into the cab of the lorry and they set off across the airfield. The heavens opened at that moment, and they drove in silence with the noise of the windscreen wipers and driving rain keeping them company. Then her companion said;

"Actually this is very fortuitous and I'm a glad of this opportunity to ask you something. I was wondering if you and the girls would like to cycle into Margate for a concert of Rachmaninov's second symphony next week? I hear the orchestra is good and I know that this second symphony is just wizard. Quite a few chaps from the camp are going and it would be nice to have a bit of female company. What do you think?"

"Yes, Sir, sounds like a grand idea. Thank you, I will ask the other girls and let you know well in time next week," Sarah promised.

"Now, that is enough of the formality. My name is Gary, and I would be pleased if you and the other girls would use it when we are not on duty."

"OK, Gary, I will tell the others – and of course you know my name is Sarah." She smiled at him. He has a lovely, friendly face, she thought.

"Yes, and it is a very pretty name too" said Gary, as they bowled along. "Do you know, you remind me of a girl I once played with when I was a youngster back in Wales. Her name was also Sarah, and I used to call her 'Sal' for short. Gosh, that was some time ago! Where did all those years go?"

The rain had stopped, the sun was out and she enjoyed being so high up in the cab and looking across the glistening fields.

"Oh, look at that magnificent rainbow," she said, "it goes right out to sea!" The clouds had parted and the rainbow was so colourful against the dark lowering sky that it became double where another faint arc shone above it. It seemed to straddle the ancient towers of Dent-de-Lion gatehouse, next to the convent. The old towers gleamed in the sun and the angry black clouds scudding out over the sea behind the rainbow created a totally magical effect.

"Looks like a fairy castle," Gary said. "The calm after the storm. Do you reckon the pot of gold is at the convent?"

"The nuns could certainly do with a pot of gold," said Sarah. "They scrape and scrimp, make do and mend, and never complain."

The lorry turned into the convent gates and drew up outside its ancient door. Sarah and the girls alighted, and with many grateful thanks they went in for lunch.

CHAPTER EIGHTEEN

"My mind is in a whirl"

Spring was well and truly sprung in East Kent. The skylarks were singing their hearts out high in the sky, feeding on the many insects rising on the wind and ecstatic in their mating dance. The mainly balmy weather and the lighter evenings made cycling to and from the 'drome really pleasant. Sometimes the girls walked back across the fields using the many footpaths which were now frothy with cow parsley, wild garlic, bluebells and fresh green alick – horse parsley – which grew in abundance by the paths. However, the weather could change in a trice; this they learned after receiving a drenching, as the cold north winds would suddenly blow rain in from the direction of the sea.

The Admin workload had eased a little but the girls were still very busy. They seem to have a ceaseless flow of signals to action, and flying programmes were constantly being typed and run off the Gestetner, which had a maddening ability to run out of ink or smudge a stencil, making the girls work even harder. Leave chits were always needed and produced, the phone seemed always to be ringing with more orders, and sometimes they had to stay late to finish up.

Mostly they were a happy bunch of girls; however, one-day sadness crept into their lives, bringing great anxiety amongst the work force, as one of their company learned the news that her home had been bombed and her parents and grand-parents had all been killed. She was distraught and immediately went on compassionate leave to stay with her aunt. It shook the girls up. They were now becoming great friends, a close unit, supporting each other, but such a tragedy made it very hard for everyone to keep their spirits up. Each feared for the well-being of their own families, and it was so difficult to keep positive whilst coping with the worry that it could happen to any one of them.

Margate and the surrounding areas of the Isle of Thanet were also subjected to raids. The railway was a target, as was Manston airfield itself. Parachute mines had flattened many houses near the 'drome, causing much devastation and homelessness.

The 'drome now had an emergency lane on the southern runway, used for planes in distress. Flying back from Europe low on fuel or with serious damage, especially to their undercarriages, they could land there with no prior warning to the control tower.

Manston was subjected to thick sea fogs which sheltered the planes from the enemy. However, most of them were disguised or housed in nearby farm buildings, so that if the 'drome was bombed the planes were safe. The fog made landing and take-off difficult so an anti-fog system was put in place. Known as FIDO, or Fog Investigation Dispersal Organisation, it was the first of its kind. It burned off the fog on a runway, enabling landings to be carried out safely. Many other RAF airfields were later fitted with this system of fog clearance. Petrol was pumped through pipes seventy yards from, and parallel to, the runway. To burn FIDO for one hour used two hundred and fifty thousand gallons of petrol, so it was expensive to run. One navigator saw it alight from one hundred and fifty miles away. Another pilot told Gary one day, as they chatted in the NAAFI, that *'the flames made him think he was descending into hell,'* but the new system saved many lives.

The very situation of Manston being near to the coast made it the closest airfield to Europe, and this fact alone was responsible for saving many a pilot who came limping home from a sortie. It provided a place to regroup and to get his 'kite' looked at before he set off for his own RAF airfield. The engineers, and especially Gary's friend Reg, were hard at it all hours of the day and night, repairing and making the battered planes air-worthy. Manston was well known for carrying spare parts for various planes, kept at the part of the 'drome near Alland Grange. Every damaged kite would be stripped down for repairs; if it was too badly wrecked, its parts would enable other planes to carry on flying. Gary was now on the list of older pilots and was occasionally called on to take up and test repaired planes. Flying was for him a welcome break from the tedium of office work.

When Sarah learned of her friend's tragedy, she longed with such an aching in her heart to go home to be with Hilda and Joe. She also feared for the safety of George. It seemed such a long time since she had been allowed home on leave for his marriage to Monica. It had been a lovely war time wedding, and Trel had been her proud escort that day. The wedding was very simply planned and her brother and his pretty new wife had looked so very happy, despite the fact that he only had a very short time on leave with his new bride. They were determined to not let the coming parting spoil their week on honeymoon, before he was posted overseas with his West Kent Regiment.

George had now been overseas for some weeks, and Sarah had only just learned from her Mother's recent letter the good news that George and Monica were expecting a baby – a sister or brother for Penny. She just couldn't wait to see them all. She wasn't due her ten days' leave for another few weeks, and she thought of them all constantly.

Letters arrived almost daily for Sarah, especially from Trel, who was a very faithful pen friend. Most evenings saw her replying to letters, or polishing her buttons, which had to be spotless for daily kit inspection. She had started to work on her embroidery, a table cloth for her mother. She was good at sewing, and after hard day's typing she felt relaxed and nearer to her parents as she assiduously stitched and wove her magic floral bouquets on each of the four corners of the cloth.

Eleanor came into the dorm. "Do you think you would like to cycle into Margate on Saturday? A few of us are going in for a concert at the Winter Gardens – Mozart and Rachmaninov I believe – to help get our spirits out of this doom and gloom. What do you say?" Eleanor looked at Sarah's curly head bent over her embroidery.

"Sounds nice, what time is it? We could get a bite to eat after," said Sarah, looking up and smiling "We need something to cheer us all up, and a concert will be great. Let's hope it doesn't rain on that day." She then threw her hands up to her face:

"Oh! My goodness me! I have just remembered, our Flight mentioned the concert to me when he gave us a lift back in the Liberty lorry that Sunday morning. There are quite a few chaps and girls going from the 'drome, apparently. In fact it was in the lorry that he told me to call him 'Gary' when we are off duty. I was supposed to ask you all if you would come and I completely forgot! I am so stupid, sometimes."

"Gary, eh? Preferential treatment or what?" Eleanor smiled as she teased.

"Oh, no! He means all of us to call him Gary, socially, and he knows our names and will use them, I'm sure." Sarah blushed and buried her head in her embroidery.

Soon it was time for lights out. The girls got ready for bed and sat chatting until the C.O. came in and bade them goodnight.

They hadn't been asleep for more than half-an-hour when the air-raid siren sounded, and almost immediately four enormous explosions roused them all with a start. "Good gracious! That was jolly close. They must be aiming for the railway again. I wish the convent was not so near to the line. I do hope those bombs landed in the sea."

The girls trooped down the stairs to the cellar to wait for the raid to be over. At least it wasn't so bitterly cold now, and the nuns kept powdered milk and cocoa in the cellar so they made hot drinks to warm everyone up. They drank their cocoa, chatted for a bit and then were allowed back to their beds and blissful sleep.

CHAPTER NINETEEN

"I just remain in silence and let the memories unfurl"

Saturday dawned bright and clear, and the sun was shining. Sarah, with other girls, carried out washing duties, changed their bed linen and were able to hang clothes and sheets out on the vast washing lines in the gardens at the rear of the convent. The girls also helped the nuns with cleaning the convent and cooking the weekend meals.

They consumed a delicious lunch of meat paste sandwiches and home-made vegetable soup made from produce gleaned from the convent's vegetable patch, which was now beginning to sprout peas, carrots and spinach. Early lettuces were beginning to push through from the seed bed, as well as radishes, spring onions and broad beans. Most of the convent garden was now down to vegetables but a small area around a quiet lily pond still had primroses, larkspur, and delphiniums. A whole variety of spring bulbs were springing up under a venerable old beech tree, itself clad in the fresh lime-green beauty of spring leaves. Later in the year the pergola would be a wonderful sight, clad in fragrant old climbing roses. The garden was protected by an ancient mellow brick wall, which prevented the cold salt-laden winds from the sea from scorching the plants within.

A statue of the Virgin and Child watched benignly from its shady niche in the convent wall. Fresh flowers or pots of spring bulbs were always placed before the statue, and a stone bench was placed for anyone in need of quiet prayerful contemplation.

The girls finished their lunch and were clearing the plates away when Jill looked out of the front window.

"Look, there are a load of RAF chaps on bikes at the convent gates!" she cried with glee. "They have come to escort us into Margate for the concert. How very sweet of them." She ran upstairs to powder her nose while Eleanor and Sarah quickly brushed their hair, glancing in the large ornate mirror by the convent door. Then they rushed round to the bike shed to fetch their bicycles.

Gary was with the cycle party and greeted the girls with a cheery wave. Sarah had decided to wear her new green dress with white buttons, and a white belt. She took her green cardigan with her and rolled it up in her saddle bag in case it was cooler on the return journey.

There were about twenty RAF girls and men in the party and they all cycled along the Canterbury road together towards Margate. The girls tended to ride together, with some of the chaps behind and some in front, acting as an informal escort. There was much banter between them all, mainly comments from the men about the way the girls rode their bikes. The girls however gave as good as they got, and the thrust and parry between them all was punctuated with much giggling on behalf of the girls as they rode along.

Soon they came in sight of the sea at Margate. Sarah was a little way behind the others. She was fascinated by the golden sands of Margate beach, now shrouded in ugly rolls of barbed wire where once it would have been thronging with early holiday makers, children making sand-castles and families making the most of the balmy spring weather. How sad war is, thought Sarah, as she rode along staring towards the lighthouse on the harbour; the tide was out, and a few desultory fishing boats rested on their sides. The seagulls were screaming and wheeling overhead and the sunshine beat down upon their heads, although there was a cool breeze blowing in from the sea to refresh them as they rode along.

Suddenly, Sarah was aware that her front wheel was not behaving normally. She couldn't move it sideways at all, and on looking down she noticed to her dismay that it was caught in the tramlines. Her back wheel followed down into the groove as well. With that Sarah began to wobble, and to her horror she lost her balance and fell with a thump on to the road. She let out an involuntary yell as she smashed into the tarmac. Her bike twisted away from her and crashed into the road, and she felt severe pain in her left arm and leg.

She gasped and began to sob, more from shock than anything, and sat on the road, shaking and trying to stand up. Most of the cyclists had carried on unaware of her predicament and she saw them merrily cycling onwards, oblivious of her plight.

Gary had been chatting to Reg as they bowled along, and was occasionally glancing back at the girls to make sure they were all right, when he noticed Sarah was not with the party. Looking back, he spied her sitting in the road. He turned round quickly, telling Reg to go on without him as he was going back to help a casualty.

A passer-by had stopped to help Sarah to the side of the road and rescued her bike from the tram lines before Gary reached her. Her wrist was extremely painful, her stockings were torn and the outside of her left arm and leg were badly grazed and bleeding. Luckily that day the traffic was light, so she had not fallen into the path of a motorist.

"Well, what have we here? Are you hurt? This is a fine two and eight, if ever I saw one!" said Gary as

Sarah gulped and sobbed quietly. He addressed the man waiting with Sarah. "Thank you so much, kind sir, for taking care of the young lady. I will take over now. She is a WAAF in my care, from RAF Manston. I am an Officer and will look after her." The kindly gentleman who had helped Sarah to the side of the road doffed his cap to Gary and went on his way.

"Well, you poor thing! Here, have my hanky and blow your nose. I think we need to get you to the first aid post: there is one nearby, at Margate Sands railway station."

After padlocking their bikes to the promenade railings, Gary helped Sarah to stand, and with one arm around her and the other supporting her poorly wrist, they walked over the road to the railway station and found a St. John's first aid centre.

A red-faced portly man in St. John's Ambulance uniform came out to help Sarah to a chair.

"Oh dearie dear! I saw exactly what happened to you. Them tram lines is evil if you get caught in them. I think you could do with a cup of hot sweet tea, my dear," he said. "You have had a nasty shock. Here, take this seat and try and relax a bit. I will have a look at that wrist of yours and the nurse will bathe your grazes."

Sarah relaxed into their capable hands, thanking them profusely. Gary stood watching the nurse cleaning her leg and winced with her when iodine was dabbed on to her wounds.

"You should go on with the others, Gary, you could still catch them up and hear the concert. I do feel such a fool and am so sorry that I have spoiled your outing. I really should have taken more care and looked where I was going," said Sarah, her tear-streaked face looking anxiously up at him.

"Not at all, Sarah," Gary reassured her. "We RAF chaps will never desert a lady in distress! I shall stay with you until you are all cleaned up, then I will go and ring for transport back to the convent. In fact, as the nurse has just brought you some tea, and if you are quite all right here having a cuppa, I will go and use the telephone now."

Gary left Sarah looking a little brighter, sipping her hot sweet tea. He walked across the station, found a phone booth, got through to the 'drome and ordered a car to take Sarah back to the nuns care.

"I cannot help feeling so bad, Gary," Sarah said, seemingly weighed down with guilt. "It is such a crying shame for you to miss the Rachmaninov, you love so much. Oh! My wrist is so painful."

"Looks like you may have badly sprained it. You will not be able to type for a while. Perhaps I could arrange for you to have injury leave and go home for a while to recover. Don't worry about me missing the concert. There will be other concerts; in fact, I will make a point of taking you to hear the second symphony myself as soon as there is another performance. I know you love that piece too, and we will both get to hear it."

Gary's kindness was too much for Sarah, and tears began to fall again. The nurse soothed her and confirmed that her wrist was badly sprained. It was quite swollen, so the nurse bandaged it up in a sling.

The transport car arrived and Gary escorted her back to the convent, making sure she was able to walk up the steps, and gave her into the care of the nuns. They scurried around her with worried faces until they settled her down into a nice big arm chair looking out onto the garden, and there they left her in peace to have a snooze.

CHAPTER TWENTY

"I thank you for your affection"

Sarah was indeed sent home to her parents on injury leave for a few days. They motored down to Margate in their bull-nosed Morris, Joe having begged some petrol from a neighbour. They picked her up from the convent, and she was very relieved to be in her mother's care again. The grazes on her arm and leg were still sore but were forming healthy scabs. However, her left wrist was still very painful and had swollen quite a bit, so the nuns had told her to rest it in a sling for a few days and to apply cold compresses.

Once back in Sydenham she was able to use her right hand to pen a few letters but resigned herself to not doing any embroidery for a while, and to using her right hand only to feed herself.

Naturally Trel was overjoyed at the unexpected pleasure of seeing her sooner than her normal leave would allow. He was avidly attentive, sitting by her side playing dominoes and regaling her with tales of the office and his fire-watching night work.

He was eager to know all about her accident, and asked if Sarah would like him to travel down to mend her bike. Sarah thanked him but replied that the Flight Sergeant, her boss, said he would get his friend Reg the engineer to see if the front wheel could be straightened out, over in his workshop.

She spoke quite a lot about her social life in east Kent. Trel felt a little left out and he began to have anxious thoughts, as Sarah seemed to be joining in with a lot of the activities, especially going to dances. She didn't hold back as she described dancing with some of the chaps who were not very good, and managed to make her feet black and blue as they hadn't any idea which way to lead her. At least I am a good dancer, Trel thought, and Sarah did admit that no-one could dance with such a light step as he. That made him feel a little better; however, the thought of another chap holding her close in his arms made him feel really uncomfortable. He realised that he was getting jealous of her life away from him and rebuked himself soundly. I must not let her know I mind what she is getting up to, he thought.

Trel wanted to spend as much time as possible with Sarah, so he asked Joe's permission to drive her back to Manston when her wrist had recovered. Joe was only too pleased to let him do so, he had very little petrol and was worried about returning his daughter. Trel reassured Joe that he had been saving up his petrol ration by sometimes travelling to work by bus, so that he may take his mother and aunt out; as they had now returned from Cornwall. He suggested that it would make a nice day out to the sea for all of them as they could stop for a bite to eat on the way.

While Sarah was at home Hilda enjoyed cosseting her, just being glad to have her back home for a while. She bought her magazines and they toasted Sarah's favourite crumpets on forks by the fire. Although it was April sometimes there was a chilly wind, and Hilda loved her open fire so much that she jumped at any excuse to light it now and then.

Hilda made her own crumpets, having wheedled a small piece of live yeast from the butchers. She also made her own bread, which tasted so good to Sarah after Mess food. Joe sat and talked to her of his work at the church and the progress of his vegetable patch. She hobbled down the garden to see Gert and Daisy, who were laying well and had lovely glossy brown feathers.

"They have really grown, haven't they? They are so friendly! Look how they know and respond to you, Mummy," Sarah remarked, as she watched the chickens scratching about in the earth for grubs. They seemed to be doing a little dance as their rear ends wiggled and their legs scraped forward one after the other. The hens ran to the wire when they heard Hilda's voice. "See how they come to greet me. That's because I am the one with the food. They are good layers, too. We have an egg each a day now and, funnily enough, as they have matured, one hen lays larger eggs than the other. I think Gert has grown much bigger than Daisy - she has quite a large comb and wattles, and she must be producing the larger eggs. The eggs have lovely golden yolks which give colour to my sponges. Having fresh eggs is such a boon and has helped my baking no end, and I can now produce the odd cake if I can manage to save up my marg and sugar ration. I shall make you some griddle pancakes today, darling, if you fancy them. I have managed to keep a pot of my home-made blackcurrant jam which will go nicely on a pancake or two." Hilda bustled away to her kitchen, pleased that she could produce treats for her daughter.

Sarah's friend Joyce was still away but their mutual school friend, Barbara, was luckily at home on leave and came across the road from her home to chat with Sarah and keep her company. They had a laugh as they both described their various experiences of the forces. Barbara had signed up to the Wrens, and kept Sarah in stitches as she described her experiences with the sailors. Barbara was a pretty girl, the same age as Sarah, with blond curls and blue eyes which shone and twinkled as she told Sarah of her escapades.

"One is very lucky to escape with one's virtue intact in the navy," she told Sarah. "Every girl for herself with that lot! You know what sailors are like; cheeky chaps, the bunch of them!"

Sarah was much cheered by seeing Barbara, and when she left they promised faithfully that they would write to each other.

Hilda came and told Sarah that she had just had a phone call from her brother. Apparently, good fortune had befallen, as George just happened to be on a '48' and was going to bring Monica, Penny and their newly born little daughter Beverley over from nearby Lee to see Sarah that very afternoon. Sarah was thrilled at the thought of seeing her brother and his family. "I'm beginning to think that this accident was very fortuitous after all," she said to her mother. "How lovely it will be to see the new babe."

After lunch George and his family arrived. Penny came skipping in. "I'm so sorry you are hurt, Auntie Sarah," she said, giving Sarah a small bunch of flowers from her mother's garden.

"Oh, thank you very much, Penny," said Sarah, and leaned over from her chair to kiss Penny's pink cheeks. "They are lovely. I'll put them in water. My, my, Penny darling, what lovely hair you have." Sarah gently patted the little girl's golden curls with her good hand.

"Hello, darling Sis," said George. "By Jove! You have come a cropper, haven't you? I say, what rotten luck." He came over and kissed his sister's head. Sarah thought George had filled out a bit. Marriage and fatherhood certainly suited him. Monica followed George into the room, carrying the babe.

"Hello, Monica, how nice to see you. Come and sit by the fire and show me your wee baby."

Monica was a tall slender young lady with finely chiselled cheek bones, and a mass of glossy black curls. She was very elegantly dressed in the latest fashion. Despite the war, she wore black court shoes and sheer stockings with seams, Sarah noted with envy. Penny was with Hilda in the kitchen, helping her to put some crumpets on plates ready for tea.

Monica handed Beverley to Sarah, resting her good arm against a cushion so that Sarah could support the little one.

"Oh, she is absolutely adorable," said Sarah, smiling down at the sleeping babe as she cradled her. "Is she feeding well? Does she sleep through the night?"

"Not really. She feeds well, but of course the bombing is not conducive to sleep, anyway, and she does cry when she is awakened by the air-raid siren. It can be very wearing and I get very tired, especially when George has to be away, and I have the two of them to look after." Monica heaved a sigh.

Sarah gazed at her little niece. What a little sweetheart she is, she thought, with her tuft of dark hair which looked as if it might curl. At that moment Beverley woke up, looked around the room and smiled at her aunt. Sarah thought her the most charming baby she had ever seen, and in her heart she hoped that one day she may have such a darling baby girl.

"Poor you, I can imagine it is not easy having a baby in war time. Do you know what? I think Beverley's eyes may well turn green like mine. They are quite a light grey colour now. I don't think they will be blue like Daddy's - or shall I say Grand-pa's - but Mummy has green eyes. They are certainly too light to be brown."

Gosh! It is funny to think of my parents as grandparents!"

"I'll take her now. Come on sweetheart, come to your Gan-gan." Hilda swept the babe away, enabling Monica and George to sit down for a chat with Sarah.

"You are not looking too bad, Sis." George kissed his sister fondly. "Life in the RAF must suit you. You have lost your puppy fat and have a nice slim figure."

"Oh, go on with you George. I certainly won't be slim for long if I just sit here eating Mummy's lovely food." Sarah laughed.

The three of them sat chatting, trying to keep the topics off the misery of war-torn London. George regaled them with his escapades in the West Kent Regiment, some of which were extremely funny as he had a very keen sense of humour. Soon Monica and Sarah were in stitches as he described his various army experiences. He was a good mimic and could take off his Commanding Officer to a tee.

His conversation kept well away from the horrors he had experienced, as no-one wanted to talk of the misery and the destruction of war, so the chatter was light and soon it was time for Beverley to be fed. Hilda brought her back into the room. Her grey-green eyes were wide open and she was sucking her fist hungrily.

"I'll pop upstairs, feed and change her," said Monica.

"I have already changed her. Poor little mite was quite wet under her pretty dress."

"Oh, thank you." Monica then took the babe and disappeared upstairs.

"Well, at least we have managed to spend a little time together, thanks to your accident."

George playfully tweaked Sarah's cheek. "How does the wrist feel, Sweet pea? I have missed your funny little face!"

"It is easing, thanks, George. The cold compresses help, and of course the fact that I am sitting here doing nothing is facilitating my recovery," smiled Sarah. "I have missed you too. Just think how much our lives have changed in such a short time."

They shared a cup of tea and some crumpets brought in for them by Hilda, and the three of them enjoyed a good chin-wag. Monica, having fed the baby, joined them later.

When Joe came home he joined the party, but they had to go and so didn't have much time with him. George took Monica and Beverley home before it got too dark, and Sarah sat by herself, thinking for a while.

She decided to try to write a few letters to Rhona, Ellie and Jill back at Manston. It wasn't easy writing with one hand, and she managed to steady her notepaper with a book whilst her left hand was kept close to her chest in its sling.

When she had finished writing to her friends, she thought about Gary and wondered if she should write to thank him for looking after her so well. She decided she would write; after all, he was her boss and would want to know how she was doing - and of course, when she would be fit enough to come back and continue with her work. At least I can reassure him that I won't be away much longer, Sarah thought. She had seen the doctor and he had said that her wrist should be back to normal in a couple of weeks. I ought to let Gary know that fact, she thought, and set to work writing to him.

CHAPTER TWENTY-ONE

"And with it to part, I shall never"

Gary grinned as he read the letter from Sarah. She came across as very anxious not to let the side down and leave him in the lurch for much longer. She is a very caring and responsible member of his team, he thought, and very kind to let me know how she is doing and when she may return to her job.

He suddenly realised how much he had missed seeing her smiling face each morning. She had been lighting up his life for a while with her sense of fun and kind acts, such as making sure he had a steaming hot cup of tea as soon as she reached the hut. She always cleaned her desk at the end of the day and once or twice had endeavoured to tidy his disorder, but he had to stop her as he knew he would lose everything. There was a method in his madness!

Manston had lately become a base for a variety of aeroplanes that were used against Channel shipping and coastal defences. Planes that were based at Manston were also taking part in escort duties for bombers attacking Germany. Gary had occasionally been involved with flying as an escort: he was very glad to get back in the pilot's seat, as he resented being desk bound all the time.

He had managed to get ten days' leave so he travelled back to Cornwall to see his family. He was so excited throughout the long train journey that it seemed to go in a trice, and soon he could see St. Michael's Mount coming into view and the full beauty of Mount's Bay lay before him. He alighted at Penzance station, noting the barbed wire all along the beach from Long

Rock, and the defensive pill boxes dotted along the waterfront. He had a quick admiring look at the magnificent green steam engine now hissing at the buffers - the beast seemed human as if it was just needing a rest after such a long haul - and he walked to the bus station and waited for the bus to his home. Cornwall was looking wonderful in the spring sunshine, and the sea was sparkling and glistening. If it wasn't for the sea defences and the odd warship in Mount's Bay you would never know that there was such evil going on in the world, he thought.

He alighted from the bus and walked down the narrow lane and paused. This was his home, and he seemed to have been away for an age. He stood looking at the modest little granite house for a while, noticing that the garden looked neglected. It was full of last year's dead straggly plants, although some colour was provided by a few tulip bulbs that had pushed their way up and were still blooming, as were the primroses and cowslips by the front door. The honeysuckle he had trained lovingly over the trellis was now dangling down and overgrown. He thought that he would have to do some serious gardening while he was on leave.

He turned the latch key in the brightly painted front door and called out: "Helloo!!! Anyone at home?"

"Daddy!!!" was the cry in unison from his children, Jared and Polly. They ran into his arms. He picked them both up and they covered his face in kisses.

"Ooh! Daddy, we have missed you sooo much. How long will you stay? Will you take us to the beach? Can we go in Trevayler woods and pick bluebells? Will you read us stories?"

Gary laughed. "One thing at a time, you two. I have missed you both very much, too. My goodness! How you have grown! We will spend lots of time together while I am on leave and we can do all the things you would like to do. Now, where is Mummy?" The children squealed with glee and hugged their father tightly. He put them down and went to find his wife.

She came out of the kitchen. He thought she looked very careworn and tired. "Hello, Helen, darling," he said, and she came up to him and gave him a rather frigid kiss.

"So, you're back then?" Helen sneered. "Well, the children are your responsibility for the next few days. I am badly in need of a break from them. It has been terrible since you have been away: I haven't been able to do any studying, and they have been on at me to entertain them all the time, as their school was bombed, and a new one has not yet been organised. They have been under my feet all day, it has been such a bind! There is a rumour that a school of sorts may be set up in the village hall, but everyone is too busy with war business to set it up for this term, anyway, as all their books and equipment was lost. Luckily it was an overnight raid and no children were hurt."

"That's all right, love," said Gary, catching her round the waist. "I'd love to be with the children, and they can help me with the garden. Come and give me a hug." She twisted away from him.

"Yes, they jolly well can be with you while you are here," she said. "I've had no time for gardening. I have far too much to do trying to keep the house together and manage the food rationing. Do you realise how difficult it is to feed our children with the little provisions we are allowed?" Her once pretty face was spoiled by her scowling at him through lowered brows.

In the background Gary was aware of frantic whining and scratching. At that moment the door to the kitchen burst open and Rusty, Gary's faithful spaniel, ran to him, licking and jumping up, showing his master just how much he had missed him by barking and wagging his tail nineteen to the dozen.

"That dratted dog of yours doesn't take any notice of me whatsoever. Luckily Bert down the road has kindly been walking him. I don't have any time for things like that," complained Helen.

With that she stumped off to the kitchen. Nothing has change in her attitude to me, thought Gary sadly. He had hoped this time of absence would make her miss him, not just as a child minder but as a loving husband, but it seemed it was not meant to be. Her books and studies were more important to her than anything. He could see that he and the children were more or less hindrances to Helen's great quest for an academic life.

Gary went upstairs to have a wash and changed out of uniform. Then they all sat down to a meal his wife had prepared, and the children plied Gary with many questions about his life in the RAF. He told them of the planes he had flown, and made them laugh when describing the mediocre camp food. It is good to be home, thought Gary, even though things did not seem to be any happier between him and Helen. He had hoped that the time apart had eased her feelings of resentment, but it seemed that his absence meant nothing more than that there was no-one to look after the children, and this fact had made her even colder towards him. She doesn't seem to want me as a husband, he thought, just a nursemaid.

He spent the mornings of the next nine days working on his garden, endeavouring to get it into some sort of shape so that Helen might be able to manage it while he was away. The children stayed outside with him, helping where they could. He pruned and tied back all over-grown shrubs, especially the honeysuckle on the trellis, the old fruit trees and the roses in the north border. He planted some potatoes to help feed the family and he gave the grass its first cut. He wondered if he should invest in some paving stones to make less of the lawn area, but thought better of it. Rusty loved the lawn on which to play with his ball, and the children's favourite game was French cricket which they could not play on paving stones. He made a little area for the children to have a garden of their own, and taught them how to look after it and sow some flower seeds. He thought the flower growing would help them be reminded of him while he was away.

In the afternoons Gary had great fun taking his children and Rusty to a tiny secret local beach. It was a glorious little sandy cove, not protected by barbed wire and pillboxes like the main Cornish beaches. Across a field he found the old back way down to the sand. All the normal beach entrances were protected by anti-tank obstacles, but he knew this secret track through the sand dunes from his childhood.

The weather was mainly fine, but sometimes a cold wind made fishing for crabs in rock pools a little chilly so running along with their dog and throwing a ball for him was preferable. They did manage to make sandcastles, topping them with the St. Piran's cross paper flags and squealing with glee, shovelling sand like mad as the incoming tide rushed in and began to demolish their work.

Gary was enjoying himself. The fresh air and azure
blue of the sea, with its rolling creamy foaming
breakers, gladdened his heart. He had missed the sheer
raw beauty of the white sandy beach, the grassy dunes
and granite cliffs, now beginning to look pink and blue
in patches of sea thrift, and wild scabious. It was too
early for the Hottentot fig to produce its hot colours of
orange, red and yellow, but the fleshy leaves of the
plant hung down the cliffs and blew back and forth in
the breeze. Gary privately thought that this invasive
plant – an incomer to the area – was quite unattractive,
but tourists seemed to love its garish colours when in
bloom. Give me native plants only, thought Gary. His
natural horticultural talent decried outlandish plants,
especially the Cordylines which were known as
'Cornish palms' but were no such thing, Gary mused.
Why don't folk realise that they come from Australia?
He loathed them, but again some local people seem to
like them. Their long brown fronds always fell and
blocked drains. He would admit that when they were in
bloom they would give off a powerful fragrance in the
evening, and the bees absolutely adored them, so he
reluctantly supposed that they had *some* merit.

Gary, good as his word, took the children and Rusty
to Trevayler woods. It was a magical place just inland
from Gulval, where the sea could be seen peeping
between the smooth beech trunks across the small
fields. They were now bright yellow with rows of
daffodils which, due to the war, had missed this year's
London markets.

This was where the children swore they could see
fairy folk hiding among the roots of the magnificent
beeches. They rushed helter-skelter down the steep
lane, next to the lodge house of Trevayler Manor.

Rusty gambolled at their heels, barking ecstatically and really enjoying his walks with the children and his beloved master. At the end of the lane was a truly beautiful sight. A magical glade opened up before them: through it a brook meandered over several small waterfalls, bubbling and chuckling over the stones into a large mysterious still pool in which swam small brown trout through the dark depths. The first baby green curled fronds of many species of ferns were pushing through the thick carpet of last year's beech leaves, and a few bluebells were waving their heads in the breeze.

The children chased each other through the trees, hiding and jumping out on one another with much laughter, and Rusty hurled himself into the pool and swam round trying to bite the shadows in the water. Gary sat on an upturned tree stump smoking a Woodbine, and watched the sun making patterns on the beech leaf carpet. He felt at peace, but at the same time his heart was sad. Helen had done nothing but snap at him since he had been home. She had lost any warmth she may have felt for him, and they had only made love once since his return. Gary felt so unwanted that he had not attempted to approach her again, and they had spent nights together with their backs to each other. Gary had just lain in his bed staring at the wall and wondering what he could do to make their marriage work. He had bought her flowers, he had arranged for a baby-sitter and taken her out for a meal in a near-by pub, but she remained cold to him, barely speaking.

I really feel that my marriage is over he thought, and felt very sad that there seemed to be no love in his wife for him. If I were an encyclopaedia she would probably be more interested in me. There and then he vowed to write to his parents in Wales about his unhappiness. Maybe they will have some good advice for me, he thought. I really need to talk this over with someone, and soon.

His last day with the family in Cornwall was rather spoilt by the weather breaking. The rain came lashing down, and that night there was a bad bombing raid on Penzance. They all spent the night in their sturdy cellar, the children snuggled up to him with blankets wrapped securely round them. They slept cuddling closely to their father until the all clear, when they were able to go back to their beds. The raids on West Cornwall were nothing like those on East Kent, but nevertheless Gary was anxious for his children's safety as he travelled back to London on the early steam train to Paddington the next day.

CHAPTER TWENTY-TWO

"What do I say, if I meet you today?"

True to his word, Trel drove Sarah back to Westgate when her wrist had mended. Sarah said goodbye to her parents, kissed them and bade them be safe, and got into the Austin Seven with Mrs. Treleaven and her sister Mamie in the back.

Sarah politely greeted the ladies, inquiring after their health, and Trel drove off. They all waved to Hilda and Joe standing at their garden gate. It was rather a cloudy day with little patches of blue sky interspersed with quite threatening black clouds.

"I hope we get to a decent restaurant for lunch before the heavens open," observed Annie Treleaven, looking skywards from her back window.

"Well, it looked like such a lovely day when I got up this morning, the sun was shining right into my bedroom, so I washed out a few things and left them on the line," said Mamie.

"Oh well, that was very foolish of you," snapped Annie. "You knew we would be out all day! They will probably be soaked. I don't know if you have any sense at all sometimes."

"I was only trying to help, Annie," said Mamie. "I knew you wanted those dusters to be clean."

"Oh well, it was only dusters, so they won't matter if they get another rinse through!" Annie grudgingly conceded, shifting restlessly in her seat.

"Now, now, Mother," said Henry from his front seat. "Auntie was only trying to help, and you really shouldn't jump to conclusions so quickly; well done, Auntie, that was very kind of you."

Trel was very fond of his aunt and would always stand up for her. Annie was inclined to pick on Mamie if her rheumatism was bad, and he didn't want his aunt browbeaten by his mother. The two half-sisters didn't get on very well, and he was sure that when he was not around that his mother probably made his aunt's life rather hard.

"Well, I think those clouds will pass over and it will be a fine day," said Sarah positively. She turned and grinned at Mamie in the back seat. "I am pretty sure they will dry nicely." Mamie liked Sarah a lot and hoped very much that she and Trel would marry one day, when the confounded war was over.

They motored on, making good time, and soon arrived in Lower Halstow in Sittingbourne where they found a lovely old pub called The Three Tuns. They parked the car and went into the whitewashed building and were met by a friendly landlord, who said the inn dated back to 1468 – hence the very small entrance door through which they all had to stoop to enter. They sat at a polished wooden table. Sarah admired the shining copper pans hanging from the walls, the horse brasses and the lovely old oak beams that criss-crossed the dining room.

Soon a friendly waitress in a crisp white apron brought their meal, which they ate with relish.

"This inn is a good find, Henry," said his mother, tucking into her lunch.

"Yes, I saw it in the AA book of good pubs in Kent. It looked so attractive from the outside in the book, and it is spacious and welcoming on the inside. The grub is good too, don't you think?"

"My fish is delicious," said Sarah. "Boy, this is wizzo! I am not looking forward to Mess food again." She pulled a face.

"Is it very bad, dear?" asked Mamie.

"Well, let's say that it is nourishing and just about edible, but lacks taste and usually looks pretty dire."

They finished their meal, each having indulged in a dessert of apple crumble and custard, drank their coffees, and went back to the car and travelled onward for a few miles to Thanet.

When they reached the convent, Mamie and Annie stayed discreetly in the car while Trel walked Sarah up the long drive to the rather forbidding red brick north frontage.

"Well, darling, when will I see you again? When is your next leave due?" Trel asked, holding Sarah's hand and turning her to face him.

"I'm not sure, Trel dear," she replied. "This injury leave has put me all out of sync. I shall have to wait to get back to work before I find out about my next '48'. I know it is a bind for you, not knowing when I will be home again, but of course I will get in touch as soon as I know myself."

"Oh, well, take care of yourself darling and don't go falling off your bike again!" Trel teased, giving her a big hug.

"You take care too, Trel, and don't forget to write!" Sarah kissed him then went running up the convent steps, just pausing for a minute to wave goodbye.

Trel walked back to the car and drove his passengers down to the beach for a quick look at the sea and a stretch of their legs in the fresh salty air before setting off for home.

"I do hope you will not let that girl slip through your fingers, Henry. She is too good to lose, and will make you a fine wife."

"I know that Mother, and I would have married her before the war if she would have had me, but she is very young. I'm fifteen years older than her, remember, and she does not want to settle down yet. We will have to see what happens when this ruddy war is over, whenever that will be, and she is eventually demobbed. All I can do is to wait for her, and that I will do, as I love her dearly."

Mamie, who was now in the front seat of the car, pressed Trel's hand with hers and smiled at him. "Faint heart did not win fair lady," she said wisely, settling down for a nap as they drove on back to Sydenham.

CHAPTER TWENTY-THREE

"It is with a grateful heart"

Sarah was soon back working her socks off with all the other girls in the hut. In fact, they all had a bit of a laugh with Gary. He was beginning to relax in their company, and there was a lot of "Go on with you! You are a scream!" As he teased the girls, making their day go a little faster with a giggle or two and a bit of good natured banter. He often pulled their legs about their boyfriends, or whoever he had seen them with at the airfield. Nothing much missed his eye and he had a fount of information from his RAF friends, many of whom envied his job being in charge of such a bunch of attractive 'popsies'.

Sarah often felt Gary watching her as she sat typing. She looked up, and sure enough he was smiling over at her. She smiled back, and he winked at her. This caused her to blush quite prettily, and made her lose her concentration until she pulled herself together and got on with her work.

Gary sometimes had to leave another Flight Sergeant, John Brown, in charge of the girls. This chap was a bit of a sour puss; he would sometimes snap at the girls thus, Sarah and the others kept very quiet and their heads down when he was in charge. The working days seemed to drag more when he was their boss as there was no joking, just hard relentless slog, and they looked forward to Gary's return.

The girls were not party to what Gary was doing when he was absent from his desk. He was, in fact, testing refurbished planes, a job he enjoyed immensely. He was not a 'sit behind a desk' sort of chap, and he

loved to be up there soaring above the Isle of Thanet.
He recently had a bit of a near miss when the kite he
was testing jammed its landing gear. Gary had had to
slide down on the new runway, almost on to the grass –
a belly-flop, he later described it as – but it gave his
insides a jolt or two, and he was relieved when she
finally slid to a standstill. He was flying again the next
day; better get back into the cockpit and ease my
nerves, he thought. His next flight, thankfully, was
without incident and went very well, this served to boost
his confidence, and made his enjoyment of flying
return.

Some of the girls had quite naturally formed easy-
going friendships with chaps they met at the 'drome.
Sarah's friend Jill had met a chap at one of the concerts
put on at the base, and had been going out with him for
a while.

"I think Jerry is serious about me," Jill said one
evening, as they sat in the dorm. Sarah was winding
embroidery silks round cardboard cards ready for use,
and Jill, Rhona and Eleanor were polishing their shoes
and buttons and sprucing up their kit ready for their
regular early morning inspection the next day.

"Go on, then, tell us more about him. Don't leave
us in suspenders!" asked Sarah.

"I met him by accident. Well, actually I spilled a cup
of coffee over him after the concert in the Naafi!"

Jill laughed at the memory. The girls stopped what
they were doing and said in harmony "Noo, really? Oh,
do go on!"

"That's the sort of thing that happens to me,
normally, clumsy person that I am!" Sarah put in.

Jill put down her polishing tin and explained. "I felt
awful about it. I turned round quickly and bumped

straight into him, and his cup went flying. I tried to mop him down with a borrowed tea-towel, but he would have none of it. Instead he cheekily asked if I would walk out with him one evening in order to make amends. He looked really nice. He is working on repairing crashed kites with Gary's friend Reg over near Alland Grange, a responsible job; and thinking about it, if I am to get involved with anyone in the RAF, I would rather it was not a flyer!"

"Can he dance?" asked Sarah, who loved to dance.

"Yep, he certainly can jitter-bug with the best of them. We went to a dance in Westgate last week and he is just an amazing mover. He helps me to dance well too – which is good, as I have two left feet most of the time and he makes it easy by holding and leading me."

"Humph, you are lucky! Good dancers are hard to find in this camp," said Eleanor, speaking from the bitter experience of having her feet trodden on and being twirled round too vigorously by some chaps.

"So, how do you know he is serious?" The two girls looked expectantly at Jill.

"Well, Jerry wants me to meet his parents," Jill said. Sarah and Eleanor exchanged knowing glances. "A bit early for that isn't it?" Ellie asked.

"I thought that too, girls, but he says he really cares for me and I feel that he is a genuine sort. I like him a lot," she said shyly.

"Good luck to you both, then," remarked Sarah. "In this war happiness can be fleeting, so you have to grab it where you can. Just keep a little bit of your heart for yourself, you never know, this Jerry may be a player."

"Oh, I don't think he is a flirt. He doesn't seem to have had many girlfriends of his own. Anyway, you sound like the voice of experience and a lot older than your years, Sarah!" said Jill.

"Well, my brother married the widow of a pilot. They now have a little baby of their own, but it must have been very hard for my sister-in-law. She already had a little girl when her first husband was shot down and killed at the beginning of the war. You never know what is round the corner these days, so you must follow your heart, Jill, and grasp whatever happiness comes your way, it seems."

Sarah gathered her silks together and tidied them away. She quickly laid out her uniform for the next day and gave her buttons and shoes a buff over. She undressed, put on pyjamas and cleaned her teeth, taking her turn in the queue for the bathroom, had a wash, and jumped into bed.

"Oh, why is the water only tepid?" Ellie complained.

"You don't really expect anything else, do you?" Rhona remarked, sweeping by in her pink dressing-gown. "I cannot find my dratted toothpaste! Lend us a squeeze of yours, Ellie, there is a dear."

Soon all were back in the dorm, snuggled up in their beds. Suddenly there was a rattle of stones hitting the dorm window.

"Did you hear that?" Ellie whispered. Jill rushed to the window.

"Oh, good grief! I forgot all about to tell you that Marjorie and some of the other girls were going out drinking after a late shift working in the Officers' Mess. She asked me to watch out for them, in case they came home after ten o'clock and were locked out. Now they are all waiting to climb up the drain pipe! Come on, let's help them!"

The girls all jumped out of bed and hung out of the window, grabbing hands and clothing where they could, and eventually the late comers were safely in the dorm.

"Oh, thank you!" puffed Marjorie, dusting herself down. She was a petite pretty girl with brown curls and stunning blue eyes. "Phew! That was a near thing – I believe the drain pipe would not have held much longer!" The other girls wiped bits of foliage and twigs off their dresses. "You have saved our lives and no mistake. It would have been jankers for us at least! We all owe you."

"That's OK, girls, we hope you will do the same for us if needs be. Hope your jaunt into the Margate drinking establishments was worth it," Jill laughed, as the rescued girls all trooped off to the next dorm.

"It was lucky that old 'Tubby' didn't hear that commotion. She will be doing her rounds soon."

Sure enough, as they jumped into their beds their C.O. arrived to make sure all was well and as it should be. She made a tutting sound as she noticed the blackout curtain flapping in the wind. She then spied the open window banging in the breeze and shut it with a firm hand, replaced the blind and left them.

"Phew! That was close! Luckily there is no moon tonight – she didn't notice that some of the ivy has been scrabbled away from the wall. A close shave for us all, and no mistake. Well, goodnight all, time for some shut-eye, sweet dreams." Sarah snuggled under the blankets.

"Good night, sleep tight and mind those bedbugs don't bite!" replied a sleepy Ellie, and soon there was silence in the dorm, as the girls slid seamlessly into the land of nod.

CHAPTER TWENTY-FOUR

"The message from music is quietly concealed"

The WAAFs were out on parade very early the next morning. It was a grey day, very windy with lowering skies threatening rain, but it kept dry for their inspection. They had already performed a bit of square bashing. Sarah always enjoyed marching, although she had to concentrate hard in order to go the right way and she was still hopeless with her left and right hands. She kept her eyes firmly on the shoulders of the girl in front, reaching out with her arms to that height as instructed. She enjoyed the stirring RAF marching tunes and felt very proud to be part of RAF Manston as they drilled. Their skirts kept blowing up in the wind and some girls tried to quickly push them down, but on seeing this their C.O. shouted: "I don't care if your eyebrows drop off, keep your eyes front and leave your skirts alone!"

At one point the wind made it difficult to hear the command "About Turn!" Thus the company kept on marching in one direction, going for too long. When finally the C.O. caught up with them, she said sarcastically: "Hello! Had a nice holiday?"

They passed their uniform inspection. It was very rigorous, but all had worked hard to ensure they presented a clean and tidy appearance. Only one girl was taken to task, for having straggly hair escaping from her cap. She had long hair, had forgotten to put on a hair net that morning and had tried to control it with borrowed kirby grips. Apart from that they were all passed as first class, their rather portly Commanding Officer informed them. The girls would make fun of their C.O. behind her back, as she was very fierce, had a booming voice comparable to any male drill sergeant and had a huge behind which wobbled alarmingly when she marched. They tried not to look at it, in case of being overcome with a fit of the giggles; hence her nickname 'Tubby'.

They were dismissed and sent back to the hut to get on with their work. Gary saw them coming and met them at the door. He had been having a break and was smoking and leaning against the hut.

"How did you do, girls?" he asked, after they had saluted each other. "I hope you didn't let me down."

"Oh, we wouldn't do that Sir, we are just the smartest ever," Rhona told her boss. "No-one can polish buttons like us!" The girls all made noises of agreement and filed into the hut.

Sarah passed Gary and smiled at him. He put his hand on her shoulder, stopping her from entering the hut and said: "Just a minute young lady, I have some good news for you. I have managed to get tickets for another performance of the Rachmaninov symphony number two. Would you by any chance be free next Wednesday evening? This time the piece is being played by a first-class orchestra, up from Canterbury, so the concert should be even better than last time. It should be a rare musical treat."

"Oh, wizzo! That will be absolutely grand! I'm not doing anything special, and you really must let me pay for the tickets. After all, it was my fault that we missed the first concert. It will be my way of making it up to you."

Gary smiled, looked down into her upturned face and said "No don't be daft, Miss Langman, I wouldn't hear of such a thing, the very idea!! I shall be very pleased to have your company."

"Well, that is very kind of you," Sarah said. "I shall look forward to it."

"Good, that is settled then. I will try and scrounge transport into Margate and will pick you up at about 18.00 hours from the Mess after dinner. Now, cut along and work some magic with those skilled typing fingers of yours."

Sarah went in and soon got stuck into her work. Her mind, however, was on other things. She was thinking about the concert, and of Gary's kindness. He is such a lovely man, she thought, and he has such a nice smile.

Wednesday soon came around. The day seemed to drag as Sarah excitedly thought about going to the concert. I wish I didn't have to go in uniform, she thought. I would love to wear my new dress.

Gary had not been in the office that day and the unpopular morose Flight Sergeant John Brown was in charge. None of the girls were on first-name terms with him; he was just not that sort of chap.

The day dragged inexorably for Sarah. At last they packed up for the day. Sarah had told her friends at lunch that she was going out that evening.

"Well, you are a fine one. Sucking up to the boss will get you nowhere," Ellie joshed.

"You do know that Gary is married with two children?" Rhona remarked in passing.

"I don't really know much about him at all," retorted Sarah. "Anyway, this is only a returned favour because we both missed the earlier concert. I'm just going out with a friend, don't you know."

The other girls teased her and asked her to let them know how she got on. Six o'clock came and Gary turned up at the NAAFI, where he had a quick snack.

"Your carriage awaits, madam," he said as he found Sarah eating rolls with her friends. "If you look sharp I will be able to drop you back to the convent to change."

"Really?" Sarah exclaimed. "That would be lovely."

"I didn't think you'd want to go out in uniform," Gary said. "However, you will have to put up with me in Air Force blue as I have no time to get back to change, I'm afraid."

They set off across the fields to the convent. Sarah rushed up to change. She donned her red and white polka dot dress and red jacket, clipped in some ceramic flower ear-rings her parents had given her, and had two minutes to brush her hair, apply a little lipstick and powder her nose before flying down the stairs to Gary, who was waiting in the large entrance hall. He was talking to one of the nuns.

"Sister Bernadette says you are a real pain in the neck," he teased Sarah. "I didn't recognise you. You certainly blossom out of uniform, like Cinderella. My goodness, can this vision of loveliness really be one of my WAAF clerks?"

They motored into Margate, laughing at his silly jokes on the way, and soon they reached the concert hall and found their seats. They were good seats, near enough to the orchestra to be able to observe their playing. Sarah always loved to watch the violinists – they fascinated her as their bows went back and forth in complete unison. She leaned forward in her seat in rapt attention.

The Rachmaninov was magical, a very passionate piece which took them to the heights and depths all in a trice. Gary looked at the expression of sheer pleasure on Sarah's face and thought what a lovely girl she was – and she shared his great love for beautiful music. Music is fine on its own, he had always thought, but to be able to share the emotional highs and lows of a particular piece with another person, well, that was something really special.

Afterwards he asked her if she would like to have a coffee with him. Sarah looked at her watch: it was early, so she said that would be a good idea. She still wanted to talk about the music, so Gary drove them to Birchington where there was a little café called Clovellys. It was set in an old red brick building, with exposed beams inside and chintz curtains at the window. They sat at a small polished table by the window. Sarah settled herself comfortably in a window seat on a soft cushion, also covered in flowery chintz. This is charming, she thought to herself as Gary fetched two coffees for them.

"Would you like a piece of walnut cake, Sarah?" Gary asked. Sarah thought that the cakes looked delicious and, since it was quite a while since she had eaten a roll, she replied in the affirmative.

The blackout boards were put up and curtains pulled while they sat there, munching cake and sipping coffee. Little lamps were lit on each table and, as they chatted about the concert and music in general, Sarah realised how much she was enjoying Gary's company.

"Have you been home on leave lately?" She asked Gary. She knew he came from Cornwall, and realised what a long way from home he was.

"Yes, I had ten days at home while you were off sick," said Gary.

"Did you have a lovely time? I expect Cornwall is beautiful this time of the year, despite the ugliness of barbed wire on the beaches."

"Yes, Cornwall certainly is stunning, as usual. It was mostly good weather, too, but rain is never very far away in the West Country, I'm afraid. I took my children and my spaniel Rusty down to a tiny local cove that I knew from childhood. It is hidden and sheltered; no-one knows of it and there was no barbed wire. They had a grand time. Rusty always digs holes, which makes the children laugh as he showers them with sand. Luckily, he races into the sea and that washes some of the sand off, otherwise my rather house-proud wife gets very cross if he brings any mess into the house. Once, after a beach trip, I didn't realise that he had a load of seaweed in his mouth which he had carried back. He spat it on the kitchen floor, so you could imagine that my name was mud. But then it always is, these days."

Sarah missed Gary's rather pensive sad expression at that time, as she was stirring her coffee and looking down.

"What are the names of your children? How old are they?"

"They are called Jared and Polly. Jared is the elder of the two by a couple of years. He is nine and Polly is seven. They are good kids, and I miss them very much," said Gary with a sigh. He produced his wallet and extracted two faded photos of a boy and girl.

"Oh, they look really sweet, and the boy looks just like you! Tell me more about your life in Cornwall."

"There is not much to tell. I used to work as an engineer at the Camborne School of Mines and spent my spare time at Land's End Airport. There, in exchange for maintenance work on the planes, I was able to have a few flying lessons and test the planes when they were repaired – a bit like now, only those planes were much smaller."

"I live in Hayle, which is way down in the westernmost tip of Cornwall, near Penzance and not far from Land's End. Our home is a small granite cottage with a large overgrown garden that needs my attention constantly. I did what I could when I was at home for that short time on leave, as my wife, Helen, cannot manage the garden on her own. She even complains bitterly about my beloved little spaniel, Rusty, and has a chap in from down the road to take him for walks. I do miss my Rusty, I must admit, and he goes potty when I go home. He never leaves my side for a minute."

Gary looked at Sarah. "Sorry Sarah, I have been going on a bit, but talking of home just makes me sad. May I fetch you another cup of coffee?"

"No, I think we had better make a move now, thank you all the same," said Sarah. Strangely she didn't want to hear any more about Gary's home life; she wasn't sure why.

They left the comfort of the warm café and went out into the dark night. Many stars were twinkling in the sky as they walked to the car.

"It has been a quiet night, so far," observed Gary, as he opened the car door for Sarah. "I hope it stays that way and we don't have any bombing raids."

"Thank you so much for a lovely evening, Gary. See you tomorrow."

He watched her walk up the long convent drive. He suddenly realised he hadn't enjoyed an evening with a member of the opposite sex so much for a long, long time. Why cannot Helen be more like Sarah? He thought sadly, and drove away to his billet.

CHAPTER TWENTY-FIVE

"The kiss is akin to the embrace"

As the weather had been fine each day, Sarah had been walking back and forth to the 'drome from the convent. Her bike was still being repaired as Reg just hadn't had the time to look at it. She was quite relieved that it was still under repair as she had lost her confidence in riding it.

However, the day finally dawned when Gary told her that Reg had put a new front wheel on her bike, straightened the handlebars and carried out whatever else repairs were needed, and now it was ready for her over at Alland Grange.

Sarah thanked Gary and realised that she should fetch her bike fairly soon although felt a little apprehensive at the thought of riding it again

A normal day working in the hut finally ended, and all were packing up.

"Would you like me to ride back beside you this evening?" Gary asked.

"Okay, that is kind of you, as I am a little nervous about riding it again. Maybe I will go over now to get the bike from Alland Grange and I'll meet you back here," said Sarah gratefully.

"Very well, that suits me as I still have a lot of work to do. So that will be fine, gives me a bit more time to finish up. By the way, did you know there is an underground RAF hangar at Alland Grange? Also, nearby there is a chalk pit into which cow byres have been cut, to keep the cattle safe from bombing raids. The house, or Grange, was taken over as an Operations base. Reg may have time to show you around sometime. The Grange itself was once owned by the monks at Minster and has a very old cellar which looks like a crypt. It is really very ancient and fascinating."

The days were lengthening as April slid seamlessly into May. Sarah had been enjoying her walk back over the fields each evening, sometimes with other girls and sometimes on her own, depending on what was going on at the 'drome. She occasionally hitched the odd lift from the Liberty bus, if the weather had turned inclement. However, having her bike back would certainly save time, especially in the morning, when she had to have a quick breakfast at the 'drome before getting to her desk bright and early, or she was due on uniform inspection or parade.

Sarah walked over to the old Grange at the southern end of the airfield and met Reg, who explained what he had done to make the bike road-worthy once again. He had also given the bike a lick of paint so it looked grand. Sarah was thrilled with it.

"Thank you very much, Reg. You have made a wizard job of the bike. Why, it looks like new! I owe you a pint next time I see you in the bar. Our Flight told me that you have an underground hangar over here."

"Yes, Alland Grange Farm was requisitioned by the RAF and now is an official extension to the main 'drome. If you are interested, you and a couple of other WAAFs could come over sometime and I will show you round. Meanwhile, just go carefully this time, Sarah. Keep your eyes on the road!"

Reg was a lovely chap: always friendly and cheerful, even though some of his work was very grim. Recently he boarded a badly hammered plane that had arrived at

Manston after a raid. The rear turret was a mass of twisted metal with hits on the fins, rudder and tail plane. When Reg had boarded her, he recognised the smell of death and found that there were tattered pieces of flying gear and uniform. Considerable amount of blood and some flesh were evident. The sad thing was that the plane had contained a new crew on their first op. That meant that the fatalities were all young. Such a tragedy and an evil waste of life, Reg thought sadly.

Reg naturally kept these details from Sarah, glossing over the true nature of his work, but he often had to have time with his friend Gary over a beer, and that was when he off-loaded the horrors of his duties. Luckily, Gary was a very good listener and acted as a counsellor for Reg, who simply had to try to clear his mind as best he could of images too horrific to imagine and just get on with his job.

Ironically, neither of them knew, of course, but the tables were to turn and Reg would end up as a sympathetic ear for Gary one day in the not so distant future.

Reg had recently started a romance with one of Sarah's fellow WAAF girls, Connie, and this really helped to lighten his load. They were getting really close as a couple. Reg had realised that she was the one for him, and taking her to dances and getting out to shows when they were both off duty did him the world of good – especially if there was a good old fashioned sing-song and a really funny comedian to lighten his mood.

Sarah knew of Connie, although she was in a different dorm at the convent and she worked in the camp telephone exchange. Sarah had been detailed to cover at the exchange once or twice and Connie had shown her the ropes. She thought that Connie and Reg made a lovely couple.

"There you go, Sarah, your trusty bike is as good as new. Mind that you give my love to Con if you see her back at the convent. Sadly, I am too busy to take her out at the moment."

Sarah walked a little way back with Reg. He was on his way to the control tower and she didn't want to get on the bike in front of him in case she wobbled. It was a lovely evening, still and quite warm, and they were chattering when they heard over the tannoy that an incoming damaged plane was approaching the airfield. Reg said: "Look over there, Sarah!"

They could see an American B17 Flying Fortress bomber approaching the airfield, from the direction of the sea. It was making very heavy going, with one propeller smashed and feathered and one just wind-milling uselessly. The pilot fired a red distress signal and the plane lobbed down on the grass almost in front of the tower and rolled to a stop in a few yards. Some of the crew climbed out of the plane almost before it had halted.

Reg and Sarah rushed forward and could see that the crew had taken a lot of punishment. They got out and some even kissed the ground, they were so grateful to be alive. They slapped each other, shook hands, and some offered up a prayer on their knees. It looked like they hadn't expected to see Blighty again. An ambulance arrived and medical teams helped to lift out a couple of injured airmen. Both Reg and Sarah were very moved by the crews' emotions at being safe.

After looking at the damaged plane – yet another for his crew to sort out – Reg and Sarah parted ways and he walked on to the control tower. When he was safely out of sight Sarah hopped on to her bike and began pedalling back to meet Gary. Once she got going she was fine and relaxed into cycling again; however, although she realised she could probably manage to cycle back on her own, she really wanted to be in the company of Gary again, so she met him back at the Admin hut.

He had heard the tannoy so she told him of the B17 coming in, and how she and Reg had watched the emotional relief of the aircrew when they were on terra firma. It was the first time Sarah had witnessed such an amazing landing and she questioned Gary about it while they rode back together. She wanted to know more about how one could land a crippled kite, and how he had had to make a forced landing only a few weeks' back. He explained what he knew about Flying Fortresses and in no time they were back at the convent. At the gate Gary dismounted his bike and said:

"There you are, Sarah! I'm very glad you are now confident on your bike again because tomorrow is Saturday, and I wondered if you would be free in the afternoon and would care to ride over to Reculver with me? You know, just to make sure you will be okay on the main road."

Sarah was inwardly very pleased that she may see Gary the next day, when they were not working.

"That is such a good idea, Gary. I need all the confidence I can muster, and main roads are a bit daunting to me at the moment. We could take a picnic. I will ask the nuns if I may make some sandwiches and we could get some lemonade to drink in Birchington on the way."

"Righty-ho! See you at about 14.00 hours tomorrow. I'll wait round the back, near the bike shed. I don't want the other girls to pull your leg about coming out for a bike ride with me. Cheerie-ho for now."

Sarah realised how sensible he was, she didn't want any silly tattle tales about her amongst the girls. Why, there was nothing in the fact that she was going for a bike ride, after all!

CHAPTER TWENTY-SIX

"My trust in you is all I've got"

When Sarah awoke the next morning the sun was pouring in through the dormitory windows, and it looked like a lovely day for a cycle ride.

There had been excitement in the dorm the night before. Jill had come in late from a date with Jerry and just missed being shut out of the convent. The girls were busying themselves with a good book or, in Sarah's case, her embroidery.

Marjorie said: "Hmm, it's not fair! We have to be back in the evening by 22.00 hours, but for the airmen the curfew is midnight!"

"That's because they think we are precious little flowers, ducks! Little do they know we are tougher than we look. Come on Jill, spill the beans, then!"

Jill regaled them with her news. She sat down on her bed and told them that Jerry had taken her out for a meal, and when she went to drink from her glass she realised that there was something in the bottom of it. She fished around in the glass feeling a little daft, and pulled out a diamond ring. She looked at it with shock as the beauty of the three perfectly matched precious stones shone and glistened in the light. At that moment Jerry had leaned forward and taken her hand, saying:

"How about it then, darling. I love you so very much, so will you be mine, will you marry me?"

Jill gasped once or twice out of amazement, but then recovered herself enough to say: "Oh darling Jerry, yes, YES," and then added "please," out of politeness.

At this the girls fell about laughing, and much congratulating and hugging took place.

"Do show us the ring," Sarah asked, and they all waited while Jill pulled a gold chain from round her neck. It was hidden by her dress and totally concealed, as she had felt too nervous to wear it on her finger. Jerry had placed it there but when Jill reached the convent she hid it from view.

"It is a big bit for me," she exclaimed as they all gathered round and emitted lots of "Oohs!" and "Ahhs!" in admiration of its beauty. It was a cross-over three stone diamond ring, set in gold in the latest fashion. "I'll put it on a chain around my neck until I can get it re-sized. I really do not want to lose it!"

"There is a really good jewellers called Cuttings in Margate market place," said Rhona. "I saw it the other day when I went for a walk into town. It looks old and very reputable. They have their own workshop at the back, so they could re-size your ring in two shakes of a lamb's tail, I'm sure."

"You remember that I met his parents a little while ago?" Jill continued, settling back onto the bed. "They came over for the day from Whitstable and took us out for lunch. His mother is a real sweetheart, she is a very nice, neat, little lady with twinkly eyes just like my Jerry. His father lives away for most of the time, at the moment. He does voluntary work for the war effort but managed to get some time off to meet me; he is tall and handsome with grey hair and a small moustache. They both greeted me with a kiss, and I felt at home with them straight away. I suppose this marriage will mean a lot to them as Jerry is an only child, and in a way I will be the daughter they never had. Well, that is what his mother told me, anyway."

"Jerry did everything in the correct way, he phoned my father and asked him for my hand in marriage. I knew nothing of this until he told me, and I still haven't phoned my parents. They will be wondering if I said yes or no!"

"That is just so sweet," said Ellie. "You are a very lucky girl, Jill. When will the wedding take place?"

"I'm not sure, we haven't yet decided. We may wait till after the war, but on the other hand why should we wait so long? This conflict could go on for years."

The morning passed quickly. There was nothing but wedding talk amongst the girls, and it was so good to have something happy to celebrate at last.

Sarah had a lot of chores to catch up with, and letters to be written home to Trel and her parents, as well as Barbara and Joyce, who were both now away on duty. Stockings needed to be darned and damp washing to be hung on the line, making the most of a fine drying day.

Finally, chores accomplished, it was time to get ready. There was a cool breeze despite the sun, so she decided to wear a thickish blue skirt with a pale blue blouse which she hoped complimented the skirt, and to take a navy pullover. She checked that she still had a roll-up mac tucked into her saddle bag, in case of inclement weather. Better to be safe than sorry, she thought, though she squinted at the blue sky that stretched to the horizon and not the tiniest bit of cloud was in view.

She got her bike from the shed and was walking down the concealed side drive when she saw Gary walking up through the trees, pushing his bike. Her heart was thumping. Now don't be daft, she told herself, you are not going to fall off again; but she knew that that was not the only reason her heart was behaving stupidly.

"Hallo there!" said Gary. He was dressed in light brown cavalry twill trousers, a check open-necked shirt and a brown sports jacket. "I hope I am not going to be too hot in these clothes, but it is deceptive because there is a keen breeze blowing off the sea. Are you ready to go, Sarah?"

Sarah nodded. How handsome he looks, she thought, and how different out of uniform, much younger really. She mounted her bike and they set off down the Canterbury road for Birchington.

CHAPTER TWENTY-SEVEN

"I will keep it close to my heart"

The ride went well, and Sarah felt fine back in the saddle. She did, however, keep a wary eye out for the tram lines which were all along the main road. They stopped to get a bottle of lemonade and set off out of Birchington village, into the countryside. Luckily the road was very quiet. They could hear skylarks flying high above them, heralding the summer which was just around the corner.

It was about five miles to the village of Reculver from the convent, all told. They cycled along the main Thanet Way, which lead eventually to London, and turned off after two miles into a tiny country lane which undulated gently down to the sea. They passed a large black painted wooden windmill, its white painted sails turning slowly and creakily in the light breeze. They saw magnificent elms sporting fresh green new leaves, their huge branches turned up to heaven as if in supplication, standing stark and proud against the azure sky, and a few new-born lambs gambolling in the fields. They paused for a moment to laugh at the antics of these young creatures, full of the joys of spring.

The twelfth-century twin towers of St. Mary's Church loomed up ahead of them on the coast. Soon they arrived in Reculver village and, passing the King Ethelbert pub, they dismounted from their bikes and padlocked them together in the pub car park.

They walked up the slope towards the ruined Anglo-Saxon church and stopped to peruse a sign informing them that there was once was a monastery there, known as Reculver Abbey. In the seventh century, they read,

Reculver had become a landed estate of the Anglo-
Saxon kings of Kent.

They walked around the church yard and saw that
much of the ground on the seaward side of the church
had been lost by coastal erosion over the years; it was
now very near the sea edge. They also saw the remains
of the large Roman fort, Regulbium, which had stood
on the cliff overlooking the sea. This once guarded the
entrance from the North Sea to the Wantsum channel,
which now was not more than a gently trickling stream.
It was once a navigable channel and made Thanet a
true island.

"This is a really historic site," Sarah said, looking up
with interest at the mighty twin towers. "I was top in
history at school. I really enjoyed the subject, so the
story of these ruins is very interesting to me. I always
wondered why Thanet was called an island, when it is
not obviously so. Now I know."

"Great stuff!" laughed Gary, as he helped Sarah up
the slope. "I surely didn't want to bore you with
historical details. I will point out the Wantsum channel
today, as we will cross it on our way back. It flows out
into the English Channel near Richborough, where
there was another Roman Fort.

They sat down on a rug that Gary had thoughtfully
brought with him. He had placed it on the top of the
grassy slope and there they relaxed, both grateful for a
rest after their exertions.

"Phew! I'm quite hot now," said Sarah, taking off
her pullover.

"Me too," replied Gary, removing his sports jacket.
"This sea breeze is lovely and cool. I hope your legs are
OK, Sarah. I didn't realise it was quite so far. We have
probably ridden about five or six miles."

"It was a lovely ride, Gary. I feel fine about riding my bike now. It was good to get on the main road, because that always worries me a bit. It was reassuring to have you riding beside me. Would you like a drink of lemonade?"

They sat sipping lemonade together and just looking out to sea. The sea was fairly calm, with just a few ripples created by the light breeze. There were no waves of which to speak. In the near distance a couple of sailing smacks pootled along, and the seagulls wheeled and screeched overhead in the sunshine. Gary pointed out that the fishermen were probably gutting their catch, as one of the boats had a large contingent of seagulls following it. A few people were walking around on the cliff top, and the beach itself was protected by barbed wire. A protecting sea fort that had been built off the coast of nearby Herne Bay could be seen from where they were sitting.

"Funny to think people are manning that fort and are living in the middle of the sea, isn't it? Must be a lonely old existence. Dangerous too, in this war." Gary pointed towards the fort.

Just then, a narrow pulling boat called a Thanet Wherry appeared, rowing along from Herne Bay to Margate. Gary had heard of these boats, which were about eighteen feet long, and he was able to tell Sarah that they were used mainly for fishing and were unique to the area. Sometimes they erected a sail, but today there was little breeze to power the boat. As an occasional flyer, Gary had to learn about local boats and shipping in order to identify them.

"Have a sandwich, Gary." Sarah offered him one from a paper packet. "Only spam, I'm afraid, but they also contain a bit of early lettuce from the convent's greenhouses, and I managed to pinch a bit of salad cream to liven them up."

They munched their sandwiches in the sun, which was really quite warm on their backs despite the sea breeze.

"Did you know that this is where Barnes-Wallis tested his bouncing bomb prototypes?" He asked Sarah.

She said she didn't know much about it, only what she had heard on the radio, and she had seen Guy Gibson briefly at the 'drome when he had visited recently.

"I must have missed him," said Gary. "Perhaps he came when I was away flying. I have heard that he drops in to Manston to see some of his old chums occasionally. It was totally amazing what they achieved with the unique bomb. Just shows we English have brilliant minds for invention, if you ask me. Apparently, a square mile just east of here was cordoned off and Guy and Bob Hay, who was the bombing leader of 617 squadron, chose Reculver Towers as a release point and as a valuable navigation aid for the final approach in the Lancaster before releasing the bomb. After the testing, Barnes-Wallis picked up fragments of the bomb by boat and brought them back to Manston, where engineers – Reg was one of them – worked in a guarded hangar to strengthen the outside casing of the bomb. Various trials took place until Guy flew out of Manston with a five-pound bomb and it bounced over the heads of watchers, can you imagine that? It came to rest here at the old Roman remains! I heard that the whole thing was named Operation Chastise. Rather apt, don't you think?"

"Goodness me!" exclaimed Sarah. "Just think it was all tested in the sea just in front of us. How fascinating!"

"Well, as you probably know the exercise was a complete success. It resulted in the destruction of two large dams in the Ruhr area, and Guy was awarded the VC, the DSO and bar, as he was the first Commanding Officer of RAF 617 Squadron. He always receives a huge welcome when he comes back to the 'drome. Those dam busting men are just so brave. Guy is young, only twenty-four. Do you know he has completed over 170 bombing operations? I am an oldie to be flying, really, that is why I am not sent on many important missions. At thirty-five one is over the hill, according to the RAF."

They walked a little way along the sea wall above the beach, which was a no-go area.

"The cliffs here are no longer chalky. Look towards Herne Bay," Gary pointed out. "They are now brown. They actually look like sandstone to me. Of course, in Cornwall all the cliffs are craggy granite. You would love Cornwall, Sarah. Have you ever visited the West Country?"

"Oh yes," said Sarah. "Not Cornwall, exactly, but I have spent a lot of time in Plymouth with my maiden aunts, Ella and Ada. My mother was born in Stoke, Devonport. Although, the cliffs there are not made of granite. I have only been on the Hoe, where it is all grass; and of course the huge naval dockyard is there, so one cannot see many cliffs."

"So, you are a West County lass on one side of your family. What about your father?"

"Daddy, who is called Joseph, is from Glasgow, and is a true Scotsman."

"Well, you are Celtic, even though you may have been born and raised in South London – you have Celtic blood in you as I have. I was born in Wales." Gary stood up. "Brrr! It is getting a little chilly. I think we should head back."

They packed up their things, picked up their bikes and rode back to Birchington. As they neared the village Gary hailed Sarah, and they stopped just before they reached the roundabout.

"Would you like to have supper here?"

"That would be a grand idea," replied Sarah. "I'm getting hungry and don't really fancy supper at the convent."

They went to a restaurant just over the road from All Saints Church, known as Rushes. It was run by Mr. and Mrs. Rush, which had a good reputation for serving tasty food.

Gary ordered bacon and eggs and Sarah ordered some local haddock.

"At least some local fish is still being caught," she said to the waitress, and they ordered a pot of tea for two.

"Yes, a few boats manage to set sail, mostly inshore out of Margate rather than Ramsgate. No fishing goes on over there; it would be too dangerous in the English Channel."

Their food was brought and they ate contentedly.

"This fish is scrumptious. How are your bacon and eggs?"

"Top hole," said Gary. "My, how I have missed a decent piece of crisp bacon. I've got fried bread and tomatoes, too! This is really delicious. So Sarah, tell me, have you anyone special in your life at the moment?"

"Yes, I have," said Sarah. "His name is Henry and he is an older man, like you, in fact he is the same age as you."

"You mean over the hill?" Gary teased.

"Henry is not old, just mature. He is a lovely chap, a very good dancer, and I have been walking out with him for quite a while now. He is known as 'Trel' as his surname is Treleaven, and that is his nick-name at the Bank where we both worked."

"Are you madly in love with him? Are you intending to marry him?" Gary felt that he really wanted to know the answer.

"I wouldn't say madly in love. He is very kind to me. I know he wants to marry me, but I am not really ready to settle down yet. I am very fond of him, but I love my home life with my dear parents and brother, and I don't want to leave them until I am a bit older. Although of course the war has split us all up. George, my brother, is off serving with the West Kent regiment. We are very close as brother and sister, although he is older than me by eight years."

They chatted on as they ate their meal.

"Tell me about your wife, Gary. You have not really spoken about her yet. Would she mind if she knew we were having supper? I hope not!"

"I doubt if Helen would mind. She doesn't seem at all interested in anything I do, except when I am around to look after the children." Gary looked down at the table, and Sarah could see that a faint pall of misery was etched on his crinkled brow.

"I'm sorry to hear that, Gary," said Sarah compassionately. "I'm sure she must miss you, and be worried about you."

"She is too busy with her books and studying to miss me, and the children just seem to get in her way and prevent her from getting on with her first love, of academia. She was fine when we first got married, because she didn't work and had more time for studying. She always wanted to go to university, and I'm sure her ambition would be to become a doctor or professor, not the wife of a fairly non-academic man of average intelligence, and the mother of two children."

"At first she was good fun to be with, but she changed when the children came along. It is a miracle that Polly was born, because she hated dealing with Jared so much. He was a nuisance to her and took her away from her studies. In fact, I do know she did all she could not to have a second child, but luckily Polly came along anyway. All her resentment at being what she called 'trapped' was turned on me, and I ended up doing what I could for the babies. When they were little, they were with me all the time. They were both bottle fed; this upset me, as I believe breast milk is better for babies, but it meant that I was the one to change and feed them. She refused to breast feed them at all. It was as if as soon as they were born they were my sole responsibility."

"Of course, the war was no-one's fault – well, blame Hitler – but what I mean is that I had no choice but to join up and go away from her, and she even resented that fact. So, returning home is not really happy for me, although I adore my kids."

"I am sorry to hear of this, maybe things will get better as the children grow up and become independent, and she can carry on with studying or go to college, or something." Sarah was a bit at a loss as to how she could comfort Gary with helpful suggestions. She was saddened to think his home life was not happy.

"My parents are very supportive," said Gary, smiling wryly. "They live in Wales but keep in touch by letter and the odd phone call. They know I am not happy and they try to cheer me up. My mother especially cannot understand Helen's attitude to her own children. She was such a good hands-on Mum – well, just look how I turned out!" He smiled for a moment.

"The happiest time we have spent is when I used to take the children to Granny and Grandpa's lovely Welsh cottage in the summer holidays. We all had such fun together. My parents loved having them. Now that is all over for the moment, but hopefully we will continue after the war. Oh! This blessed war. It has caused so much misery to so many people."

Gary noticed that Sarah was looking really concerned and realised he may have upset her.

"Come on! I do not want you to be miserable as we have had a lovely afternoon, and now I will settle up and we must get you back to the convent."

Gary got up and went to pay the bill. Sarah felt very special to have been privy to his unhappiness, and during the ride back along the Canterbury road to Westgate, and she tried her best to lighten the mood and to make him laugh.

"Thank you for a lovely afternoon, Gary," she said, as they reached the convent gates.

"Take care and sleep well, young Sarah, and I hope you now feel more confident about riding your bike," he said, waving as he rode away.

Sarah walked up the convent drive pushing her bike, her mind going round and round thinking about what Gary had said. That poor chap, she thought. No-one would know of his unhappiness; he is such a cheerful fellow at work. I won't say anything to anyone else about his marital misery at the moment, they do not need to know. He had given her a lot to think about.

She put her bike away and went into the convent.

CHAPTER TWENTY-EIGHT

"So soon my cares will vanish"

The next day at the 'drome, as the girls were working, the tannoy blurted out a warning and the next minute there was a tremendously loud rumbling noise, followed by a thundering crash that sounded really near to them.

All jumped up from their desks.

"Oh my giddy aunt, what on earth was THAT?" Eleanor gasped. When all was quiet they trooped out to have a look at what had caused the noise.

They were amazed to see that an American fighter plane, a P-47 Thunderbolt known colloquially as "the Jug", had crashed into a nearby RAF building. It had been badly shot up by German guns. The word "Smoocher" had been painted on the side, but was now almost obliterated.

The pilot had been aiming for the emergency runway but had over-shot, ploughing into the building, which looked like it had acted as a brake and was now partially demolished. The Jug, which served with 487 Squadron, had sustained a tremendous battering, it was literally a sieve, with gaping holes and jagged tears through the fuselage, wings and tail. The pilot was alive but injured, and was standing propped up nearby surveying his battered plane. Luckily it did not burst into flames. The airman said ruefully: "Well, she will never fly again," and when Reg and his crew arrived he told them before he passed out that one shell had actually exploded in the cockpit. Reg said that it was a miracle that he was still alive. A camp ambulance, or blood wagon as it was known, arrived, and medical staff took the pilot away on a stretcher for emergency treatment.

Reg and his crew towed the Jug off the collapsed building to see what parts of her could be salvaged.

The girls went back to the hut, all feeling very shocked.

"Gosh! Another few yards and we could very well have been under that plane," Rhona said with a shiver, and she shook her head ruefully. "It doesn't bear thinking about, and sometimes it is very hard to just stay sane with this madness going on around us. It was amazing to see the pilot still alive. He was extremely lucky."

The girls filed into the hut. They were still visibly shaken and they took a while to settle down to their work. Sarah gratefully typed out her own leave chit for a weekend '48' that was coming up.

Gary had not been in the office for a few days since they had their outing. He had been detailed to another part of the 'drome. She didn't know what he was doing and missed his ever-present cheerfulness, which helped the day along. After what he had confided to her about his home life she was amazed that he was able to be so happy-go-lucky. I suppose he just shuts it all out of his mind, Sarah thought.

The girls cycled back to the convent and Rhona suggested that they all go to the flicks that night. So after supper they walked to nearby Westgate, where the cinema, The Carlton, had recently been converted out of the old Council buildings. It was doing well, replacing the main Margate Cinema which now was just a bomb site. The seats were blue plush and there was popcorn on sale. They watched Ingrid Bergman,

Charles Boyer and Joseph Cotton in "Gaslight". It was a gripping thriller and the girls enjoyed it very much.

On the way back to the convent they chatted. "Ingrid Bergman is so beautiful, isn't she? I think she is my favourite actress."

"Oh yes, mine too," Sarah joined in enthusiastically. "I have a scrap book at home with lots of photos of her. She is absolutely stunning when she smiles, and she plays her parts so well portraying the character of Paula with such panache."

"I think Joseph Cotton is just dreamy." Jill twirled around, clasping her hands in front of her and looking heavenwards. "He gets my vote, as I simply adore his shiny curly hair. I would love to run my fingers through it."

"Och away! Your hands would probably come out all covered in grease. Yuk!" said a new WAAF called Marge. She had lately joined the girls at the convent. Sarah loved her Glaswegian accent, so like her dear Father's brogue, and her amazing sense of humour. She always made the girls feel better with her funny stories, and mostly had them in stitches recounting her many escapades with the opposite sex.

The days passed and still Sarah had not seen Gary, so she prepared her kit bag for her leave and Friday evening saw her waiting for the London train at Westgate station. The train sped swiftly over the Kent countryside, passing the grassy levels on which lambs gambolled in the sun. The fields and woods were now enfolded with the bright green mantle of spring. The yellow hazel catkins swung their copious pollen into the air and white rabbit-tails or scuds of pussy willow had given way to chestnut sticky buds as the new leaves unfurled. Bluebells carpeted the woods creating an indigo haze under the trees, sharing the space with white wood anemones and yellow aconites. The birds were busy singing their hearts out, guarding their nesting sites. Nature carried on as usual, despite man's war madness.

Sarah changed trains at Bromley South and caught a local steam train. The platforms were thronging with service men and women; there were hardly any civilians to be seen. Everywhere seemed so dreary and grey after the beauty of the countryside.

Dear old faithful Trel was there at Penge East station to meet her with his car. He was so pleased to see her, held her tight and kissed her again and again.

"It is so lovely to see you, darling. Are you well? Is your wrist playing up or has it mended?"

Sarah said she was fine and, snuggling into his shoulder, she told him that he smelled lovely as usual. It was nice to be back in his arms again. She had missed hugs and kisses, and they stood there for a minute or two just outside the station with their arms round each other.

Trel took her home, where Hilda had prepared a lovely supper for her.

"Come away in, Trel," said Joe, after he had greeted his daughter. "There is supper for you, too."

"That is very kind of you, sir," said Trel.

Sarah went up to wash, took her cap off and undid her tie. She put on her cardigan and began to relax. She greeted her mother with a kiss and hug.

"How are you, Mummy darling? I do hope you have not gone to too much trouble for me?"

"And why wouldn't I go to any trouble for my darling daughter?" Hilda beamed across the table.

They sat down to a bountiful supper.

Sarah regaled them with stories of her time at Manston. Some were funny, some not so, but she glossed over the danger she might be in from crashing planes, as had happened just the last week. She didn't want to upset her parents, or Trel for that matter. Instead, she told them of the new Glaswegian girl Marge and how she made them all laugh, and of her friend Jill who had recently become engaged to be married to an airman at the camp.

After supper Trel had to go, so he said his thanks and goodnight to Joe and Hilda and Sarah walked to the front door with him. The chiming clock in the hall pronounced that it was 10.45. She was very tired and kissed Trel quickly.

"What would you like to do tomorrow, Sarah? Would you like to go to the flicks? There is a very good Bette Davis film on at The Rink cinema."

"That would be grand Trel, thank you. See you tomorrow evening at about 6.00, then."

Sarah shut the door and ran upstairs to the comfort of her old bedroom. She threw herself on her little bed, felt its softness take her weight as she sank into her paisley eiderdown, and felt really glad to be home again.

CHAPTER TWENTY-NINE

"I will keep this close to my heart"

Trel took Sarah to the flicks the next evening. They watched '*Now Voyager*', a film that Sarah absolutely loved.

It featured Bette Davis at her best playing, a young lady who falls for a married man with a child, and she kept remembering the quote " *We have the stars, don't let us ask for the moon*", relating to their affair.

Sarah thought it was such a romantic, passionate film. She couldn't help herself from thinking about Gary at that moment. She blew her nose as the tears had come unasked, tumbling down her cheeks. She pushed these thoughts out of her mind and turned to Trel, sitting beside her and held his hand.

They went for supper afterwards at nearby Cobb's restaurant. Trel was so glad to be with Sarah. He knew she had twined herself around his heart, and this enforced parting made every moment with her doubly precious.

Over their supper Sarah chatted incessantly about her life at Manston and Trel noticed she was mentioning her boss, whom she referred to as "Flight", quite frequently. She recounted their cycle ride to Reculver, saying how very kind he was to escort her on her first bike ride after the fall, and his solicitousness to her.

Just as they left Cobbs and were walking home, an air raid siren began its mournful wailing. They broke into a run and made for the Twentyman's cellar. Hilda and Joe were already down there with Jessie and Mary,

Mr. and Mrs. Eacott from number 18 and the Pendreds. They were playing cards.

"Come on in, you two," said Hilda. "Will your mother and aunt be OK, Trel?"

Henry helped Sarah to a seat and they greeted the other occupants politely and enquired after their health.

"They are in Cornwall at the moment, thank you, Mrs. Langman, staying with friends. Auntie wasn't very well and so Mother thought it best to take her down to Truro. They still have raids down there but not so many as London, and Mother thought that getting away from this nightmare may make her recovery quicker".

"Very sensible," said Hilda. "I worry so much about my sisters in Plymouth. There have been some terrible raids on the city, and they live fairly near the docks which also received a tremendous bashing recently."

"Oh drat it! What a bind! I've laddered my last reasonable pair of stockings, caught on a splinter," Sarah interjected. "I do like to wear a decent thin denier when I go out, and not those thick service issue passion killers. Now I shall have to save up my clothing rations for another pair."

"I think there may be another pair of yours in the airing cupboard, darling," said Hilda, as Joe dealt another hand of rummy. The staccato of ack-ack was heard in the far distance.

Trel was pleased to be spending a bit more time with Sarah; although down in a cellar full of people was not his ideal venue, as he had hoped to walk Sarah slowly home after their supper. He felt that he wanted to talk to her seriously about their future, but Sarah neatly avoided any serious talk, and he was afraid that she was getting too fond of this "Flight," as she called her boss. She seemed to talk about no-one else, and although she had told Trel that he was married, with children, he felt very jealous of her enthusiasm when talking about what they did together. I'm not sure about her feelings for this chap, he thought. I certainly don't want to share Sarah with anyone else; but maybe they are just friends, and I am getting upset over nothing. If I press her too hard about him, she may get cross with me. Perhaps I will just let things lie for a bit, and wait until her next leave to say anything.

The All Clear siren sounded. There had been a few loud local explosions, but they wouldn't really see the damage until the morning. All hoped that their homes were left intact. Sarah and her parents thanked the Twentymans, and wished them a good night. They walked up the hill to their home. Trel went with them a little way, holding Sarah's hand. Fires were burning in the distance but their road seemed to be, thankfully, untouched.

"Good job I'm not on fire watch duty tonight," said Trel, much relieved.

Sarah was her usual jolly self in those last moments they shared together. She cheerfully kissed him, thanked him for a lovely evening and said she hoped to see him on her next leave.

"That won't be for five weeks, I'm afraid. That is when my next ten days is due. I hope you won't be lonely, Trel. Perhaps you should ask out one of the other girls in the office, just to keep you company."

"I don't really want to walk out with anyone else but you," said Trel, a little sadly. "Besides, all the females left in the office are at least sixty, as all the younger ladies have been called up. I keep busy with my fire-watching – and, of course, there is always Herbert with whom to have an occasional drink and game of billiards. He is still working in the city while Violet is tucked away in the country, so he is quite lonely too. It is such a pity we can no longer have a round of golf or two. I so enjoyed playing with him at Beckenham Place Park, and the odd round would be so relaxing, especially now the days are warmer and there are much longer and lighter evenings. Sadly, that is not to be; the golf club is closed for the duration."

Trel stopped and held Sarah's shoulders for a minute, turning her to face him.

"Look here, darling Toodles. You happily spoke at supper of your friend in the WAAF who has just got engaged, so why can't we? I know it seems more urgent in the Air Force, with men and women being killed all the time, but we in Civvy Street are also in danger, and it would make me very happy if at least I may ask your father for your hand in marriage, and put a beautiful engagement ring on your finger."

Sarah's face fell. She really wasn't expecting Trel to talk about marriage. He was looking at her so earnestly, and she felt very uncomfortable and didn't want to hurt his feelings, so she said gently "Oh Trel dear, I really cannot think about getting engaged or married at this point in my life. Everything is so topsy-turvy at the moment! How on earth can I possibly think how I may feel when I have finished my tour of duty? At any rate, I have had to sign up for at least four years, so it would be a very long time before we could have any sort of married life. It is different in the RAF; personnel can marry and live in married quarters together and still be in service to their country." Her face creased into lines of anxiety.

"Besides, as you know, I don't feel ready to settle down yet, even though I am very fond of you, so please don't be upset. We just have to wait, and I know you have already been very patient with me. It is such a pity that you are not the same age as me, because you wouldn't be wanting to settle down yet either! Just be assured for now that I will want to get married at some point in my life because I really want to have children. Now be a dear and kiss me goodnight! We have had such a lovely evening, and I thank you for that."

Sadly he left her with a kiss on the forehead and a quick bear hug. Heaving a long, drawn out sigh he walked down the road to his mother's house. He was keeping an eye on it while she was away in Cornwall. I shall just have to be patient, he thought, but it will be very hard to keep a cap on my loneliness and longing for Sarah to be my wife.

He regretted once more that he was not on active service in one of the forces. At least then his time would be fully occupied while Sarah was away. He just missed her so much, especially as he now wouldn't see her for at least five weeks. Trel suddenly decided that he would take some of his holiday leave and travel down to Cornwall to be with his mother and aunt, and to visit some old friends of his in Truro.

"Well," he thought. "It is a great pity, but I shan't be needing my holiday allocation for a honeymoon in the near future, that is for sure."

CHAPTER THIRTY
"Armours me with such true protection"

It was a bright sunny day. The birds were very busy feeding their young, and were singing their hearts out warning others away from their nesting sites. The sky was blue, and spirits rose with the return of the warm weather.

At the 'drome someone had thoughtfully filled a couple of large old tins from the Naafi club with soil and had planted spring bulbs in them. Presently cheerful yellow daffodils were nodding their heads in the breeze; they followed some small dark blue irises, which had just finished blooming. There they sat, either side of the hut door, gladdening the hearts of all who entered.

Sarah returned to the Admin hut. For the past few days she had been detailed to help out in the Post Office kiosk, to fill in for a sick WAAF. She quite enjoyed sorting stamps and serving personnel: the joshing interaction with airmen really made her day. They always had a friendly way of flirting as she dealt with their postal needs. Her cheerful outward-going nature, often whistling or singing while she worked, made her popular, and she was a natural at sorting out parcels and weighing letters, which was always a tedious job. She had great fun with the American airmen stationed at Manston as they sent various packages back home. Sarah just thrived on their friendly banter.

However, now she was back at her desk getting stuck into typing warrants for the sick bay. She looked up and was pleased to see Gary come in and sit in his usual place. He smiled at her and then rose to speak generally to the girls, explaining that while he had been away from Admin he had been testing a new Spitfire Mark X1V which he reckoned was the tops. He explained to the rather bemused but interested girls that this new kite had a 2,050 horse power 2-stage griffon engine, and that it could reach nearly 450 mph with an improved ratio of climb, and it was excellent for intercepting flying bombs. He had also been allowed to once fly anti-flak to draw enemy planes away from German bombers. This was only because they had lost a lot of young pilots lately, and he was called on as a reserve. He said he knew it was very dangerous but he just loved to fly; however, with a grin he said he was glad to be back amongst his 'girls'.

The WAAFs said they had missed him and his silly jokes, and all felt glad that he was back safely on the ground.

Sarah had been detailed 'duty stooge' that evening, which meant she had to stay late and finish up after the others left. She was a bit fed up as her friends had arranged to attend a play entitled '*While the Sun Shines*', which was being put on by a London company who had come down to Manston from the Globe Theatre, and she had been looking forward to their performance.

The day dragged on, only livened up by shrieks from some of the girls as Sarah tripped up and sent the in-tray flying. To the horror of all, this disturbed a plague of earwigs which had been hiding underneath the papers, and the insects were sent flying in all directions.

"Oh drat it, I am so clumsy!" laughed Sarah, as she brushed herself down and removed the odd earwig or two from her skirt. Lots of giggles ensued, and screams of "Yuk! Get those horrid things away from me!" came from Eleanor, Marge and Jill. Sarah, being very practical, fetched a dust-pan and brush. She swept all the rogue insects into it and threw them with great aplomb out of the nearest window.

"The warmer weather must have brought them all out," observed Gary, wryly. "We have had them in the huts before. Thanks for doing that so capably, Sarah."

"That is OK – after all, it was my fault. My father is continually warning me, ' *You've got to watch!* as at home I tend to drop tea cups, or spill milk on laden tea trays. I am just accident prone, and have to live with that fact. Look how I fell off my bike, for instance!"

She threw her hands out in a gesture of resignation at her hopelessness.

"Never mind dear, we all love you just the same," said Jill, kindly. Calm ensued as all settled down to their work once again.

The day wore on. Sarah was beginning to feel tired – there was so much work to do – but she made a coffee for herself and Gary and they carried on. Soon it was time for the others to go to the Mess for their evening meal before the performance of the play.

"Be a dear and bring me back some sandwiches before you go to the play, would you Ellie? I shall be here for at least another hour or two. I have simply loads of flying programmes to type."

"OK, ducks," said Ellie. "Spam and tomato do you? Don't work too hard!"

They left the hut giggling and chattering. Gary came over to Sarah; he said he had lot of catching up to complete too, and would keep her company. Sarah was very pleased that he would be staying behind with her, and she found that her work took no time at all. Ellie dropped her off a pack of sandwiches, and one for

Gary. They both ate at their desks, Sarah brushing the odd earwig off her desk, away from her food. They worked in companionable silence.

When it was finally time to go, Gary came over sat on the edge of her desk and said. "I'm sorry you missed the play, but I'm glad to have this opportunity now we are alone to ask if you would fancy another bike ride? I thought we could ride down to the lovely village of Wingham and have some tea this coming weekend. What do you say to that?"

"That would be great fun, thanks Gary. I could do with more bike riding practice. Is Wingham very far?"

"Well, it is a bit farther than Reculver, but we could take it easy and the country roads are fairly quiet, as no big army lorries will be passing us that way. I'm just about finished now, so would you like me to walk you back to the convent as it is such a lovely evening?"

"Yes, that would be great. I'll just put my work away."

Gary locked the hut and they walked across the fields, now covered in lush spring grass, and saw the green shoots of winter sown wheat waving in the wind. There was a farmer still working his horses: they were pulling a drill attached to a hopper feeding barley seed into the newly raked furrows. Sarah and Gary paused a while to watch the mighty Clydesdales straining into their harness as their driver clucked and called out to them by name, encouraging them with every step. They made a splendid sight against the pink, yellow and blue sky created by the dying sun.

The two sauntered on, chattering about this and that. Mainly Gary talked of his recent flying experience, and Sarah was happy to listen and interject now and again to ask questions. She was really interested in what

the pilots got up to on sorties. Gary said he may even
be able to take her up for a short flight some time,
perhaps when he was detailed to carry out a flight of
one of the planes newly rehashed by Reg and his
engineers. He thought he may be able to clear things
with his Adjutant, but he would have to wait for his
decision on the matter.

"It may well be that they think it would be too
dangerous," he said, ruefully. "Although Reg and his
crew are superb engineers. Pity we can't go down to
Land's End Airport. I could take you up for a flight,
then!"

They strolled on happily together. Gary lit a
cigarette and offered one to Sarah.

"I don't really smoke, but I could try one."

Sarah took a lighted cigarette from Gary and
tentatively puffed at it. She immediately broke into
paroxysms of coughing. Gary patted her on the back,
laughing as he did so.

"I think you need a little practice at smoking," he
chuckled. "It is really relaxing when you inhale the
smoke. It will come in time. Here, have a peppermint –
that will help with your cough."

Sarah wiped her streaming eyes and gratefully
sucked on the peppermint.

"Smoking always looks so sophisticated," she
remarked. "My father smokes a pipe and my mother
smokes, well, I would say puffs, at a cigarette as she says
'just to be sociable'. She does not inhale, as she has
bouts of bronchitis which I have inherited, so perhaps I
shouldn't smoke at all."

"Oh, everyone smokes these days. It won't hurt
you."

Just then, seemingly out of nowhere, a Messerschmitt was seen by Gary coming in low and fast towards them.

"I don't like the look of him, Sarah. GO! Quickly run as fast as you can for those trees!"

They both began running towards the edge of the lane where there was a copse. The German plane screamed nearer and began to open fire on them. Gary threw himself forward in a rugby tackle and pulled Sarah down on the ground, under the trees. He shielded her with his body. The plane swooped low but had to bank steeply to avoid the towering elms in the copse.

Within minutes two Merlins came screaming over from Manston. They were on the German's tail and chased the alien kite out over the North Sea. He wheeled round, and a thunderous crash was heard coming from the direction of Birchington.

Gary rolled off Sarah's back, propped himself up and helped her, as she had been lying face down. As she sat up she burst into tears and was shaking like a leaf. Gary put his arms around her and held her tightly against his chest, where she sobbed and sobbed.

"You are OK now, little one." Gary rocked her in his arms for a few moments, then drawing her away gently he gave her a clean hankie to wipe her eyes and blow her nose. He then took the hankie and carefully wiped away the mud sticking to Sarah's cheeks.

"We are quite safe now. That damned German has gone, chased by a couple of our planes. It sounded as if they caught him, as a plane crashed, I'm sure of it. Now then, try to stop crying – it is all over."

Gary smoothed Sarah's hair back from her face, noting how very pale she looked. He retrieved her cap from the ground and placed it on her head. He helped her up and carried on holding her hand as they walked a little unsteadily away from the copse that had saved them, and down the lane which led to the convent.

Sarah was so shaken up inside she couldn't think straight. All that she knew was that Gary's arms around her had felt so strong and comforting in her moment of abject terror, and that his hand in hers as they walked along seemed so natural and right.

He escorted her in to the nuns who, once they had learned what had happened, took her in and made her a cup of hot sweet tea. They also offered Gary a tot of brandy as he was as white as a sheet, and they made them both sit down in a quiet room overlooking the garden.

"We live in such a mad world, don't we Gary?" Sarah said at last, revived by her strong tea.

"We certainly do, but it cannot last for ever. This war will end and peace will come eventually, I'm sure of it," Gary remarked reassuringly. "For the present, I really must be off. Now, I hope you are feeling a little better. Don't forget our bike ride this Saturday afternoon, will you?"

"No I won't forget, and yes thank you, I do feel a lot steadier. How on earth can we think of going on a bike ride with maniacs like that German pilot out there?" asked Sarah, her green eyes looking anxiously up at Gary.

She is so young and vulnerable, he thought, and he felt very protective towards her.

"What happened today was a one-off, remember, we cannot live our lives in fear. We have to grasp our happiness every day. On Saturday I will meet you at the

end of the convent drive at fourteen hundred hours –
mind you don't be late!"

Sarah watched Gary drink his brandy and thought,
he shielded me today with his body, and he could have
been killed. That was so brave of him. She didn't want
him to leave.

"Thank you for looking after me yet again, Gary. I
think you may have saved my life."

"Nonsense! It was the copse of trees that saved us. If
they hadn't been there, well, we may have been shot to
smithereens. Now you get a good night's rest, and try to
forget what happened. I'll say goodnight for now. By
the way, I meant to ask you if you would like to go and
see "Now Voyager" with Bette Davies one evening next
week? It is meant to be a corker of a film."

Sarah said she would love to go. She didn't mention
she had already seen it, as she thought it would be good
to watch it again with Gary. She watched him walk away
down the convent steps and stride down the drive, and
sat alone with her thoughts for a while.

CHAPTER THIRTY-ONE

"If you count happiness by a smile or a kiss"

Sarah was surprised that she slept very well. She had been tired from the extra work, but after their encounter with the German plane, she thought she would never sleep again. She thought that maybe the nuns had slipped a mild sedative in her tea, to help her with the shock, and that was probably why she went out like a light. How kind and thoughtful of them to do that. She asked the nuns when she came down that morning, and Sister Benedict affirmed that that was what they had decided to do.

"You looked so poorly," she said. "We felt that you needed to rest your mind and body and didn't think you would agree to take anything, so we took over and dosed you unknowingly for the effects of shock."

Sarah thanked the nuns and said it was the right thing to do. She told the girls what had happened. They were aghast, full of questions and very supportive. Most came over and gave her a kiss and hug as they drank their early morning cuppa.

"Fancy, if you had come to the play this would not have happened to you!" Rhona observed, putting her arm round Sarah. "It was very good, by the way, but never mind that! Luckily you had Gary with you, he was very brave."

"Sounds like something out of a film, the way he shielded you from harm with his body." Marge stirred her tea. "Och away, it was very decent of the wee man, he could easily have been shot!"

Sarah thought about it all over her breakfast, and was glad that as it was the weekend she would see Gary that afternoon for their bike ride. I seem to be getting very fond of him, she thought. I really cannot help it. He is always putting himself out for me, and taking care of me, but it is not just that. I feel really drawn to him as a person. She decided that she wanted to make him as happy as he made her feel, and perhaps she could lighten his load by being a good friend to him.

It was a lovely, sunny day with just a few odd clouds floating in a clear blue sky. After they had all finished lunch, as she had heard that the forecast was for rain later she prudently checked that her mac was still in her saddle bag and then walked her bike down the convent lane to meet Gary.

They set off down the Canterbury road to Sarre, cycling slowly, taking in the very pretty little village of Preston with its mellow old church and continuing to Wingham. It was quite a long ride, and they mainly had to go in single file and so couldn't chat. Sarah was glad of that, so she could concentrate fully on not falling off. They rode over the bridge spanning the Nailbourne River, and paused to look down into its dark depths, watching for a while the long fronds of river weed snaking back and forth like tresses of hair. They even spied a few small fishes, hiding in the shallows and swimming in the dappled sunlight.

When they finally arrived at Wingham, they parked their bikes by the side of the grassy verge, locked them together and walked through the village looking at the many white and black timber-framed buildings bending into the path.

Wingham was a very unspoilt typical Kentish village. Sarah and Gary strolled along, looking at two of the ancient inns which dated back to the 13th century. 'The Dog Inn' was once part of a monastery, they read on a plaque. Further on they passed the 'Eight Bells', and at the end of the village turned the corner to see the lovely St. Mary's church built of local flint and possessing inside rare wooden pillars unusually made of chestnut. It also dated back to the 13th century and had been visited by Queen Elizabeth the First. They stopped to read all about the church on a notice board outside.

It was very pleasant to saunter in the sun among the beautiful higgledy-piggledy old buildings. There were antique shops with interesting and enticing things displayed in their windows, and a couple of book shops in which they had a quick browse. Soon they spied a nice looking tea shop and they finally stopped for a rest.

"Would you like to sit outside in the sun?" Gary asked Sarah. She said she would, as one never knew when the rain that was forecast would come. He ordered tea for two and they sat together, enjoying the warmth at a little table covered in a blue polka-dot cloth.

They chatted, but both avoided discussing their ordeal the previous day, with the exception that Gary said he had found out that the Messerschmitt had been shot down. It had crashed into Shuart Farm land, at Minnis Bay. The pilot had ejected and was now in custody. Gary reassured Sarah that their encounter with a German kite would not happen again in a hurry, as the fly-boys at Manston were now on high alert and would intercept any incomers before they did any damage.

Gary realised that Sarah needed taking out of herself and decided to suggest a treat for them. "If we start back early enough, we could make that film tonight if you would like," Gary suggested, as they partook of some delicious little home-made honey cakes. "What a wizzo idea!" Sarah said, her face aglow at the thought of spending a little more time with Gary. Watching Sarah's happy face, Gary realised that his suggestion seemed to be just the ticket, and was glad he had thought of a visit to the flicks.

They walked back to their bikes after paying for their tea; again, Gary insisted on treating Sarah, even though she protested, so he relented and said she could buy them some popcorn or an ice that evening. She agreed with a laugh and said that she would buy him an extra-large double scoop of ice cream.

The sky had clouded over a bit while they had been eating and quite a wind had started to blow. The ride home was more difficult as it was mainly uphill. They stopped half way at Sarre because it had started to spit with rain, and they put on their macs. A soft slow mizzle began to blow in from the sea.

Gary eventually left Sarah at the convent. She was quite wet and was pleased to change her clothes. She freshened her face with a touch of powder and lipstick, thinking what a fright she must have looked in Wingham after the wind had played havoc with her hair, and it had given her very red cheeks.

Why should I care what he thinks of me? She wondered. I *do care*, however, and I am getting very fond of him. She had no thought of caution, she was young and her emotions were being stirred by this lanky curly-haired man with the wicked sense of humour and engaging smile. When he winks at me I go all weak at the knees, and I know, I just know, that I blush.

Gary called for her that evening and they walked to the Carlton Cinema at Westgate. The rain had blown away and the sun was out again, making the wet pavements glisten.

They had to queue outside the cinema with lots of other airmen and women. Sarah spied Jill and Jerry further on in the queue and waved at them, but hoped they wouldn't leave their place in the queue to join them. She wanted Gary to herself.

True to her word, she bought them both huge double-scoop ices in the interval before the main feature. In the first half they watched the supporting feature which just happened to be a Donald Duck cartoon, which made them both rock with laughter.

Sarah really enjoyed the Bette Davis film the second time. She knew what was coming, and as it was sad she found herself quietly dabbing away tears. She tried to hide it but Gary noticed and slipped his hand in hers. That felt so wonderful! The story involved a married man and a single girl, so it was very relevant to their new-found friendship. He let her hand go quickly as the house lights went up and all stood up for the National Anthem.

They walked back to the convent chatting about the acting and actors. It had begun to rain while they were in the cinema and Gary held an umbrella over them both, Sarah was delighted for the excuse to put her arm through his.

"Are you going to church in the morning, Sarah?" Gary asked. "Yes, I thought I would go with the girls. Sometimes Rhona comes with me, but some of them do not care for church."

"Would you care to accompany me to a local church I have found? It is tiny, and reminds me of a chapel back in Wales."

Sarah said that would be very nice, and he arranged to pick her up in a RAF car the next day. He said that his C.O. didn't mind him using it occasionally, as long it was only for local trips and he paid for petrol or used his own coupons.

They parted at the convent gates and, when he was saying goodnight at the convent, he took her hand in his and lifted it to his lips, brushing it quickly with a light kiss before he turned and walked away. Sarah walked slowly up the convent drive holding that hand to her cheek, and smiling.

CHAPTER THIRTY-TWO

"A year is like a chime in all eternity"

Gary picked up Sarah a little way from the convent
gates the next morning. They were both in uniform:
although Sarah would have loved to wear 'civvy'
clothes, uniform was more correct.

They motored to the little hamlet of Acol and pulled
up, parked next to a field and walked a few yards to the
tiny church dedicated to St. Mildred. It was set down
from the road, in a dell, and was prettily constructed of
flint with small lattice windows. One bell clanged away
in the bell tower on the roof calling the faithful to
worship. The gravel path leading to the door was
flanked with primroses and violets.

They entered, and heard the cabinet organ playing
softly. The sun streamed on to the wooden pews
through the south windows, making it very light inside.
The church was quite full, and Gary escorted Sarah
into a pew, having obtained prayer and hymn books
from the sidesman. They knelt together and bowed
their heads in prayer for a moment or two.

At the east end of the church was a neat white apse
in which the altar stood. To the left of the altar was a
colourful statue of Mary and the infant Jesus. The dark
beams of the roof showed up well against the white
painted ceiling and the stunning triple stained glass
windows of the apse threw coloured patterns on the
floor lit by the sun. The communion rails were of dark
wood, and green embroidered kneelers depicting white
crosses were placed along the rails. A large brass
chandelier with half-burnt candles hung over the altar
in the middle of the apse.

"What a pretty little church," Sarah whispered to Gary after their prayers. He nodded in assent, and soon they were standing for the first hymn, a favourite of Sarah's: 'Eternal Ruler of the ceaseless round', set to a beautiful tune Song 1 by Orlando Gibbons.

They sat side by side listening to the sermon, preached by a bald-headed kindly looking clergyman who looked over the top of his glasses at the congregation and stopped periodically to blow his nose with a loud trumpeting sound. They stood for the creed, and after prayers went up and knelt together to partake of Holy Communion.

Sarah felt the comforting warmth of Gary's leg beside her as they knelt in the pew after they took communion. She was so pleased to be in church with him, and prayed for him and his family as well her own parents, George, Monica, their girls and Trel.

After they sang the last gentle hymn, 'In heavenly love abiding', they said goodbye to the vicar, thanked him for his sermon and stepped out into the warm sunshine.

"Well, that was a very nice service. I just love that last hymn. It was one of my Grand-father's favourites, back in Wales," said Gary. "Not many people know of this little church. They mainly go to St. Catherine's Church in Manston, known locally as the RAF church; in fact, I saw you there once with the girls, didn't I? Of course, I remember, I gave you all a lift back to the convent. I found Acol Church one day when I was on a bike ride, and have been to a couple of services. I came to Evensong recently. Reg kindly came with me, and I thought you may like to worship here, too."

They sat in the sun for a moment on a bench outside the church, enjoying the spring flowers planted along the path.

"What are you planning for this afternoon? Would you fancy a walk along the cliff top just down from the convent?"

Sarah said she would love that, so they parted and went back to their respective billets to change and have some lunch, meeting again afterwards to walk down Domneva Road towards the sea.

It was a glorious afternoon with just a little breeze, and the sun which shone on their backs as they walked along had the comforting promise of summer.

Sarah had changed out of her uniform and wore a pretty lemon frock with a matching cardigan. Gary wore a blue short-sleeved sports shirt, open at the neck, and carried a light jacket. They chatted as they walked along, mainly about what had happened in the hut during the preceding week.

Sarah had recently been struggling with the Gestetner. It had been playing up, and she had ended up with very inky fingers. She showed Gary that the ink was indelible and still stained her hands despite much vigorous scrubbing on her part. Gary said that the Gestetner was due for replacement: it was causing too much trouble and he had put in a requisition for a new one. However, with the war on, the new stencil machine would probably be a long time coming.

As they reached the sea front they noticed that lots of Air Force personnel had the same idea and were happily strolling along the undercliff promenade. Some were hand in hand and a few were sitting in little niches in the chalk cliffs, enjoying a smooch or two. They recognised one or two of the couples, and Gary said he could see Reg and Connie sitting together enjoying the sun.

Sarah and Gary decided to walk along the top of the cliff on the grass, away from the others. The sea was sparkling, there were no clouds in the clear blue sky and gulls wheeled about them shrieking their raucous cry. Gary said that was because there would be nests just under the grassy top of the cliff and the gulls were only protecting their young. Warships were seen miles away on the horizon making their slow way up to the Thames from the North Sea.

Suddenly, and most unexpectedly, a Spitfire appeared over the sea flying along the coastline from Margate, hugging the contours of the cliff. The plane passed them flying quite low. Gary said he could see the pilot, who happened to be a chap he knew, in the cockpit as he flew so close, and he waved.

Sarah jumped at the sight of the plane but was relieved to see it was a friendly kite from Manston.

"He is just carrying out a test run," he explained to Sarah. "I would normally be doing this sort of flying. Possibly Reg had just patched up this kite and the test pilot, Bill, was just seeing if she was worthy to be back in action."

The Spitfire flew out to sea. They watched it from the cliff, and then suddenly it wheeled round and came back close to where they were standing. The pilot waved and made the wings of his plane dip both sides alternately, rocking in salute as he roared back towards Margate. Everyone laughed and cheered.

"The cheeky devil! By Jove! I reckon old Bill was virtually wolf-whistling at all the canoodling that was going on!" laughed Gary. "I'll catch up with him later."

They carried on with their pleasant walk, stopping for a while to sit on the grass overlooking West Bay.

"How can there be such evil as Hitler in the world when we have been given such a beautiful place in which to live?" Sarah looked thoughtful. "I just don't understand why people want to rule others, to dictate, mould, and to discriminate between one race and another. We are all human and have been given the fantastic chance to appreciate the beauty of our surroundings and to live in love and peace. Why, oh, why some people have to cause so much devastation, the deaths of many people, and heartache, I shall never know. Why can't they be glad for what they have?"

"It does seem like madness," said Gary, sadly. "All you need is a sunny day, love, good food and happy folk, and in that you find true contentment. People always want more than their allotted share in life; always more money, always more praise or fame, or as in Hitler's dream, a master race of blond Aryan people to rule the world. Thinking about that – he has dark hair anyway!!!! I wonder if he has Jewish blood in his ancestry – now there's a thought!" Gary winked at Sarah.

Sarah laughed. "Go on with you, that is quite a novel theory! Changing the subject, have you heard from home lately?"

"Yes, I had a letter the other day. Jared has had the measles, so Helen has had to nurse him and that has made her even crankier towards me. Her letter tore me off a strip for not being there to help. I have written to my son, sending a few comics and my love. I hope Polly doesn't get it too – that will just about finish Helen, to have two sick children taking her away from her beloved books! Perhaps it is a good job that I am here and well away from her wrath at the moment. Have you heard from your Trel?"

"Oh, yes, he writes almost every day. He is so lonely, poor chap. He got so fed up that he went down to Cornwall to be with his mother and aunt for a couple of weeks, but he is back now and they stayed on in Truro, so he is alone. I do feel sorry for him. He misses me so much."

"Well, I would miss you, too. I couldn't be without your lovely smile to cheer me for very long, and I must say I feel sorry for the poor chap. It is quite ironic that he comes from Cornwall, isn't it?"

They sat pleasantly in the sun for a while, watching the tide coming in.

"It is such a shame not to see happy families picnicking on the beach, people swimming and children building sandcastles. Oh, I do wish we could all get back to normal. Sometimes it feels like this war will never be over," sighed Sarah.

"Well, you know, Manston is getting all geared up for a special event. You must have seen the signals coming in through Admin. It is top secret, so I won't speak much about it, but soon you will be aware at work that something big is about to happen, this could well tip the balance in our favour and may go a long way towards finishing this bloody conflict. In fact Helen wrote to me about President Eisenhower staying at Tullimeaar House at Perranarworthal near Falmouth. He met Winston Churchill there, she had heard, and this meeting is all to do with the event coming up soon. She just listened to local gossip – which really shouldn't have happened – but she knew that I probably was wise to it all anyway, and she was correct. At least we are well supported in this op. by the Americans, our friends, and allies.

Now, to change the subject, I think it is nearly time for me to go back to my billet. I have a game of snooker booked with Reg and the boys tonight."

They stood up, Sarah brushed the grass from her skirt and they strolled back to the convent, where Gary left her with a cheery wave at the gates.

CHAPTER THIRTY-THREE

"Forget it, for each has a heart of gold"

After supper Sarah went up to the dorm with Rhona and took out her embroidery. She carried on working on the table-cloth for Hilda; she had now completed all but one corner, embellishing it with a design of various intertwined flowers and leaves.

"That is coming on beautifully. Your mother will be very pleased with it," Rhona observed. "I wish I could embroider. I am so cack-handed, I would be sure to prick my finger hundreds of times and get blood all over the spotless white cloth!"

"Go on with you, Rho, it is not that difficult. You know how accident prone I am, yet I can do it; so can anyone, with a bit of practice. I could help you to have a go on a small piece of cloth if you like," said Sarah. "It is only a matter of learning how to execute the different stitches, French knots, stocking and back-stitch, etcetera. I mean, look here – these hollyhocks are composed mainly of French knots, and they are very easy to do."

"That is OK, Sarah. I have got to mend my uniform and polish my buttons, so perhaps another time, thanks all the same. At least I can just about darn things without making too much of a mess."

They worked away for a while, listening to the wireless.

"Oh, I love that tune," said Sarah, as '*After a while*' came on the radio.

"Sarah, while we are alone, I simply must ask you. Are you falling for our boss, Flight? You seem to be spending a good deal of time with him. I know he was helping you with your bike riding, but is there more to it all? You know Jill, Ellie and Marge have all noticed the way he looks at you across the hut."

Sarah started: she didn't expect that question, but really it would be very nice to just discuss her feelings with a close friend.

"Well, I think he is such a nice chap, and he seems to like spending time with me. We are really just friends, but I must admit he is figuring more and more in my thoughts lately. He makes me laugh, so I feel happy when I am with him. It is such a relief to talk about it with you, but please, this is just between us two. I don't want any teasing from the others, or insinuations going on. He is a married man, albeit he is very unhappily married.

The fact of the matter is; he always seems to be looking after me. I mean, when I fell off my bike, who was it who bothered to turn back to see if I was OK, helped me to first aid, and then escorted me back to the convent and thus missed the concert?

Then last week, when we were nearly killed by the German plane, he really saved my life at the risk of his. I cannot help being drawn to him, but it is not just that he looks after me. Oh, Rho, I just have to admit that when he took me in his arms after I was so frightened by the plane, I just wanted to be there for ever. My feelings for him have just grown from friendship. I realise it is wrong of me and it is very easy to forget that he is married, as being with him is just so natural. His caring for me is a bit like my brother George, who has always looked out for me. With Gary it is not really what you may call a 'brotherly' feeling that I have for him. I am really fond of him. Do you understand? It is difficult to explain, and because he is unhappily married it makes it even more complicated!"

"Really?" said the intrigued Rhona. "I had no idea – tell me more."

"Well, it is very sad, is wife is totally cold towards him. She seems to have no love for Gary at all. She just needs him to look after the children as she had ambitions to be an academic, and anything that comes between her and her studying gets short shrift. Poor Gary went home recently and was simply used as a baby-sitter – not that he minds that, because his children, Jared and Polly, are his life – but he was looking for some warmth or love from his wife, and he received none."

"No, really? Good grief, the poor man! One would never guess, would one? You would think she would be so pleased that he hadn't been killed testing kites or whatever he gets up to when he is not with us! I cannot believe he is carrying round such sadness inside, as he is such a happy chap in his capacity as our boss, always laughing, joking and teasing us. How very rotten for him. This puts things in a totally different light. However, I must say, I have also noticed how much he looks at you when you are working. He is drawn to you and no mistake, and you could be treading on dangerous ground, especially if you care for him too."

"Oh, I do care," said Sarah passionately. "It is all very hard because when I am with him and he is so kind to me, and such fun, I am always laughing and am in seventh heaven. I am beginning to forget all about Trel, although of course, I still write to him. I find it difficult to think of anyone but Gary. Oh, Rho! I am so glad I am talking to you about all this. I have wanted to broach the subject for ages, but there always seemed to be lots of other girls around. I have not had a chance to talk to anyone alone. I so wanted to tell Jill about it the other day, just to talk it all out with someone, really, and now you know. Phew, what a relief this is!"

"Has he kissed you or anything yet?" asked Rhona.

"No, nothing like that, he is a real gentleman when we are together, and we are just friends. Trel doesn't make me feel the way Gary does. There, I have said it – and what a relief to admit that fact. Gary treats me with honour, but he did kiss my hand the other night in a gallant way when he left me at the convent. And, well, quite honestly, I would love him to kiss me, you know, properly." Sarah looked at Rhona in a sideways manner. "Do you think that is dreadful of me, Rho dear?"

"No, of course not, I would feel the same way. He is a very good-looking chap. Plus, of course, we are all here together miles away from home in a very perilous situation. We could all be bombed or shot at or invaded and taken prisoner at any minute. One has to grab what happiness one can. I must admit I admire Jill and Jerry going ahead with their wedding; I mean, why wait, when it could be too late. Everyone is on edge these days with such bad news all around them, it is not surprising that we cling on to each other – normality goes out of the window during war time, and some say morality too. You only have to watch some of the girls with the Yankee airmen at a shakey-do. Anything goes these days, especially when they have been drinking. Lots of the girls have men friends at the 'drome, some of them must be married too! It is only a natural result of us all having to be together in this maelstrom of unhappiness that is war."

"Not that I am advocating that you let things go too far in that direction, young Sarah, but to fall in love is the easiest of things when one is under great strain. It makes life seem worthwhile. You obviously have a great compassion for Gary, and his sadness at his being married to the equivalent of a fridge!"

Sarah laughed at Rhona's words. "You are incorrigible, but please, *please,* I beg of you, keep this as our little secret, for the moment at least. I don't want to be the butt of any jokes, and I certainly don't want the other girls watching Gary and I at work."

"Well, come to think of it, it is obvious, if one has any sense at all, that the chap is crazy about you – but if I hear the girls chatting about you two I will do my best to put them off the scent, if you like."

"Oh Rho, you are a dear! I'm sure that will help parry any rumours that may go around about myself and Gary. The last thing I want is for him to be hurt any more."

"Well, that settles it then. I will keep mum, and be your *confidante* when you need me. By the way, changing the subject, did you see that there is a big Service Ball to be held at Westcliffe next Saturday? It has been organised for everyone to boost morale. Do you fancy coming? The Yanks will be out in full and we should get a few good dances. They are very fast on their feet, it should be a grand shakey-do! We need to let our hair down and have a good time and there should be tasty eats and a decent band."

"That sounds like great fun, Rho. Will all the girls be going?"

"Most of them, unless of course they get stung for duty-stooges that night. Just make sure you volunteer during the week, then they won't make you work at the

Jill Hogben

weekend. I'll let you know what time the Liberty bus will be coming for us, it will be making several stops on the way to pick up personnel. What do you think you will wear?"

Sarah thought for a moment. "Well, I have my pale blue silk dress, the one with a lace bolero. I bought that before the war and have it with me. Luckily I can still get into it, in fact, it will probably need taking in as I have lost weight since joining up. Do you think that will be too posh?"

"That sounds just the ticket, dear. It is in the large ballroom, so it is not just a 'squeeze' at the local palais de dance! I will have to wear my navy pleated dress again. I have no clothing rations left, but at least I have some new dancing shoes."

The girls talked about the dance for some time, then others came in and all made their ablutions ready for bed.

CHAPTER THIRTY-FOUR

"When you put your arms around mine"

The week passed fairly quickly, interrupted only by
copious air raids on Manston. These disrupted the lives
of the WAAFs but they cheerfully got on with their
work, treating them as interludes of nuisance. Running
to shelter was disruptive but to a certain extent, they
had become inured to the raids.

One of the WAAFs had written a poem dedicated
to the airmen, their heroes, and it was posted up on the
wall:

> *"He is so young and joyous,*
> *yet he bears the fate of nations on his shoulders now.*
> *His roaring Spitfire thunders up the sky –*
> *to him the drone of engines seems a song.*
> *He rides the cloud pavilioned lists*
> *that lie between earth's surface and the evening star.*
> *His feats of arms are such*
> *as men have dared never before.*
> *His brief reports can vie*
> *with ballads of those knights and kings,*
> *whose deeds were red-hot news in Camelot.*
> *He has a threefold England in his charge:*
> *The old-world England we have loved so long,*
> *And then the splendid England of today,*
> *and finally the England yet to be.*
> *We pass him in the street – a knight who wears not*
> *golden spurs, perhaps – but shining wings!"*

Everyone at Manston admired the courage of the brave
pilots, most of whom were very young, and many knew
of faces they no-longer spotted at the 'drome, those

who had given the most precious thing they had, their lives for their country. The fly-boys were heroes indeed, and often the WAAFs were seen scouring the skies for the return of squadrons that had set off to defend the nation's liberty.

Dances were a chance for all to relax, to get away from the stress of conflict and everyday RAF life, and to mingle socially. So when at last Saturday came, the day of the big Service Ball, there was much excitement at the convent and a flurry of activity in the dorm. Girls were vying for baths and needing hot water for hair washing; there was never enough, bath water was shared, and some girls resorted to the new invention of dry shampoo in desperation.

Those who owned fine denier stockings hurriedly washed and dried them and those who had none made do with staining their legs and getting a friend to paint on a seam at the back. The dorm was awash with make-up and the air was heavy with various scents and perfume that the girls were trying out. The girls manicured each other's nails, and plucked eyebrows to cries of "Ow! That hurt!"

Chaos reigned, and shouts of "I've lost my flames of passion red lipstick!" Or alternatively, "Who has taken my powder compact?" Everywhere the scurrying of girls caused chaos, as they tried dresses on and borrowed petticoats from those who unluckily were 'duty stooges' that evening and couldn't go to the ball.

Rhona and Marge helped each other set their hair, Jill and Sarah managed to put their own curling papers in, and all came together to brush out the finished hair-dos, hair spray being wielded liberally. Marjorie kindly ironed dresses and passed them to various girls.

Soon the girls were ready and Phil yelled "The Liberty bus is here!" which made them hurry to clip ear-rings, fasten necklaces and get their wraps on before gingerly going down the stairs in their high-heeled shoes.

Marge reached the hall and called out "Come on lassies, the lads are awaiting us!"

The smiling nuns waved them off and told them they all looked lovely. There was much giggling and chattering as they got on the bus and met several of the airmen already on-board. Those who had men friends paired up. Sarah sat with Rhona, having scoured the bus for Gary, but she couldn't see him.

"I hope Gary comes to the dance. He is not on this bus," she whispered to Rhona. "He has been absent from Admin for a couple of days, hasn't he? Perhaps he is busy testing kites. Oh, I do hope not."

Sarah spied Reg and Connie at the back of the bus chatting animatedly. Maybe I could ask Reg where he is, she thought, but then I had better not. I don't want people to know I care for him. She looked rather sadly out of the window into the dark of the night as the bus trundled along the lanes to Westcliffe.

They parked outside the venue, shrouded in darkness; one would never know a dance was being held inside. However, when they reached the darkened porch and the front door was shut firmly behind them, they were soon dazzled by the bright lights and glittering decorations of the main foyer.

They left their wraps at the cloakroom and made their way to the magnificent ballroom, lit with sparkling chandeliers. The windows were firmly cloaked in blackout blinds and heavy blue velvet curtains, so as not to show one chink of the bright scene inside. The RAF band The Squadronaires was playing, and one or two couples were already on the dance floor, whirling round.

A long table ran down one side of the room on which were sandwiches, dainty cakes, jellies and many other good things to eat. There was a large silver bowl at one end of the table with little cups round it attached on hooks and a ladle to scoop out the punch, heavy with fruit. There was a bar with plenty of beer for the men, and some of the girls who liked a stiffer drink.

The band started playing dance tunes, those of Glen Miller. This encouraged the American airmen to approach the girls and lead them onto the dance floor.

Sarah loved to jitter-bug, but some of the Yanks were very rough and threw her all over the place. She danced happily for a while, and then had to sit the next dance out to get her breath back.

"Phew! I had a right tussle with that Yank," she said. "He was all hands and kept grabbing me by the waist and holding me just a little too tightly for my liking."

"They are all the same, ducks," a friendly girl remarked. "Just keep them in their place. They mean no harm, and they always are very generous with their gifts of sweets, chewing gum and fags. I have just had a dance with that tall lanky chap over there. He threw me up in the air, then I went through his legs, I lost my grip on his hands and went skidding across the dance floor!"

"I saw you," laughed Sarah. "Did you hurt yourself?"

"No, thank you, only my dignity was bruised showing my all. Luckily, I had no stockings on to ladder," she giggled.

Sarah was asked to dance again, this time it was Reg who spied her alone and came over. Connie had gone to have something to eat. Reg was a good dancer, very gentlemanly after the Yanks, and Sarah took the opportunity to ask him if he had seen Gary.

Reg said he hadn't lately. He thought Gary was involved with some top secret job. They hadn't even had a game of snooker for a while.

The dance floor was getting really crowded and a 'Paul Jones' was played. Both sexes joined hands and went round in circles in front of each other in opposite directions. In that way Sarah found herself dancing with lots of different chaps, whichever one she was opposite when the music stopped, and had experience of the tall, the short, the sweaty and the smooth dancers. Some were good dancers, some trod on her toes. At the end of the Paul Jones she sat down with the others for a breather, and then went to have some punch as she was thirsty.

She was standing on her own having a drink when the lights dimmed and a slow dance started. She thought she would go to the ladies to freshen up and she made her way to the cloakroom. She had to wait for a cubicle as there were many ladies with the same idea. There she saw Rhona.

"Grand dance, isn't it Rho?"

"This certainly is one of the better dances I have attended," said Rhona. "The Squadronaires band is the tops, isn't it? The singer has a dreamy voice – I think he is called Jimmy – he is good-looking too, a bit of all right and I wouldn't say no to him in a dark corner!"

"Rho, really!" Sarah pretended to be shocked, and pulled a disapproving face.

They walked back around the side of the dance floor, now full of close couples waltzing together. Sarah shivered with delight when she suddenly spotted a familiar figure coming towards her.

"May I have the pleasure of this dance?" Gary asked. Rhona glanced back and smiled at the two of them, and walked on.

"Goodness! You startled me," said Sarah. "Where did you come from?"

"From heaven on the wings of prayer," teased Gary. "Actually, I was sitting down, over there. I had looked out for you but couldn't see you anywhere and thought perhaps you were on duty and not here. Being away from work I had no clue who was duty stooge tonight, and I hoped it wasn't you."

"I was in the ladies. I looked for you too, and even had the gall to ask Reg where you were. He is here with Connie, but he had no idea if you were coming or not."

The Squadronaires played '*As Long as there is Music*', and Gary took Sarah in his arms and skilfully steered her around the floor. He was a good dancer, holding her gently but firmly. Almost as good as Trel, thought Sarah, but she pushed away thoughts of Trel at that moment, and savoured being once again in Gary's arms.

"I have been away on a project; I expect you have some inkling of it by now in Admin but we mustn't speak about it. I was trying to get back in time to ask if I may escort you to this dance, but I hadn't a hope."

"And I didn't think you were coming at all when you weren't on the Liberty bus." Sarah looked up at him, her green eyes sparkling in the dim light.

"You look really lovely tonight in that beautiful dress," Gary said softly, and they whirled around in silence for a while. The lights were dimmed and they felt able to show their closeness in the dark.

Sarah leant her face against his chest, closed her eyes momentarily and savoured their closeness. Gary put his head gently on hers and they danced together as one.

When the lights went up and the dance was finished, Gary escorted her back to a seat tucked away at the end of the ballroom, where they were partially concealed by a large fern and aspidistra.

"Well, that was very nice," he remarked. "You are a good dancer Sarah, but then I thought you probably would be by the way you walk. Do you know that you have a very lovely flowing walk, feminine and graceful, so I imagined that you would be a natural on the dance floor."

"You old flatterer! Graceful walker indeed – I am liable to trip up at any moment, as you know to your cost in the office."

"Well, it doesn't show when you trip the light fantastic." He winked at her.

They spent a pleasant while talking and then got up to jitter-bug. Gary was so funny: he hammed it up in front of Sarah, throwing his arms and long legs all over the place. Sarah kept up with him, and they cut a fine dash on the dance floor as he picked her up and whirled her around.

They had a couple more slow dances towards the end of the evening, Sarah just loving to be near Gary and to feel his arms around her. The last waltz was played and everyone clapped and cheered, thanking the band, and made their way to the cloakrooms.

"I have an RAF car, as I came from Dover way, so would you like a lift home?"

Sarah said that would be grand. So they set off together. The night was calm and clear, there was a crescent moon and the myriads of stars above twinkled gaily.

"I am going to do a little detour. Do you mind?" asked Gary, looking down at Sarah beside him.

"No, not at all. I am far too awake anyway. In my mind I am still dancing with you."

Gary drove to Kingsgate Bay and stopped in a car park at the top of the cliffs. There the moon was reflected in the sea, making a magical silvery path to the shore below, where gentle waves were slowly bringing the tide in over the wet sand.

"We could have a walk," said Gary. "I do think, however, that it will be a bit chilly for you out there. It is a clear night, and the temperature is quite low."

"No thanks, I'm quite cosy in here with you. Besides, I have danced so much this evening I don't think my feet could carry me any further." She turned to look up at him and smiled.

"My, you are so pretty. Your face looks radiant tonight." With that Gary, leaning forward, gently caught her under the chin and, lifting up her face to his, planted the softest tenderest kiss on her upturned mouth. Sarah responded and lifted her arm around his neck, drawing him to her.

"There, perhaps I shouldn't have done that," Gary queried as they looked into each other's eyes. "Maybe it was wrong, and presumptuous of me, but I have been wanting to do that for a long, long time. The moment was just magical and I hope I haven't upset you in any way. I didn't mean to take advantage, it is just that you look so beautiful and your perfume is absolutely delicious."

"I wouldn't have let you kiss me if I hadn't wanted you to." Sarah smiled up at him. They kissed again and then sat in companionable silence for a while, holding hands and looking out to the moon and the sea.

"I'm not sure how to tell you, and this may seem a little sudden, but, I believe I have fallen in love with you." Gary took her face in his hands. "Your sweetness has seeped into my poor unloved heart and has begun to heal it from within, warming the emptiness there with your kindness, and thoughtful caring ways."

"I, too, have feelings for you, darling Gary" responded Sarah. "I have treasured our times together lately, and gradually I have begun to care for you very much. I-I think I am in love with you too." Sarah spoke softly and her heart beat madly as the words came out of her mouth. She was still very young and inexperienced in relationships of the heart, but she so wanted him to know how much he meant to her.

"That is absolutely wonderful, darling. I cannot believe you care for me too. Oh, *if only* I were free."

Gary's unhappy marriage loomed large in their thoughts, but they both pushed it to the back of their minds. He leaned over and put his arm around her and she rested her head on his shoulder, and they sat together in silence watching the glittering silver moon-lit sea.

"As much as I want this moment to last forever, I'm afraid I think it is time for us to go back. It is nearly your witching hour, although I understand that just for tonight there is to be an extension for WAAFs, because of the ball. We don't want you locked out of the convent, do we? It does seem a bit mean that we men are allowed out till midnight."

They drove back and Gary kissed her again at the convent gates.

"Goodnight, my little one, sweet dreams. Are you going to church in the morning?"

"No, I think I will have a lie in tomorrow, but I am free in the afternoon. Perhaps we could get together?"

"I have got the car for the weekend, so we might motor out somewhere for a spot of tea. How about that? Or, we could have a game of tennis, at the 'drome, whatever you would like to do."

"I think a drive out would be an absolutely grand idea. I am too tired for thoughts of tennis at the moment. See you after lunch tomorrow." Sarah blew him a kiss. "Goodnight, my dearest."

He drove away and Sarah floated down the convent drive, and met all the girls who had come home on the Liberty bus. They were all chattering but she just kept quiet, savouring the moments she had shared with Gary, wrapped in a warm glow. I cannot believe it, but he actually loves me, she thought, and hugged herself happily.

CHAPTER THIRTY-FIVE

"When did my love for you take place?"

The warm sun streamed in through a tiny chink in the blackout curtains and shone directly on one of Sarah's eyes as she lay sleeping. It woke her up and for a moment she lay listening to the soft breathing and some gentle snoring of the other girls, all tired out from last night's dancing.

Then she suddenly remembered what had happened. Oh my goodness! Gary loves me! She wriggled down under the covers and stretched out luxuriously with a smile on her face. It just seems like a dream, she thought. Last night's dance and the subsequent ride in his car came flooding back into her morning memory, and she savoured every last moment of the warmth that pervaded her heart.

She slipped out of bed had a quick wash, dressed and went downstairs for a cuppa. At the weekends the girls ate meals at the convent, so after getting herself a bowl of cereal she took her teacup and bowl out into the garden and sat in the sun, eating.

Rhona had meanwhile risen and had come down for a cuppa. She joined Sarah, and was all agog to know what had happened after the dance.

"Well! You know that Gary had a staff car from being away at Dover, so he was able to take me home."

"I saw you weren't on the Liberty bus with everyone else – you were missed, you know. Anyway, what happened?"

"He took me on a detour to Kingsgate. Oh, Rho! It was such a lovely evening, the moon was shining over the sea, it was magical and..."

"Yes, yes, go on – don't keep me in suspenders!" Rhona urged her friend, putting down her tea cup to listen intently to the details.

"Well... he kissed me," Sarah said, shyly.

"I'm not a bit surprised. I could see that was coming a mile off when I watched you two dancing last night. You both looked as if you were floating along in the clouds. Anything else?"

"He told me he loves me!!!! I told him I loved him, too!"

"Oh, goodness me, did you really? Well, that puts a new light on the whole situation. You both seem to have jumped in head first!" Rhona lent forward and took her friend's hand.

"Now my dear friend, you must be very careful! You are so young and inexperienced in matters of the heart. Gary is older and not free – he should know better – but I do understand, he is unhappy and unloved in his marriage, and there you are in front of him, caring and sympathetic to his marital plight and looking radiant, and, well, men will be men. I do feel that you could well be opening up a hornets' nest of troubles."

"I'm too happy at the moment to worry about anything else," said Sarah dreamily.

"I can understand you, of course I can, but you are treading on dangerous ground, you know. Most of the girls missed you in the Liberty bus going home. Now, we must think of a plan to explain your absence."

"Is that really necessary, Rho? I simply don't want to tell lies to my friends. Can't we at least bring Jill, Marge, and Ellie into the picture? They may well be sympathetic, as you have been, to a couple in love."

"Hmm. I'm not sure. I will have to think about that," Rhona replied after a pause. "It could get

complicated if more people are in the know – but I can
see that if you go on seeing Gary, they will not fail to
notice something going on. They are all our friends, of
course, and should be trusted. Perhaps you are right,
better to have them on board at the beginning. Maybe
we should go and find them now, explain, and swear
them to secrecy. I cannot actually think that this could
be kept from them, as we all work together and live
together; they have already asked me if anything is
going on, and I, of course, threw them off the scent as
we had agreed."

"OK. I would certainly feel better not to have to lie
to my friends. Let's go and find them," said Sarah,
impulsively.

"Just a minute, Sarah. What about your Henry or
Trel or whatever you call him these days? Had you a
thought for how this may affect your relationship with
him? I mean, he is not here, and unless you say
something, he has very little chance to find out what has
happened. So where does that leave him in the scheme
of things? Will you finish with him, or keep him in the
dark?"

"Oh! I really cannot think straight; I haven't even
given him a thought! I am so wrapped up in the fact
that Gary loves me. Maybe I will tell him on my next
leave, but that will be very difficult. He has been so
kind to me and I know he loves me and expects us to
get married after the war. He has been trying to get me
to agree to an engagement for ages – in fact, he
mentions it every time I go home.

I have a '48' coming up soon. I shall have to think
carefully about what to say. I really don't want to hurt
him, I care for him a lot, but it is just that my feelings
for Gary are much more powerful and passionate. Oh,

Rho! I've never been in love before! This emotion has swept me off my feet, and that's for sure!"

Rhona put her arm round her friend as they sat chatting in the sun. "I do understand how you feel, and how falling in love is such an amazing feeling and shouldn't be marred by worries. However, you and Gary have plenty to think about. At the same time as advising caution, I do want to say 'enjoy this feeling': it is the most exciting lovely warm feeling of all, to be loved and to love. There is nothing like it, and at this time of war it can make emotions much stronger, because of the danger in which we all have to live. Of course for you two, there are the complications of his wife and family. Still, I think we will just see how it all pans out for now. Shall we go and find the others? They may well have risen out of their pits now, and you can explain all to them."

"I really don't want anyone to get hurt, especially Gary's children, Oh goodness, that has really thrown a pall over everything."

"Well, not to worry about that now! This is early days – just enjoy your love, but be aware that there may not be any future in it. In fact, if I were you, I wouldn't say anything to Trel just yet. Be cautious: after all he is there, waiting for you, offering a good life and secure future, and you don't want to throw that all away just yet. Just try and be sensible and keep a little corner in your heart for Trel. You never know when you may need him."

They gathered up their tea cups and plates and went in to find the others. The girls were still in the dorm, some still in bed and others were just getting washed and dressed.

Rhona gathered Jill, Marge and Ellie together and they all sat on their beds as she explained what had happened last night between Sarah and Gary. Sarah sat listening with a smile on her face.

"Wow!" Jill interjected jumping up and down in her seat. "That is absolutely amazing, you two are in love. Gosh! Just fancy that! How absolutely wonderful!"

"Well, of course, it is lovely," Rhona said cautiously. "However, the thing is this has to be kept quiet, as you understand Gary is married, albeit very unhappily – I'll explain another time about that – so this cannot really come out into the open. Jill, you mustn't even tell your Jerry. We must all act as normal, especially at work, and fend off any questions from any of the other girls who may want to gossip."

The girls all gathered round Sarah and kissed and hugged her, saying they would certainly keep 'Mum' about her love for Gary and would support the couple in any way they could.

"Och away! I love a love affair!" Marge joined in. "This will brighten up our days no end, and we will do everything to make it easy for you, lassie, and Gary – he is such a dear, and he deserves your affection, he surely does." The girls carried on chattering to Sarah until lunch time. After lunch Sarah got ready to meet her love.

CHAPTER THIRTY-SIX

"These times should be so complete"

Gary drew up a little way away from the convent. Sarah spotted him and ran along to jump in his car.

"Hallo, you pretty lady! How are you today?"

"Floating on a cloud, thanks, and how are you darling?" said Sarah, shyly.

"I am very well thank you. In fact I am feeling just tickety-boo, and the whole world is rosy, because you said you loved me last night!"

They drove off up to Minnis Bay and sat for a moment over-looking the sea.

Gary switched off the engine and turned and took Sarah in his arms, and kissed her again and again.

"I have been longing to do that all night. I simply could not sleep. I kept realising that you returned my feelings and, well, that was heady, like drinking the best champagne!"

"Me too – I woke up and thought about you immediately!" Sarah put her head on his shoulder.

They sat for a while chatting and over-looking the sparkling sea, then headed off for Canterbury. They parked the car near the city walls and felt safe enough to walk hand-in-hand through the cathedral gardens, bedecked with colourful flowers and abundant with trees snow-covered with palest pink cherry blossom, like ballerinas in long floating tutus. The old cathedral stood magnificently proud in the afternoon sun, its mellow stone glowing warmly. They stood for a while and looked up at the Old Harry bell tower.

Gary pointed skywards. "It is just incredible that this wonderful building was constructed before they had cranes and modern building techniques. Just think of the effort it must have taken to get those huge blocks of stone up to the top of the tower!"

They strolled on through the cathedral grounds and out through the mediaeval gatehouse into the high street. They did some window shopping as they walked along, admiring beautiful china or dapper menswear, antique and curio shops. They passed smart women's modes, and even in war time one could see a wedding dress in the window, for sale, a beautiful gown for a spring bride.

"Jill should see that dress, Gary, and I bet it would take a lot of clothing coupons," remarked Sarah. "She and Jerry are getting married at St. Catherine's church next month and she doesn't know how to get hold of a wedding dress. We are all saving up our coupons for her trousseau."

"That is very kind of the girls," said Gary. "Hey! I know where I can get my hands on some parachute silk. Reg has a stash of it over at Alland Grange, taken from prisoners of war. In fact, the last lot came from that ruddy pilot who nearly killed us, the one that came down at Shuart Farm. Reg and his men went over to see what they could salvage from the crashed Messerschmitt and were there when the pilot was captured. He was wandering around in a dazed fashion still attached to his parachute, so that should do. It would need a good cleaning, but there is plenty of it for a dress, I would think – not that I know about these things, of course." He laughed, shrugging his shoulders at the general ineptitude of men when consulted on women's clothing.

"That is fantastic news for Jill, I will tell her to go and see Reg as soon as possible. You don't think he could have got rid of it yet, do you?"

"I doubt it. He has far too many other things to do. Last I saw it was rolled up and stashed in a cupboard."

They came to the end of the high street and turned into a walk that ran beside the river Stour. They could hear music, and as they walked nearer a bandstand came into view with deckchairs arranged in a circle around it, and a brass band playing merrily.

"Shall we sit and listen to the band for a while? I love to watch people play brass instruments. I nearly took up the tuba, you know, but I was too small to carry it!" Gary laughed and gently steered her towards a deckchair and helped her settle.

Sarah laughed at the thought of Gary behind a tuba. They found deck chairs and sat side by side in the sun, their hands joined, listening to the music. The brass band played a lot of wartime tunes from the Great War, '*Pack up your troubles in your old kit bag*' and '*Hang out your washing on the Siegfried line*', as well as Vera Lyn's 1942 signature song of '*There'll be blue birds over the white cliffs of Dover*'.

It was so pleasant, sitting there with Gary stroking her hand. Sarah closed her eyes, relaxed back and said, "I'm in heaven, I want this to go on forever. Just think that the evil of war has brought us together. Out of a bad thing has blossomed our love for each other by bringing us together across England to Manston."

"I know, darling, and to think I was dreading coming over to Kent from Cornwall. I really didn't want to be posted far away to Manston!" Gary laughed. "How did I know that the sweetest angel of a Clerk GD was waiting for me there?"

They sat in the pleasant afternoon sunshine, listening to the band for a while.

"I had to tell Rho about us," said Sarah, during an interval in the music. "She noticed us dancing and knew I hadn't been on the Liberty bus. She asked me point blank this morning and I couldn't lie to her. We talked it out and realised that we couldn't really hide anything from the others in our dorm, Jill, Marge and Ellie. I don't have to worry about Phil, now, as she has been posted away. You see, we live in such close quarters and they may have realised I had been with you, or at least have been suspicious. They had already discussed us, actually, as they had noticed the way you look at me at work – something I hadn't thought about and wasn't actually aware of myself."

"Oh darling, good grief! Was I *that* obvious? I cannot believe my girls were watching me at work. I didn't think that I was letting my feelings for you show so much. I do realise that you are now in an awkward position. It will be fairly easy for me to keep our love from the chaps. I mean, Reg may get an inkling, but Bill, Jerry and the others probably won't realise anything is going on. We men are more private about our lives. You women discuss everything! I shouldn't worry, as your friends are good sports. I am sure they will only chat amongst themselves about us. After all, everyone loves a lover, or so the song goes!"

They carried on enjoying the band for a while, then Gary suggested they go and get a cup of tea, so they walked back up the high street and stopped for a while at a tea room. They shared a pot of tea and enjoyed a doughnut each. As they finished their tea, Gary asked: "I have had an idea. Would you like to go to Evensong in the cathedral? It is nearly six o'clock and it starts at half-past, so we are in plenty of time."

Sarah had never been in such a huge sacred building and was very pleased that Gary suggested they attend the service.

They walked back together through the cathedral gate and over the grass to the ornately carved huge cathedral entrance. The organ was playing, and it was difficult for a minute to see inside after the bright sun shining outside. They made their way to a couple of chairs just off the main aisle. Sarah was in awe of the beauty and magnificence of the soaring pillars and intricate fan vaulted ceiling, which stretched so loftily above them.

The evening sun poured through the magnificent window behind them and lit the choir as they processed into their choir stalls.

"This huge sacred space is a bit of a change from our tiny Acol Church, isn't it? Talk about the sublime to the ridiculous. Just look at those dear little boy choristers," Sarah whispered. "No men to speak of though, such a pity. I can just spot one or two older men."

"All the lay clerks are away on active service. Only those too old to be called up are left to balance the harmony," Gary explained quietly.

The Service opened with the prex:

"Oh Lord, open Thou our lips". Gary and Sarah sang in response "And our mouth shall show forth Thy praise".

The service continued. Sarah tried hard to concentrate, but the sheer beauty of the building took her breath away, and most of the time she just looked around and tried to read the wording on the many monuments on the walls nearest to her. They sang a psalm together. Sarah thought that Gary had a lovely baritone voice, probably from his Welsh heritage, she deduced.

The choir sang an anthem, one of her favourites, Bach's '*Jesu Joy of Man's Desiring*', and while their treble voices soared to the roof Gary quietly slipped his hand in hers. I feel so happy, she thought, and said a quick prayer to the Lord above for their new found love. I wonder if He minds us being together: after all He brought us both to Manston. If Gary had been happily married I would have still fallen for him, but I would have not kissed him. I would have just been a friend and tried to lighten his load, she realised, trying to find some justification for their love in her mind.

After Evensong, and as the organ thundered out the recessional voluntary, Gary and Sarah walked around the cathedral for a while, marvelling at the immense space in this mighty mother church of the Anglican Communion, absolutely central to the Anglican faith. They felt proud that they were part of an RAF unit that was responsible for endeavouring to protect the cathedral, intact from the Luftwaffe.

"I wonder why we didn't see the Archbishop?" Sarah queried, looking closely at a large stately tomb. "Gosh just look at the intricate beauty of the stone carving, it looks like pink marble."

Gary moved closer to peer at the tomb. "It's alabaster. Oh, he is probably busy elsewhere in his See. There are a lot of other clergy people in a cathedral, for instance the Dean, Hewlett Johnson who preached this evening. He normally takes more services than Archbishop William Temple. The Archbishop may have taken Matins or Holy Communion this morning. He is getting on a bit now."

Gary led Sarah out into the waning sunshine, which touched the topmost pinnacles of the cathedral and turned them to gold, and they walked back through the delightful gardens to the car and drove back to the convent. Gary parked in a side road and he and Sarah enjoyed a kiss and cuddle.

"Well, goodnight sweetness, sleep well. My, how things have changed between us since we were last in the Admin hut together. That was probably only about a couple of weeks ago. We will have to be very professional when we meet tomorrow, but it will be hard not to want to kiss your lovely soft mouth."

"Oh, I know, darling Gary," said Sarah, clasping his hands in hers. "I shall find it difficult to concentrate, knowing you are so near yet so far away. When may we be together again like this?"

"Things are a bit difficult at the moment, because of this important operation coming up. I may be called away, and the workload will be very heavy." Gary pondered for a moment.

"I suppose it wouldn't hurt to meet you one evening, or to walk you home when we are both in the office.

I tell you what, to make us both feel better, we will make a provisional date for Wednesday evening. We will walk into Birchington straight from work, and have bite to eat at Rushes, that lovely café, or we could try "The Pinot". I have heard a good report from that eatery, but of course that is further away at Minnis Bay. Then there is The Clovelly Café. Oh, I don't care really which one we go to, as long as we spend some time together! We will choose which one on

Wednesday, depending on the weather. I have just realised that it would be good if you cycled, rather than legged it to Manston that day: then we could go on to Minnis Bay, without worrying about getting back."

He kissed her hand, winked and smiled at her, and they parted.

CHAPTER THIRTY-SEVEN

"Your presence will not be in vain"

At the first opportunity Sarah told Jill where she could get some parachute silk for a wedding dress.

"I'll walk over with you, after work to see Reg about it, if you like Jill."

Jill was over the moon at the thought that she would be able to wear a decent wedding dress after all; she had resigned herself to wearing a suit. She was so happy when the other girls were told about the silk and they said that between them they would make a dress for her. No were coupons needed, so there would be more to spare for her trousseau.

Gary wasn't in the office the next day. Sarah was glad, in a way, so that she could concentrate on the mound of work she had to get through. A WAAF called Kitty, also a 'Clerk General Duties', had compiled a poem for them all to assist in learning the different forms, from Form 575 Shoe Repair Label to RB 12 & 8 Ration cards that the clerks had to produce. She stuck the memory-nudging ode on the hut wall where it was used and admired by all the girls:

I must have used a lot of forms, and yet had no idea,
that had I cared to glance,
I'd find a number printed there.
If someone named a 575 it wouldn't mean a thing.
Yet often the cobbler
my down-trodden shoes I'd bring.
Form 292 I know quite well from last year's course PT,
I little thought, "Result of Course"
could mean so much to me.

And quite soon now Form 413 will take me on my way
back to Record Office Manston, Kent
but not for long I pray.
I'm hoping that Appendix B for RAF 1020A
will be the means of helping me
to better things someday.
Then filling in Forms 318 the Record Card of Leave.
I'll thank the Clk/GD of course
for the numbers up my sleeve!
I'll never use a 252 I hope but if I can
I'll hand out heaps of 295s to every girl or man.
And so until that special form, that's 1394
close up the AP 837 for forms won't win the war!
1672s in plenty, and RB 12 and 8
would help to while the time away
in a very pleasant state.
We trust that someday soon we'll raise Form 1755
and bury all these books and forms,
which cause us all to strive so hard to reach the
standard, that's required to suit the RAF,
and be a perfect Clark GD while serving in the WAAF!

Jill and Sarah walked over to Alland Grange after work, on the south-west side of the 'drome. Jill was full of her love for Jerry and their plans for their future together. Sarah kept quiet but wished she could talk more about Gary, and in her heart she knew there would be no future for them as he was tied to another. So she just listened to Jill's happy chatter.

They found Reg and he took them to the 'chute. It was ivory colour, and very soft, yet strong enough to support a man. Sarah, who had an eye for sizes of material, said that they probably would only need the best large panels from the 'chute, and Reg offered to box it up after cutting off the harness and to transport it over to the convent when he had a moment.

Jill was really pleased with the creamy ivory colour of the silk. It would need good wash before they could use it, but if they could get hold of a piece or two of lace to adorn it, she was sure it would look lovely.

"We need a dress designer," said Sarah to Jill. "I wonder if Marge is any good at that. I know she makes her own clothes, so she would be the best person to ask."

They walked back to the convent together, and a few days later, Reg turned up with the silk. Marge said she would be pleased to think up a pattern, as she was used to making clothes for her mother in these straightened times.

All the girls had great fun drawing various wedding dress shapes. Designs were forthcoming as they put their ideas on paper: some slim and clingy, others fuller, feminine and floaty. In the end they came up with a pattern that Jill really loved, so the girls carefully washed, dried and cool ironed the material ready for cutting out and sewing together. They borrowed an ancient treadle sewing machine from the nuns, working hard together tacking the dress into shape and soon it was ready for a first fitting.

They all gathered round Jill, who stood on a stool in her petticoat, and the dress, was slipped onto to her slim figure. They inserted padding in the shoulders as the fashion for wide shoulders which emphasised a slim waist was 'all the rage'. The silk clung beautifully to Jill's lovely figure and the hem dipped down at the back, creating a small train. A length of lace had been found: Marge remembered that she had some at home and her mother kindly it sent down from Scotland, and she was now embellishing the sleeves at the cuffs. A small matching piece was tacked round Jill's slim waist.

"Oh, girls! How can I ever thank you. This dress will be perfect!" Jill looked at herself in the mirror, twirling around as much as she could on top of the stool.

"Just be careful you don't fall." Ellie reached out and steadied Jill. "There is more lace left than I thought, Jill. We could perhaps fashion it into some sort of veil with a tiny head-dress. I wonder if we could get hold of a cream artificial flower, too? You will need something to adorn your hair."

"Ow! Ouch! Something just stuck in my hand," exclaimed Jill, sucking her palm. "Yes, I do need something. Not a full bridal veil, though, that won't be me! I like simple things."

"You have found one of the many pins that kept the dress together, Jill. Sorry about that lassie," Marge apologised. "My, you do look grand! I'm so pleased you like the style."

They helped Jill out of the dress. Within days Marge had sewn it together, finished the trimmings, and fashioned a little lace and flower head-dress, complete with small veil– and the bridal gown was complete.

It was lovely for the girls to look forward to and help organise a wedding. Their RAF life had been pretty grim lately and they all needed cheering up. The wedding was set to take place within a month or so; it couldn't be fixed until the happy couple had seen the vicar. Naturally the girls talked of very little else, which took the pressure off Gary and Sarah, as their liaison was forgotten for a while.

CHAPTER THIRTY-EIGHT

"Happiness was this – just this"

It was a nice evening, with no sign of rain, so Gary and Sarah cycled to Minnis Bay after work and went to the Pinot Café for a bite to eat. They hadn't seen each other for a couple of days and were very pleased to be alone at last, away from anyone who would know them.

Gary took Sarah's hand across the table. "Your lovely face is such a blessing to me, I could just gaze at it all day!"

"Well, I have missed being able to hug you when I see you, but gazing at me all day would be very boring for you," teased Sarah. "The girls, though sworn to secrecy, would notice you looking at me."

"I know, I know, but I have to glance your way sometimes. I just cannot help myself."

"Did you know there is a Camp Talent Show being organised? You should go in for it and play one of your Chopin pieces."

"That is very kind of you to say so, but quite frankly I just haven't had enough practice lately to be confident enough to play in public. We only have a ropey old Joanna in the Sergeant's Mess, and most of the time it is used to play popular songs, or a bit of ragtime. I would feel very exposed playing at a talent show. Well, serious music anyway. I wish there was a decent piano somewhere that I could go and play sometimes. My music is a great release from the harsh realities of wartime."

"Can you play ragtime, then? Or boogie-woogie?"

"Yes, I love to extemporise. I am lucky that I can play classical piano from musical scores. I can also play by ear, and pick out any popular tune – well, on a good day that is! Did you know I can also play the accordion?"

"Are there no end to your talents, darling?" Laughed Sarah, sipping her coffee. "I can play the piano too, but I am not very good at it. I used to play duets with George. Gosh, those were the days, the happy days before this blooming war. How it has disrupted our lives! I hardly ever see George these days, and I miss him. Of course, he has his family to consider, now, but we were so close. I do feel a little bereft of his company, sometimes."

"Oh, don't say that! You have me now, you know – and remember, if it wasn't for this war, we would never have met. Neither would Jill and Jerry, Reg and Connie." Gary looked thoughtful for a moment.

"I do realise, of course, that you must miss George. I would love to have had my sister with whom to have a good chin wag. She sadly died when we were quite young. It must be comforting to have the closeness of a brother."

"I didn't know you had a sister," said Sarah, surprised.

"Well, there are a lot of things we don't really know about each other yet, aren't there?"

Their meal arrived and they ate in companionable silence for a while.

"By the way, I have ten days' leave coming up soon so will be going home to see my parents."

"What about your Trel? Will you see him too? How will I manage without you for ten whole days?" Gary looked a little quizzically at Sarah.

"Yes, I will see him; after all, I am walking out with him, and he is lonely without me. He writes every day,

I cannot go home and not see him. In fact, thinking about it," Sarah put her head on one side and looked at Gary over their table, "You know, you have a lot in common with Trel."

"You mean the fact that we are both head over heels in love with you?" Gary threw back his head, laughed and playfully chucked her under the chin.

"No, I mean that he, too, is thirty-seven. He also plays the piano very well; in fact, he bought a new upright mahogany piano just before the war and spends almost every evening when he gets home from work just playing it for relaxation. You will never believe this – he also plays the accordion!"

"Good grief!" Gary exclaimed. "We do have a surprisingly lot in common, I must say, he sounds like a man after my own heart, and I certainly concur with his taste in women, anyway!!!! How will you act in his company?"

"I cannot act in any way other than as normal. We will probably go out somewhere to a meal or show or something, and he will probably be asked back to eat a meal at our house. My mother and father are very fond of him. They can see he makes an excellent suitor, and my mother likes to feed him up as he is very slim and she knows he is lonely. In fact, most weekends he is round at my parents' house, playing cards with all their friends and neighbours."

"Your mother is very kind to include him and welcome him to your home, even though you are away. I wish I could meet your family. They sound so warm and loving. It is such a pity that that I cannot be introduced." He looked glum for a moment then asked:

"Have you been Trel's girl for some time? I'm beginning to feel very sorry for him. After all, you are here with me, and you love me. What do you think he would make of that?"

"Well... of course he is rather possessive - even about me dancing with other chaps down here. I know he wouldn't like to know I had met and fallen for someone else, and would be very hurt, I wouldn't like that to happen at all.

We met in Barclays Bank head office, and worked in the same department a couple of years before the war. That is another coincidence: I met him at work, too! He was very kind to me, and helped me tick up my ledger as I cannot add up for toffee!

As for when I get home, I shall just be friendly as per normal, and keep him in the dark about you and I. I don't want to lie to him, but I shall have to just bend the truth a bit about what I have been doing down here. You have your wife to think of too! Oh, why could you not be single – then I would be able to come clean to Trel and you and I wouldn't have to have a furtive relationship!" Sarah looked downcast.

"I know, darling, it is going to be difficult. Well it already is, seeing you at work every day, and I do think we have done very well at ignoring each other in company. However, not bringing me my favourite cup of coffee – well, that was taking things a bit far! As for Helen, pah! She just couldn't care less about me, and would probably be very pleased to think I wouldn't be bothering her any more."

They had a cup of coffee, with a quick sandwich and left the café to cycle back to Westgate. Halfway there Gary called out to Sarah. She stopped and he motioned her to take her bike and lean it against a hedge. He then pulled her behind the hedge and gathered her in his arms passionately. "Couldn't take you back to the convent without a smooch, now, could I?"

"Certainly not! If you hadn't, I would have had to take you into the shrubbery!" They stood in the waning evening light and held each other tightly. His lips were soon on hers.

"I have been wanting to kiss you all day, to touch you, to smell your lovely fragrance." They stood together in each other's arms for a while. "Oh, Sarah, darling, you are so much my perfect girl, and I do love you so, you know." He gave her one more hug and then said "Hey ho! Come on then, sweetness, it is probably time for your cocoa!"

They mounted their bikes and rode on together. When the convent was reached Sarah turned into the drive with a wave and called out "Goodnight, see you tomorrow!"

She put her bike away, thinking how Gary's kisses really made her tingle. I am just so attracted to him. She smiled happily and went into the kitchen to find her supper. After she wandered into the common room, from whence jolly music was emanating. Lots of laughing greeted her.

There she found a hilarious sight. Ellie and Rhona were trying to tap dance together to a record on the gramophone. '*Shoo-shoo Baby*' by the Andrews Sisters which was belting out, the girls were trying to work out a routine to the music. This was accompanied by much giggling and faulty steps.

"I didn't know you two could tap dance?" Sarah laughed at their attempts.

"Well, we didn't know that the other could either, if that makes sense?" Rhona gasped, now very out of

breath, and she flopped down onto a sofa. "Oh! I jolly
well have stitch in my side now. I came in to listen to
the gramophone when Ellie came in and started to
dance, so I got up and joined her. Do you think we will
be good enough for the Camp Talent Show?"

"Maybe, with a bit of practice. It certainly would be
fun to watch the two of you!"

"What about you. Sarah? Can you sing or
anything?"

"Heavens! No! The only talent I have is in reciting
poetry. I used to attend elocution lessons and won
various prizes for my 'upper class' voice."

With that Sarah climbed onto a stool and launched
into one of her elocution exercises. With a mock
solemn face she clasped her hands before her and
recited:

"Father's car is a jaguar, and Pa drives rather fast.
Castles, farms and draughty barns
we go charging past.
Arthur's cart is far less smart, and can't go half as fast
But I'd rather ride in Arthur's cart
than my Papa's fast car!"

"Good grief! Lah-de-dah!" Ellie exclaimed. "I always
thought you were common as muck!"

"You rotter!" Sarah laughed and threw a cushion at
Ellie and said she was tired, so left them to it and went
up to bed.

CHAPTER THIRTY-NINE
"Abundantly sentimental"

On Friday evening Sarah went home on leave. Gary went with her to Westgate Station and saw her on to the London train. He kissed her and said he had plenty to keep him busy, but told her to hurry back as he would miss her, and then waved her off. She said she would write to him, and leaned out of the window to wave to him until he was out of sight in a cloud of steam and smoke.

She sat back and looked out of the train window at the flat fields leading to the sea. This is the first time I haven't really longed to go home, she thought. Of course, I really want to see my parents, but leaving Gary is very hard. I have 'got it bad', she thought, and she realised her feelings for Gary were colouring her whole life.

Trel met her as usual at Penge East station, they kissed and began to make plans for the weekend. I have been going from one to the other, Sarah thought, this is all very strange – and she didn't really like the idea.

"I thought I would take you on a run out to Ightham Mote tomorrow, darling," Trel mentioned, as they made their way to Sarah's home. "I have been saving my petrol rations for an outing, as I haven't seen you for so long and have missed you so much. I have taken a few days leave, I couldn't get the whole ten days off as we are frightfully busy at the office but I hope we can cram in as much time together as we possibly can in the next ten days."

"OK, Trel, going out in the car would be fun. However, please do remember that I must spend some time with my parents, and also if George is around I want to see him and his family. I am actually a little tired now, so I won't ask you in, if you don't mind. Will you pick me up tomorrow afternoon?"

"Yes, I will be there, and the forecast is good, sunny all the way! We can go shopping in Lewisham or go to a show, whatever you would like to do. Oh, it is so good to have you home!" Trel leaned over and kissed her. "See you tomorrow, then, Toodles."

Sarah walked up the path, flagged on both sides by late pansies, primulas, and cowslips the latter of which came from her aunts' house in Plymouth. The front door was framed with a froth of white blossom from the pyracantha bush. Sarah lifted the letter box and called "Coo-ee!" before letting herself into the welcoming hall. There, fresh flower heads were floating in a pretty glass bowl on a paper mache chinoserie table, and their perfume wafted through the house. The old chiming clock struck the half hour. All was warm, welcoming and homely.

Hilda came rushing out to meet her. She hugged her daughter, and her familiar fragrance enveloped Sarah, making her feel at peace.

"How lovely to see you darling, it has been such a long time. Let me look at you."

Joe came out from the dining room. "Hallo, ma wee bairn." He took her in his arms.

"My! It is good to see you – you are a feast for the eyes and no mistake. Come and have your meal. Your Mammy has roasted an especially large chicken for you, we haven't had one for ages. No, it is neither Gert nor Daisy! She managed to save up her coupons and cajoled Mr. Smith the butcher into finding her one.

Cost a pretty penny, too." Joe's Scottish frugality showed through for a moment.

"We saved it just for this meal, to welcome you home on leave."

They sat at the large table, covered in a snowy white lace table-cloth. Joe began to carve the chicken, and Hilda poured out a steaming hot cup of tea for her daughter.

"I am very spoilt, this is really scrumptious. Thank you darling Daddy and Mummy, for all your love for me."

"Och away! We adore you lassie and need to spoil you now and again. You are a very precious wee girl to us, you know. Besides, chicken is my favourite meat and a special treat for us all these war time days. Your Mammy will make soup with the bones, so none will go to waste."

They tucked into their meal, accompanied by Joe's carrots and the last of the sprouts freshly gathered from the garden that morning, as were the crispy potatoes, roasted in lard by Hilda till they sizzled. On the table there stood a steaming boat full of rich gravy, made from boiling the giblets, and the chicken was accompanied by tasty sausage and parsley stuffing made to Hilda's own recipe.

"We didn't ask Henry to dine with us, this time" said Hilda, watching with great pleasure as her hungry daughter tucked into the meal she had prepared. "I must say I feel a bit mean in not doing so, but we rather wanted you to ourselves this evening. After all, we haven't seen you now for ten weeks, and that seems like a lifetime. You are looking very well, all rosy cheeked. That seems surprising, since you are mostly shut away in a hut at your typewriter."

"Ahh, but I cycle or walk to and from Manston every day," explained Sarah. "I do get plenty of fresh air, sun and sea air which quickly tans the skin, even at this time of the year. Mummy, this chicken is so delicious, and I *am* seeing Trel tomorrow."

"Yes, it is a lovely tender bird, isn't it? I was afraid Mr. Smith would only have broilers, but I think I am a favourite customer of his, and he made sure this was a young 'un."

Joe paused in his eating for a moment, laid down his knife and fork and looked with a concerned expression across the laden table at his daughter. "Now, what is all this about you being shot at? George wrote and told us, I must admit, we were worried sick."

"I wasn't going to tell you. I was fine, well protected, and I'm cross that George worried you. He had no right to do that, I confided in him being my darling brother, but in no way wanted you two dear folks worried. I will explain:

It happened as I was walking home one evening across the fields to the convent. I had a companion, my boss, a Flight Sergeant. We had both been working late, the others had left early as they were going out that evening. He was also on his way back to his billet, near the convent in the Canterbury road and we were chatting generally. Suddenly a German plane came out of the blue and dived towards us.

'Flight' saw the plane, and shouted at me to run like hell for a copse of tall elm trees, thankfully, we just got there as the plane dived nearer and began to shoot at us. He pushed me forward in a rugby tackle and threw his body across mine to shield it. He saved my life! The plane then had to swerve upwards to miss the tall trees, and was chased by a couple of planes from Manston which also suddenly appeared, and we heard an explosion and Flight found out later than the German plane was shot down over Birchington, but the pilot ejected and was captured!"

Sarah leaned back and looked at her parents' worried faces. "There, I knew I shouldn't have told you. I was very frightened, but Flight looked after me and took me back to the nuns, who made us sit in a quiet room. They gave me strong sweet tea, and he had a shot of brandy before he went to his billet."

"What a brave man your Flight Sergeant is!" said Joe. "You must let me know his name and I will write and thank him for saving my precious wee girl. Is he the same chap who helped you when you fell off your bike?"

"Yes, he is. He always seems to be looking out for me."

"He sounds like a really kind man. I just thank God that you are safe, darling," said Hilda, leaning over and taking Sarah's hand. "I do understand that we are all in danger these wartime days, but we all hope that nothing will happen to those we love, and when one learns of such a narrow escape, well, one can only praise the Lord that you are unhurt. It's no good, I need a hug!"

She got up from the table, walked around and held her daughter tightly. Sarah placed her head on her mother's ample form and enjoyed being held in her arms.

"Well a nice thing came out of our fright - and that is we used the parachute silk from the ejected pilot, who was taken prisoner, to fashion my friend Jill's wedding dress! We have all been involved in making the dress, which has been a lovely experience, very therapeutic, and has kept our minds off the horrors of this war."

"That is very kind of you all, I can imagine you had
a lot of fun sewing together!

Right then – home-made apple pie and clotted
cream for pudding!" Hilda bustled away to the kitchen.

The rest of the evening passed pleasantly, with Sarah
regaling her parents with funny anecdotes, such as the
plague of earwigs in the hut and Ellie and Rhona's
efforts to tap dance together.

"Do you know if George is on leave by any chance?"
Sarah enquired of her mother.

"No, sadly, darling, you have missed him. He was
here a week or two ago. But we could always motor
over to see Monica, Penny and baby Bev. She has
really grown up, and has a mass of dark curly hair."

"That would be lovely! I am looking forward to
seeing that darling babe and her sister. However,
tomorrow I promised I would go out with Trel for a
run in the car, probably to Ightham."

"We are glad to hear that. You know, he has missed
you so much! He will enjoy your company for a while.
Please ask him to come over for Sunday lunch. You
know that he often joins us and the Twentymans for a
hand of whist on a Sunday evening. I must admit I treat
him as if he were a future son-in-law." Hilda threw a
questioning sideways glance at her daughter.

"I know you do, Mummy, and you are very
welcoming and kind to him, and his mother and aunt,
but I just don't want to be tied to one person yet.
Maybe in a few years, after the war, who knows? I
mean it is difficult, because he may not be the man I
wish to marry. I just don't really know my own mind
yet. I haven't really experienced life, although the war is
a baptism of fire – I mean in relationships – I haven't
had a chance to see how I would feel about another

man. I do care for Trel very much, he is a sweetie, but he is so serious sometimes. I do feel a bit trapped, as if I am expected to marry him, and him alone."

Sarah had Gary in mind the whole time she was talking to her mother but could not talk about him to her; not yet, anyway. She continued: "You see, darling Mummykins, my relationship with Trel is not really tickety-boo, as RAF life has opened up other possibilities. I have other male friends now and have been dancing with lots of chaps, especially the Yanks, and they are good dancers and lots of fun. I don't want to keep Trel hanging on waiting for me, but I'm afraid that is the way it will have to be. Even if we weren't in a war-time situation, I would be interested in going out with other chaps too. I just cannot be tied down at the moment, and, really, the fact that I was conscripted and am away gives me a breathing space. Although, of course, I look forward to seeing Trel and going out with him, I really don't want any more than that from our relationship at present, and I certainly don't want to be engaged!"

"I suppose you have to look at it from Trel's point of view. Of course the war changes things but he is certainly of an age to marry, he has a job secure enough to support a wife, and he is a good Christian chap.

Although I do understand how you feel darling. I am sure I was a bit like you, at your age. Your Daddy wanted me to settle down, too, but I was also not keen and he had to – as he put it – 'lay down the law', and as I really loved him, I did as I was bid and we were married. We have been extremely happy, so it was the right thing, but you must just let Trel know simply that you may marry him some day. Hmm... I may see if I can have a word with him too, but I will wait until you are back at Manston. He just needs a bit of reassurance, I suppose, and that is what you cannot give him at the moment."

They packed away the dinner things and, after washing up, Sarah dried dishes for her mother amongst much laughter as the odd plate slipped from her grasp and went flying. They sat down for a little while in the front room with their cocoa, and Boocles the cat came in and sat on Sarah's lap. She stroked him and he purred contentedly.

Sarah started yawning, so she and Hilda repaired up to bed, Joe first winding the old chiming clock as usual in the hall. That clock's chimes are just sounds of home, thought Sarah, as she climbed the stairs to her welcoming room.

CHAPTER FORTY

"To these moments I oft times cling"

The next morning Sarah woke up in her own little bed, and as she lay snuggled under her pink paisley eiderdown she pondered on how lucky she was to have such a loving home to return to on leave. Not like Gary, she thought, he gets no love when he goes home, except from his children.

She put away thoughts of Gary for the moment, and went down to breakfast after enjoying a long hot bath.

"You don't know how lovely it is to have copious hot water for a bath. In our ablutions one is very lucky to find the hot water geyser working properly. Mostly the water is tepid. Rho and I discovered a place to have a hot bath once, a hidden set of six bathrooms at the 'drome, and there seemed to be bags of hot water. It was probably erected when airmen and women still lived on site, before the bombings of 1940. Those bad raids on the 'drome are the reason why the airwomen are now living at the convent and the chaps went to their present billet at the old Hockeredge Hotel on the Canterbury road. I don't think many these days know of the existence of the secret wash room. Thank goodness for your old boiler in the kitchen, Mummy, it certainly heats the water beautifully, and keeps the kitchen and hall very warm, too."

"Yes, we are very thankful for that boiler. I dry my clothes on the pulley above it, and so it doesn't matter if it rains on wash-day. Actually, looking at the pulley, one end is lower than the other. It is all skew-whiffety, and I really must ask Joe to fix it before it falls down. By the way, I have already done some washing today. I

wonder if you would give me a hand to put it through
the mangle after breakfast, darling?"

"Certainly I will, Mummy. This boiled egg is deee-
licious – is it from one of our hens? By the way, do you
remember Auntie Ada or was it Ella, who would always
say an egg was deee-licious?"

"I think it was Ada who made that remark. Yes,
yours could be Gertie's egg. She is a very good layer,
they are usually a bit larger than Daisy's, and they both
make my cooking very tasty.

Your aunts are coming up from Plymouth to stay
later on in the summer, at least, I do hope they can. I
haven't seen them for so long. It all depends if there
will be travelling restrictions. They will probably come
by coach, but it is such a long way. The train is quicker;
however, in war time one can never be sure if they are
running or not."

"Oh, please let me know when they may come. I
will try and get a '48' to come home and see them. I do
love my dear aunties. They are so funny when they
disagree, all in their broad Devonshire accents!" Sarah
chuckled.

Sarah happily helped her Mother with the huge old
mangle, turning and pressing the bed linen through the
rubber rollers to remove as much moisture as possible
after it was boiled in the old copper. They hung the
sheets on the line and Sarah walked round the garden
in the sun.

"Daddy's vegetables and fruit are coming on a treat,"
she observed, bending down. "Looks like you are going
to have a good crop of strawberries this year; in fact,
some of the fruit has already set." She picked a
strawberry. "Mmm, this is heavenly, so sweet! The
blackcurrant bushes are really growing healthily too. I

love the little grass path around the back so that one may pick them easily! That blackcurrant smell so reminds me of home."

"Yes, the little grass path was a good idea of Daddy's, wasn't it? We may well get a bowl of those strawberries before you go back off leave, so let them be now!"

Hilda laughingly admonished her daughter, and they walked around together, looking at the lovely roses that were just coming out over the trellis, the perfume of which wafted in the morning air. Hilda's speciality blue delphiniums were looking superb; in fact, the whole garden was coming to its peak of May-time beauty. The old apple tree planted by Joe was fair bursting with blossom, enveloped in a drift of pink and white. Bees bumbled about in the flowers, fertilizing each bloom and sipping the nectar. Hilda said they would probably get a decent crop of apples in the autumn.

They went to see Gert and Daisy, the chickens, busily pecking about in their run. Sarah threw them some crumbs of bread she had saved, and said they had certainly grown, and Gert was much bigger than Daisy. They both had changed their feather colour slightly. Hilda said that was because they had gone through their first moult and often the feathers regrew with slightly different variations of colour. Joe had given them a caterpillar-ridden cabbage crown with plenty of green leaves and they were attacking it with gusto.

A pleasant morning passed. Joe came out with some deck-chairs and they all sat in the sun, and chatted.

After lunch the doorbell rang and there was Trel, looking very smart in a tan sports jacket, check shirt, green tie and cavalry twill trousers. His brown shoes shone with much polishing. He presented such a dapper image, and Sarah could smell his lovely cologne as she kissed him on the cheek and he came in.

"I'll just get my cardie and bag," she said, and ran upstairs. Trel waited in the hall.

Joe had gone down to his vegetable plot and Hilda came in from the garden. "Hello, would you like to come to Sunday lunch tomorrow?" She asked him.

Trel thanked Hilda and said he would be very pleased to do so. Just then Sarah ran down the stairs, carrying her cardigan and a scarf.

"Have fun, you two," Hilda called, and disappeared off into the kitchen.

"Bye, Mummy! We won't be late," shouted Sarah. "Cheery-o, Mrs. Todd!" called Trel.

Trel escorted her down the garden path to his waiting car, and they set off through Beckenham and West Wickham, towards Ightham.

Sarah chatted gaily in the car about helping her mother that morning. Trel kept asking her what she was doing at Manston, so she did speak about 'Flight' as she called Gary when she was away from the camp. He figured so much in her life, as her boss and her companion, that it was hard not to mention him. She did try hard to steer the conversation away from her RAF life, and kept asking Trel about the office, his colleagues and any interesting tit bits of bank gossip that there may be.

However, Trel was a quiet, private man, and wasn't one for gossiping, so couldn't really give Sarah many details about the staff. His tormentor, Mr. Cochrane, had been called up, making his working life easier without having to endure snide remarks all the time. Trel talked more about his Fire Watch duties, and the latest difficulties of travelling to work in war-torn London.

They reached the little village of Ightham and had a stroll in some woods near Ightham Mote. On their way back to the car they paused to gaze down into the water-filled moat and stood wondering at the amazing half-timbered old building. Trel told Sarah that Ightham Mote was renowned as one of the most beautiful ancient manor houses in England. It was built in 1320, and, amazingly, was still standing after nearly 700 years, despite Hitler's bombing raids so far. He said he had planned to take Sarah into the house as it would normally have been open to the public but, because of the war, sadly it was shut.

They walked around the moat, admiring as much of the outside of the ancient house as they could see, then on to the car. Trel drove them to Featherbed Lane for a bite to eat.

Over their meal of quiche and salad, they chatted.

"I am so lonely without you darling." Trel reached out and held Sarah's hand across the table.

"Oh, I know, I do realise that fact, and I'm really sorry. Oh, look over there at that bird, hasn't it got unusual plumage?"

Sarah did her best to distract Trel from getting what she called his 'grave face' on and talking about their future. She could not cope with that at the moment. Her heart was full of Gary, but she must not show it. She tried to be light and flippant, but that only seemed to annoy Trel, and he accused her of not being able to be serious for one minute. He accused her of being 'so casual' about everything.

She said that she was young, and there was enough sadness and devastation brought by the war that she didn't want to be serious at all.

Trel knew what he meant. He was so longing to make her his own, but she was like a flibbertigibbet, laughing and smiling and chatting about nothing in particular. He just gave up with a sigh at the effort of trying to pin her down.

Sarah steered the conversation round to his mother and aunt, asking after their health.

Trel replied that they had been to Cornwall for a while, and Sarah knew that he had joined them. It had been good to see his old Cornish friends, but he couldn't be away for long. In war time any leave from the bank was only very brief, as there was so much financial business to sort out with too few staff.

He said that there had been a serious raid on Truro railway station, the Germans tried to bomb a train, and several people were strafed by machine guns in the streets. So his mother and aunt had returned to Sydenham, by coach, as they both wanted to be near him.

"Auntie Mamie had a bit of a cold which had gone on to her chest," said Trel. "Luckily, she has recovered and is right as nine pence now, and is taking advantage of this lovely weather to do some spring cleaning and wash the curtains. I do worry about them both, however. Auntie is rather frail, and in her eighties now."

"I know how you feel, Trel. I fret a lot about Mummy and Daddy. Mummy does suffer from bronchitis most winters, and Daddy - well, he is not a strong man and works so hard being an Elder at his church, as well as his job at the bank, and of course tending our lovely garden. Isn't it funny that all our life our parents worried about and cared for us, and now they are getting on in years, and it is our turn to worry and care for them."

"Actually, darling Toodles, I would like you to be fully occupied in caring for me, and for any children we may have. So, how about it? Let me at least put a ring on your finger so that no marauding amorous American airman may think you are fancy free."

Trel leaned forward and smiled at Sarah. She inwardly shuddered: he had very skilfully had turned the conversation around from his mother and aunt to their future, and she felt rather trapped.

"I am not interested in amorous Yanks. They are loud and brash, not my cup of tea at all, although it is fun to have a bit of a flirt with them. Flight said we WAAFs should give them a wide berth."

As soon as she had said that, she realised that was like a red rag to a bull.

"I mean a bit of a smile and a joke is good for morale." She wriggled out of her gaff swiftly. "One cannot go around with a miserable face. Flight instructs us to gee each other up, and we have to make light work of the sheer slog of everyday RAF life, where airmen are lost each day on bombing raids. A bit of harmless banter each day enables us to get through our work and, hopefully, this war."

"I just don't like the thought of other men flirting with you, darling. Surely you can understand that?"

Trel sat back and got his wallet out to pay the bill. Sarah said nothing for a while, realising she was on sticky ground. She had meant to tell Trel about her brush with death but she realised that would worry him unnecessarily and in telling would also bring Gary to the fore as a hero, probably upsetting Trel on two counts, so she just kept quiet about it. He already knew about the bike incident, and as it was only natural that her boss should look out for her, and he accepted that rescue.

They walked to the car and she commented on the glorious sunset, turning the world golden as it shone through the trees. Trel held her hand and said that nothing would take his eyes away from her that evening, as to him she was more attractive than any sunset.

Near the car he stopped and kissed her.

This is very peculiar, I should feel something, she thought, but I feel rather numb. His lips are soft, his moustache still tickles me, his gentleman's cologne is as attractive as ever, in fact, all is the same as normal, but I don't feel anything inside. She returned his hug: she did still care for him, but she felt so mixed up.

They drove home through the golden evening, and Sarah tried her best to be cheerful and talk about anything that came into her head. Trel was a little quiet. He could feel that there was a strange coolness coming between them, and he didn't know how to take it. He thought it was probably his fault. He realised he must not push her into making any plans for the future even though he was desperate to make her his fiancée.

They reached her home and Sarah thanked him for a lovely evening, and said that her mother wanted him to come to lunch the following day.

"How about you?" He looked quizzically at her, holding her hand. "Do you want me to come?"

"Yes, I would love you to come, as long as you leave your serious face at home." Sarah playfully tapped his nose. "How about a game of tennis in the morning? I need the exercise and I can skip the morning service and go to evensong instead."

"All right, I will call for you about eleven tomorrow. Then we can go to the Forest Hill tennis courts, gosh, that will certainly be fun!" He leant over and kissed her, stroking her hair fondly and smiling.

"I do love you Toodles, so very much, you know." Sarah kissed him on the cheek, and got out of the car. Trel walked round and opened the garden gate for her. "Goodnight, darling," he said.

"Goodnight Trel, sleep tight" she replied, and with a cheery wave she ran to the front door and let herself in.

CHAPTER FORTY-ONE

"My mind is in a whirl"

Sarah's ten days' leave passed quickly. She spent a lot of time with her parents, going out with them for lunch at Cobb's restaurant and over to nearby Lee, to visit Monica and her children. Baby Bev was growing fast. Sarah noticed a great difference in her, she was chuckling merrily to herself and her dark hair which had grown quite a bit was in tight curls. Her eyes had stayed grey-green, just like mine, thought Sarah proudly. Penny had grown, too, and was very sweet playing with her little sister.

Sarah made sure that she gave some of her time to her father. She took their home-made green garden bench down to the vegetable plot as Joe was working and sat on it whilst chatting to him: 'chewing the fat' Joe called it, as he leaned on his spade and smoked his pipe. He did note at the time that she was mentioning her boss 'Flight' quite a lot, but just accepted it as part of her life in the RAF, especially as the chap seemed to be taking good care of his daughter. He made a mental note to remember to pen the letter of thanks for saving her life. Both he and his wife had been horrified at Sarah's tale of being attacked and shot at, but realised that they had to accept this danger was part of being at war. So they didn't dwell on the subject, but kept it in their hearts.

She went with Hilda to watch Joe play bowls in a local park. He was very good at it, and she thought how dashing her father looked in his bowling 'whites'.

Sarah presented her mother with the completed embroidered table-cloth and watched with pleasure as

Hilda opened it out, smiled and admired her neat stitching. She knew that anything she made was doubly precious to her mother, because of the time and effort that had been put into its inception. Although, for Sarah, carrying out her embroidery was no effort: she just loved creating flowers with the coloured silks, and Hilda was absolutely delighted with it.

Hilda and Sarah went shopping in Chiesmans in Lewisham. She had saved up some of her clothing rations so she could buy Sarah a couple of pretty summer frocks. They had lunch out, and after their repast enjoyed choosing a pair of light summer sling-backs to go with the dresses.

On a few evenings she went out with Trel, when he could spare the time from his fire-watching duty.

Fortuitously, during her leave, there were only two night-time raids, entailing more card games in the Twentyman's cellar. In general, their short family time together had been as relaxed as it could be in the war-time suburbs.

She managed to catch up with her best friend Joyce, who was also on leave. They went off together and had lunch in a café. Sarah really wanted to sound Joyce out about her feelings for two different men.

Joyce was always a great laugh; she had a tremendous sense of the ridiculous, and teased Sarah when she heard her story.

"Coo!" said Joyce. "Two men after you at once! Just fancy that! I don't suppose you have seen Barbara this leave, have you? I saw her recently, and she was also in a two and eight about some naval chap or other. You both should keep your hearts well and truly locked up, and just have fun with no emotional involvement, as I do."

Sarah agreed with Joyce, but explained it wasn't that easy – feelings just happened.

"I know, you duffer! I do understand that if someone had saved my life and was very handsome to boot, well, I could never resist a man I uniform anyway." She gave her friend a knowing look.

"The main thing to realise, my very dear old pal, is that the answer to this situation is obvious, and two main facts point to the sensible route to take. One chap is married with children, one chap is single, eligible and a dear, (Barbara is very fond of your Trel you know). So the way forward is clear: you stay with Trel, keep him happy on leave, and have fun with Gary while away, but just don't get too involved.

That is called hedging your bets! None of us have really had the chance to experience serious relationships yet, and I know that if one does not keep one's heart intact, one is asking for a load of misery when things go wrong. Your Trel is a good steady chap, and anyone can see he is head over heels in love with you. Why, you have been walking out for at least a couple of years already, and, truth be told, Trel has the patience of a saint to wait around for you! You are lucky that most of the eligible women at the bank are away at war – he is a dashing handsome chap. you know, and a very good catch. After all, he doesn't drink to excess and I should imagine he is very good with money. You would have a very comfortable life as his wife."

Sarah knew her old friend spoke sense, and she pondered over her wise words. However, something was about to happen that confused and challenged her loyalties even more.

That terrifying moment came when Sarah knew that Trel had been late in having his evening meal at Cobb's restaurant and, to her horror the very next morning, word came through that Cobb's had been bombed. Sarah's heart was in her mouth, and she shared her worries with her parents, who were also concerned as they had grown close to Trel.

They tried to find out more information from neighbours. Captain Pendred came up the hill and said he had heard that the restaurant had gone, so Joe walked up Sydenham High Street to look at the devastation. The whole of the back of the department store where the restaurant used to be was now just a pile of rubble. The front was still standing, with its cupola announcing 'Walter J. Cobb and Company 1902', and some parts of the department store were unscathed, but they looked forlorn with their windows blown out.

Joe sent an arrow prayer up to the Lord for Trel's safety, but came back looking very worried as he could get no information about survivors. The kitchen and waiting staff were all killed, and he didn't relish telling that to his daughter.

After a few agonising hours, finally Trel managed to get the time to ring Sarah from work and reassure her that he was unhurt. It had been a close shave, he told her, as he was the very last person to eat a meal there. The raid had happened very soon after he left. She cried when she heard his voice, and he was moved by her worried response, she does really have feelings for me after all, he thought happily.

The frightening incident at gave Sarah a sharp jolt. I do still care for Trel, she thought, and she knew she would have been devastated if he had been killed or injured. This narrow escape made her even more mixed up inside, and her emotions were all in a turmoil. Is it really possible to love two people at once, she wondered, because that seems to be my lot! I am beginning to feel like piggy in the middle.

Now that Trel knew she still did care for him, he realised that in order to keep Sarah in his life he should endeavour to make their time together light and jolly and quell his natural desire for future commitment from her. Thus he bent over backwards to make her happy, and took her to a Harold Lloyd comedy at The Rink cinema, so they had a good laugh together, and to a couple of local dances. He knew she loved to dance, and sure enough they thoroughly enjoyed their evenings together before she was due to go back to Manston.

However, Trel felt in his heart that there was still something coming between them, marring their former happiness, which he found very hard to understand. She has changed, he thought – all because of this ruddy war. In fact sometimes he felt so miserable that he even considered finishing their relationship altogether. I cannot tie her to me in any way, he thought sadly, she always seems so casual. He knew he was ridiculously jealous but hadn't a clue how to control his feelings. Better to end it, even though it seems that she cares for me, then I could have peace of mind and I needn't worry what she is getting up to while she is away from me.

He had made his mind up to do just that, however, when she slipped round to say goodbye to him she was so sweet, and brought him some tobacco for his pipe and a magazine. After her visit he felt better, and told himself not to be so sensitive. Once again he put his emotions on hold.

"I'll write to you, and I hope you will write to me? I am so glad you are safe," was Sarah's parting shot. Her farewell kiss was tender on his cheek, as she left him to go and pack her things for her return to Manston.

Reaching home she closed the front door behind her, leant against it and thought how difficult it was to have feelings for two men. With Trel she felt she was living a lie, because at least she could be honest with Gary – he knew about Trel, but Trel could only really suspect things. He had no proof, and that was the truth.

Sarah was not a dishonest girl and didn't like deceiving anyone. Coming home and seeing Trel again always put her emotions into such a muddle. She thought a lot about the advice Joyce had given to her, but felt that it didn't really help. Sense goes out of the window when one is so attracted to the wrong person.

"Is that you, dear?" Hilda called from the front room where she was listening to some singing on the wireless. "Do you like Mario Lanza darling? He is my favourite, he has such a beautiful tenor voice you know."

Hilda put down her mending and patted the chesterfield seat beside her for Sarah to join her.

"Come and tell me where you have been."

"Oh I popped up to say goodbye to Trel. You know I really do love him in my way, and couldn't bear anything to happen to him."

Sarah went and sat by her mother, putting her emotional difficulties to one side, and they chatted pleasantly until it was time to go to bed.

CHAPTER FORTY-TWO

"Like shadows on the grassland"

It was the beginning of June and a lovely sunny day
when Sarah watched and waved to her parents from the
train, which steamed out of Penge East Station. Her
mother, with tears in her eyes stood trying to smile,
while her father doffed his hat and waved it through the
steam.

She sat back in her carriage, blowing her nose and
wiping her eyes. I just hate to leave them, she thought.

She changed trains at Bromley South for the fast
service to Westgate. As she waited for her train the
magnificent Golden Arrow locomotive, splendid in
green livery with shining diagonal arrow across the
front, roared at speed through the station, bound for
Dover. It made the waiting passengers step back as the
wind whipped around them taking newspapers, hats
and stirring up dust into the air. Someone said it was a
special one-off run, ferrying troops to the south coast,
as the regular Golden Arrow service had been
suspended during the war.

There were a few airmen and soldiers on Sarah's
coast-bound train, as well as civilian passengers, some
of whom were stoically taking time off to visit the coast
on such a lovely day.

Sarah settled down into a corner of the carriage,
having been helped to heave her kit bag up into the
luggage rack. This contained clean clothes lovingly
laundered by Hilda, and her new summer frocks. She
pulled out a packet of egg, tomato and cress sandwiches
and a large slab of her mother's fruit cake. She tried to

read a book her mother had lent to her, but her mind was thinking about Trel and Gary.

She knew she couldn't wait to see Gary again, but still wanted to hear from Trel. She sighed, and thought, I'm too young for all this serious romantic nonsense. Joyce is quite right: I should just treat them like a couple of boyfriends and have fun with them with no heavy involvement. She decided to do just that. From now on she would keep her emotions firmly in check.

However, most of her resolution went out of the window when she leaned out, hanging onto her cap, and espied Gary waiting for her on Westgate Station.

She alighted from the train. He took her kit bag and whispered, "I just couldn't wait to see you again, so I found out when your train would arrive. I'm absolutely dying to kiss you, but we must wait for a less public place. I have missed you so much! You look really well, darling."

They walked along the sunny platform and out of the station. Gary had borrowed a jeep, which Sarah thought great fun if a trifle bumpy! They parked on sea front where they sat for a while.

He took her in his arms, knocking her cap off, and kissed her resoundingly. Her whole body reacted to him. Her tummy turned over and her heart was beating madly. She remained in his arms for a few moments and knew that this was where she wanted to be, and that dear Trel did not make her thrill this way.

"How are you?" She asked Gary when they finally sat back. She held his hand and stroked it softly. "Oh, look! You have my lipstick all over your face!" Sarah laughed and wiped his face with her hankie.

"I don't mind at all. I have been totally bereft without you, my little sweetness. Now you are back, my

cup runneth over with delight!" He kissed her again.
"How I have missed your smile, and your absence in
the Admin hut has been hard to bear. Just knowing you
will be back in your seat just a few yards from me each
day makes me feel so happy. By the way, we have been
devilishly busy. I can tell you now, because I know you
have signed the Official Secrets Act and will not
breathe a word. We are not parked near any other
vehicles so I can safely explain:

You will notice a lot of information coming through
the office. You may spot the name 'Operation
Overlord' – it's the code name for the Allied invasion
of North West Europe, commencing with the planned
invasion of France. This should take place very soon
on what will be known as D-Day. I won't mention the
actual date, but you will find this out when you return
to work. After a couple of missed opportunities, largely
because of bad weather, at last all systems are go. This
is the project with which I have been very much
involved, and about which I could not tell you until
now. This was the reason for my trip to Dover, where
troops are secretly being mustered. I probably will be
needed on standby to pilot whatever kites may be
required. I think Typhoons will be involved, so I will
not be around after tomorrow in the office. I have got a
lot of admin to tie up beforehand – although no leave
chits, as all leave has been cancelled for a while!

All your WAAF chums will be in the know. They
have only been given sketchy information, for safety's
sake, so you may talk among yourselves about it as long
as you are very, very discreet, and only when you are in
the convent dorm. Do not say anything, even in front of
the nuns, please. There must be no chattering in public
places. This is an extremely important strategic move

and, if successful as planned, could well go towards ending this blessed war."

"Goodness me! That is amazing, I cannot wait to find out more," said Sarah, wide-eyed. "Oh, how wonderful it would be if the end of the war was in sight. Actually, thinking about it, I saw the Golden Arrow thundering through Bromley station, full of troops, and I wondered what was happening. Now I understand."

"Well, this op may well contribute greatly to finishing this bloody conflict once and for all, but there is a long way to go yet. I can tell you one interesting piece of information," said Gary, mysteriously. "That is, as a secret act of preparation, the BBC ran a competition for French beach holiday snaps. It was actually a ruse to gather as much information as possible about beaches, so that the choice of the right landing sites were made."

"That is very clever, very few would suspect anything," said Sarah. "How is Manston going to be involved?"

"Well, we are designated as an invasion support group. Kites are to be scrambled; as I said, they will mainly be Typhoons from Manston. They are all standing ready, in order to be a formidable enemy to the German army if it makes any moves towards shifting tanks and other vehicles to the front, once they realise what is happening. The Typhoons will make their lives very difficult.

This is all to be a big surprise for old Jerry! He is going to get his nose bloodied, and no mistake. If it all goes to plan it will be England's largest seaborne invasion in history. Over 7,000 ships are to take part – in fact, the naval part is code named 'Operation Neptune'. Rather apt, don't you think? This is a serious attempt to win the war! The information re several false planned ops have been allowed to get through to the Germans, to confuse them, so hopefully they will not be expecting the Allied invasion. The date has been fixed because the tides are right; as are the phases of the moon, to enable the best vision. If the weather holds it should be perfect timing."

Sarah put her hand to his lips. "Dearest, sorry to interrupt! The plans sound really fascinating, but I really think I must away back to the convent now."

"Sorry, darling! I forgot you have had a journey, and must be tired. I just love to be back in your company, and the time just whizzes by when I am alone with you. You are right; I think it is time to get you back to the convent for a meal and to an early night, as tomorrow there will be a tremendous lot of typing. Just think you, with the others, will be carrying out important parts in 'Operation Overlord', and you should be proud that you are oiling the wheels (so to speak) towards victory, through your nimble fingers figuratively walking miles on that old typewriter."

They had another kiss and cuddle, then Gary took her to the convent, and he went back to his billet at the Hockeredge Hotel.

CHAPTER FORTY-THREE

"These times should be so complete"

The next day Rhona and Sarah got their bikes out of
the shed together and rode to Manston. Some of the
way they could ride abreast, and Rhona asked Sarah
how her leave had gone.

"Lovely thanks, Rho: the folks are well and we
managed to spend some quality time together."

"And Trel? How is he? Did you see him?"

Sarah couldn't answer for a while, as they came to a
narrow lane and had to ride one after the other.

They reached the 'drome, dismounted, and walked
the last bit together to the hut.

"Yes, I spent time with him, but it was very difficult
to steer him away from any serious talk – of marriage,
and our future together. He just wants to get engaged to
me, to keep me away from the Yanks!"

"Well, it is a good thing he has the wrong end of the
stick, then! Have you seen Gary yet? He has been
extremely busy with 'Operation Overlord', as I expect
you know; in fact, my girl, you won't know what has hit
you at work. We have more to do than ever before. I
think wars run on paperwork, you know!"

Rhona laughed, and wheeled her bike into the shed.

"We will have to chat later, we are here now."

They went into the hut, already a hive of industry.
They saluted Gary, who stood up and returned their
salute.

"Morning, girls," he said, winking at Sarah. "Good
to have you back, Miss Langman. We have missed
your cheerful presence, and I especially have missed

your lovely coffee, so perhaps you would be so kind as to fetch me a cup?"

Sarah scurried away, smiling, to make the coffee, and the morning wore on without incident. Gary managed to discreetly slip her a note asking her to walk back with him that evening.

Jill, Sarah, Rhona, Marge and Ellie were just settling down in their desks after a very quick lunch in the Mess, when the wail of the air raid siren started its mournful cry.

"Right, everybody to the shelter, NOW!" Gary shouted, and all ran like hell and dived down into the underground shelter.

They scarcely had time to get their breath back when they heard the explosions of bombs dropping. One explosion was very loud and close to their shelter. They huddled together. "Blow this for a lark!" one shivering new recruit observed. The other girls tried to reassure her that all would be fine.

When finally the All Clear sounded, they came out to see that a large crater now gaped near the shelter, and they had to climb over clods of earth and rubble to reach the hut. Ellie stumbled and fell over. Jill, who was near to her, helped her up. "Another pair of RAF-issue passion killer stockings have bitten the dust," Ellie said ruefully as she brushed herself down. "I have more ladder than stocking now!"

Gary had gone to a different shelter and, when they were back at their desks in the hut, he said that he had ascertained that several German Dornier Do 17s suddenly came in low from the Pegwell Bay direction and swept round the 'drome twice, dropping bombs. He said that Hurricanes were scrambled to chase them off, but it was extremely windy and they had a job to take off. They finally managed to get airborne and saw the Dorniers away from Manston and out to sea.

The rest of the afternoon was fairly incident free, just extremely busy, and all were very pleased when it was time to knock off. Gary waited for most of the others to leave. Sarah told Rhona that she was going back with Gary, so Rhona departed with the others.

Gary and Sarah wheeled their bikes along because of the strong winds, and both had to put their caps in their saddle bags, once they were off the 'drome, because they kept blowing away. They decided to go to their favourite Pinot Café in Minnis Bay. They struggled to cycle against the wind, but eventually got there and settled down to order a meal.

"I don't know about you, but I am famished." Gary perused the menu. "I feel like a good old-fashioned fry up. Now, what about you, my sweet?"

"I could definitely murder egg and chips, maybe with a sausage if there is one, and some tomatoes."

"I am also having chips with mine, as I don't know when I will get another square meal. Tea OK for you?"

He ordered a pot of tea and some toast. "Bit like breakfast!" Sarah remarked, smiling.

"I must admit I love a fry-up now and again. Beats the runny gravy and soggy vegetables of the Mess! I just long for a good bit of fat now and again."

Their pot of tea arrived and Sarah poured out two cups and said "Do you know that I have given up sugar? I simply cannot bear saccharine, so I decided as it is so difficult to get sugar on ration that I would give it up. It is not good for one, anyway."

"Well, I'm sorry, but I cannot bear tea without sugar. It is so bitter, I find." Gary put in two heaped spoonsful and stirred vigorously.

"Now then, tell me all about your leave. How did it go? How are your parents? How is Trel?"

Sarah told Gary of the outings she enjoyed with her mother, and how she visited Monica and the children. She hadn't managed to see George, sadly, but she did have time to watch her father play bowls.

"Sounds like you had a good relaxing time. Were there any bad raids while you were in Sydenham?"

"One or two, but luckily it was fairly quiet most of the time. However, I must tell you, I had a scare when Trel nearly got killed in a bombing raid." She explained what had happened over their meal, which had arrived steaming hot and looked most appetising.

"So you see, although I missed you all of the time, when I nearly lost Trel, it made me realise that I still care for him too, and that has made me feel very confused."

"You poor dear, I understand completely. It must have been a terrible shock for you, knowing he was the very last to leave the restaurant. Why, I would be in pieces if Helen were hurt in any way. I know she has no love for me, but she is the mother of my children, and my wife, and naturally one cares."

Gary sighed as he tucked into his meal.

Sarah paused in her eating. "This is really so tasty! Cycling always makes me famished. Oh, Gary, you are so perceptive. You seem to be just on my wavelength, and I feel I can share anything and everything with you. You are so compassionate and understanding about Trel – I don't think for a minute he would be like this about you. He would never be able to comprehend that it is possible for one person to care for two people at once.

When I am with you everything feels so different, I feel truly alive and just want to be near you every moment of the day. I don't feel that with Trel, even though he loves me so much and keeps asking me to get engaged. I am very fond of him, and he wants us to marry as soon as possible. He thinks I fancy the Yanks! He wants to tie me to him, so he feels I won't stray with any other airmen – whom he presumes are lining up to take me away from him!"

"I'm not surprised he thinks that way! You do have such a lovely smile, you know," Gary interrupted. "Sorry, darling, do go on."

"I think he has felt there is a little coolness between us. I do try to act normally, but I keep thinking of you when he kisses me. His caresses do not make me tingle as yours do; his kisses are nice, but don't make my heart beat fast. I feel very pressurized by him. I daren't talk to him about you saving my life, he was jealous when he heard you had taken care of me after the bike accident. It is all very difficult, really, and I am not good at handling the situation. I have never had two men in my life before and it is all very, well, wearing!" Sarah laughed and made a face.

"Also," she continued, "The plain fact is, we women can only really *love* one chap at a time. That is totally different from just caring for someone. I now have learned that fact. It is all in the kissing, you know – one kiss is pleasant, but the other means so much more. I really don't know how some girls string along a load of chaps. I know I really couldn't cope! I would rather be with you and honestly finish with Trel, but as you are married with children, well, we just have to take our happiness while we are here together.

There can be no future for us, and that is the plain fact, as much as I hate the thought, because all I want to do is be by your side. If I stopped seeing Trel – which would be fairer to him, even though it would hurt him – then I may not get such a chance for a home and family eventually, with such a nice eligible chap. That sounds totally selfish, I know, how I hate being dishonest!"

Sarah tilted her head to one side and looked at Gary across the table. He immediately reached out and held her hand.

"Maybe I am not being fair to you, darling. Telling you that I love you has put you in an awkward situation with your Trel. I feel sorry for the poor chap, I must say: he must miss you terribly, and then when you go home on leave he perceives a coolness in your demeanour. One cannot choose with whom one falls in love, it just happens, and I knew the moment you walked into the hut on your very first day that you would signify greatly in my life. I had no idea you felt that way about me, too." They gazed at each other's eyes across the table, then continued to eat in silence for a while.

"You see my darling, dearest, sweet one, I cannot offer you any future. Even though I, also, find it difficult when you talk about being with Trel.

If I just had Helen, well, I would grab my second chance of happiness with you gladly. You already mean so much to me, and your caring for me too has just turned my life around. You have brought light and joy into my lonely existence, and to know that you love me, well, it seems just unbelievable, really and means the world to me.

Helen has made it quite plain that she cares not a bit for me. However, my little Polly and Jared are also my life. I would never hurt them, so I couldn't contemplate divorce; although it has crossed my mind several times, and, I hasten to reassure you, that was long before you came along. I have been very vulnerable to falling in love with someone else, just from the sheer longing for human warmth, since Helen has been so cold towards me."

Sarah drank deeply from her teacup and said:

"I confided in my best friend Joyce, at home, about us, and her advice to me was very sensible. She said, I should not finish with Trel, at the moment, just have fun with you, knowing that there can be no future in our relationship."

"I think that is the only option we have," said Gary sadly. "We know we can only be together like this as long as possible, and we will just have to make do with the little time we have together. Really, our days are numbered. Therefore, I think she is right in advising you to keep Trel happy. He is probably going to be your future – as much as it makes my heart break to say so."

They finished their meal. Sarah had a tear in her eye but she hid it from Gary. I love him so much, she thought, but I must let him go one day, but not yet, please – not yet!

The wind had dropped, so they were able to ride back to the convent.

"Remember, I will be away for a few days now," Gary reminded her as they parked their bikes and stood together in each other's arms in the shrubbery, holding each other tightly. Gary stroked Sarah's head and, after kissing her, placed her cap back on her head.

"Don't be sad, little one, we will have lots of good times together yet. We will have outings to look forward to, and dances, I simply must jitter-bug with you again, soon. We will go to the cinema, perhaps back to Canterbury. We will really make sure that we enjoy this summer of 1944 together, to the best of our ability. After all, this blessed war has actually brought us together. I really did not want to come to Kent when I was posted here, and now I don't want to be anywhere else! Goodnight now my love, sweet dreams."

They parted at the convent gates with a smile and wave.

CHAPTER FORTY-FOUR

*"When problems become pressing
and my mind is in a whirl"*

The next few days held an uneasy air of expectation. It was as if all the staff were supercharged, and there was a very strange atmosphere at the 'drome.

The girls reported to work as usual. Sarah was sent to the Post Office to fill in. She enjoyed working over there, as it used different skills and got her away from her typing for a while. Gary was away – she had no idea where, but knew it was something to do with D-Day. Flt.Sgt. Brown was in charge at the hut, which made the girls very fed up. Sarah was very glad she didn't have to endure working under him. He was such a sour puss, a stickler for regulations and very particular. Everything had to be just perfect, which sometimes was not humanly possible in the little amount of time allotted, considering the burden of work there was to complete.

Everyone was asking for information at the 'drome. All were hoping and praying that the invasion was going as planned, but not much real news filtered back to them.

A couple of Messerschmitts, returning from a London raid, flew in low and offloaded their bombs onto the 'drome, and strafed the ground with machine gun fire. Luckily the tannoy had warned everyone and all had taken cover in time, so they didn't do much damage.

Later that evening Rhona and Sarah were alone in the common room getting their gas masks ready for next day inspection. This gave them a chance to have a chat, as the other girls had gone to an ENSA show. The entertainers had come down to Manston especially to boost morale, but neither of the girls had felt like going.

"Now then, Sarah, we have some quiet time together, so how was your time with Trel?" asked Rhona, cleaning the visor of her gas mask.

"Pass me that cloth, dear," said Sarah. "I cannot get this dratted thing clean. I'll tell you what happened on leave. It made things doubly difficult for my emotions, I must say! Trel was nearly killed in a bombing raid! He had just about left a local restaurant after his evening meal, and he was actually the very last person to dine there when it was hit. I knew he often went there for an evening meal, and next day I was beside myself with worry, as I heard that the kitchen and waiting staff had been killed. I waited in agony for ages, because I had no way of contacting him, and finally it seems he was allowed to ring me from the office as he realised that I may be worried. Oh, Rho! It was so good to hear his voice. You have no idea how I felt when I heard him say 'Hallo'."

"Good heavens! I can imagine how you felt, but that means you still love him?" Rhona looked up at her friend, pausing in her vigorous polishing.

"Well, yes I do in a way. Oh, really, Rho, I am so mixed up! This incident made things a lot worse in my head. I know I am in love with Gary – he just makes me tingle when he kisses me – but I also know I care a lot for Trel. I am fond of him in a different way, that's all! Do you understand me, because I'm blowed if I do?"

"Of course I do. It is a very sticky situation in which to find oneself and all to do with the chemistry between twin souls."

"My best friends at home have advised me to enjoy my time with Gary while I can, knowing that there is no future for us. In the meantime, I have to keep Trel on a back burner, as he probably holds my best chance of marrying and having children of my own when this war is through."

"Do you think you will be able to keep your emotions in check?" Rhona looked anxiously at her friend. "I mean, the advice is very good, and you do have to think of Gary's children in all this, but this won't stop you loving him and wanting to be with him. You do run the risk of being very hurt one day, you know. Will you then really and truly be able to give Trel the love and support he needs as his wife?"

"Well, to be honest with you I really have no idea how I shall feel when it comes to marrying Trel. I suppose I shall just have to keep a stiff upper lip and not think of Gary. I mean, I would not want him to be parted in any way from his children It is the thought of those two little ones that will help my resolve. For the moment, anyway, I am jolly well going to enjoy this time we have together. It is too late to say 'do not let one's emotions get involved', because they already are, so I shall endeavour to keep things light between us – although Gary may not agree with that! Oh, goodness, Rho, quite honestly I have no idea how things will pan out. I am just living for today, and the chance of being near Gary."

"How true that is, Sarah, we don't know which day may be our last. Think of what happened to you when you were walking home. You have to take your happiness whenever you can, these days, so go for it, and you know I will support you in any way I can – you can be assured of that – and, at the very least, you can pour your heart out to me in complete confidence."

"Yes, Rho, you are such a dear, thank you so much. It means a lot to me, having you as a *confidante*." Sarah got up from the table and went round to give her friend a big hug. "Now, tell me – what has been happening while I have been away?"

"Well, one of the best things was the Camp Talent Show."

"Oh, no! Did I miss you and Ellie tripping the light fantastic? What a shame! How did you get on?"

"We weren't booed off the stage, at least, and I think we did really well, coming third in the dancing section of the show. At least we kept our timing together and made it to the end without tripping each other up. It was really great fun!

Your Gary did a turn too: he played Chopin's Polonaise in A-flat and then turned it into the latest song, which I love, '*Till the end of Time*'. I think he was singing that for you, you know. He won his heat, he was very popular, and of course he is such a very good-looking chap and a talented pianist."

"Well I never did! He had told me some time ago that he was no good at playing because he couldn't find anywhere to practise and didn't want to make a spectacle of himself. What a shame I missed him – I would have clapped and clapped. Maybe he will sing privately for me sometime.

Right, that's it! I've had enough of this cleaning. My gas mask is in A1 condition and my buttons and shoes are polished within an inch of their lives, so how about some cocoa and then bed?"

"Sounds a great idea, Sarah. My hands are worn out with rubbing and I've got polish all over them. Actually,

I think someone was taking photos at the talent show, so you may well see Gary playing the piano in them and even, perhaps, Ellie and I tap dancing in the camp rag. They will probably also be pinned up on the Mess notice board."

They made their way to the kitchen for cocoa, and took it up to bed with them.

"Oh, by the way, Jill and Jerry's wedding is in two weeks' time. The dress is finished, and we have been helping her with the last-minute preparations. She doesn't know it, but the girls are going to form a guard of honour for her as she comes out of the church. We will all sit at the back and then slip out as the organ voluntary plays. I think Jerry's airmen friends will also be joining in – it will be a long guard of honour!"

"Oh, I shall look forward to that," smiled Sarah. "A spring wedding. How lovely and romantic."

"You know she wants you for her bridesmaid? Oops! I can see you didn't know! Oh gosh – me and my big mouth. Perhaps I shouldn't have said anything. Please act surprised when she approaches you about it.

The reception will be over the road from St. Clements Church at 'The Jolly Farmer', you know, the pub we went to that time after church. Your Gary is a friend of Jerry's, isn't he? I think he is going to be the best man."

With those happy thoughts they got ready for bed.

CHAPTER FORTY-FIVE

"Then the look, the well-known sign,
when you placed your hand in mine"

It was at least a couple of weeks before Gary was back
at his desk in the Admin hut. Sarah had finished her
relief job at the post office so they were working
together again. Neither had been home on leave for a
while, and things had got back into a more normal
routine slog of paperwork after the frenetic pace and
burden of work at the beginning of June.

Gary still couldn't say much about the invasion to
the girls, who quizzed him about it, because of security,
but he could say that it had been a major offensive
against the Germans, and was successful in that the
Allies now had a strong foothold in Normandy.

Manston planes had played their part valiantly in
maintaining Allied air superiority. Altogether, Gary
said, over one thousand three hundred RAF planes had
been involved from bases all over England, as well as
over four thousand ships and several thousand smaller
craft. Some one hundred and fifty-six thousand Allied
troops had landed on the five chosen French invasion
beaches. He had heard that Winston Churchill himself
had wanted to board a ship and sit in the English
Channel, watching developments, but when the King
also said he would join him, Winston realised what a
fool-hardy thing it would be and stayed in London, in
order to dissuade His Majesty. Mr. Churchill had
hailed the invasion and said that it had been
"undoubtedly the most complicated and difficult
operation that has ever taken place."

The June weather had turned really warm and the girls were sweltering in the hut. They had, with permission, discarded their heavy uniform jackets, and wore short-sleeved blue blouses with ties – which they hated at this time of the year. They had all the windows open to catch any breeze, but the sun beat down mercilessly on the tin roof. Gary had managed to find a small fan which he set up to blow cooler air across the hut. This helped a little to make them feel more comfortable as they worked.

When they walked over to the Mess for lunch they were wolf-whistled by passing airmen, who were not used to seeing WAAFs without their jackets.

Although the warm days were more enjoyable than the winter, the best part was later in the day, when it became a bit cooler. The evenings, in the main, were long and beautiful. The sunsets over the sea at West Bay were magnificent to behold, with stunning mixtures of pinks, oranges and yellow, interspersed with little white clouds streaking across the waning sun, which threaded a path of shimmering gold across the calm dark sea.

Gary accompanied Sarah in walking along the cliffs most evenings. It was very pleasant up there in the fresh sea air on the cliff tops, as the barbed wire protecting the beaches was out of sight and, if it were not for the presence of warships making their way out to the English Channel, there would be little to tell that there was a war on.

It was good to get away from everyone, a quiet time for them to be together. Although there were other couples walking in the evening sun, most of them walked towards Margate to the pubs. Gary and Sarah wanted some privacy, so set off westwards towards the quieter Epple Bay. This enabled them just to enjoy each other's company, as they had enough of being with others during the day. They spent a lot of time when they were well away from anyone else just clasped in each other's arms, romantically. They watched, transfixed, as the setting sun created a magical door effect as it reached the sea. Sarah whispered that looked like the portal into a fantasy land of light and joy, and it seemed as if one could just row a boat out and disappear through it. They remained together, watching the sunset making a path of gold across the sea until it disappeared, leaving many pale yellow sunbeams reaching up into the darkening sky.

During their private times they often chatted about music, and whenever possible attended local concerts, enjoying being together and being transported by their shared musical passion.

One magical moment when they were alone Gary sang '*Till the end of time*' for Sarah, as he had at the Talent Show. The romantic tune based on the Chopin Polonaise, in A-flat Op. 53. Gary said he could also play the original tune, but he loved the adapted song with its very poignant words:

> *"Till the end of time as long as stars are in the blue*
> *As long as there is a spring*
> *and birds do sing I'll go on loving you."*

His rich Welsh voice sang out to her. He told her that this was the way he felt about her, and she said she felt the same. Their feelings for each other seemed to deepen with every day that passed.

They went on bike rides to Broadstairs and walked around the streets lined with Victorian houses, trying to

imagine Charles Dickens writing in 'Bleak House' up
on the cliff top, over-looking Viking bay.

They rode past the southern outskirts of the 'drome
and observed the Mosquitoes parked up, with their tails
high in the air. Gary explained that they had come in
on the grass runway, and their nose wheels were so
heavy that they had stuck in the mud, making their tail
ends stick up. They reminded Sarah of birds with
heads down, tails up, pecking at corn.

Another evening, when they were cycling along by
Cliffsend, they heard a low rumble and a Lancaster
bomber came in very low over Pegwell Bay near
Hellfire corner. It obviously had been involved in a
bombing raid and was peppered with shot and
damaged. They watched transfixed as it came in lower
and lower, bits of its fuselage were falling off. It slewed
onto the grass near to them; luckily it came to a
standstill, and all of the crew managed to get out safely.
Gary went over to see if he could do anything for them,
but considering their crash landing, amazingly the chaps
were all OK, and they radioed to Manston for
assistance.

The two of them left the crew and rode on to
Ramsgate, parking their bikes on the cliffs. As the
evening grew darker they could make out flashes of
light, gunfire and explosions coming from France.
Allied troops had made great inroads into Normandy,
but there was still tremendous battles raging in north-
east France.

"We are lucky to be over here, darling. Thank
goodness we have managed to keep our shores safe
from the Nazis."

They rode home quickly before it became really
dark.

Sometimes, after work, they walked into Birchington for an evening coffee at The Clovelly Café in Birchington square. They were just so ecstatically happy in each other's company, on a high, intoxicated by their love for each other. Gary always made Sarah laugh so much with his funny stories, and the tenderness she showed him gladdened his heart.

He wondered if they could get away somewhere together for a weekend, but that seemed impossible. Their duty rotas did not match up and his was very full, he always seemed to be needed for something or other at the weekends.

However they did manage to go to church together most Sundays. Time off was allowed for church services. They went back to Acol to the little church where they could worship together in private, away from St. Catherine's at Manston, which was frequented by RAF personnel.

People were noticing them together more and more. In their happiness they didn't realise that this could be a problem, and threw caution to the wind. Mostly, when they were together, they were totally oblivious of others. They did not realise that their love for each other was carrying them into a time of great sadness, but for the moment, the warm summer months, were theirs alone.

CHAPTER FORTY-SIX

"Keep your sense of humour flowing"

The day of Jerry and Jill's wedding dawned bright and sunny. Jill was the centre of attention at the convent where the girls fussed around her, curling her hair and helping with make-up, and everyone was buzzing with the excitement of a wedding.

Sarah assisted her in putting on her dress and adjusted the small flower and lace veil on her head, pulling dark curls around her face. Sarah had lent her some pearl ear-rings, and Marge had fastened her own pearl necklace around Jill's slim neck.

Rhona had fashioned a lucky horse shoe out of silver paper and hung it over Jill's arm, and Ellie had stitched an Air Force blue and white frilly garter.

"Let me see – '*something old, something new, something borrowed and something blue?*' Have we got everything?" Rhona asked.

"That is something blue – your garter I mean – something borrowed, well you have two items of jewellery, something old, ummm, oh yes! The parachute silk! Now what is new?" Marge thought for a moment.

"Why her prospective husband, Jerry, of course, he couldn't be newer, you dope!"

Gales of laughter ensued, and, as they helped Jill down the steep staircase to the reception area of the convent, all the girls sang:

"*Here comes the bride, short fat and wide, see how she wobbles from side to side!*"

Jill stooped slightly and went out through an archway of nuns, who stood on paving stones and reached over

her, holding their hands together. The bride then
stepped into the waiting shiny black staff car.

Jill had chosen Sarah to act as bridesmaid for her.
Sarah wore her own cream silk frock and she held a
small posy of summer daisies peeping out from a circle
of ferns. She also carried Jill's larger bouquet of cream
roses, with trailing asparagus fern. Sarah turned to help
the bride into the back of the car and then slipped into
the front seat, sitting next to Reg, who was wearing a
borrowed chauffeur's cap. The car had been decorated
with white ribbon on the bonnet, and an arrangement
of flowers adorned the back window.

"All in and sitting pretty girls?" Reg enquired when
they had settled.

"Yes thank you, you may drive on, my man!" said
Sarah cheekily. "I must say, Reg, you really look the
part in that hat, you know!"

"Thank'ee most kindly, Miss." Reg saluted as Jill
and Sarah waved to the nuns and they drove off to St.
Catherine's Church in Manston village. The other girls
followed closely behind in an RAF transport vehicle.

They reached the church and Sarah helped Jill to
get out of the car. She adjusted her hair, pretty tendrils
of which had escaped the small veil, arranged the small
train at the back of Jill's dress, and gave her the
bouquet.

"Are you ready?" she asked the bride. "You really
look radiant, so very pretty. How is your tummy
feeling?"

"Thank you, my friend. Yes, I'm absolutely fine, my
nerves have all gone, I'm about to marry the man I love
and I couldn't be happier. Now be a dear and go and
see if you can see my father anywhere? He promised to
meet me here."

"Yes, I can see him near the church porch. Come on, I will take you to him." They walked along the church path together and joined Jill's father, who was beaming at the sight of his daughter.

"My, oh my, but you look beautiful, my darling daughter." He smiled and kissed his daughter. "By Jove! What a lovely day for a wedding, isn't it Sarah? By the way, you look smashing too!"

The other girls arrived, and chattering and giggling they made their way into the church.

"Is Mother here?" Jill asked her father. "Have you seen Jerry?"

"Yes, he is here, and he looks very nervous to me, and your mother is safely in the front pew, hanky at the ready!" Her father replied, smiling at his daughter. "There is just one fly in the ointment: the small choir is in place and the bell is ringing, but we have no vicar at the moment."

"Are you sure he is not in his vestry?" Sarah asked Jill's father, as she pulled Jill's veil forward to partially cover her face.

"Well, the best man, Gary, I believe he is called, has been sent to find out if he is anywhere in the church as no-one has seen him yet. The verger is here – he is ringing the bell."

At that moment, Gary rushed out of the church. "I'm just going to check the vicarage next door. It's almost time for the wedding, but no vicar as yet!" He smiled and winked at Sarah before he ran off.

To his amazement as he approached the lovely mellow old Victorian vicarage, he could hear someone singing a psalm at the top of their voice. He went round the side of the house to the back garden, and there he found the incumbent singing away lustily whilst digging in his vegetable garden, wellies on and mud on his hands.

Gary coughed politely. "Excuse me, Sir, you are wanted at the church for a wedding, you know. The bride and groom are already waiting for you."

"Oh great jumping Jehoshaphat! I completely forgot, the RAF couple is it not? I will be there in two flicks of a lamb's tail. Silly me, what a thing to do!!"

He left his spade and ran into the house, discarded his wellies, washed his hands, grabbed his vestments and ran with Gary to the church. He entered through a small 'late vicar's door' in the side of the church, which led directly to his vestry, so no-one spied him in his haste.

Gary returned to Jerry to reassure him he had found the vicar. He came back out momentarily to tell Sarah, who was waiting outside the church with the bride and her father.

The next minute the organ struck up the voluntary and the bridal procession solemnly walked into the church and up the aisle. The vicar met them with a beaming face, slightly red and perspiring from his rush to robe up.

While the vows were being taken, and after the ring had been given by Gary to Jerry, Sarah and Gary made their way to the pew behind the mother of the bride, who by that time was dabbing her wet eyes with her hankie and blowing her nose frequently.

Gary smiled down at Sarah and whispered that she looked lovely. Sarah went off into a reverie, thinking how lovely it would be if she were marrying Gary.

The small choir sang an anthem, '*Ave Verum Corpus*' by Mozart, while the register was signed. The bride and groom came out of the vestry, holding hands

and looking very happy. Gary and Sarah signed as
witnesses to the marriage. They then formed up
together behind the bride and groom, in front of Jill's
and Jerry's parents, who walked down the aisle behind
them. Sarah took Gary's arm and proudly processed
with him. This is heaven, she thought.

The newlyweds were greeted by an archway of RAF
airmen and women, and they ran through, laughing,
while copious amounts of confetti wafted around in the
summer breeze. Once the photographer was satisfied
with the photos he had taken, the wedding party made
its way across the road to the reception at The Jolly
Farmer.

Gary and Sarah sat on the top table but at opposite
ends, Gary by Jerry's father and Sarah by Jill's mother.
They kept smiling at each other down the table, but
couldn't talk while the wedding breakfast was eaten.

The speeches followed, with lots of wisecracks by
best man Gary about Jerry's RAF life. The toasts were
drunk, and the cake was cut. Then the tables were
cleared for dancing.

Gary sat at the old Joanna and played a romantic
waltz for the first dance of the newly married couple.
Then he slipped into a boogie-woogie, and everyone
got up to dance.

Sarah went over and leaned on the piano, watching
with admiration his skilled fingers flying over the keys.

Later on, another RAF chap took over playing the
piano and Gary and Sarah were at last able to have a
dance together.

"I just love to be in your arms, darling," Sarah
whispered.

"Me too," said Gary. "I am very proud to be dancing
with the best-looking girl in the room."

The afternoon became evening, some sandwiches were put out and Gary and Sarah slipped out into the pub garden for a little privacy.

"I love a wedding," sighed Sarah. "When you think that this is wartime, a time of austerity, we still have managed to have a grand time – and dress the bride without using up too many clothing coupons, thanks to that parachute silk."

"Well, it is the finest silk, you know, probably much better quality than goes to make normal dresses. It has to be first class, and not too heavy, in order to take the weight of a man's body when he jumps."

"I think she looks really lovely. I do hope they have many happy years together, and just think they met through this dreadful war. Happiness flowering out of dark days." Sarah turned towards Gary.

"Same as us, darling," smiled Gary, quickly stealing a kiss from her upturned lips.

The wedding had made their love all the more poignant, as they both realised that there would be no happy marriage for them.

They put these sad thoughts away, went back into the reception and danced the night away.

CHAPTER FORTY-SEVEN

"The past is crystal clear, like a diamond in the sun"

It was a sweltering 15th June, when a strange noise was heard in the East Kent sky. People came out from their houses, still wearing their dressing gowns, disturbed at the unfamiliar droning sound to watch what they thought was a German plane in flames. They rejoiced that another German bomber would probably crash, destroying its cargo of lethal bombs before they could do any damage to the people of England. However, when the engine suddenly cut out and the strange 'plane' dropped out of the sky like a stone and exploded, they realised that this was something different.

Gary explained what was happening to his WAAFs, as they had heard the droning and some had seen the unknown pointed craft whizzing through the sky.

"Right, girls, I have learned that this is a deadly new German weapon, sent to wreak havoc by causing as much sudden death and destruction as possible. The first V1 flying bomb, nicknamed 'doodlebug', was thankfully shot down from Manston by a Flight Lieutenant, a friend of mine. It is basically a pilotless plane; these are sheer evil, as they cannot be detected as easily by radar, and can just arrive one at a time – mostly missed by our searchlights until it is too late.

This recent V1, probably signifies the beginning of Hitler's new weapon assault nightmare, and was possibly launched by the Germans from a French or Dutch coastal area, directed towards London. No-one can predict where these bombs will land. You are safe all the while that you can hear that whistling, droning sound, but when it cuts out – it drops – then one has to run for cover like hell."

At Manston there was talk of these new weapons in guarded whispers at the 'drome. The paperwork was piling up in Admin, with the first jet-fighters arriving at Manston. Seven Meteors from 616 Squadron were sent to engage the doodlebugs. They achieved this by flying alongside the evil bombs and trying to nudge them with a wing tip, thus sending them off course, so that they crashed harmlessly onto farmland below. Gary gave this information to the girls. "Not that this brilliant outcome is easy to accomplish – it requires very skilled flying."

"My, that must take some seriously precise manoeuvring, and all at tremendous speeds no doubt," remarked Ellie.

"You are right, Eleanor. Meteors can clock about 380 mph, they are fast. Changing the subject, there are a lot of daylight raids happening from Manston at the moment. These are in addition to night raids, and you must have noticed the daylight raids when compiling flight schedules."

"Yes, we have realised that the offensive seemed to be stepping up. We actually thought it was probably as a result of the D-Day invasion."

"You are pretty damn near in that supposition. I'm glad that my clerks are so intelligent!"

Later on that evening, Sarah and Gary were walking together through some sunlit woods near to Minster.

"I haven't told you, have I, that I had a really nice letter from your father, thanking me for rescuing you on the way home that evening." Gary looked down at Sarah.

"Oh, so he wrote to you, did he?" She said, as they strolled along holding hands. "I had to tell him what you had done for me, and how you were so good at looking after me and taking me back to the convent, both times, when I fell off my bike and when we were attacked by that dreadful German plane." She shuddered at the thought. "I didn't say anything about it to Trel, though, he would have become jealous again. It doesn't take much to start him off, so I erred on the side of caution and kept quiet about it. So what did darling Daddy say?"

"He just wrote a short note saying that you were a pain in his neck, and that next time you were in trouble I was to look the other way!!" Gary laughed.

"You rotter, here take that!" Sarah let go of his hand and made out to take a swing at him. Gary deftly caught her hand and used it to catch her up in his arms, and for a moment they stood under the leafy canopy locked together, lips firmly upon lips, oblivious to the world around them.

When they let go of each other, Gary held Sarah's hands and looking down into her eager face said. "You don't think I'm going to tell you what was in the letter, surely? I mean it is private, between your father and I."

"OK, but you are such a tease, that is all."

"Well, if you really want to, you can read it for yourself. I just happen to have it with me now."

Gary reached into his jacket pocket and took out the letter. Sarah recognised her dear father's writing instantly.

"No, thanks. You are quite right, the letter is your private business, and I don't really want to read it. Do you know, I am sure that Daddy knows that you are more to me than just a boss. He is very perceptive, and it could be he has picked up that I speak about you quite a bit. It is hard not to when I am away from you, because you are so very dear to me, and you are on my mind when I don't see you every day."

"My sweet one, you have quite a wise head on your beautiful young shoulders, eh?" He quickly bent down to place a kiss on the top of her head. Sarah looked up at him.

"I am very worried about my folks in London. They must be terrified, because of the V1s, which have brought a further horrific nightmare to anyone who lives in the suburbs. I think I need to apply for a '48' to check that they understand that they must take cover when the drone cuts out. Oh, I just feel so anxious! It is piling up like a pressure in my head, there just seems to be one dreadful weapon after another." Sarah put her hands up to her face.

"Don't let them get to you, sweetness! That is their aim, remember, to erode away one's resistance with fear. I could sort you out some extra leave, if you like. I will do that as soon as I can, although that means you will be away from me again." Gary pulled a wry face, and made Sarah laugh.

"By the way, old Reg says Alland Grange field is fairly bursting with shot up kites, and that more bods have been sent down to give them a hand.

On a lighter note, darling, I must tell you that the happy day of Jill and Jerry has stirred matrimonial feelings in Reg, and I do believe he intends to propose to his Connie. I know she does not work with you, Sarah, being a wireless operator, but please keep Mum about this. Reg confided in me that he was thinking about taking the plunge the other day. He sees a lot of carnage over at Alland Grange and realises that life can be very short during wartime, and he just wants to get on with making Con his bride, in case it never happens. I wish I were single too, then I would make you Mrs. Scrivens as soon as you could say thruppence!"

Sarah realised the sadness of this statement, something that could never be. Watching the marital bliss of newly-weds didn't help, but of course she was a girl with a generous heart and was very pleased to learn of Reg's proposal to Connie and to see Jill and Jerry when they returned from their short honeymoon, as they looked so happy together.

Jill found Sarah one evening in the dorm, and sat down on her bed.

"Sarah, dear, I just wanted to thank you so much for being my bridesmaid on our happy day. I knew you would be a good choice. You are always so calm and collected, and you certainly allayed my nerves on the day. What about the best man then? Gary certainly supported my Jerry very well. He played his role as aide to the groom with great panache and sensitivity, and as for finding the vicar in his vegetable garden – well, that was absolutely spiffing of him, he showed much presence of mind. Whoever would have thought that would happen!" Jill laughed.

Jill then looked at Sarah quizzically.

"Hmm. You two are getting closer aren't you? In fact, it is very apparent to me that you are even more entangled emotionally, am I correct? I know you confessed ages ago to us all that you were in love but please dear, just keep your head. He is such a lovely man, we all adore him as our boss, and I do hear from Jerry that he is genuinely unhappily married, but that is where the danger lies. He obviously cares for you a great deal and I have spied you looking at him with stars in your eyes. I am so sorry he is married. You make such a lovely couple, just right for each other, but I and the other girls are a bit concerned that you two are heading for an almighty prang, as Jerry would say."

"I know, Jill, I understand what you are saying. Rho has been my counsellor for some time. It has been good to be able to offload my feelings to a close friend, and she has been marvellously unjudgemental. However, I have resolved to just enjoy this time we have together. It is very difficult, because I do care for him with all my heart, but we both have faced the fact that we can never be more to each other than passing ships. I still have my Trel in the background; he knows nothing of all this, and I do try not to hurt him in any way by speaking about Gary when I go home on leave. Please don't worry about me. I just have to think about his children back home in Cornwall and how much they need their father, and because I adore little ones, I just couldn't be the one to part them from him. I keep focussing on that fact, but, do you know, I do believe my heart will break when we finally have to part."

"How sad for you, but on the other hand, also happy because you actually met him and can spend a short time in your lives together. At least you are falling into all this with your eyes wide open. I don't envy you a bit; I would have died if I couldn't have been Jerry's wife."

The girls changed the subject as they could hear voices approaching. The others came in, and all flocked round Jill, chatting happily about her wedding and reliving the day together, before she left to join her new husband in the married quarters.

CHAPTER FORTY-EIGHT

"These joys are lost to me I know
without the pleasure of your sight"

Gary pulled strings and Sarah was allowed home for a
'48' and was able to chat to her parents, and reassure
them that much was being done at Manston to combat
the doodlebug. They had been informed about their
possible appearance by public service announcements
on the BBC Home Service, and Joe had actually seen
one of the monsters flying northwards from his back
garden.

The Twentyman sisters, Mary, in particular, were
very upset and very nervous about them, and Joe had
asked the ladies to walk up the hill for a cup of tea and
chat so that he might allay their fears and steady their
nerves. It just seemed that everyone was at breaking
point. The war had been going for five years now, and
although the British Bulldog spirit was still there, it was
wearing a bit thin. People had endured quite enough.

Sarah went to see Trel, but it was not a happy visit.
She did her best not to talk about Gary, but Trel
questioned her incessantly about 'Flight'. Sarah had not
told him of the walks, outings and suppers she had
enjoyed with Gary, only the social times they had been
together with lots of others, such as at dances or at the
pictures. Trel just couldn't stand the thought of Sarah
being with anyone else, and he was obviously very
unhappy. Sarah did find the situation a little hard to
handle. She tried to be light and gay and make their
time together fun, but she ended up going back to
Manston feeling rather sad, and virtually went straight
into Gary's arms as he met her off the train.

She didn't hear from Trel for at least three weeks after she returned to Manston. She continued to write him chatty newsy letters, as she would to her brother George. Nothing came back from him, until finally, he wrote to her a stern letter more or less proposing that if she persisted on talking about, or being with 'Flight' in any other capacity than RAF business, then he would finish with her. It was a mild warning that she was to be more committed to their relationship. Sarah just got cross with him, and replied about anything she could think of: the weather, general day-to-day RAF life, the food, the nuns, her friends – anything at all but their relationship. She avoided and side-stepped anything serious, with a nimble flick of her fountain pen.

Sarah had been quite shocked by Trel's letter. She knew that Trel was a sensitive soul, rather over-sensitive, really, but she had no inkling of his deeply possessive nature. In a way it drove her even more towards Gary, although she couldn't get much closer to him emotionally. Trel's over-blown reaction to her chatting about routine socializing at Manston, made her very wary of him. She thought she had been very careful to play down any involvement with her boss. He is stifling me, she thought, and then when she saw Gary she forgot all about Trel.

Trel had a feeling that he was driving her away and just didn't know how to handle the situation. He thought the hard-handed approach would help Sarah to see how much he cared; he had no idea that it would have the opposite effect. Annie had always doted on him, being widowed so young: he was the apple of her eye and to certain extent got everything he desired, and lots of attention from a mother and aunt who both adored him. He was used to being king bee in a relationship, not second best.

He jotted down in his diary that Sarah was always '*so casual*' when he tried to pin her down to some sort of commitment, and that he should really finish with her, but the thought of that made him, as he wrote, '*feel rotten*'. In all truth he really didn't want to end it, he just didn't want to be hurt, and he felt helpless and totally out of control in their relationship.

Any little kindness that Sarah performed for him, such as coming round to his flat and tidying his room, or bringing a packet of his favourite Garibaldi biscuits – 'squashed flies', as she called them – made him curtail his resolve to end it between them. '*She does love me!*' he wrote, with joy, in his journal.

Thus the summer wore on. The weather had been in the main hot and sunny, with a few odd thunderstorms which cooled the dusty air and refreshed the parched earth. All were heartened by the good news that the German garrison in Paris surrendered on the 25th of August to the Allies. The successful capture of Paris heightened the goals of the British and U.S. Armies to push forward and reach Berlin before the Soviet Army. All were cautiously optimistic that the Huns could be routed, and it seemed that the end of the war in Europe could be in view.

In Thanet some sandy beaches were partially opened again, with some restrictions. Gary and Sarah, enjoyed sitting with a picnic on St. Mildred's Bay beach, bathing together in the sea when the weather permitted, and walking along the sands, paddling together as the sun set over the sea. These were the heady days of their love.

They were able to enjoy being together at dances, listening to an orchestral concert or attending ENSA shows at Manston. Their favourite music, Rachmaninov's second symphony, is very passionate, and reminded them of the very first time they went to a concert together. It became a theme of their love for one another. They became inseparable during off-duty hours, except when Gary went home on a short leave break. He enjoyed spending time with his children, but couldn't wait to rush back to Sarah's arms.

They had a great time going out and about into the countryside, or to Canterbury to listen to the band on a Sunday afternoon, sitting side by side in deck chairs and eating very rarely found ice-creams. They attended the new camp cinema and laughed until tears streamed down their faces at Bob Hope in '*The Cat and the Canary*'. They were just having fun rejoicing in each other's company.

They often went for cycle rides. One trip saw them biking over to the south side of Manston 'drome, near what was colloquially known as 'crash or Hellfire Corner'. Gary showed Sarah the new Horsa gliders which were now parked up near the grass runway. They were loaded on to tripods, and Gary explained that the pilot would sit in the glider and a Halifax or Albemarle bomber would fly low and hook them up and tow them as near to Holland as possible, releasing them at 1,000 feet.

Sarah was amazed and said that when the glider hooked up it must have made the pilot experience a tremendous jolt as his flyer was towed upwards and away. She loved the fact that Gary knew so many technical details about flying and different planes, and was able to explain everything to her. He had wanted to take her up on a test run, but realised that would not be allowed in war time. Romantically, in private, they didn't hold back in their feelings for each other. There was no longer any need for subterfuge: they were in love, and that was all that mattered.

Sarah's father, Joe, knew from the tone of her letters that something was going on, and wrote to her, a loving letter, but with a cautionary message:

"Well darling, I have long ceased to believe in platonic friendship between the sexes, as sooner or later one or the other may fall in love which only leads to unhappiness if there is no response, or if the other be not in a position to respond. It seems to me that you must cut this friendship even though this may make you unhappy for a time. But it is better than heaps of unhappiness later, and remember one has to make some sacrifices in life for the sake of principles, honour, and regard for others. We want you to be happy and contented but on a proper lasting basis, and knowing more of life than you, we wish to protect you from its perils and dangers.

Now about Trel, really he did not say much, in fact, I had to get it out of him which as I already told you came from the remark in your previous letter. I was sorry he had not written to you as this might have eased matters, as I know from my own courting days when I had at times to lay down the law. Poor chap, he seems quite broken. Have you ceased to care for him?

At times seeing you with him made me think you were very happy together and might ultimately get engaged: he seems a nice steady fellow and in a good position and quite eligible. And I have never noticed any change in your attitude when you have been home from time to time, so all this has come as a great surprise. I suppose your going away has made a difference and your regard and love has been affected, however, you must settle this part yourself as you are the party concerned and Trel. I wonder what will be the upshot of it all."

He was obviously worried about Sarah getting hurt, and also thinking of the loyalty Gary should be showing to his wife and children. He did not know that Gary had an unhappy marriage and cold wife; perhaps he could have better understood his daughter's emotions if he had been a party to the whole story. However, as an Elder of the Presbyterian Church he had to uphold the sanctity of marriage, no matter what the circumstances. He dealt with the matter sensitively and with much love. He didn't talk of his fears to Hilda, only to say that he had perceived that Trel was unhappy and it worried him.

Sarah was quite startled to receive the letter from her father. She knew her parents had been kind to Trel, and were fond of him.

Sarah felt very guilty about Trel when she re-read Joe's letter, and the thought of him being a '*broken man*' touched her, making her sad, but her love for Gary was so strong that after considering it for a while she shrugged it off, rather selfishly.

During one of their walks, Gary and Sarah had discovered that next to the convent was a little leafy path, at the end of which were a couple of grass fields. One led into the other. The second field was totally enclosed by high trees and looked as if it may have had a crop of hay cut from it, but apart from that it was untouched. By the hedgerows, wild flowers were

growing; little mauve thistles reminding Sarah of her
Scottish father, yellow ragwort, and masses of tall
daisies. In this secluded field, Sarah and Gary found a
place where they could meet and be totally alone, a
secret haven for the two of them well away from anyone
else, a little space of their own. They used to walk
there, or take a picnic and a rug and just sit together
listening to the peace and quiet of the birds singing.
There their passion for each other could run its natural
course, away from prying eyes.

On such a visit Gary spied some small red fruits on
the ground. The plums were just ripe, and there were
many still remaining on the trees.

"I do believe these are cherry plums," he observed.
"I heard one of the local lads talking about them
recently, but have never seen such a fruit. Here, Sarah,
try one." He picked a tiny plum from the tree, and
brushed it off with his hanky and handed it to her.

"Gosh! They are so tasty. They certainly look like
cherries at first glance." Sarah gathered some of the
fruit into her pockets. "I must find out about these
delicious plums. Look, there are some golden ones,
too. They must be peculiar to this area, I have never
seen them before."

"They certainly don't grow in Cornwall, that is for
sure," observed Gary, biting into the tiny crimson
plum. "They are just right for popping whole into one's
mouth. I expect one could make jam with them. Shall
we gather a few for the nuns? I'm sure they will be
pleased to have them. I have an old paper bag in my
pocket, which would certainly suffice to tote back a
pound or so."

"Good idea. Oh, look! You have plum juice all
down your chin," laughed Sarah. She tip-toed up and

wiped his mouth – her hanky falling to the ground as
he suddenly kissed her.

These were happy days, when their time together
seemed to stretch eternally.

One lazy sunny afternoon in late summer, when the
crickets were chirruping in the grass and bees were
buzzing in their bumbling way in and out of the late
wild flowers around them, they sat together on a rug,
under a clear blue sky. Sarah's head was resting in
Gary's lap, and he was stroking her face with a long
piece of grass. "This is bliss, my sweet one. Just you
and I in our own little world. I wish this could go on
forever." He leant over and lifted her up to kiss her and
hold her in his arms.

"Do you know something? I'm sure my parents in
Wales would have loved to meet you. Under different
circumstances, they would have taken you into their
hearts so easily, as they could have seen how much you
make me feel alive and loved; my mother especially,
for true love is all she ever wanted for me. She knows
only too well that I get no love or affection from Helen.
In fact, I am going to tell you a secret. My parents
already know about you."

Sarah sat bolt upright, "They do? How on earth did
that happen? Did you meant to tell them? Didn't you
risk their severe disapproval?" Her eyes looked
anxiously up at Gary.

"Well, when I went home recently, they were staying
with Helen to help with the children as usual. My
mother and I went for a walk, and, well, I sort of told
her about you."

"Wasn't that like a red rag to a bull?"

"No, darling Sarah, remember my parents love me a
lot, and have been very sad that I have not been happy

with Helen for a long time. They wouldn't approve of
us, naturally, but they understood how and why I have
fallen in love with you. They knew I was starved of
affection and warmth, and could see that it would be
very difficult for me to resist someone as sweet and
loving as you, they are very, very understanding. My
father especially, being more worldly wise than my
mother, says nothing, but I know he would not
condemn me for loving you. Besides, only a mother
really knows her child and she perceived that
something wonderful had happened to me. Why, she
said I was almost glowing and no longer had a lost look
about me. So you see I just had to tell her about you."

"Did she warn you off me?"

"No, not in so many words – she merely warned me
to be sensible, and careful with my heart. So here I am,
entrusting its care to you!!!"

Sarah sighed. She looked down and gathered Gary's
hand in hers.

"I love you with all my heart, but I know we cannot
ultimately be together. So although I will cherish your
love always, please leave a little place in your heart
marked 'my own', because we will both need to draw
on our strength of purpose one day, when we will have
to part. I'm afraid my father has written to say he has
observed Trel looking very miserable, and has asked
me if I have stopped caring for him. He is a very kind,
but astute man and has noticed my animation when I
talk about you, even in the capacity of my boss. He also
noticed that I had written about you quite a bit in letters
home. I couldn't help it, because we spend so much
time together at work and off-duty. I so wanted to tell
both of my parents just how happy I am to be with you.

I stopped myself saying exactly that in so many words, but they have picked up my emotions, anyway."

"Well, our love is hard to hide. I can see that, our folks are bound to notice our happiness. So what has he said about it?"

"He has advised me to finish with you now, so as not to cause too much unhappiness later, but, Oh Gary, it is too late for that. I couldn't bear to be without you now."

They stood up and started to pack up their picnic things. The sun had sunk behind the trees and the air suddenly felt a lot cooler. Sarah put her cardigan on and then Gary swirled her around and clasped her in his arms. His mouth clamped down upon hers, desperately and with deep longing.

They clung there together in their quiet secret place for some time, until finally they walked back hand in hand to the end of the fields, then separated to face the world.

CHAPTER FORTY-NINE

*"And now the hour has vanished,
and the time has slipped away"*

August Bank Holiday Monday dawned a little
disappointingly, with grey clouds scudding across the
sky and rain lashing down. Sarah and Gary had
arranged to go for a bike ride to Wickhambreaux, a
tiny little Kent village near their favourite Wingham.

Sarah donned her mac and went out to meet Gary at
the end of the convent drive. Luckily when Gary spied
the rotten weather, he managed to get the use of a staff
car; that feat in itself was almost a miracle on a Bank
Holiday. Gary said one of his superior officers owed
him a favour, and so he pulled some strings.

Sarah settled into the car. "Thank goodness you
managed to get the car! What a shame about the
weather, and on a Bank Holiday too. Just think of all
those day-trippers wanting to go on the beaches, now
that they are open again."

"Never mind, darling. I think it may clear up later,
but of course at the moment it looks pretty grim." He
leant forward and squinted through the windscreen at
the leaden sky. "Oh blast the rotten weather, but I
suppose, really, all that matters is that we can share this
time. As the song goes, *'never mind the weather as long
as we are together!'"*

They bowled along through Plucks Gutter and
Grove Ferry, quaint little Kentish hamlets, and
eventually came into the village green at
Wickhambreaux. There to the side of the green stood
the 13th century thatched inn called "The Rose", which
normally looked very pretty with a red rose clambering

up its white front, and many colourful hanging baskets. They noticed the flowers through the rain, but had no time to enjoy them, as it was teeming down.

Gary parked the car and they both made a dash for the inn door, and arrived inside laughing and dripping wet. Once they had taken off their wet macs, Gary escorted Sarah to an intimate table in the corner, a little nook well away from the main bars. The old beams had been festooned with hundreds of hop vines, which hung down all around the pub creating a sweet smell and adding to the ambiance of the interior. The rain lashed against the bottle-glass windows.

"Goodness me! It is coming down in buckets. We got so wet in such a few yards! Well, this is very cosy. Look at the little orange lights on the walls, makes it feel warm even though the weather is atrocious. Certainly doesn't feel like the blazing August Bank Holidays of the past."

"What would you like to eat?" Gary scanned the menu. "Myself, I think I will go for the steak and kidney pie."

"Hmm, I think I would like the fish in a cream sauce, with spinach," Sarah decided.

They leant forward and held hands across the table, gazing with delight into each other's eyes. Gary removed a wet lock of hair from Sarah's forehead.

"Look what I received today, all the way from Cornwall." Gary took out two rolled-up pieces of paper from his inside jacket pocket.

"Jared and Polly have coloured in pictures for me. It is so nice to think they are thinking of their old Dad. I will put them up in my billet, on the wall – makes me feel nearer to them."

"What do your children look like?" Sarah asked as she perused the brightly coloured drawings. "I note that Jared has sent a picture of a steam train, and Polly sent a colouring in of her dolly, by the looks of it."

"Well, you never know, unless they sign the pictures. I'm amazed that Polly sent her dolly picture, as she loves steam trains as much as Jared. They often beg me to take them to Eastern Green to watch the steam engines thundering through from London to Penzance. However, to answer your question, you saw the photos, remember? The children are both fair-haired with blue eyes. I agree Jared looks a lot like me, and I think Polly takes more after Helen. Although Jared takes after me in character."

"Pity I shall never meet them. Have you still got the photos with you, I'd like to see them again?"

Inwardly Sarah thought that she must keep these children in mind and how much they needed their Father all the time. They must come first.

Gary took the photos out and handed them to Sarah.

"Oh, I remember them now, what darlings! Is that Helen in the background?" Sarah was really curious.

"Yes, that is my wife. As you can see she is scowling at the camera, because I wanted her to hold the children for a moment. Do you know, I really have great difficulty in understanding her. We have two wonderful kids, yet her books are always more important to her. I don't think she should be married. She would have made a wonderful bookish spinster, never happier than when she is delving into her studies. She is the daughter of a local chemist, and I suppose that is where her desire for academia came from, her father. Her mother is a nice soul, very cheery and not a bit like her daughter, but I must admit her father is a bit of a dry old stick with not much of a sense of humour. Yet she used to be fun when we first met, at a dance in Penzance.

You'll love this bit Sarah: on a Sunday evening some years ago, after church or chapel all the local chaps who had battered old cars would line them up by the sea on the prom. Then local young maids would parade in front of the cars on the other side of the road, in their Sunday best finery, bonnets, the lot. If a chap liked the look of one of them he would shine his headlights on her as she walked along the prom, to indicate that she had taken his fancy. If the maid was willing, she would go over to the car, get in and drive somewhere quiet for a bit of 'slap and tickle'!"

"Sounds like a novel way for farming and fisher folk to meet each other," laughed Sarah.

Their food arrived and they tucked in. Sarah had a bitter lemon to drink and Gary had a shandy. After they had eaten their dessert, the skies outside seemed clearer, so Gary paid the bill and, as the rain had stopped, they went for a walk round the quaint village. It had many little thatched cottages, all huddled together as if they were leaning on one another, and a large handsome Queen Anne red brick mansion next to the inn. Wickhambreaux still had a mediaeval mixture of church, manor house, mill and rectory, all facing on to the village green.

To the north-west of the mill stood the 14th century flint and stone church of St. Andrew. Gary and Sarah walked to the church and had a little peep inside. The sun had come out and was quite warm, so they decided not to spend too much time inside, but to get out and enjoy the better weather.

They went back to the car and drove away. Gary said that he had noticed earlier that there were a couple of folding chairs in the boot, so he suggested a drive to their special spot at Reculver where they could sit on the cliff to watch the sea, in the warm afternoon sunshine.

Sarah thought that was a grand idea, so they motored northwards through the country lanes, refreshed by the rain.

"Generally, it doesn't rain very much in Thanet, does it?" Sarah observed that the passing fields still looked quite parched and the earth still was cracked, despite the downpour.

"Not really, that is why you often see fields being irrigated. It really is something of a dust bowl, with the strong winds off the sea taking the precious top soil. Also when it rains hard after a long time, the earth is not able to absorb it and the surface water just runs away."

"Do you know, Sarah, it is very different in Cornwall. It rains so much in the westernmost part of England, and, of course, in my native Wales. Here, I should imagine, you have to keep watering the gardens all the time! The damp conditions encourage an abundance of the most enormous slugs in Penwith, you would never imagine their size. They consume everything and anything in their path, you know! So it is a constant battle for the gardener to protect his plants. I have tried using copper pipes: they don't like copper, as it sets up an electrical shock when their slime comes into contact with it. One still has to closely watch one's plants like billy-o, though. Hmm, I wonder how my garden is faring in Hayle? It is probably completely overgrown by now. Oh, well!"

"I should like a garden of my own to tend," said Sarah, wistfully. "I'm not really into growing vegetables like my father, but I love sowing packets of larkspur, poppies, nigella and my favourite pinks. Daddy lets me have a small patch of his garden to tend, but again, like your garden, it had been neglected this year."

"In our thoughts we could create our own little dream cottage, darling. You could imagine furnishing the interior and sowing your flowers, and I could be the handyman, putting up trellises for beautiful old climbing roses." Gary smiled as they motored on.

"Oh, Gary, what a lovely idea! Somewhere we can go to in our mind's eye, a place for just us two. Plus of course, your children could visit!!"

"Don't forget a small rough patch of grass for my beloved spaniel Rusty, although if we made it in the countryside - he would have plenty of rabbits to chase through the woods and fields." he laughed.

With these pleasant thoughts in their heads, they reached the car park at Reculver and walked up to the top of the cliff by the ruined church, carrying the chairs and a bag of iced buns that Gary had thoughtfully brought with him. There they sat together, holding hands, staring out over the sparkling sea, chattering about this and that, both in seventh heaven.

There were a lot of people about, being a Bank Holiday; all looking pleased to be out in the sun after the dreadful morning. They had no thought for others around them. They laughed and joked and occasionally Gary would tease Sarah, then she would pretend to sulk so that he had to pull her to him in an embrace of forgiveness.

It was as if they were in a bubble of happiness all of their own. Nothing could touch them at that moment, sitting in the sun.

Sadly, they were very wrong.

CHAPTER FIFTY

"Turn just once more, before you go,
I'll try not to let the tears flow"

The next day was warm, dry and sunny, and a complete
contrast to the wet, dismal morning before. Sarah
enjoyed her ride with Rhona to the 'drome, she felt
very happy to be seeing Gary soon. She parked her
bike and began to walk to the hut. Suddenly, she was
called over by her C.O., 'Tubby' who was walking by.

"A.C.W. Langman, come with me!"

Sarah saluted and followed her C.O. into the
Orderly Room. There, sitting behind her desk, was the
Warrant Officer for the WAAFs at RAF Manston.

"At ease, Langman, please sit." Sarah saluted again,
and sat in front of the desk.

The C.O. and Warrant Officer were looking grave,
and for an awful moment Sarah thought "*It's my
parents, or George. Please God, not that. Something
must have happened.*" Her heart was in her mouth.

"I am sorry to have to tell you that you will be
leaving Manston in an hour. You have been posted to
RAF Castle Camps in Cambridgeshire. When I have
finished speaking, you are to go straight to Ursuline
Convent and pack your kit bag. A car will be waiting to
take you to Cambridgeshire."

Sarah went white. Well, what a shock! At least her
dear family were safe! She didn't know whether to be
relieved, or horrified at the thought of a posting away
from her friends, away from her love.

"You are not to discuss this with anyone. You can
write to your fellow airwomen when you settle in at
Castle Camps, to say goodbye."

"Ma'am, may I query as to why I am being moved so quickly?"

"I think that you must know the reason, Langman. You have been seen holding hands in public places with Flight Sergeant Gary Scrivens, a married man with a family. The RAF will not tolerate such affairs, so you have to go. For us at Manston it is a great shame, as we will be losing, in you, a very conscientious, popular Clark G.D. You will be commended for your hard work while you have been with us, and for that diligence RAF Manston thanks you. Now go and pack."

"Attention!" Sarah stood and saluted. The officers returned her salute. "Dismiss."

She marched out and walked to her bike in the shed. Tears had started to prick her eyes, and by the time she was cycling back to the convent she was crying. In the wind tears were streaming down her face as she rode on.

Gary had also been called in to see his superior Officer. They dealt with him more leniently because he was vital to them at Manston. He could not be spared, so he just received a severe reprimand, and any leave he may have had planned was cancelled.

He stumbled back to the hut. He was told not to say a word to the other girls, but they saw that he was very pale and upset. He didn't speak, but quietly got on with his work, communicating only when necessary. The girls couldn't believe his glum demeanour, and they talked about it among themselves over their lunch in the Mess.

"Oh I hope nothing has happened to Gary's family?" Jill looked shocked."

"No, I don't think so, he would be relieved of duties if that were the case, I think that something has happened to Sarah," Rhona remarked. "She was just behind me on her bike this morning, and now where is she? I saw Tubby leading her away. Oh, I do hope it is not her family that have bought it."

"Och away! Observing Gary, I think they have both been given a roasting. He is one miserable chap. I don't think it is about Sarah's family," said Marge, astutely.

"Do you really think so?" Ellie was horrified. "Do you think Sarah has been posted away from us? To another camp?"

"I wouldn't be surprised," Marge said, shaking her head. "They have not been very discreet lately – I have spied them kissing in the shrubbery next to the convent."

"Surely she would have been allowed to say goodbye to us? Oh, life will never be the same at Manston without Sarah. She has become my very best friend." Jill began to cry.

That evening, the girls could see that Sarah's locker was cleared out, all her possessions had gone, and there was no note for them anywhere. On Sarah's bed was a single rose from the convent garden. They realised that Sarah had left it for them.

"I wonder where she has been sent, and who could have betrayed them?" Rhona said sadly. She already missed her good friend, but in her heart she contemplated that maybe she could have prevented the affair.

"They just fell in love, simply that," said Ellie. "Gary was unloved by his wife, Sarah was so pretty, with such a warm friendly nature, he just felt drawn to her like

iron filings to a magnet. He so desperately needed
someone to care, and Sarah was too young and naive to
resist him. We did our best girls, come on, we warned
her; but of course, everyone loves a lover. It was good
to watch them so happy in each other's company. It is a
text book wartime love story, and sadly now we have to
watch the aftermath. We must really buoy Gary up. He
is going to take it very badly."

All Sarah's friends felt very miserable at her
immediate departure. They could see Gary was torn up
about Sarah's absence, they thought they would wait
awhile before tackling him about Sarah's posting.

The Admin hut was a very sombre place for the next
few days, Gary just got stuck into his work. He didn't
laugh and joke much, he was polite but there was no
camaraderie. Ellie took over Sarah's duty of making
sure he had a decent cup of coffee in the morning. He
thanked her but hardly looked up.

He applied to carry out his duty in another part of
Manston, and sadly for the girls Flight Sergeant John
Brown was detailed to take his place. Their working life
suddenly got a lot more difficult, and Gary was gone
before the girls had a chance to speak to him properly
about Sarah.

A fortnight passed, and a letter arrived for them all
at the convent.

"Goodness!" Rho exclaimed. "She is way up in
Castle Camps, Cambridgeshire, near the small town of
Saffron Walden. She sends her love to us all and says
how much she is missing us. She apologises for just
leaving, but she had no choice – she was ordered to
pack immediately. She also says it is not too bad up
there, and at least she will still be able to get home on

leave fairly easily. She will just have the bother of crossing London, from Kings Cross Railway Station."

"Do all of you realise?" Marge pointed out, "There is a modicum of comfort in all this? That wee lassie will now have the chance of a decent future with her Trel? Poor chap, he has taken a back seat, but now no more. Really, for her it was the best thing that could happen. Gary and Sarah would never have had the strength to split up, it had to be done for them."

"You are right, you canny Scot!" said Jill. "Gary will get over Sarah, and she will be free now to devote her time to Trel - after the war, but for the moment, I know her heart will be breaking."

CHAPTER FIFTY-ONE

"I just remain in silence, and let the memories unfurl"

As soon as Sarah had settled in at Castle Camps, she wrote not only to her friends at Manston, but to Gary.

She found it very difficult. She missed him dreadfully, and she shed one or two tears over her letter to him.

Of course, she knew that they had been foolish, but what happiness and joy that foolishness had brought into their lives. She didn't regret their time together: the spring and summer of 1944 would always hold a dear place in her heart.

She had thought a million times when and how their parting would eventually take place, but the shock and immediacy of her enforced departure and consequential posting to Castle Camps took the wind out of her sails for a long time.

She eventually settled into RAF life again, she had no choice but to make the best of it, but as Jill predicted, inside her heart was breaking.

One 'drome was very like another. She was still a general duties clerk, inundated with chits of paper, typing various documents, and having to use the ubiquitous Gestetner, which she hated with a vengeance.

She thought of Gary constantly, and wondered if she would ever meet him again. She thought that he may try and wangle a meeting, after all, they never even got to say goodbye. If *only* they had known that Bank Holiday Monday was to be the very last time they would be together.

Trel was very surprised to learn in her letter of her immediate posting, but he knew that sudden postings could happen at any time during the war. He did not suspect that there was a reason for her speedy departure. He was, in the main, really pleased that she would be away from 'Flight' – he really feared that her boss had come between them and driven them apart emotionally. Perhaps she will come back to me now, perhaps I will have her undivided attention and may once again claim her as my girl, he thought.

Hilda and Joe were pleased that she wasn't too far away, especially as George had recently been posted to an army camp in Dorset and couldn't, therefore, get home very often.

Sarah missed Gary so much. She was bereft without his cheerful voice teasing her, and loving her. It was as if a part of her body had gone, suddenly, and she couldn't pull herself together. She tried to tell herself that this was the parting they knew would come one day, some airy-fairy time in the future, but all the while that day had been unfixed she was able to ignore the approaching pain of separation that was their inevitable destiny.

Back in Manston, Gary was a broken man. He had lost his dear sweet girl, so savagely, so quickly. He couldn't bear to be in the hut without her, and so was relieved when his transfer to another part of the 'drome came through within days. Luckily, Reg needed more men over at Alland Grange, and Reg knew that Gary had some engineering experience in maintaining planes so he enabled the transfer by requesting that Gary joined him in working on war-battered kites.

As usual, they were extremely busy over at Alland; lately there had been a tremendous number of planes

on which to work, and other engineers were arriving all
the time to lend a hand. Battered planes were stacking
up. The fortuitous position of Manston aerodrome,
almost on the coast, was often a pilot's first port of call.
A more than welcome refuge for kites limping home
on the return from a difficult sortie. RAF Manston
prevented many a crippled kite from a ditch in the sea,
especially if low on fuel. Undoubtedly Manston
aerodrome saved pilots' lives.

This move was very good for Gary, not only
because he was on hand to take refurbished planes up
to test them at a moment's notice, and the engineering
work was hard and physical, but because he could
confide in Reg. Every evening after the day was done,
they went to the NAAFI club for a drink and snack and
Gary talked endlessly about Sarah. Reg just let him get
it all off his chest. He listened but did not judge. He
had known the pain of lost love years before, when his
fiancée ran off with another man. Reg knew the searing
hurt inside, and that the worst thing for Gary was that
he knew Sarah was in love with him – she hadn't hurt
him and left him for another.

Gary was driven mad just knowing that she was up in
Cambridge, so near yet so far, longing for him. Reg
tried to dissuade him but Gary felt he had to do
something about it.

Late one afternoon on 25th September, Reg and
Gary had just packed up for tea on a fine sunny day.
Suddenly the sky was full of Spitfires, and in came 124,
118 and 229 squadrons to join Manston's 504
squadron wing. Their duty was to provide escort for
three major bombing operations. The tannoy
announced that volunteers should to report to R and R
– rearm and refuel – helping to service the hordes of

Spits that had lobbed in. Reg and Gary both worked very hard with bowser crews until almost nightfall, getting kites up to speed. This vital work took Gary's mind off his sorrow for a few hours.

However, his longing to see Sarah again did not abate and, after a month or two of exchanging letters, he wrote and asked Sarah if she would mind if he visited her at Castle Camps. He needed to check whether she would want to see him again as he mused that maybe she had begun to cut him out of her life, and wouldn't want to resurrect their relationship. Although her letters were always warm and loving, it might be a different matter, actually seeing each other once more.

Sarah couldn't get time off until it was nearly Christmas. She then wrote to tell Gary that she would love to see him, and of course he must come up to Cambridgeshire. She said she would try to find a suitable hotel in nearby Saffron Walden where they could stay. She synchronized her '48' leave with his, and he arranged to travel up to meet her. His heart was bursting with longing, just to see her sweet face again.

Reg had warned him against going – he could see this would only prolong the agony of separation for both of them – but he knew he was fighting a losing battle. '*Love always finds a way*', he thought. He told his old friend that he would be waiting for him at Manston, and would be ready with a pint and a friendly listening ear when he returned.

CHAPTER FIFTY-TWO

"I still feel your arms around me,
and your cheek so close to mine"

Sarah strained her eyes for a sight of the train that was bringing Gary to her. There was no sign of it, and it was very cold waiting at the railway station. A bitter wind played round her legs, but she didn't mind: she was glowing with the thought of seeing him again.

She had known in her heart that he would eventually travel up to see her. They just couldn't be parted the way they had, it was too horrible to bear, to be cut off so finally and quickly like the slicing of a sword, and just as wounding to the soul. As soon as they started corresponding, she could hear that he was suffering as much as she had been at their brutal separation.

She didn't give a second thought to the fact that this sudden cruel parting could have been the best thing for both of them in their doomed love affair. She could have chosen not to see him again, and turned once more towards Trel, but her pain overwhelmed her, and she chose just a little time more with her Gary. Love is not sensible.

She was well wrapped up against the freezing cold in her new beaver lamb fur coat, bought for her by her parents. She had had her hair freshly permed and wore her new brown court shoes. She spent ages in front of the mirror at her billet wondering which ear-rings to wear, which necklace; in the end she plumped for a cultured pearl necklace and matching tiny seed pearl ear-rings. She wore just the touch of L'Aimant perfume on her wrists and behind her ears, the latest in red lipstick was on her pretty mouth, and her clear young skin was enhanced with just the lightest trace of face powder. She had to look good for her Gary.

The new WAAFs with whom she had made friends wondered what she was about.

"I reckon our Sarah is off to meet her sweetheart, girls, what do you say?" A rather plump, motherly looking girl called Doris observed to the others.

"Well, I may tell you all about it after my '48'," said Sarah. "But then, I may not!" She smiled enigmatically and skipped out of the billet.

At last a whistle shrieked in the distance and afar off Sarah spied the smoke belching out of the train's funnel as it rounded a bend, and her stomach turned over with nerves. She walked towards the end of the platform and back in her excitement.

The train pulled into the station, and with a belch of smoke and steam came to a halt.

Sarah glanced anxiously up the platform and down again, not sure in which carriage Gary would be travelling. Then she spied him. His head was stuck out of the window, and he was waving frantically.

"Sarah! Darling!" he yelled down the platform.

"Gary – Oh my Gary!" Sarah ran to his door and they could hardly get it open quickly enough before they were in each other's arms.

"Yes, darling! Yours today, and in my heart only yours for all time."

The world around them passed by, and the train departed in clouds of smoke and steam, chuffing merrily.

There they stood, locked together in an embrace, lips on lips, alone on the now-deserted platform.

"Oh dearest, I have so looked forward to this moment!" Gary gently held Sarah's upturned face in his hands. "Let me look at you now, let me stare into your glorious green eyes, and let my poor sad heart be warmed again by the dazzle of your lovely smile."

The tears began to fall softly from Sarah's eyes. Gary gently wiped them away.

"The light has departed from my life since I have been without you. I didn't think we would ever be able to see each other, or be together again. Not even being able to say goodbye has been so hard. Your letters, so warm and full of your sweetness, have more than helped me get through these months without you. If only we had known on that happy Bank Holiday Monday what was to happen, would we have been more prepared?"

"Probably not," replied Sarah, reaching into her handbag for a hankie. "I don't think either of us could have foreseen the shock we would have that morning. Oh! I must look such a fright, and I spent ages doing my face so that I would look pretty for you, and now I have spoiled it, and look!" She glanced into her powder compact. "My nose is really quite red. I'll just pop into the station rest room and powder my nose for a minute, shan't be a tick."

Gary lit a cigarette and wandered down the platform while Sarah made her repairs. She was only five minutes, and came out smiling.

"You looked fine to me, Darling, you don't need make-up," said Gary, and they strolled towards the station exit.

Sarah glanced at Gary sideways, stopped and turning to him said:

"Let's look at you then, have you lost a little weight? Well, well, well, what a surprise, what do we have here?" Sarah put her hand up to Gary's lips and softly caressed his new moustache. "I thought something was tickling me when we kissed! You kept your new facial addition very quiet. You certainly look the part of a jolly old RAF pilot now, what? What!!!" She teased him. "It is absolutely spiffing, old boy!"

"Yes, I thought I would keep the old 'tash a secret until we met again, I really wasn't sure you would like it – after all, your Trel has a moustache, and I thought it may confuse you when we kissed!"

"Don't be a dafty, you two may have similarities but I would never confuse your kisses, no way!"

Sarah stepped back and scrutinised Gary's new acquisition. "I quite like your effort, it makes you look distinguished, I must say, and it has more than a touch of ginger – or should we say strawberry blond – about it. Have you been practising twirling the ends and saying 'Popsies at twelve o'clock', then?"

They both laughed and held hands and walked out of the station, Gary pausing to give in his ticket to the inspector.

"So, why did you grow a 'tash?"

"I was so blue when you left, I just felt I should change something about my sorry situation; and as my life is not really my own at the moment, and I seem to belong to the RAF, I thought I would try and look more like an airman than before. Anyway, darling, instead of talking here let us think what to do next. Let us not waste a minute of our precious time together. What shall we do? Where shall we go? Is it far to RAF Castle Camps? It would be interesting to see where you are now living."

"We could get a bus there if you really wanted to. I don't really want to go too near the 'drome site, though. In fact, I have an idea: we could get a double-decker bus which goes straight past there and you can look out over it. It is very like Manston, only a bit smaller, really. The girls here said that the place was crawling with the Canadian Air Force, 410 Squadron, earlier this year, and that they have only just left. We also have 68 Squadron's Mosquitoes; they have also just arrived, along with 151 and 25 Squadrons."

"Hmm, Canadians eh? I'm glad they have gone! They may have taken a fancy to you, too! Couldn't have that, my girl."

They walked along the road to a bus stop, and boarded a bus bound for Castle Camps village. Gary was able to get a quick glance at the RAF base from the upstairs window, and that seemed to satisfy his curiosity.

Alighting at the village, they decided to take a walk around. It was a small hamlet, pretty, but not in the same way as their beloved Wingham. It was good for them just to relax and hold hands again, knowing that they were strangers to the area and no prying RAF eyes would be watching their every move.

They made their way to the 15th century church of All Saints, which was shut as it was winter time, so they walked for a while around the churchyard. Pausing at a large headstone they noted it was dedicated to a past rector, John Ernest Bode. The gravestone also informed them that he was the writer of the popular hymn '*O Jesus I have promised*'. Gary and Sarah agreed that it was one of their favourite hymns, and Gary immediately burst into a verse. His rich Welsh baritone rang out into the deserted churchyard.

"O Jesus I have promised to serve Thee to the end,
Be Thou for ever near me my Saviour and my friend

I shall not fear the battle if Thou art by my side
Nor wander from the pathway
if Thou wilt be my guide."

"That was lovely, darling! I shall always think of this moment in the future when I sing that hymn," clapped Sarah. "Now, however, I'm fair perished with cold, so let's go to that lovely looking inn we passed on our way to the church."

The inn was very welcoming, with a large log fire burning in the grate. The landlord was a friendly affable chap, and they ordered some food. Soon the warmth of the fire thawed them out, and they sat back in comfy chairs and relaxed in each other's company.

"I could just sit here for ever, gazing at you, sweet one, I wouldn't want to do anything else." Gary stretched out his long legs in front of the fire, and lit a cigarette. "You never got on with this smoking lark, did you? You could have one if you wanted." Sarah smilingly declined his offer.

"However, to practicalities. We discussed where to stay tonight in our letters. Is it far to The Abbey Hotel in Saffron Walden? Were you able to make reservations for us?" Gary asked Sarah, as they sipped warming coffees.

"No, it is not far, just a short bus ride away. I visited the hotel one weekend and was able to secure two rooms for us," Sarah said, her hands gratefully cupping the warm coffee. "Gosh, I would almost be glad just to hold this cup, never mind drink its deliciousness. It is unnumbing my fingers beautifully. Luckily my chilblains have not started to flare up yet, even though I think it is much colder up here in Cambridgeshire.

Did you notice from the train that the terrain is similar to Thanet, with flattish fields? The sea is further away, here, of course. They do say the sea keeps the land warm, and here we are in a landlocked county – plus we are that much further north – and I'm sure it is icier. There are some jolly hard frosts in the morning. They look stunningly beautiful, often with mists floating about like wraiths suspended over the white fields. It is very Christmassy, but no snow as yet. Sometimes the sun breaks through above the mist and then it looks totally magical, like a winter fairyland!"

"Have you forgotten last winter, darling, in the hut?" Gary reminded her. "That was pretty Arctic. Do they have more efficient heating apparatuses up here, or tortoise stoves as we had?"

Before Sarah could reply, they paused in their conversation, as the plump red-cheeked landlady brought them over two steaming bowls of vegetable soup and a plate of sandwiches, daintily decorated with sprigs of fresh parsley, mustard and cress.

"Now, my dears," she said, putting down the tray. "I've found you a piece each of my fruit cake. They are only small pieces, mind you, as I can only spare the ingredients for baking once a fortnight now, due to rationing. You are welcome to these slices, anyway, and I hope you enjoy them."

The two thanked her profusely for her kindness, then carried on eating and chatting by the fire. For both of them it was bliss. This simple time together was all they desired.

Gary munched contentedly and then said: "You know, I have moved away from Admin. I am working with Reg now, over at Alland Grange. Oh darling, I just could not have survived without you among the other girls. I would have just been such an old misery guts, and of course all the girls were also so stunned and missing you, and wanted to talk about it. That was all too much for me, so I just had to get out of that hut. We were all suffering your loss together. I'm afraid I left them in the not too jolly hands of miserable old John Brown, too. They loathe him – he is a difficult cove – but I was selfish, and knew I couldn't be efficient any more. I didn't mention the move in my letters, because silly things like that can be intercepted and used against us. I don't have to see anyone now, back at the main 'drome, very often. Reg and I, together with old married man Jerry – when he can get away from Jill (just joking darling!) – spend our evenings in the NAAFI club.

I tend to eat there most days, chew the fat figuratively speaking and maybe have a game of billiards. Those two have been my saving grace since you left Manston. Also, Bill – you remember my pal, the Spitfire pilot – has been kind, too. They have listened to me wittering on about you till they were fair blue in the face. They never judged me; they know my home circumstances, and they are just three jolly decent chaps that I am proud to call my good friends."

"I'm very glad you are over with Reg, and are probably carrying out brilliant repairs on those bashed-up kites," Sarah said, finishing her soup. "Being there on hand to test them too, that must be very useful to the RAF. I know your age was against you flying, but you were often called over, and it meant you had to leave us in Admin. It all seems a much better set up for you. Reg and Jerry are both such darlings, so kind and non-judgemental: they are ideal chaps to have as friends. Mind you, I do know it is grim over at Alland

Grange. Some of the sights inside the crashed kites are not for the weak-stomached. Reg told me that, but the job you will be doing is vital, so really it was a good move all round."

Gary grinned at her over his soup and winked at her.

"Oh, I say!" Sarah had a sudden thought while munching on her sandwich. "I wonder if you could fly over to Castle Camps on some pretext or other. That may be a possibility; after all, it is not far, and shouldn't take two minutes in a Mossie!"

"What a damn spiffing idea, darling!" Gary laughed. "Probably totally out of the question, though. I have to fly the kites where I am told, and they are sorely needed, so it is usually a 'once round Thanet coastline job'. Then, if they are fit, they are off to the younger pilots for use almost immediately. I am considered too old these days – even for a rear gunner, or navigator!"

They finished their lunch and to their amazement realised it was getting quite late, almost three-thirty.

This precious time together was racing by at an alarming speed. They had no inkling of it, and its passage meant nothing, only that they had very little.

CHAPTER FIFTY-THREE

*"All that mattered, all that counted,
must be still until another day"*

They alighted from the bus at Saffron Walden and
walked up through the old market town to The Abbey
Hotel, which stood on the corner of the High Street
and Abbey Lane. They checked into the Georgian
hotel, and were shown their adjoining rooms, which
looked out onto fields at the back. They looked very
comfortable, with chintz curtains and matching
counterpanes giving the rooms a very homely feel.

They went downstairs and asked the manager what
time the evening meal would be served.

"In about half an hour you can make your way to
the restaurant. Meanwhile, would you like an aperitif?"

"Yes, please. I would love a small sweet sherry,"
Sarah asked, and Gary ordered a whiskey and soda for
himself. They sat down at the bar.

"Why is this called 'The Abbey Hotel'," Sarah
asked of the manager.

He explained that once, long, long ago, there was a
Priory, called Walden Abbey, which was founded
under the patronage of Geoffrey de Mandeville in
around 1136. The Abbey was separated by the town of
Walden by Holywell field. Just behind the hotel, Abbey
Lane led to it from the village. After the dissolution of
the monasteries by Henry VIII it was converted into a
house. He said that the hotel was named after Abbey
Lane.

"So why is the town of Walden, now called Saffron
Walden?" Gary, asked joining in while sipping his
drink and lighting a cigarette.

"Well, now, it is really nice that you two young people are interested in our history," he smiled. "It is my private passion. I will explain: the crocus that yielded the precious saffron – *crocus sativus* – grew very well in this district, owing to the local soil and climate. It is a pale blue colour, not yellow as one would imagine, and the long pistils which yield the saffron are bright red, but produce a yellow colour when dried. A cottage industry grew up, extracting the precious saffron spice from the dried pistils and selling it, hence the name 'Saffron' was added to the village of Walden. It was used as an expensive yellow dye, a spice and even as an aphrodisiac in the 16th and 17th centuries. The Cornish use a lot of it in 'saffron cakes and buns'; it is grown down there, too."

With that piece of erudite information he left them to their drinks.

"I have certainly eaten plenty of saffron cake and buns at home, but never gave their yellow colouring a thought. Now I know!" Gary sat holding Sarah's hands, and they gazed into each other's eyes.

Sarah smiled and then her voice put on a graver tone. "You know, dearest Gary, that we cannot really see much of each other in the future. It will not be possible." Sarah brushed her hand softly on his face, caressing his cheek and looked sadly at him.

"I know darling, I am only too aware of the distance between us, but maybe we can wangle the odd weekend such as this one. It depends on how you feel. I know your folks are against us having any relationship, and really, I don't blame them – being in love with a married man is not much of a future for their daughter. Especially when she has an eminently eligible suitor already on tap, as it were. Thinking about my daughter Polly, I'm not sure I would want this for her, either!"

"But it is you who are in my heart," said Sarah leaning forward caressing Gary's hand. "One cannot love to order! Yes, I am very fond of Trel, but all my passion and longing is for you. It is all very difficult, emotions cannot be called up just like that. Yes, the plain truth is that my father has advised me to cut you off, no letters, etcetera, but they are the only things that keep me going at the moment. I cannot stop wanting you to write. They just prevent my days being so empty without you. Even the sight of your handwriting on a RAF envelope makes my tummy turn over with pleasure. However, it seems that I should tell you not to communicate with me. In fact, I'm so afraid that this will probably have to be the very last time we spend together. I am trying so hard to be strong."

"Please don't say that, my sweet one, I cannot bear it. I have been so afraid you would say that, dearest Sarah. I just don't know how I will go on without the thought of us meeting again soon, and the comfort of receiving your wonderfully cheerful and loving letters. Even if we cannot see each other very much, or be together, surely writing does no harm, and brings much joy to my lonely soul. Besides!" Gary said a trifle crossly, "I simply refuse to believe we cannot work out a way to see each other again."

They finished their drinks and were called to the restaurant for their meal. The room was very opulent, all done out in green and gold with a beautiful plush carpet and dark green velvet curtains tied back with golden swags at the windows, which were criss-crossed with anti-blast tape. It was getting dark, and the waiters were just fixing the black-out blinds as they sat down at the table, which was in a corner near a blazing log fire.

There weren't many other diners that evening, so it was pretty quiet and very intimate. This happy time together was tinged with the sadness of their situation. Neither of them wanted to say that they should not see each other again – it was just too painful – but the spectre of their parting hung over them both like the grim reaper.

They enjoyed their meal and chatted inconsequently about things, not wanting to dwell too deeply on the futility of their love.

Gary ate whilst watching Sarah intently. He wanted to drink in her very being, the way she tilted her head, the way she would suddenly laugh as she dropped her napkin, admonishing herself for being so clumsy, as usual. All the little nuances of her personality he tried hard to capture, and place in a corner of his mind for future reference. He just couldn't bear not to be near her, but didn't want this happy time to be tinged with the sadness of future loss.

Sarah was feeling the same. Dear Gary, she thought, as she watched him eating his meal, chuckling at his own jokes. How he absent-mindedly rubbed his head if he was thinking deeply about something. Suddenly a radio was turned on, and in the background to their amazement they could hear their favourite Rachmaninov symphony starting to play.

"I cannot believe it! Our music! See even the BBC are on our side!" They both laughed. "This was meant to be, Sarah, we were meant to meet." Gary gazed at her. "This music will run through my soul for ever, and every time I hear it, it will bring me closer to you. Wherever we are, we will be together in my heart and mind because we share its beauty. It means so much to both of us."

Eventually, wearily, they decided to go up to bed. They climbed the stairs together hand in hand, and many years later, Sarah wrote this poem about their night together:

Secrets

When oft in solitude and languid state
Where sleep escapes each weary lid
I sometimes recall and often relate
Where once we were twain and there did bid
Sweet memories make when you were my own,
Where secret happenings were one's alone
For the sheets cannot talk and the pillows are mute
And nobody knew of our amorous pursuits!

O dream of delight that faded at dawn
O song of songs, O night of bliss
When you were my whole world of love alone.

CHAPTER FIFTY-FOUR

So think of me sometimes Darling,
remember though we're far apart,
I won't tell a soul I love you, though
I'm left with a broken heart

The next morning was cold but bright and sunny. Sarah and Gary asked the maître d' what time the service would be at the local church. He told them, and after partaking of a hearty breakfast they walked up the hill along the frosty pavements to St. Mary the Virgin church. It was most magnificent, with a tower and spire of 193 feet. A sidesman told them that it was the largest church in Essex, and dated back to the 15th century, as he gave them their prayer and hymn books.

It was Advent Sunday, and so the Service took the form of Advent Carols. Gary and Sarah were able to join in singing '*The Angel Gabriel*' and the '*Cherry Tree Carol*', along with '*O come, O come Emmanuel*', one of Gary's particular favourites.

They felt closer than ever, having spent this time in a different place, miles away from Manston, and were happily chatting and laughing as they made their way back to the hotel for Sunday lunch. They decided to indulge themselves a bit and have a roast dinner. They thoroughly enjoyed the rare taste of best roast beef, roast potatoes, parsnips, and Brussels sprouts with lashings of hot tasty gravy poured over Yorkshire puddings, home-made by the landlady. This was followed by crème brulee and coffee, over which they held hands and smiled at each other, trying not to think of their impending parting.

After lunch they had a short walk around the fields at the back of the hotel, but it was extremely windy and began to sleet, so they returned to the warm hotel, sat by the fire and ordered a pot of tea, scones and strawberry jam with cream. Sarah couldn't believe her eyes when the waitress brought out the pot of tea with two matching cups and saucers – they looked very familiar to her.

"Good gracious!" She exclaimed with astonishment. "This is the very same tea service as my mother uses at home for Sunday afternoon tea. I cannot believe it! Look! It has orange flowers, with blue and green leaves all over it. Well, I never did! I shall have to write and tell Mummy straight away."

"Perhaps you should not mention me, though, darling, and just make out that you were having tea with one or two of your WAAF friends, eh?" said Gary, wisely.

"Hmm – what a pity. I would love to be able to tell my mother about you. She would love you as I do, just as you say your parents would have loved me. Oh, it is all so sad, really."

"Now, now, don't get downcast in our last few precious hours together." Gary endeavoured to lighten the moment.

"We knew of the difficulties we would face in the future, but all that seemed too far away during our time at Manston, although the horrors of war were all around us, all the time. We could read of the devastation in the documents we had to process, or be shot at by marauding German kites, but nothing else could touch us because we found each other, and our love is strong. This separation by miles is the hard bit to endure. We can no longer see each other every day.

Oh! If only we had been more careful not to be affectionate in public. We will never know who saw us, who reported us. We could have enjoyed a little more time close together."

"Maybe there was someone in 'The Rose' at Wickhambreaux that magical Bank Holiday Monday; after all we both came in for a roasting the very next day, so perhaps someone saw us then. I wasn't looking around for anyone from the camp, I only had eyes for you, and it has been extremely difficult not to kiss and caress you more openly in public. Or it may have been later at Reculver, as we sat on the cliffs. We will never really know." Gary sighed with exasperation.

Sarah agreed, and Gary continued. "What makes me so cross is that my C.O. just said we were seen holding hands? Holding hands! Good grief! Such a heinous crime! It just seems so innocuous, but it started our enforced separation and thus prevented our day-to-day meetings. I was really hauled over the coals, but they didn't post me then as I am deemed too important to Manston to move, so I'm afraid my sweetness that it was you who were subjected to that dreadful shock. Not allowed to say goodbye to anyone, and almost frog marched off the camp and up here, tout suite!"

"Oh Gary, it was very hard not being able to explain things to the girls, Rho, Jill, Connie and Ellie. I had little time to pack, but I managed to leave a flower on my bed for them, and hoped they may see it as a little message of farewell."

"Yes, they did mention that. They were totally stunned, and couldn't imagine where you were, and I just couldn't bring myself to tell them or talk to them in any other way than work. It was a truly great shock and a dreadful day; that is why I transferred to Alland

Grange as soon as I could. I knew if I spoke to the girls I would probably show my emotions too much."

"They would have understood, darling Gary. I'm not sure how they would have comforted you, though."

The evening was drawing in, and Gary told Sarah he had to be on the 17.30 train. So they collected their things and caught the bus to Saffron Walden station.

"We have had a super weekend together, and the memory of this time will help me to get through the lonely hours without you until we can meet again." Gary held Sarah tightly in his arms, his nose buried in her sweetly smelling hair. "Now, no tears please – I want to remember you like this always, standing waving to me on the platform, with your lovely smile lighting up your face."

At that moment, the train pulled in with a roar and hiss, belching out steam like a monster. Gary kissed Sarah passionately one last time. They broke free and he boarded the train, immediately winding down the window.

"God bless you, my love. Until we meet again, remember you are always in my heart." He looked down at her. "My dear sweet love," he whispered.

Sarah, hand on the train window, looked up at him and said "Goodbye, my dearest one, always keep safe and God bless you too!"

The whistle blew, the guard waved his green flag and the train pulled slowly out of the station. Gary waved from the window for as long as he could, watching the little figure of the woman he loved receding into the distance.

Sarah stood on the cold, bleak, windy platform, tears coursing down her cheeks, her heart breaking.

Jill Hogben

CHAPTER FIFTY-FIVE

'My dearest my loved one, oh what can I do?
Your sweet face is vanishing now from my view'

Sarah was cheered by receiving a Christmas card from
Gary, but early in 1945 she was posted again, this time
way up north to RAF Acklington, in Northumberland.

As she was so far away, with no chance now of them
meeting up, Sarah took the plunge and bravely asked
Gary not to write to her again. Although it hurt her so
much, she was trying her best to do the right thing, as
her father requested.

She also tried to write more loving letters to Trel,
although they still sounded very much as if she was
writing to her brother George, without any passion, but
with a lot of care for his health. She asked him to make
sure he wore his warm vests, and to eat plenty of hot
meals. She did care for him, and faithful Trel just kept
on writing to her regularly.

She hardly went home on leave, the journey was just
too far this time.

Gary tried not to write to Sarah but his longing for
her was too strong, and occasionally Sarah still sent him
little things in the post. He sent her a letter after much
thought on his part, and enclosed a sprig of daphnia,
first harbinger of spring, and a book of poems. He
wrote:

"*Yes, I did promise not to write to you again darling,
but it has been a hell of a job trying to keep my
promise. I promised my folk that I would cut out this
letter writing, you promised your people too, didn't you
Sarah, that you wouldn't see me again, now, this makes*

*two of us in the same boat. My people, of course, know
that I am not so terrifically happily married, but I
suppose they have come to the conclusion that two
wrongs will never make a right, my Mother especially.
My Father, who is, perhaps, a wee bit more world wise
says nothing but thinks. Don't imagine for one moment
Sarah that I have got into a row. I haven't, they would
never censure me, or cross me, only try and point the
way out. They would lead and not drive. So now you
know what has gone wrong Sarah, a rather lame excuse
at not writing. Perhaps though, I was thinking of your
feelings a wee bit too, as I say, I didn't want to re-
awaken your feelings towards me if they were sort of
dying a natural death. I am not very good at expressing
myself, although you say I am a past master, but I do
hope you know what I am driving at. I think you do, for
we almost thought the same, and wished the same
during the year 1944.*

*Needless to say, you have been constantly in my
thoughts. I have thought of you each day, at the
beginning, and at the ending of every individual day. I
cannot seem to forget you. You are always with me, in
thought. I often wonder where you are, and what you
are doing. If I could drive you out of my being a little,
things wouldn't be so bad. If I saw you now, at this very
moment I am afraid I would just have to rush up to
you, and hug you ever so tightly and I am afraid that
that desire and feeling will be part of me right to the
end of the road. I don't know why you have got under
my skin so Sarah, but there it is. The more I try to
think the bigger muddle I get into. I wish you were
back at Manston, or alternatively I was with you,
especially with the advent of spring. I am afraid I am
going to be a sort of lonely soul these next few months,*

without you. Of course I still have memories, but nothing more tangible than memories.

I am still struggling away at the book you sent on to me. I am afraid I do very little reading these days. I try and crowd as much as ever I can into the day in order to have no time for thought.

I have a field day every now and then, and dig your letters out, and read them all and perhaps have a look at your photograph. You will see, I haven't destroyed them, not one of them. As you say it would probably be advisable to destroy them, for if some-one else read them they would most probably misconstrue the whole meaning of each and every one of them. I cannot seem to part with them though. Another of my traits of sentimentality showing itself. We have certainly been very outspoken in our correspondence, haven't we sweet one.

Well my darling, Good Night and God Bless you. I do miss you, so very very much. I often wish I could see you again. Look after yourself, and keep smiling.

With my fondest Love, Hugs and Kisses Eternally 'Your'

      Gary xxxxxxxxxx

Sarah really resisted the temptation to reply to Gary even though on lonely evenings in her billet she thought of him constantly. Instead she sublimated her longing into privately writing poetry about her feelings. She poured out her heartbreak through her pen, often sitting head bowed over her note book and the tears trickling down her cheeks.

More than a Memory

People slip into our lives and snugly seem to fit
and then by freak of fate again they vanish out of it.
This is not all,
for they have left an imprint on the mind,
A lasting signature that has been boldly underlined.
The interest and laughter shared will oft be recollected,
Sights and sounds revive
the past by something dear connected
Not easily forgotten nor erased
though dimmed by time,
For they have left a fragment of
themselves that is sublime.

CHAPTER FIFTY-SIX
"For every day I could kiss you"

Because she hadn't replied to Gary's last letter, Sarah didn't expect to hear from him again and was amazed later on that year to get an RAF air letter from Egypt where he had been posted. Manston had let him go at last.

Gary tried not to communicate with her, but missed her so very much. He knew that once she was demobbed he would no longer be able to write to her. He really wanted to let her know he had finally been posted. His very last letter to her came from the middle of a desert, so they had no chance of another weekend together. Distance separated them but their love continued.

My very Dearest Sarah,

I don't know whether you will be surprised or annoyed at again receiving a few lines from me. I have toyed with the idea for several days, now, as to whether I should write to you again. My better self said "no", but my heart said "yes" and so, here it is.

I hope if you are annoyed, that it is only a wee bit. It is the wrong thing to do, I know, but there, I invariably did the wrong thing where you were concerned, as far as judged by human society.

And so, I am going to lose you now, am I? I am going to miss and lose your friendly letters and all your little expressions of affection. I knew it had to come through some-time or other and was sort of semi-reconciled to the fact. However, when the blow did fall, I felt it very keenly. I read and re-read that passage several times.

Do you know Darling, out here where one's only link with England is a letter or two, you acquire a very critical and keen sense. You read and re-read a letter so many times that you can always feel what is unexpressed in the letter itself. You acquire a sixth sense, and so it is with me. I can see how you felt about telling me not to write to you again. I can feel that you didn't know quite how to express yourself, and at the same time be very diplomatic. I am correct, ain't I? Still if you say not to write any more, it is as you say and this will be probably the last letter I address to you, unless you say otherwise.

Another thing that prompted me to write to you was the fact that to-day is August Bank Holiday. Yes, the first Monday in August, do you know where you and I were this time last year? No doubt you do. To me last Bank Holiday is as vivid in my mind's eye as if it were yesterday. A lot has happened since that day, hasn't it? Quite a lot of water has flown under the bridge. I don't suppose I will ever re-capture those happy days of 1944. They will just remain a very treasured memory. I so often wish I could see you again, though, you pretty thing you. But as you say it would be fatal. I am afraid I would have to give expression to my feelings. Silly Chump ain't I? Although I haven't seen you for what seems an age, your face is still engraved in my mind's eye and I would recognise you anywhere. Why? I don't know. I know your every little trick of walking and standing, and I would be able to pick you out anywhere. Now, though, I don't suppose that occasion will ever arise.

Do you know, Sarah, I can read you like an open book. I always seemed to be able to do it, why, I don't know. I understood you better than I understood

*anyone else living. I could almost read your thoughts
and now, although I am thousands of miles away from
you, I can still do it. You feel so near to me sometimes.
Just as near as if you were sitting down by the side of
me at our little spot. I knew you were going to say that
you thought it advisable to stop writing to each other. I
even knew too, that your Trel was going to ask you to
get married. Don't ask me why I knew Sarah, for I
cannot tell you. But, nevertheless, there it is. Maybe
you will have sensed that fact, from the tone of my last
letter and the varied remarks I made. Isn't it strange? I
hope you could never read my thoughts, for sometimes
they didn't run along channels that would conform with
the standards of decency. Still I expect you could –
couldn't you, for I made myself so obvious at times,
didn't I? I wouldn't be a very good poker player would
I?*

*And what do you think, of all days I am duty N.C.O.
on this particular day. What a come down from last
August Bank Holiday, isn't it? I have mounted the
Guard and shortly will be making a tour of the Camp
with an Orderly Officer so as to ensure that all the
Guards are posted. Yes, I do duties in this dump but
really I don't mind doing them, for it is a field day for
me and takes me out of the Orderly Room for a few
hours. Nevertheless, I still flannel my way out of all the
horrible and distasteful duties. You always said I was a
flanneler, didn't you darling?*

*And so once again, sweet one, and possibly for the
last time, I will wish you good night and God Bless,
never forget that through all the long years to come I
will walk beside you. I'll cherish your dear memory,
and think of you often, too often I am afraid. Never
was I happier than when with you. I could say quite a*

*lot more things, but under the circumstances I think
they had better remain unsaid. I hope you are happy,
very happy in fact throughout your life, and should you
marry, Trel, I do hope the partnership will be a
success.*

*If any time you feel like writing to me well, you
know or should know, how welcome your letters will be
received. Give my best wishes to your brother George
please. Take great care of yourself, always. I'll say a few
words of prayer for you each and every night, you will
always occupy a dear corner of my heart. I wish I could
see you again, just for once, but it appears it is not to be
so. You are always in my thoughts. I often have a look
at your photograph. I still have it near me, in a frame.
May God Bless you Darling, throughout your life.*

*With my fondest love, hugs and kisses, eternally yours
Gary xxxxxxxxxxxxxx*

This letter tore into Sarah's heart. She kept it along
with his photograph and the other letters, secretly
stashed away, for no eyes but hers and she sent no
reply.

The war ended in 1945, much to the relief of all.
Sarah had signed up for four years' tour of duty and
wasn't demobbed from Acklington until 1946. Gary
promised he would destroy Sarah's letters before he
was demobbed and went home to Cornwall in 1948. In
an earlier letter he suggested that they should meet
again in 1948 before he returned home.

Sarah married her Trel in 1947. He had waited so
patiently for her. They became engaged when she was
demobbed, as she realised that her future lay with Trel.
Although he had remained faithful to her, things had

cooled between them. Sarah went to see him and more or less asked him if he still wanted her for his wife.

Trel was overjoyed, as were Annie, Hilda and Joe. Trel took Sarah to an expensive jewellers and bought her the biggest three-stone diamond engagement ring in the shop. Sarah would have preferred a smaller ring, but Trel insisted she had the very best. After all, he had waited nearly seven years for this moment, and now Sarah was to be his wife at last.

They married in March 1947 in Holy Trinity Church House, as the church had suffered bomb damage to the east end apse. Their photos were taken outside the west door, which was still standing. Her friend Joyce was a bridesmaid. They honeymooned in Bournemouth and moved in with Trel's mother and aunt. Sarah began her married life at No. 113 Tannsfeld Road at the bottom of the hill, living in the same road as her parents, at No. 15.

In March 1948 Sarah gave birth to her first child, her longed-for little girl, whom she named Jill after her WAAF friend at Manston.

She settled into domestic life, living with Trel's Aunty Mamie and Annie. She found it very hard to share a kitchen with her mother-in-law, but was very fond of Mamie, a sweet Cornish lady, who was very homesick for the West Country. She told Sarah that *"she was the only friend she had in the world."* The birth of Sarah's baby girl made Mamie much happier; she blossomed in caring for Jill, as she had looked after Trel and his sister Violet all those years ago. She just loved children.

Sarah was not happily married to Trel. He was very much in love with her, but Gary was ever present in her heart. She tried to be a good loving wife to Trel as he

provided well for her, her life was really centred around
her little daughter and her parents, with whom she
spent a good deal of time, just up the hill in her old
home.

She didn't have much time to herself but, when she
had a rare moment, she secretly carried on writing
poetry. This way she was able to sublimate her hidden
feelings, as her longing for Gary was still like a knife her
heart. She wrote before she was demobbed, on RAF
paper from Acklington:

*'I feel assured that there is no such thing as ultimate
forgetting. Faces once impressed upon the memory are
indestructible. A thousand accidents may and will
interpose a veil between our present consciousness and
the secret inscriptions on the mind. Accidents of the
same sort will also rend away this veil. But alike,
whether veiled or unveiled, the inscription remains for
ever.'*

This dream is mine
As you stand here above me
This love is thine
When you whisper you love me
Don't lose heart
If the dream is fading
Keep the tryst over
E'en with sorrow pervading
For this is our charter
No-one can borrow or barter

Sweet is your kiss
And sweeter your responses
My heart beats fast
As I melt at your dear glances.

Fade not dear dream
But invade all my visitations
This is not a plea
But an earnest invitation
My love supreme
Make reality my dream

"And now the summer has gone, alone am I"

Oh my darling don't you know that
I love you with a love that will never let me go

How I long to crush you in my arms
Be near, to you as close as close can be
How can I go on without you?
Life is nothing unless you are near
Come to me in my music enter my whole being
Let me kiss your arms, your hands, your mouth
How dark are the days without you?
Without you the days are endless
And the nights are lonely
All your loveliness surrounds me,
All my longings will they ever be realised?
How sad I am
My tears lie salty upon my cheeks

Are your longings the same as mine?
Let me pretend we are together
Let me feel your arms around me

And my lips enjoy your sweet kisses
We are now dancing together
I am turning you round and round in my arms
To this beautiful music

We are sitting down alone
My hand is on yours
My fingers now are pressing up your arm
You shudder at my touch
Do I thrill you so much?
I will never relinquish you
I shall endeavour time and time again
To win you

I know in the end I shall conquer all ...
....and you will be mine.

CHAPTER FIFTY-SEVEN

"I just remain in silence and let the memories unfurl"

In 1949 Auntie Mamie died. Sarah had become very fond of her, and missed her kindness. Trel and his sister Violet were devastated at her loss, as she had virtually brought them up when Annie was widowed and had to go out to work.

Sarah's second daughter, June, was born. She now had her two girls, all she had ever wanted, and in the children she was fulfilled.

In 1953 Trel and Sarah went on holiday to Westgate. Sarah didn't really want to return to Thanet, but Annie had become ill with leukaemia, and Trel didn't want to go too far from London. He wanted to take Jill on a safe sandy beach, so they stayed at the Rowena Court Hotel, Sea Road, which had a lovely garden overlooking the sea.

On their way to Westgate they drove through Birchington and Sarah saw The Clovelly Café and Rushes restaurant, where she and Gary would often dine. She looked miserably through the car window at the path by the road that they would walk back to the convent, and when she passed the convent and saw the little nook where she used to say goodnight to Gary, the tears fell freely from her eyes.

Trel didn't understand why she was so sad. He said crossly, "Well, I suppose you are tired out with our two. I cannot understand why on earth you are crying, when I have brought you away for a sea-side holiday!"

Sarah dried her eyes and concentrated on the children, and they spent a pleasant few days, taking Jill on the beach, tucking her skirt into plastic pants so she could paddle in the sea. June slept in a pram borrowed from the hotel, and was wheeled on to the beach. The weather was pleasant enough, and when they sat on St. Mildred's beach, Sarah tried hard not to look at the twin towers of Reculver Church in the distance, but her eyes were inextricably pulled to the west, and her heart was filled with sadness.

Annie suddenly took a turn for the worse, and Violet sent word to Trel to come home.

Sarah was left in a place of memories with two small children. It was not a happy time for her. Returning to Thanet was very painful, and she realised that her love for Gary had not abated with the passing of nine years since she had seen him in Saffron Walden. She longed for him with every inch of her being, and sublimated her sorrow by pouring all her love and affection into looking after her little girls.

Many years passed.

Sarah still wrote poems when she had a spare moment. She and Trel made the best life they could for their daughters, and they were happy in their way. Sarah had learned to count her blessings and not dwell on what might have been. However, fate stepped in, and at certain times in her life she found herself surrounded by memories of her time with Gary.

In her teens June was not happy at her school and it was recommended that she was sent to be a boarder at the Ursuline Convent at Westgate. Sarah went down to settle June into her new school and walked through the large reception hall, noting that it had not changed a bit. More memories came flooding back: of her WAAF friends, of Jill's wedding. Sarah looked at the stairs and her mind took her back to that happy day, and she could imagine Jill coming down, looking radiant as the bride.

Life seemed determined to make sure that her memories of Gary would not fade. She looked down the convent drive and imagined him standing there, waiting for her with his bike, ready for a ride. She tried hard to smile at the memories, as they were still so clear in her mind. She wondered what he was doing, and if he was happy. She hoped fervently that he was at least contented, that maybe now he was home his wife was able to study and that would make her happier.

Changes happened in the family, Joe contracted T.B. and died, leaving a heart-broken Hilda. Three-year old Jill caught T.B. from Joe causing quite a scare, luckily she recovered.

In 1968 Trel retired from the bank. In that year Sarah's beloved mother, Hilda, died from pneumonia contracted after breaking her hip in a fall and Sarah was distraught with grief.

In 1970 Jill left home, and she and June both were engaged to be married.

Trel became ill after a bout of the 'flu in June 1970 and died quite quickly. June was still living at home, and Jill came home from Brighton where she was sharing a flat.

Trel's funeral was held in Holy Trinity Church, across the road from where they married. That evening Jill asked her mother how she was feeling and Sarah said she was fine and not to worry about her. She seemed to be acting as normal, and not as if she had just lost her husband. She didn't seem sad at all. There was such a marked difference in the way she behaved after Hilda's death – then she had been shattered with misery. June's fiancé Mike also noticed that Sarah did not seem to be grieving in any way for her deceased spouse.

It was true: a large weight had been lifted from Sarah's mind with Trel's death. She was fond of him, and tried to love him in her way, but they had not enjoyed a happy marriage. She had spent a lot of time with her mother Hilda after the death of Joe, and Trel resented this time because he felt neglected.

She did her duty as a wife, cooking and cleaning for him, and occasionally they would go to the pictures or to a concert together, but in the main they were not happy. Sarah tried hard to be loving towards her husband, but found it difficult sometimes. Trel loved her and didn't understand her coldness towards him; this made him very bitter, and he was often critical of the way Sarah did things. So when he died she was released from living a lie. She could enjoy her family and not have to try to be a good loving wife any more.

Her thoughts returned to Gary. She could now openly write her poems about him, indulge in her longing for him, and face her continuing love for him quite freely, without guilt, knowing she was not being disloyal to Trel. She was free.

She even confessed to Jill one day that she had not been a good wife to her father – she had been cold and unloving to him. Jill couldn't understand that, as her mother was such a warm loving person towards all the family, and coldness was so against her caring nature. It was as if her mother had needed to tell her, to explain and to get it off her chest somehow. Maybe Jill would have understood if she had confessed to being in love with Gary all her life, but Sarah just couldn't bring herself to say she was in love with a married man, so

Gary remained her 'friend', with little significance to both her daughters.

Jill and June both married.

Jill's family moved to Westbrook, near Margate, to give space for their growing family. Thus once again, Sarah was required to visit Thanet.

During visits to Westbrook memories were triggered, and at last she could speak freely about Gary although she still alluded to him as 'my friend', so that her daughter still had no idea of the depth of love that had existed between them.

Jill listened with interest to Sarah chatting about her RAF memories. Sarah recounted that Gary had been a Flight Sergeant, and was her boss. She laughed about her accident falling off her bike, catching the front wheel in the tram lines, and how her friend Gary had come to her rescue. She also spoke of their cycle rides, especially to Reculver village and Wingham.

They took a trip out to Manston so that Sarah could look again at the RAF base, which was still in use. Sarah chatted animatedly about freezing ablutions, and dreadful food in the Mess. It was very cathartic for Sarah to just let her memories flow to her daughter, memories that had been pent up inside her for years and years.

Sarah asked her daughter if she would accompany her to a service in the little church at Acol. Jill said she would be pleased to take her, and left the children with her husband, so that they could go to a morning service. It never occurred to Jill just how much this meant mother, she just thought it was a charming little church. Sarah sat beside her daughter and saw Gary, so clearly in her mind's eye, sitting in the pew as he had done with her all those years ago.

She told of how they were seen holding hands by someone in the RAF, and how she was posted away to RAF Castle Camps.

Jill thought it was sad that they parted, but again didn't give it any significance, because Sarah always held back from telling her the truth. She just thought it was nice that her mother had memories of an old friend, and that her moving to Thanet meant her mother could relive happy memories of their RAF days.

Jill often travelled up to visit her mother's house in Sydenham. Once, they were sitting together enjoying a cup of tea when Sarah went to a cupboard and brought out some old sepia photos of a smiling chap resplendent in an RAF airman's uniform, sergeant stripes on his shoulder. Jill thought he looked pleasant enough. Sarah did keep stressing that he was married with children, and said his name was Gary, and that they had fun together, but that came to an abrupt end when Sarah was posted away, for holding his hand in public.

Looking back Jill castigated herself – after all, one didn't usually hold hands with just a 'friend'. The signs were there, but Jill missed them completely.

Sarah also showed her a book on life as a WAAF during World War Two, given to her by her friend Jill, for whom she was named.

Some while later, Jill was walking past an antique shop in Margate and noticed a lovely tea-pot in the window, decorated with orange flowers and blue leaves. Jill recognised it as the tea-pot that her Granny always used for Sunday tea with Uncle George, Auntie Monica, Penny and Beverley, her cousins. She thought that it would make such a lovely present for her mother, so she went into the shop and bought it for her. She wrapped it up and felt really excited at the pleasure she was going to bring to Sarah, on opening and spying Granny's tea-pot again.

On her birthday, Sarah was sitting in her usual comfy chair by the fire in her Sydenham home. Jill couldn't wait for her to open the present she had bought. Sarah looked at the box and said "Oh! I wonder what this can be?" Her daughter smiled in anticipation of her pleasure.

Sarah removed the paper, looked into the box and her face fell. "I cannot have this, darling," she said to her daughter with a sad expression on her face. "You have it, I really have no room for it, here you are."

Sarah quickly handed the box back to her daughter. Jill was stunned and hurt at her words.

"Why ever don't you want it? What is wrong, it is Granny's tea-pot. You remember, surely? It is 'Fantasy' – Royal Tudor Ware, Granny had the whole tea service. We always had it on the table at Sunday tea I thought you would absolutely love it!" Jill said, now totally bewildered and not comprehending at all.

Sarah looked at her daughter wistfully.

"Look here, darling, I know you meant well, but a tea-pot, in 'Fantasy' pattern, was part of the tea service on the table when Gary and I had our very last few moments together. I know it was also the same as your Granny's, but the memory of that day is just too painful for me. It would always remind me of our parting."

Jill was totally shocked at the strength of her mother's feelings and certainly didn't want to upset her, so for years she kept the tea-pot high up on a shelf in her house, where it remains to this day.

"All day I have thought of you, savoured
the joy which we spent,
Yet if each day I could see you
it would not mar, nor pall,
For every day I could kiss you, I would not mind at all,
My dear one, how I long to embrace you,
Encircle, encompass and encase you
For your image is burned on the mirrors of my mind
And lights the lamp in quiet corridors of time."

CHAPTER FIFTY-EIGHT

"Keep your love forever growing"

Jill, her husband and family moved to Cornwall and
bought a house at the top of a hill in Newlyn when
Sarah was in her eighties.

Sarah came down to stay with Jill, and one lovely
afternoon they were sitting together at a garden table
over-looking a beautiful sea view across the bay to St.
Michael's Mount, showing the harbour at Newlyn, and
stretching round to the Lizard. Suddenly Sarah said:
"Do you know that Gary lived in Cornwall, although
originally he was born in Wales?"

Jill was amazed. She asked her mother whereabouts
in Cornwall he lived. Sarah said, "He and his family
lived in Hayle".

Jill said that was very near, and she suddenly had an
idea. This man Gary obviously meant so much to her
mother, so she thought it would be a great thing if they
could meet again.

She quietly asked Sarah what Gary's surname was,
trying to be casual, so that Sarah wouldn't understand
what she had in mind.

Sarah told her Scrivens was his name. So Jill left her
in the garden and hurried inside the house to fetch the
phone book. She wrote down all the Scrivens' phone
numbers she could find and went to her bedroom and
started to ring them all methodically.

There were about six or seven people of that
surname listed in the phone book. So without really
thinking it out, Jill rang each one. Her only thought
was, wouldn't it be wonderful if I could find Gary for
her mother, and they could meet again. She tried a few

numbers, but was met with "Oh no, my 'andsome, there is no-one who was in the RAF in our family".

Jill was beginning to feel she was being daft at trying, until the very last person on her list answered the phone.

Jill asked: "I'm very sorry to bother you, but may I ask if by any chance you have a Gary Scrivens in your family, who served at RAF Manston in the war?"

The chap at the end of the phone said: "Yes, he was my father. Why do you ask?"

This question threw Jill for a moment, she hadn't thought of the next move, so she said: "My mother is presently staying at my house in Newlyn. She knew your father during the Second World War, at Manston, where she served as a WAAF, she worked for him, and she often wonders what he is doing now. I don't suppose he is still alive, is he?"

"No, I'm afraid he died in the 1980s." Jill's heart sank at this news. How terribly sad. Now they would never meet.

"Well, I was wondering if you would mind telling me a bit about him, what he did after the war, that sort of thing, and maybe if you have any photos of him in later life that I may borrow and show to my mother. She would be overjoyed to see them, as they were good friends."

The chap said he was called Jared, and he would look some photos out of Gary, and that his father worked at the Camborne School of Mines for many years before he retired.

Jill asked if she could pop over to St. Just and pick up some photos, and she promised she would bring them back safely. Jared said that would be OK. So they said goodbye and Jill put the phone down, wondering with trepidation just how she could break the news to her mother that Gary had passed away.

About half an hour passed, and Jill had just sat down to talk with Sarah in the garden, when she was called to answer the phone.

It was Jared. He said he had been talking things over with his sister Polly and they both decided that they would like to meet this friend of their father's. So Jill, invited them over for tea the next day.

She told Sarah, who was absolutely amazed that she would be meeting Gary's children and wondered what they would make of her. However, the news that he had died came as a shock to her; stabbed her in the heart. She always felt comforted that he was living somewhere in Cornwall, but now she knew that her true love was no more. She hid her profound sadness from her daughter.

The next afternoon was sunny, so Jill set the garden table and served tea and cakes. Jared and Polly arrived and June came over from her holiday home at St. Just, to be with them all.

The conversation soon became animated, Sarah chatted merrily about going to concerts and outings with Gary. Jared was very interested in hearing of his father's time in the RAF, and asked Sarah lots of questions, which Sarah was very pleased to answer. Polly was a little more cautious; she knew her parents had not been happily married, but could see by the way Sarah was talking of her father that there was probably more between them than just a friendship. In fact, at one point she was moved to say huffily: "Well, this wouldn't have happened if there had been married quarters at Manston."

Jill took photos of Jared, Polly and Sarah sitting together. Jared kindly brought over copies of photos taken of his father in later life for Sarah to keep, and one of him at work at the Camborne School of Mines. He told Sarah that two more children had been born to Gary and his wife, after the war, but sadly one son was killed in a road accident. Sarah was inwardly pleased that Gary had made a go of his marriage.

When at last they left for home, Sarah sat on her own overlooking the sea in the garden holding Gary's photos in her hands, and smiling at his friendly face, much older than when they parted, with a tear in her eye. There was the dear face she had sorely missed seeing for so many years, the kindly visage of the man she had loved all her life.

Sitting alone, her thoughts went back in time, seeing in her mind's eye their happiness: the two of them walking along the cliff top at West Bay, cycling to Reculver or sitting in deck chairs listening to the band at Canterbury. The theme from their beloved Rachmaninov's second symphony played in her mind, and all her happy memories of Gary came flooding back as she looked once again upon his dear countenance.

A year later, when she was eight-eight, her grandsons Chris and Jamie interviewed her and filmed her answers to their questions about her life. She was asked about her time at Manston and her friend.

Sarah said quietly "Oh well, he was married, but I never forgot him."

He had always held a place in her heart. She remembered: 'Now Voyager' –
"We have the stars, don't let us ask for the moon."

Jill Hogben

Sarah's words written for her love:

The Kiss

Your lips on mine tear a page from time
The pressure remains, uplifts and sustains,
And then, anon, I will muse upon
This timeless event, so heaven sent,
To capture and to seal,
This moment so ideal,
The total eclipse, of our two lips.

Recollection

And now the hours have vanished
and time has slipped away,
I still recall your laughter,
and remember what you say,
I still feel your arms around me
and your cheek so close to mine,
I still recount the moments
which infuse each part of time.
Like shadows on the grassland
as they dance across the glade,
The shadows still remain there
when the sun has ceased to fade,
When problems become pressing
and my mind is in a whirl,
I just remain in silence
and let the memories unfurl,
They bring me to such gladness
they bring me to such bliss,
Like the pleasure of a handshake
or the pressure of a kiss.

They smooth down all rough edges
and iron out every crease,
They bring back sweet contentment,
and a mind so full of peace.
So just remember, when you think you feel your age,
You have written a memory on my memory page.

Treasured Weekend

You can make me laugh, you can cause a sigh
By the tilt of your chin, or the look in your eye
By the touch of your hand, or the squeeze of your arm
Each characteristic vibrates with your charm
Did it really happen?

Or was it just a dream
having you beside me, enhancing every scene
Now you're gone I'm left with just a memory
but treasured and pleasant it will always be.
Precious and magical ensconced in our eyes
And no one else has the gift we are left to prize.
For it's ours and ours alone which we can express
When days maybe drear and thoughts are suppressed
So let's give a warm glow to Fate, who was so kind
And gave us such a cherished time
in our twin minds.

CHAPTER FIFTY-NINE

"Alone am I and alone I shall be,
unattached for you have gone from me"

Sarah lived until ten days after her 90th birthday. She
was tired and hadn't been in the best of health lately,
and her body was frail. She enjoyed her birthday, but
was overwhelmed by the amount of presents and cards
she received from family and friends. She was a very
popular lady, always cheerful with a ready smile, and
she remarked she had been very blessed, but she didn't
want to live to be 100. She had had enough.

Shortly afterwards she became ill very suddenly and
died in hospital.

Her family were all shocked to the core at her
sudden passing: when one moment they had been
rejoicing with her on her birthday, the next they had to
deal with her funeral, whilst still surrounded by her
birthday presents, which was very sad and hard for
everyone.

The day after her death, June, Jill and her husband
Trev went to Sarah's house, to go through her papers
and to inform all of her passing.

June went into Sarah's front room, to a little
bamboo cabinet where she found a folder containing
photos of a man in Air Force uniform, various hand-
written documents, signed off by Gary from RAF
Manston, and some letters on RAF paper written by
him to Sarah. She called out to Jill, and they looked
through the folder with amazement. There was also a
book of poetry from Gary to Sarah, inside was a sprig
of dried Daphne. *'to remind of us of the spring.'*

The letters from Gary were passionate and full of love and longing, pouring out feelings, emotional and sad. The sisters read them and soon tears were coursing down their cheeks.

"She was really in love with Gary and he was with her," Jill said, wiping away her tears.

"He says he will walk beside her for the rest of her life. They weren't just friends. Her poems must have been for him. I often wondered for whom she was writing, so full of aching and loss. How sad it all was that they never met again, and that we never realised the strength of their love for each other."

"Till the end of time as long as stars are in the blue
As long as there is a spring
and birds do sing I'll go on loving you."

Thus this story of their unrequited love was written.

One of Gary's sayings was written down in a little note book by Sarah, alongside mundane every day jottings, in dark letters and underlined to emphasise was:

'Our days are numbered'

THE END

Jill Hogben

About the Author:
Jill is an historian and has written and published two
church histories to date and is presently working on
another, the history of
St. Peter's-the-Apostle in Thanet.

The History of St. John the Baptist Church, Broadclyst,
Devon was published in 1999 together with a paper on
the discovery of the Church House, Broadclyst
published in 'The Devon Historian' and
The History of the Church in Paul Parish, Cornwall
published in 2006.

Jill Hogben

Our Days Are Numbered